I0674291

OWN

by

K.I. Lynn

&

N. Isabelle Blanco

Own

Publication Date: November 28, 2016
Genre: FICTION/Romance/New Adult
ISBN-13: 978-0997514032
ISBN-10: 0997514035

PART 3

"When a deep injury is done us, we never recover we forgive." - Alan Paton

"I've loved her my whole life, and I'll love her for the rest of it. To be with her forever is the only way I'll ever find happiness." - Brayden

"They say to love is to forgive, but how do you forgive the one you love? How do you move past the pain and into happiness? It's a struggle, but I'm ready to fight." - Kira

PROLOGUE

BRAYDEN

Eight years ago

I glare at the little imp outside my window, half-tempted to not open it and leave her out there.

As if I ever would.

I'm so pissed at her for climbing that tree again and putting herself in danger, yet looking at her is the first spot of happiness I've had all day.

Storming up to my window, I slide it open, lean out, and practically fling her skinny little butt against me.

Kira squeals and wraps her arms tight around my neck.

My heart is about to explode and it won't slow down until I have her inside and safe.

Once I do, though, my heart is beating harder than ever. And when I put her on her feet and she doesn't let go, moving closer and hugging me tighter instead, I swear I'm going to have a heart attack.

Damn, she always smells so good.

1

Swallowing nervously, I push her back and glare down at her. "You're the most annoying ten-year-old in the world."

She slaps me in the chest hard. "And you're the most antisocial, thirteen-year-old jerk alive! Why have you been ignoring us all day?"

Shrugging, I turn away from her and walk to my bed.

She follows me, of course.

She's always following me.

It should annoy me.

Despite what I said, I wouldn't want it any other way.

How weird is that?

Whatever. She's my best friend. Of course I want her around, even when I'm too embarrassed to show my face.

The lights are off in my room though, and I have no plans of turning them on.

She doesn't need to see.

No one needs to see.

My face is still red from earlier. I was freaking crying and I'd rather die than let anyone know that.

"Brayden." Kira climbs on the bed next to me. "What's going on?"

"Your mom is going to flip if she wakes up and realizes you aren't in your room."

"You were ignoring us all day. And I know what it means when you do that."

Of course she does. She *knows* me. All of me. There's nowhere in the world I could ever hide from this girl, including inside my own self.

"It's nothing, Kitty. I just wanted to be alone."

"You never want to be away from me, so stop lying."

I glare at her cocky, adorable ass, wondering why I put up

with her.

Her hazel-green eyes turn soft. Man, I hate when she looks at me like that. It makes me feel like both a king and a peasant at her feet. Like I can take on the whole world, but at the same time like I'm weak and powerless in front of her.

I don't get it. I know I love her. I've loved my best friends since I met them. Both her and her brother. And I have no problem admitting that.

But why does what I feel for her feel so *different* than what I feel for Ryan?

"They were fighting again, weren't they?" she asks me softly.

The question makes me itchy. Literally itchy. My skin crawls at the reminder and it's a struggle to remain seated.

She's ten. I don't want her knowing about bad things like this.

But of course she knows. Ryan knows. Sometimes it feels like the whole world knows. There's no way the neighbors don't hear the epic blowouts.

My mom accused my father of cheating today.

He denies it up and down.

She told him that if she ever catches him, that'll be the day she leaves him.

There was something weird about the way she said it. As if it were something that had happened before.

But of course it hasn't. My mom would have left him if it had.

Right?

My throat closes up at the thought. I know my mom would be better off without him. That I would be, too.

But I must still be a stupid little boy, because thinking of them separating *hurts*.

Please. Please. Don't let my dad cheat on her . . .

Kira places her small hand on my cheek and I jump. She's caressing me, that soft, loving expression aimed at me, and I want to melt into her.

How does she do that? How does she make everything okay in my world just by touching me?

The understanding in her eyes is too mature for a little girl like her.

"Did he hit you?"

Her question surprises me. "Why would you think that?"

"Because I'm always waiting for it to happen."

So am I, actually. All the time. I walk around here waiting for the day that he aims that rage at me.

But that's another line he knows he can't cross. My mother made it clear. Touch me and she will end him.

Damn. My life is so fucked up. How many kids' mothers have to warn their fathers not to hurt them?

"He didn't," I assure Kira, grabbing her hand and holding it in mine. We twine fingers and just look at each other in the dark.

"Brayden, I'm going to ask you something but don't get mad."

I sigh. "You know you tell me that every time right before you ask me something that ends up making me really, really mad, right?"

She giggles then goes back to being serious. Placing her other hand on my cheek, she stares sadly into my eyes. "You were crying, weren't you?"

Knew it.

I let her hand go and turn around so my back is facing her

4

and I'm sitting with my legs dangling over the edge of the bed.

I *hate* being seen as a weakling. My father already treats me like I'm pathetic.

Kira comes up behind me and shoves her legs underneath my arms. She curls them around me, crossed over my lap, and her arms come around me too.

I feel her press her cheek against my back as she hugs me from behind.

I'm angry at her for bringing up the fact I was crying, but I can't push her away. She's the only thing in this entire world that can comfort me.

"I'm sorry," she mumbles. "I just had to know."

"Yeah," I whisper.

"What?"

"Yeah . . . I was." I can't even add in the last part, *crying.* The word gets stuck in my throat and I can't get over how bitter it tastes.

Kira curls around me tighter, like a baby boa constrictor.

She's so tiny. I wonder sometimes if she'll always be. I'm only thirteen and I'm already almost a foot taller than her.

"I hate that he makes you cry. I wish I could hit him with a lamp right in his nose."

I burst out in a quiet laugh. "Me, too. Trust me." I reach up and hold one of her arms in my hand.

"There has to be something we can do, Brayden."

We. She always talks like that. Makes me feel like a part of her family. Her brother is the same way. They act as if they have never imagined a life where I won't be a part of it.

I freaking love them for that.

"There's nothing we can do, Kira. I just gotta grow up and

move out."

She tenses all around me and somehow squeezes me tighter. "Without us?"

"No, silly. We're all going to be together. Always." I realize some people would think it's dumb that I'm promising her that without knowing the future for sure.

Screw that. Somehow I'm keeping that promise. Kira, my mom, and Ryan are all I truly have.

"I wish your parents would break up now so you and your mom could be happy."

Her comment hurts me. I don't reply. I'm ashamed of the fact that them possibly breaking up brings tears to my eyes again.

Damn. My father might be right. I am weak.

Kira let's me go.

I hate it so much that I fling around without thinking, searching her out so I can bring her back to me.

She urges me to relax back against the headboard. Then she lays her upper body on my lap, facing away from me.

Instantly, I start caressing her hair. I love her hair. Don't know why, it's just hair, but I do.

"Brayden, you need to start calling us when these things happen."

I say nothing. What can I say? I know I should. That they're my best friends and are there for me no matter what.

I don't know why I isolate myself when things like this happen. Maybe it's just that I hate anyone seeing me emotional.

Kira pinches my leg.

"Ow! What the heck?" I tug lightly on her hair. "Why'd you do that for?"

She doesn't turn around. Just snuggles back into her comfortable position on my lap. "You're not promising. Promise it, Brayden."

Lying to her kills me. Unless we're playing a prank on her, I can't deal with lying to her. I hate it for some reason I can't explain. "I'll try my best," I promise honestly, smoothing my hand down her hair.

It's good enough for her. I can tell by her content silence. Kira believes in me. Thinks I can do anything.

I hug her from behind. I should leave it alone. She's happy with my response. The conversation should end here.

"Kira?"

"Hm?" She mumbles sleepily.

It's eleven-thirty at night. We both have school tomorrow. Of course she's tired.

"I need you to promise me something, too."

She turns a little bit on my lap and stares up at me with those sleepy, big eyes. "Anything."

Kira has a direct connection to my heart. Everything she does speeds it up. It's so weird that it disturbs me sometimes.

I ignore it and focus on finding the right words to explain what I need from her. In the end, all I settle for is, "Please don't push me away."

She blinks up at me, confused. "Brayden, you're never getting rid of me. BFFs for life, remember?"

I shake my head, frustrated with the tight knot in my throat. Why is asking her for this so hard? "You don't get it. One day, I might be a huge jerk to you."

That makes her sit up and face me fully. "You're always a jerk to me."

I'm still shaking my head. "No. I mean, worse of a jerk."

Her little brow furrows. "Worse?"

She's not getting it and this is harder than I imagined. I'm asking her . . . Damn, I'm asking her not to abandon me.

Even though one day I have a feeling I'm going to give her a good reason to do so.

Kira places her hand on my cheek and I instantly fall still. "Brayden, you annoy me all the time. But I'm your friend. I'll always be your friend. Forever. I mean it."

"What if I hurt you one day like my dad is always hurting the people around him?" The words leave me fast, real fast, but at least I finally got them out.

She seems offended on my behalf. "You're not like him, silly."

"I am," I admit in a low voice. I've felt that violence stirring inside me. It's there, waiting, like a dark shadow on the edges of my vision.

She slaps me on the shoulder and I hiss. "Don't you ever say that again. It's not true. You're my bestest friend in the world and you wouldn't be that if you weren't awesome."

I throw her against me and crush her in a hug. *Thank you. Thank you. Thank you.* I can't force the words out to let her know what that comment means to me, even though I'm screaming the words in my head.

"Can't breathe, dummy," she says against my neck.

She doesn't sound like she's suffocating, so I don't let her go.

I can't.

"Don't ever push me away, Kira. I mean it. I won't let you."

"You're never going to give me a reason to push you away."

8

But I am. No matter what I do, one day I'm going to mess this friendship up just like my dad ruins everything around him.

I'm wired to do it.

And no matter how hard I try, I won't be able to avoid it.

ONE

Kira

Present

Minutes.

Hours.

I don't even know anymore.

Time passes by at an interminable pace. Looking outside the window, I know we're speeding, Jenna pressing down on the gas like her life depends on it.

Not her life. Mine. Everything that I am has been taken from me, thrown in cuffs and put in a cell. Like an animal.

He fought Austin like one. I can't deny how bad it was.

It's all my fault.

I have no idea what I'm going to do with Brayden. No idea what to do with all this love inside me, a love I've finally admitted to myself still exists.

Of course it exists. The love is the reason why the hate still pounds strong. Without it, the hate could have never existed. I'm consumed by both, and they're trapped inside my anxious, racing heart.

I want to urge Jenna to go faster, but I can't. Brayden's phone remains clutched in my cold, sweaty hand. I refuse to let it go. There's no way I can.

It occurs to me that I feel the same way about the owner.

"Almost there," Jenna says, as if she can sense that I'm falling apart one insane piece at a time.

I don't say anything. My vocal chords feel frozen. Closing my eyes, I pray for the strength to keep myself together. The guilt is choking me. I don't know how I'm ever going to live with it, but I do know I'll have to live with it for a long, long time.

The car turns and then jerks to a stop.

I'm out the door instantly, eyes glued to the entrance of the precinct. It's the only one in town so I know for a fact this is where they brought Austin and Brayden.

Inside, it's pretty empty. Calm.

The crime rate here isn't very high so I'm not surprised.

Trembling, I walk up to the main desk and address the female officer sitting behind it. "Excuse me." She takes her sweet time looking away from her computer and meeting my eyes. "Two guys were just brought in—"

"They're in holding cells and we've just started processing their paperwork. You'll have to wait."

Wait? While I'm barely keeping it together?

Absolute torture, but the woman looks away from me and back at her computer, making it obvious that I have no choice.

Like an idiot, I don't move, frozen here before the podium. The phone's still where it's been the entire time—against my heart as if doing so will erase the fact that Brayden's not with me.

"Come on. We should sit." A hand lands on my arm.

I jump, startled. It's Ashley, and she's staring me at me compassionately.

"Come on, hun." She gently leads me toward the row of chairs against the wall.

I let her, in a daze. We sit right as Jenna and Marilyn run inside. It may be fucked up of me, but I don't pay them any attention.

I can't.

It's amazing how an event like this can slap some sense into a person. For weeks now I've been fighting not to admit to myself that I'm falling apart for that man once again.

Now all I want is to be with him. Even if it's just to stand outside the cell, at least I'll be near.

Minutes pass, each one dragging by. I lose a little piece of my mind with every second.

"It's going to be okay, girl," Jenna says.

I nod without looking at her, although I don't really believe her.

"I doubt the charge will be anything crazy."

But that's the problem. There's going to be a charge regardless. Brayden's life will never be the same after this and it's all *my* fault.

Austin's life won't either.

How could I do this to the both of them? I should've been firmer with Austin. Made it clearer to him that we would never happen.

A voice inside reminds me that nothing I said was going to get through to him. He suspects about Brayden but I couldn't bring myself to confess that he was right.

I never told him who I'm addicted to and because of that he thought he still had a chance with me.

It's obvious now what I have to do; as soon as I see Austin, I have to be clear with him once and for all.

Have to break his heart once and for all.

An hour passes. Then another. Halfway through the second hour I'm so close to tearing out my hair. "I can't take this anymore. What's going on?"

"That's it. I didn't want to have to do this, but this is ridiculous." Jenna gets to her feet and starts dialing on her cell.

I know immediately what she's about to do and I want to tackle hug her for it.

Her dad's a judge here in town. She's going to use her connection with him to get me in to see Brayden.

"Hey, Daddy? Yeah. Listen, don't kill me, but I need a *huge* favor." She walks away so we can't hear the rest of the conversation.

Oh my God, I have no idea how I'm going to ever repay her.

She comes back about five minutes later and smiles at me. "My dad's not happy having to step in about this. And he's definitely not going to be willing to help Brayden out with his sentencing so I didn't bother asking, but he said he should have you in there in a few minutes."

I jump to my feet and throw my arms around her. "Thank you. Thank you so much." A single tear leaks out of my eye.

She hugs me back even harder. "Anytime, girl. But after this, you and I are going to sit down and have a serious talk."

I don't have to ask what she means by that. It's pretty obvious that they've all realized my drastic change when it comes to Brayden.

I'll worry about that later. For right now, all I care about is getting in there.

The captain of the precinct exits his office and walks to the lady at the front desk. They speak in hushed tones and their eyes cut in our direction.

I'm pretty sure my eyes are pleading with them both.

The captain walks away and the woman turns to us fully. "Which one of you is Ms. Roth?"

I rush forward.

"Fifteen minutes max." She motions for another officer to come lead me to the cells.

Throat tight, I nod and start walking toward the small swinging door that separates the back of the precinct from the waiting area.

"No personal items," the lady says before I can cross through.

Jenna comes up to take my purse, phone, and Brayden's phone.

My heart thunders against my ribs as I follow the officer past the admin area and out into another hall. It's bare, stark, and obviously this leads to where the holding cells are.

We reach a heavy door with a key scanner. "Don't get close to the cells. Absolutely no touching." He swipes the key and I hear the door unlock. He pushes it open and steps aside so I can go through.

There's only four cells, two on each side, facing each other down a wide hallway. It only takes two steps for me to see them both.

They're sitting in their own separate cells, facing each other.

Both of them are still bloodied. There's still caked blood on their faces. They haven't been given any sort of medical attention.

They're glaring at each other, and it's obvious by the hatred in their eyes that those bars are the only thing stopping them from going back at it.

Brayden's name leaves me on a whisper.

His head snaps in my direction and his swollen eyes widen as much as they possibly can.

They both say my name at the same time.

I'm only focused on one of them.

Brayden shoots to his feet.

I run to his cell, forgetting all about the instructions I was given to not get too close. My hands wrap around the bars.

His hands wrap around my own, squeezing them.

That's all it takes for everything to come barreling out of me. I hear a sob break free, and my vision blurs as tears flood my eyes.

"Kira. Baby. No." Brayden looks wrecked by my tears. "It's okay, Kira. It's okay."

I shake my head, my voice breaking with each sob. "N-no. No it-it's not. Th-this is all my fault."

"Stop." He leans down enough to get eye level with me. "This is not your fault."

"He's right, Kira," Austin says behind me.

15

The rage leaks into Brayden's eyes once more and he snaps his head back to scowl at Austin. "She's not fucking talking to you, so leave her alone."

"See? This is why I broke your face in. Because you don't know when to step the fuck off."

"Says the man who doesn't know how to take no for an answer. And newsflash, you pathetic fuck, you're the one with the gash on your forehead."

"Stop!" I cry. "Both of you just stop already!"

They fall silent.

The door at the end of the hall opens. "No touching!"

Brayden glares at the officer like he wants to kill him, too.

Hastily, I step away from him before he ends up saying something to the officer that gets us into even more trouble.

His eyes snap to me, and the anguish of a million lifetimes shimmers in his emerald eyes.

My heart shatters and my self-control almost dies with it. But I have to stay away from him. No matter how much I just want to tear at those bars and wrap my arms around him, I can't do anything that's going to make his predicament worse.

There's also something else I need to accomplish. Something that's been a long time coming.

I don't know what the future holds for Brayden and I, but it's time I set Austin straight once and for all.

The officer gives us one last silent warning and the door closes behind him again.

"Kira, baby—"

I shake my head at Brayden and step backwards away from him.

His expression falls.

I know what he's thinking. There's no time to explain anything to him. I'm on a time limit and I can't leave here without making some things clear.

As if Brayden calling me "baby" doesn't go a long way toward clearing things up with Austin.

When I turn to Austin, his light blue eyes are as devastated as Brayden's are.

He already knows. He knows what I'm about to tell him. His eyes *plead* with me, and I can almost hear his voice in my head.

Don't do this. I love you. *I'll never give up on you.*

But how? How did this man fall so deeply in love with me? I'm so stupid. I should've seen the signs. I was selfish and ignorant, and now I'm going to tear him apart because of it.

As more tears leak out of my eyes, his name leaves me on a whimper, "Austin."

His hands tighten around the bars.

Behind me, Brayden groans with anguish.

I know he hates this. I'm hurting him too because I do care for Austin and it shows in the way I just said his name.

I keep destroying them both and no matter what I do it'll always be like this. All I can do is try to set one of them free and hope that one day he'll forgive me for my immature foolishness.

Crying, I open my mouth again—

"It's him. You're picking him," Austin says through gritted teeth.

I start to nod, but I catch myself before doing so.

"You love him?"

Lips pressed together, I refuse to answer Austin's question. Brayden is behind me. Even if I've admitted to myself that the emotion still exists within me, I'm not ready to divulge it to him.

And why should I? Regardless of what I feel for Brayden, I can never have him. There's too much behind us. Between us. Too many bad notes, too many mistakes.

Not to mention the largest obstacle of all, and Austin is aware of that.

"How are you supposed to be with him when he's your fucking stepbrother, Kira?"

Ding. Ding. Ding. I'm not. Brayden and me, we're not meant to be. It can never happen, I know this.

Brayden doesn't. Or he doesn't care.

"What the fuck do you care? She's making it clear she wants me and it's none of your fucking business how we work things out."

Austin ignores him, his eyes *on fire* as he stares at me. "Exactly how are you planning on working this out? Or are you going to just continue hiding?"

I flinch. Low blow, yeah, but I know he isn't being malicious. It's a valid point.

He narrows his eyes in Brayden's direction. "What are *you* going to do? *Hide* her all the time?" Brayden starts talking but Austin focuses on me again and cuts him off. "I can give you so much more than he can, Kira, and we both know that."

Austin never hurt me, never tore me apart. He's also right about being able to *openly* be with me. His love is pure. Untainted.

And I want no part of it.

If I'm going to decide on anyone's love, I know whose I want. Stained, dark, sick, painful, and obsessive, and yet it's the one I'd pick if I could.

Tears continue to silently leak down my face. I press my lips together and look up into Austin's eyes. The words won't leave me. I know exactly what I have to tell him to end this once and for all, yet I can't.

Not just because Brayden's here and I'm not ready to let him know everything happening inside me. Hurting Austin like this is one of the hardest things I've ever done.

I can't speak, but I have to end this here and now and there's only one way.

When Austin asks me one last time, "Kira, be honest with me. Fully honest. You can't see yourself ever trying with me?"

All I can do is shake my head no.

The look in his eyes is too much. I close my own like the coward I am, unable to see it anymore.

"So that's it. You want me to just leave you alone?"

I nod, but I'm crying so hard at this point that I doubt my response is believable.

The door opens out in the hall and the officer calls me out. My time is up.

"I'm sorry, Austin. It just can't ever happen between us."

His jaw clenches stubbornly. I'm breaking his heart and yet the defiance in his stare tells me he's not finished with me.

Until another man actually claims me, he's never going to let me go.

I spin around to talk to Brayden one last time. He's staring at me with both hope and betrayal in his expression.

He can't tell if I want Austin or not. I know. My inability to shut down Austin entirely is giving off mixed signals.

I'll fix it later, I promise myself.

I run up to him and ignore when the officer yells that it's time to leave. "I'm going to call your dad, okay? Make sure everything is fixed. I'll be waiting for you at home when you get out, I swear."

Some of the hurt leaks from his eyes. "Call my mom instead."

I nod and walk down the hall before the officer decides to come drag me out. Once outside, I pause on my way to the front and try to wipe my face clean of tears.

Futile. They won't stop. I'm destroyed by what's happened to those two because of me.

The girls are anxiously standing, waiting for me with worried expressions. As one, they come around me and hug me tight.

I let them, needing their support more than ever. Without them here, I honestly don't know what I'd do.

TWO

Kira

"Call my mom instead."

The words are still ringing in my ears as I sit on the hard bench, waiting. Why in the world I said his dad . . . Force of habit, most likely. That, and his mom lives two hours away.

She should be here soon, which is good for two reasons— she's not Steven and she's a nurse.

Brayden's wounds need some actual attention. The officers literally left both he and Austin like that.

My knee bounces up and down as I bite on my thumbnail. Jenna, Marilyn, and Ashley whisper around me, but I'm too focused on Brayden and all I didn't get to say. All that I *couldn't* say to Austin.

That was two hours ago. The first hour I spent filling the girls in on my history with Brayden.

I started from the beginning.

It was brutal, but in the end, they understood why I'd never told them everything.

The history between us isn't pretty. It's jagged and jaded. Filled with every emotion under the sun magnified by a strength only hormones can induce.

Scary. Frightening. Overpowering in how it affects me . . . affects us both.

I've been trapped in my brain, left to stew about the night's events. The cataclysmic result of something I started seven months ago when I tried to forget him and gave Austin a piece of me.

It was a way to forget Brayden, but also an attempt to hurt him.

Our toxic relationship only thrived in the chaos.

In the end, it doesn't matter.

There's only one man I've ever wanted.

And yet, ultimately, to the world I'm Brayden Hunt's little sister.

"Kira!"

I blink up, staring at a woman walking toward me that I haven't seen in years. The one who used to be my neighbor, who was always so nice. I wonder if I can even look her in the eyes knowing *why* she isn't my neighbor anymore.

My mom is the one her ex cheated on her with.

"Mrs. Hunt." The name sounds strange to my ears. Even though my mom didn't change her last name because of me and Ryan, she is the current Mrs. Hunt. I stand to greet her, my posture stiff, unsure of what she thinks of me after everything.

She smiles at me as the gap between us closes and she wraps her arms around me. "That's not me anymore. Just call me Abby."

My muscles relax as she guides us to sit a few feet from my

friends.

"I'm sorry you had to come all this way. He didn't want me to call Steve." The words fly from my mouth before I can stop them.

She stares at me, then pats me on the knee. "It's okay, I'm glad you did."

I'm surprised by her calm. The last times I'd seen her she looked worn. Tired and angry and sad. Staring at her now, there is worry, but she looks . . . happy. Not happy about the situation, but that maybe her life is better than it was when she was married to Steven.

"How did you know?" I ask.

She raises her brows. "Know what?"

"That I was calling about Brayden? You immediately asked if he was okay after I said my name."

She studies me for a moment, trying to gauge something. "Well, because *you* called me."

"Why me? What does that matter?" What has he told her?

"You have no other reason to call me."

"And you aren't curious why it was me?"

Her eyes twinkle. "Kira, if you're referring to if I know about my only son's undying love for you, I do."

"Y-you do?" Wait . . . undying love?

She nods. "I've known for years how he feels about you."

"How?"

"You're full of questions. Shouldn't it be me asking what got my child in lockup?"

I sit back and cross my arms. "You two are the same. It's like trying to pull teeth!"

Her head falls back with a laugh. "So true." She bumps me with her shoulder. "He was always sweet on you. I know my

23

boy, so when he came to live with me before college, I knew something was up. A little molasses cookie torture and he caved, telling me everything. Ever since then, I'm the only one he could talk to about you."

"He talked about me?"

She nods. "He left out some details, the kind moms just don't want to know, but the deep feelings for you have always been there. I hoped for both your sakes that it would turn out to be a crush, but after a while, after he said he couldn't go home the next summer, I knew it was more. Your age difference was hard on him."

"But he never . . . He's always been against love." And now he seems devoted to me. It's odd, goes against the Brayden I grew up knowing.

Her lips form a thin line. "That's our fault, his father and me. I'm afraid the example we gave him poisoned him on the idea."

"It did. Long ago, when we were kids, he told me."

Abby gives me a sad smile. "Now you're older, adults, not as ruled by teenage hormones. He's at your mercy. He'll do anything for you."

"Anything?"

"To keep you, protect you, there's nothing that would stop him."

Oh, God.

I can't stop the image of his beaten, pleading expression through the bars as I moved to talk to Austin.

The pain he'd been exuding made a small vindictive part of me happy, because I saw it as balance. But the part that always tried to soothe him took over and had me running to him.

I will always run to him, even after everything.

"But . . . we can't even be together."

She studies me for a moment. "Legally, there's nothing separating you two."

"Maybe not, but to society he's my brother."

She purses her lips. "I wish I could argue against you, because the last thing I want is an obstacle in front of his happiness, but you're going to college with a lot of your classmates who know you as Brayden's younger sister. Even if it is by marriage."

"We can't be a real couple."

"I wouldn't say that, but I also wouldn't say it's going to be easy."

Nothing between us has been easy in years. Easy was when we were kids. Now everything is hard and emotionally draining.

"Why don't you go on home? I'll deal with getting him out and finding out what the damage is."

I nod and stand, my mind already whirling with how bad it could be. Will he go to jail? I don't even know what the charge is let alone if it's a slap on the wrist kind of one or more serious.

I turn back to her and smile. "Thanks, Abby."

Walking up to the girls, I can tell right away something is off. The expressions and whispered words as they all tuck their phones away set off alarms.

"What? What is it?" I ask.

Jenna tries to give me a *it's nothing* smile, but fails.

"Let's get you home," Marilyn says as she stands and takes my hand. "Besides, I think you've got more to tell us."

Diverted, but I let them take me away.

My heart tears in my chest with each step away from Brayden. The image of him locked in that cell all beat up kills me, but there's nothing more I can do.

Let his mom handle it and I'll try to handle any damage on the other end.

As we walk out, Marilyn wraps her arm around mine and Jenna throws her arm over my shoulder.

I love my girls. Not only are they standing by me and up for me, but it's after one in the morning and they're next to me as we walk out of the police station.

We all slip back into Jenna's car and I look back to the station in defeat and worry.

"Stop that," Marilyn says, swatting at my hand.

I'm about to snap at her, my brow furrowing as I almost unleash some bitchiness, when I realize what I'm doing.

Damn, six nails down. Mangled by anxiety. On occasion, usually in times of stress, I chew on my nails.

I smile sadly at her. "Thanks. Looks like I need to get a manicure again."

Jenna hasn't even thrown it into gear when Ashley lets out a low hiss from the front seat.

"Oh, shit."

The way her words come out makes the hackles on the back of my neck stand up.

I pull out my phone, assuming whatever she and Lyn are staring at is on Facebook, and open up the app.

At the top of my newsfeed—*"Incest is disgusting! What the hell is wrong with people?"*

The blood leaves my face for a fraction of a second before it erupts into a boil, my hand clenches down around my phone.

26

Jennifer has dealt the first blow.

I have to force back the posts my fingers want to type.

It's not incest, bitch.

Shut your cunt mouth.

You don't know what the fuck you're talking about.

Jealousy doesn't look good on you, slut.

Only the tip of the iceberg I want to shove up her ass.

I'm typing out letters before I can stop myself, but come to my senses before I hit enter.

I can't respond. It'll look suspicious.

I have to ignore it. Swallow it all down.

My pride.

My anger.

My protectiveness.

My love.

"Is she fucking serious?" I say with a stressed laugh. I look up from my phone to the three sets of eyes watching me. "Bitch has some balls saying that shit without proof."

The expressions that are watching me with such love and worry don't change. Looking back down at the screen, I see why.

"Craig Randall and 1,046 others" have reacted to her post. "268 shares."

"Fuck . . . that's most of the school."

And all in the last four hours since her post.

"Dad has a whole bunch of knives from his military days. We can go cut a bitch up and feed the parts to sharks," Ashley says in an almost serious tone.

It's enough to make me let out a small laugh through the tears that are forming.

"Yeah, but the nearest sharks are a thousand miles away.

That skank would stink up my car!" Jenna's brow furrows as the corner of her lips turn down in disgust.

"There's Newport Aquarium."

"It might look a little weird if we wheel in something and start dumping human remains into the tank."

"Damn."

"But in all seriousness, Kira, that fucking bitch is going to pay."

I nod, but my bottom lip is nailed between my teeth.

"Okay," Jenna starts as we pull out, "so, he broke your heart, but I gotta ask . . . What was it like kissing Brayden Hunt at fifteen?"

I let out a small laugh. "It was . . ." Fuck. There's only one way to describe it. "It was the best kiss of my life."

"The best?" Marilyn wags her eyebrows.

"I would say there have been better ones since then, but it was definitely the most memorable."

They giggle and I appreciate their attempt to lighten the mood. It really does help.

The house is dark when we pull up. They're still asleep, which means they don't know yet.

"You're going to have to sneak in," Jenna says.

There's one way to do that, or there used to be before Steven had my climbing limb cut off the tree outside Brayden's window.

I shake my head. "Front door or back door."

Jenna's head tips back in laughter. "That's what he said."

I roll my eyes, my lip twitching as I push on the back of her seat. "Perv."

Grabbing onto the handle, I open the door and climb out. The windows roll down and my girls lean toward the openings.

"Good luck," Marilyn says.

"We'll form a plan of attack in the morning," Ashley calls from the other side of Jenna.

Jenna smiles and reaches for my hand. "Love you, girl."

I smile at her. "Love all of you, so much." I blow them a kiss as they pull away, watch as they disappear around the corner.

Left alone in front of the house, I stare up at the building that has never felt like a home. A residence. A place to sleep.

A place I endured because my mother was happy.

I miss the ranch home to the left. The one with the tree house. It was my sanctuary. *My* room, *our* home.

This house was the fun place with the pool, where Brayden could be found, but inside I watched it change him. Warp him.

It wasn't the house's fault, but the man residing within its walls. His poison infected everyone. Slowly killed happiness, joy, and love with his selfish venom until everyone was miserable.

Every time Brayden came home everything seemed to brighten, the soothing light combatting the evil. He overpowers everything, which I think makes his father jealous.

After seeing his mom for the first time in years, I see where he gets it from. There's an infectious light within him, but there's also the consuming darkness from his father.

I *hate* his father. I *hate* what he's done to my mother. Sucking the life from her. Any small measure of happiness he once provided stripped away.

A miserable man who thrives on making others miserable, too. Takes pleasure in unhappiness.

With a sigh, I start up the driveway. My shoes click loudly against the pavement in the silent night air, almost amplifying and announcing to everyone my presence.

My phone provides just enough light to get my key into the lock. It clicks over, a small creak of the hinge as I push it open just enough to squeeze through, then shut and lock it again.

I cringe as my heels click on the hardwoods, resonating around the entryway. A few more taps as I pull them off and head to the stairs.

Everything is still dark when I reach the top of the stairs, only eight steps until I reach the safety of my room.

"Kira? Are you just now getting in?" Mom asks, stopping me in my sneaky tracks.

Fuck.

Busted.

I don't even turn to look at her, but I can feel her eyes burning into me. "Yes."

The padding of her feet on the carpet causes a thudding in my chest that grows harder with each step. "Two hours past curfew?"

"I can explain," I say as I turn to face her.

Her arms are folded across her chest in true you're-in-trouble mom fashion. "It better be good, young lady."

"Well . . . something happened."

Her eyes narrow. "Please elaborate on this something."

"There was a fight and I was a witness."

"A fight?"

I peer over her shoulder at her bedroom door. No sign of Steven.

"Brayden."

Her eyes widen as she lets out a gasp. "Is he okay?"

I shake my head and pull her down the hall and into my room. "Don't tell him."

Her brow scrunches. "Tell who?" It only takes a second before her mouth pops open to an O shape. "Kira . . . it's not something I can keep from him. He's his father."

"Just until he gets out."

"Of *jail*?"

I nod. "His mom is there, she's taking care of everything."

"Abigail's there? How did she . . ." The question falls away. She knows the answer, has already figured out that I called, but I hope she doesn't look further into it.

"He's pretty beaten physically, he doesn't need to be verbally bashed when he isn't even here to defend himself."

She purses her lips and nods. "I'm sure we'll hear from her soon."

There's no talk about my breaking curfew, even though I'm eighteen. It's still their house, their rules. I respect and love my mom, so I'll do as she asks.

Stepping forward, I wrap my arms around her waist and lay my head on her shoulder. "Thanks, Mom."

It seems like forever since I got a real, deep, comforting hug from her, and she doesn't disappoint. Mom hugs can take it all away.

When we part, she motions to my bed. "Get to sleep and we'll talk more in the morning."

I nod and watch as she walks out, closing the door behind her.

Unfortunately, there's no sleep in sight for me. Not until he's out, until I know he's okay.

Until I can see and touch him.

Sitting down at my computer, I move the mouse to wake it up. I'm afraid to go on Facebook, to look at Jenn's post, but at the same time I'm driven to do it.

There's even more comments than before. More people asking who she's talking about.

It feels like there are stones in my stomach. Why does she not only have to be the biggest slut, but also the biggest cunt? Is her jealousy that deranged that she thinks her obtuse words will drive a wedge between me and Brayden and have him rushing into her arms?

Talk about unbalanced.

The bitch doesn't post a single comment, because she can't. It's a theory. That, and the more she doesn't comment, the more worked up the crowd becomes with curiosity.

"Well, bitch, curiosity killed the cat. You'll fucking get what's coming to you."

The words are typed out before I can stop myself, but I force a breath, then slowly delete each and every letter.

It's nothing more than bait, but with all the attention, where will she stop?

I pull my knees up, hugging them to my chest, staring at the screen.

"I wish they'd never gotten married," I whisper to no one.

Is it so bad to wish that my mother had never had her small taste of happiness, just so I could have mine?

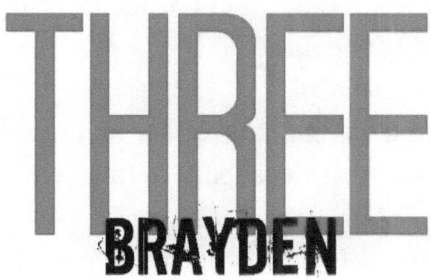

THREE
BRAYDEN

"Are you done?"

"What the fuck do you mean am I done?"

My fingers curl into fists. I fucking hate my father's voice. I hate him even more.

And if he talks to my mom like that one more time . . .

My mom has her phone hooked up to the car's Bluetooth so, unfortunately, I can hear both sides of their conversation.

"Are you done behaving like a jackass or do you want to continue acting like the fool you are?" my mother asks him coldly.

I do a double take, mouth gaping open. Whoa . . .

My mother has screamed at him many, many times before. But she's never cursed at him.

She's never spoken to him this coldly, either. Like he's shit beneath her shoe and she can't be bothered with him beyond the getting rid of him part.

My father's clearly just as shocked. The silence on his end is uncharacteristic. I can almost feel his indignation.

Pride for my mom warms my chest.

"Abby—"

"*Abigail*, Steven. And I don't want to hear it anymore. I told you what's happening."

"He has his own place!"

I want to pretend that my father not wanting me there doesn't hurt, but there's a part of me that cringes at his words.

"Yes. He does. But it's going to be easier for him if he stays there until Monday when I can get him to see a lawyer about his options."

"He wouldn't need to see a lawyer if he wasn't such a piece of—"

"Careful, Steven. Especially when someone like you has no moral leg to stand on and no right to judge him."

"What?"

"Oh, I'm sorry. You need me to be clearer? *You're* the piece of shit here, not him."

Holy. Shit.

My mother hangs up the phone on my father before he can respond. She's calm on the exterior, but her cheeks are pink and her eyes are ablaze as she stares straight ahead.

"I've never loved you more, Mom."

My comment rips a surprised laugh out of her and the tension leaves her. She reaches over and squeezes my hand. "It's about time someone told him."

We pull up to the front of the house less than ten minutes later. I'm expecting to be hit with tension of the thought of stepping foot in there and facing my father.

Fuck that. I don't care. My girl's in there.

And I think she might honestly feel something for Austin.

I swallow back bile at the thought. There's no forgetting how she looked at me when we were arrested. She stared at me with the same pained adoration back in the holding cell.

Once and for all, we're going to straighten this out. She's going to explain to me what it is she feels for that bastard.

Mom stops me before I can exit the car. "It's just for the weekend. Hopefully we can get the lawyer to see you first thing Monday."

My jaw clenches. "Mom, I'm not staying here until I have to go to work. I'm only here for one thing." I don't have to tell her what that is. She knows.

Kira's car is in the driveway. Good. Neither one of us is staying here, and we're going to need it to get back to my place.

Mom sighs but she doesn't argue. "Well, I'm going to be staying with Jolie, remember her?" At my nod, she continues. "I won't be more than twenty minutes away so if anything happens, you call me. All right?"

I nod again and turn to leave.

Her grip on my arm tightens. When I turn to stare at her, she's eyeing all my untreated wounds with both a mother's concern and a nurse's examining eye.

"Mom, it's fine. I'll get it cleaned up as soon as I'm inside."

Her eyes flicker up toward my brow. "That one's going to need stitches."

"Butterfly stitches at the most." The wound's crusted over, already beginning to scab, and it stopped bleeding hours ago.

My mom exhales slowly and for a second it seems like she's not going to let me out of the car.

Love her, but nothing's keeping me from Kira.

I open the car door and step out. "Love you, Mom. Promise it'll be okay. I'll text you once I'm home."

She nods. There are tears in her eyes.

Damn it, I hate putting her through this but I can't wait a second longer without finding my girl.

As I'm jogging up the driveway toward the house, I hear my mom drive away. I pull out my keys and step inside.

He's there. At the foot of the stairs. Waiting for me. His eyes show none of the concern that I saw in my mom's. Instead, he eyes my wounds with blatant disdain.

Whatever. I don't have time for this shit.

Staring straight ahead, I walk to the stairs and try to go past him.

He grabs my arm and pulls me back. "Where the hell do you think you're going?" His hold on my arm tightens. He wants to hurt me and this is his only way of controlling himself.

My way of holding back the urge to punch him right in the face? I grind my teeth and stare at the second floor landing. "I'm heading up to my room."

"I know where you're really fucking going," my father growls, and he pulls my arm harder.

Don't break his fucking face. Don't break his fucking face. "I just want to go upstairs and wash all the blood off."

"Do you think I'm fucking stupid?"

Don't answer that.

"I know where you're really going and I'm telling you right now—"

"Steve!"

I turn my head and see Sonia at the entrance to the living room. She's glaring at my father.

"Let him go, Steven. He's been through enough."

My father sneers at her as if he's disgusted with her as well. "Stay out of this, Sonia. He deserves everything he's getting."

One more. One more and I swear to God . . .

My father leans closer and mumbles loud enough for me to hear, "Stay the fuck away from your sister or I'll call the cops on you. I don't care if you're my son, you're legal and I don't have to accept you here."

He drops my arm.

Thank God. I don't think I can stay near him another second without ending his disgusting life.

I run up the stairs, rage pummeling my veins. I focus only on Kira's open door. If I don't focus on her I'm going to run down the stairs and find my father.

I stop outside Kira's door. She's at her desk, staring at her computer. Her brow's furrowed and there's a tiny frown on her face.

She's worried.

"Baby."

Kira jumps and flies around in her seat. Her eyes widen.

And there. There it is. What I've been dying to see in her eyes again.

"*Brayden.*"

"Come here, baby."

She's out of her seat in a flash. I catch her up against me, hugging her tight. The warmth and feel of her, that delicious scent . . . Groaning, I squeeze her tighter.

37

Can't get close enough, and I'm pretty sure I'm suffocating her.

Kira doesn't care. Her little body burrows deeper, and her thin arms are locked around my neck.

My face is buried in her neck.

She places a kiss on my temple.

There's just so damn much bouncing between us. Pure emotion. That affection and need that I've been drowning for all these years.

Choking madness of a dead man's thirst.

Saved by this. The only person I've ever needed as much as I need air to breathe.

Kira. My sweet kitty.

"Oh God, Brayden. I've been so freaking worried about you." More kisses to my temple, cheek, jaw. Sweet affectionate kisses. The kind that are meant to soothe.

I'm not thinking about that.

Sliding one hand down her back, I squeeze her ass and grind my hips into her.

She stutters my name and tries to pull back.

Refusing to release her, I take two steps into her room. Then, I put her down long enough to spin her around and press her against the wall next to the door.

"Brayden!" she hisses under her breath and tries to push off the wall.

Palming the back of her head, I hold her in place and yank down her tiny pajama shorts.

"Why are you doing this?" she whispers, trying to reach back for my wrist.

I ignore the question and ask one of my own, "Why couldn't you tell him it's *me* you want to be with?" Fisting her thong, I shove it down her hips and leave it trapped around her thighs.

No answer. Kira tenses, and I can almost imagine her pressing her lips together stubbornly.

Fine. We'll deal with that later.

I pull at my button and practically rip my zipper open.

She hears it and tenses even more. "We can't. They're downstairs. They could come up any second."

I know. Don't give a fuck. Can't think past the warmth of her pussy right now.

I yank my cock out. Tightening my hold on the back of her neck, I bend my knees and slide my dick between her plump ass cheeks.

Her high-pitched little gasp makes it jump. The head rubs into her asshole and that gasp melts into a low, hungry moan.

"Soon, baby," I mumble, using my dick to play with her ass some more.

She relaxes against the wall and turns her head to the side. Her lips are parted and her beautiful eyes are glazed.

"You want me balls deep in this ass, don't you baby?"

Her eager nod makes me smile.

Shifting my hips, I slide my cock down.

Wet. Swollen. So motherfucking inviting. A single thrust shoves me in nice and deep.

Kira barely catches her scream and she bites down into her lip so hard she draws blood.

I let go of her neck and cup my hand over her mouth. "Don't. Scream." And I start pounding into her as hard as I can without making too much noise.

I know the door is open. One of our parents can come up the stairs and see me fucking her from behind. I should've closed the door.

As if I give a fuck about any of that.

Jaw clenched tight, I focus on the open door and thrust into my girl's wet pussy. The position makes her even tighter. Every move is a slight struggle as her walls clamp down on me.

Kira whimpers into my hand, rocking her hips back in circles. I look down for a second to take in the sight. Her beautiful ass cheeks frame my soaked dick as I fuck her.

"God baby. I can't wait to fuck that ass," I whisper roughly, working my hips in circles to get deeper.

She squeezes her eyes shut, mewling quietly beneath my hand.

Yeah, she's almost there.

Fuck. So am I.

Kira grips my entire length, so wet and juicy that I hear every thrust I give her.

There's a sound on the stairs.

She locks up, eyes wide with terror at being caught.

I ignore the sound, her fear, thrusting deeper, blindly chasing that explosion.

Kira struggles in my grip, eyes on the hallway outside the door.

I shove in all the way to the hilt and rotate my hips in circles. I make sure to tilt my hips so I hit that spot inside her just right.

Her eyes squeeze shut. She's fighting this. Her pussy is practically convulsing around me, already starting to come, and she's too scared of being caught to tumble over that edge.

"This is mine, you hear me?" I hiss in her ear and press my nose to her hair so I can fill my lungs with her delicious scent. "That pussy comes when I want it to come."

A muffled whimper leaves her mouth behind my hand.

"Don't you dare scream." I remove my hand from her face and slide it down around to the front of her body. Then, I slide my thumb between her ass cheeks and find her hole.

She loves it. Doesn't matter how hard she fights this, she's giving me that orgasm.

I play with her clit and ass at the same time and speed up my thrusts, not caring anymore if someone can hear the sound of skin slapping skin.

Kira slams her hand on her mouth and claws at the wall.

"Yeah. Fuck baby." My growl's too loud but there's no help for it. She's squeezing down, pulsing, right where I fucking need her. I lean down and bite the side of her neck. "That's it. Give it to me." I bite her neck again, harder.

Her orgasm tears through her, the pulsation so powerful that I'm dragged along with her.

Pure pleasure bursts through my balls and cock, and I arch into her, head thrown back, lost in the painful bliss of emptying inside her.

The roaring in my ears recedes just in time for me to hear yet another sound on the stairs.

Definitely steps this time.

Kira hears it, too.

I slip out of her and feel all the come leak out as I go. She rushes to lift up her shorts while I shove my cock back into my jeans.

"Brayden, are you staying for breakfast?" Sonia calls from the stairs.

Kira's a hot mess, cheeks flushed, hair all over the place. The two bite marks on the side of her neck are bright red. Brutally visible.

Just like I wanted them to be.

I zip up my jeans, check to make sure there's no come stains on me, and walk to the doorway. When I lean out, Sonia's halfway up the stairs, staring up nervously.

Like she didn't want to chance coming all the way up and interrupting something.

Fuck. She knows something. I'd suspected it before, but now it's more than a suspicion. It's almost a certainty.

"I won't be staying. Just wanted to talk to Kira before heading back out to my place."

She nods with that same nervous expression on her face. Without another word, she turns and heads down the stairs.

If she suspects I'm fucking her daughter, why hasn't she confronted me about it? I'll ponder that later. I step back in the room and face Kira. "Get dressed. We're not staying."

My girl's flustered. Confused. She blinks at me and shakes her head a little. "Wha—"

"We're leaving baby."

"But your wounds—"

"Exactly. I need you with me. But not here. I'll meet you downstairs in ten minutes."

FOUR

BRAYDEN

I'm busy minding my own damn business when I feel someone behind me.

I have a feeling who it is. I refuse to turn and acknowledge his presence.

"Where do you think you're going?"

"Home." I stuff more clothes into my duffel bag and make a note to come remove the last of my clothing from here. I'll keep what's absolutely necessary but it's time to start limiting my time here. Kira can come over to my apartment instead.

"You are home." I can hear him sneering the last word.

"My apartment."

"We'll see how long you have that."

I pause and wonder: does this man *want* me to hit him? Sighing, I zip up my duffel. "What do you mean?"

"Do you honestly think that after this I'm going to continue paying for it?" he asks.

My jaw ticks. "Whatever." I mean it. I'll find a way. My mom has already offered to help me. I don't want her to but it's a last, last, *last* resort. Worst case scenario, I just have to work two jobs.

"We're not done talking about this."

Oh, I think we are. "I'm exhausted. Heading out." I'm surprised he actually steps aside and lets me through.

Then I hit the top of the stairs and hear his sardonic, disgusting comment.

"I hope her pussy's good enough to be ruining your life over. Lord knows her mother's was for me."

Red stains everything around me. Rage explodes inside my head. I whirl around.

He smiles at me, as if *baiting* me. "Go ahead. Add another incident to your record today. Let's see how good that makes you look in front of the judge."

My future with Kira. That's the only thing that keeps my feet planted on the ground. "You're fucking disgusting."

He laughs. "You're the one fucking your stepsister, *son*. Who, by the way, pretended to be on her way to see her friends, at three in the morning. As if it isn't obvious she's waiting for you down the block."

She is. I told her to.

It fucking kills me that this scumbag knows that.

The smile drops off his face and his expression turns murderous. "Go ahead. Keep fucking her. But you won't do it in this house. And if you get caught? I'll ruin both your fucking lives."

"Don't you dare threaten her!"

"Me? You're the one threatening her with your inability to stay away. Maybe you don't give a damn what everyone will

44

say, but you'll tear her away from everything she loves. Everyone she loves. And your best friend? He won't be able to show his face in his own hometown either without having to hear about how disgusting you are."

His words cut deep. Because, I have to admit, I've only been thinking about me. About convincing Kira to be with me so we could be together out in the open.

My father's right; I don't give a fuck what anyone will say. But the way this is going to impact Kira and Ryan . . .

Damn it all to hell, I'm trapped.

I refuse to let her go, but for now I'm going to have to be extremely careful until I find another solution.

And if that way somehow involves ruining my own father's life . . .

The wheels start turning and the whispers of the idea going through my mind calm me.

"Do yourself a favor before I make you regret being such a waste of skin—take Kira's name, life, and everything about her out of your filthy mouth and mind. She doesn't exist to you and you will leave her alone."

My father's eyes flash and he bares his teeth at me. "Are you threatening me, boy?"

"No, *father*. It's a promise." I run down the stairs before he says anything else and I forget all about my future with the woman I love. There's no sign of Sonia on the way out.

As I step outside, it finally sinks in that Ryan, probably Sonia, my father, and my mother all now know.

Not to mention Dana and all of Kira's closest friends.

For how long can we keep the truth from spilling out? I want to tell myself that the consequences don't matter, but Kira's happiness matters a whole fucking lot.

My phone vibrates and I know it's her before I even look.

Is everything okay? I've been waiting around the corner a while.

Yeah. I just got out of the house. On second thought, drive three blocks over and I'll meet you there.

Why? Did something happen?

We just have to be more careful for now, baby. I hate reminding her of this huge obstacle between us, but after that little conversation with my father there's no help for it.

He'll do it. He'll either find a way to throw me back in jail for visiting, or he'll be at the center of the scandal, spreading the poison while playing the martyr.

You're right. I'll be waiting for you.

I stick to the shadows as much as I can as I walk to our meet up point. When I get there, I see that Kira's parked with the ignition and lights turned off.

My smart girl.

But it burns that she has to hide like this while being with me.

Not for long, I remind myself.

Whatever I have to do, whatever it costs me, this situation will be resolved.

Kira's beautiful, hazel eyes glitter in the dark. She's staring at me worriedly while I get in the car.

I close the door and start to reach for her. Last second, I pull my hand back and clench my fist.

She nods and turns the ignition.

Her silent agreement of how careful we have to be sets off an alarm. I don't know why. It's common sense that we need to err on the side of caution.

She's always been the more careful one.

Call it simple intuition. Whatever. All I know is that her behavior is starting to worry me.

Her foot presses down on the accelerator hard and we take off like maniacs. I'm so shocked that I stare at the road with wide eyes.

Usually, I'm the devil speeding like I'm immortal. Her hurry to get us home worries me. "Kira—"

My kitty doesn't even need me to finish the sentence. "I can't stand to see you injured like that anymore. Need to get you home and take care of you." She takes a turn at full speed, narrowly avoiding the sidewalk.

God, I fucking love her.

"Baby, I'm not bleeding anymore."

"Don't care." She speeds up even more.

I smile, drunk on the speed and her worry over me. "If the cops pull us over, they might take me back in."

Annnd . . . The car slows down by at least fifteen miles per hour.

Fuck, man. She's making me hard. "I want to put my dick in you so bad." We're by the highway now. No worrying about people seeing us.

I reach over to intertwine our fingers and she lets me. I stare at her; she stares at the road, her focus on getting us to my place.

She's different. Open. *Allowing.* No hesitation in holding my hand or even squeezing it back when I squeeze hers.

Relief melts all of my tension. I'm so happy to have her back, to have her like this, that I almost forget all about the Austin issue.

Almost. Thinking his name is enough to bring a lot of my tension back.

"Kira, we need to talk."

She doesn't say anything and continues to stare straight ahead. There's no refusal forthcoming, but she isn't welcoming the idea of a discussion either.

"Tell me why you couldn't tell Austin I'm the one you want."

There. A flash in her eyes. A slight narrowing. She presses her lips tight together and shakes her head.

Her hand doesn't let mine go, nor does she look in my direction.

Stubborn little thing.

"I'm not letting this one go," I say.

"I know."

"Then why not just answer me so we can move forward." Please tell me you don't have feelings for him and I swear we'll just move forward . . .

"We have bigger problems."

"Problems bigger than you having feelings for that pussy?" I ask, incredulous.

"Later." She says nothing more, and it's fucking obvious that she considers the subject closed for now.

I'm so frustrated I'm tempted to let her hand go. But that's not what we need—definitely not what *I* need.

I drop the subject for now and silence descends. It's not an uncomfortable silence, but it's not ideal either.

It's fine. I'll let it rock. The feel of her hand on mine is enough to keep my impatience at bay. As soon as we're in my house, I'm going to get her to talk about Austin and whatever is on her mind.

"Are you in any pain?" she asks as we get on the highway.

"No, baby."

Her eyes flicker to me and there's a hint of disbelief.

"I swear. I'm good."

"Looking like that? Yeah, okay."

I smile at her. "I got you with me, though. Don't I?"

Warmth shines in her eyes. We fall back into silence and remain that way for the next thirty minutes.

That's how long it takes us to get to my apartment. Even when worried for me, she can't help but rush to get me home and take care of me.

Fucking hell, please tell me this means we're finally heading in the right direction.

Kira parks the car and we head upstairs. She takes my keys and leads the way, running up the stairs in small jean shorts. By the time I hit the second floor landing, she already has my apartment door open.

I smile at her determined expression and walk inside. She closes the door behind us and heads straight for the bathroom.

I know what's coming. And I also know I'm not getting anywhere with her while all her protective instincts are engaged like this.

My woman needs to take care of her man and nothing is going to stop her.

Smiling, I sit back on the couch and remove my shirt. I'm so damn happy that I don't even feel the pain of the cut on my lip stretching.

Kira exits the bathroom, her small arms full of first aid supplies—alcohol, peroxide, wipes, cotton, and the small kit that has extras.

Her eyes bounce all over my tattoos—all carvings in honor of her. Every single one of them. She sees me smiling and scowls viciously. "This is by no means funny."

"I'm not smiling because I think it's funny."

Dropping all the items onto the coffee table, she opens the small first aid kit. "So why are you smiling?"

"Because you make me so damn fucking happy."

A pause. A deep inhale. An even slower exhale. Then, she squares her shoulders stubbornly and opens one of the gauzes.

"What's going on with you?"

Of course, she ignores my question.

She wets the gauze with peroxide and comes up to me. On her knees before me, she starts slowly wiping away the crusted blood on my brow. "I'm starting here because it's the worst one. Then I'll do the one on your lip."

I make sure I stay utterly still for her. "Baby, talk to me."

"Brayden, it's bad."

My heart accelerates. Just like that, I'm nothing but rage, adrenaline, and testosterone, all primed to protect my woman from whatever is threatening her. "Who's fucking with you?"

Kira pauses, blinking at me in surprise. "How—"

"I know my girl. Always have. Don't forget that." The pink blush that stains her cheeks almost distracts me. "Now tell me who messed with you and has you like this."

Sighing, she wets the gauze in peroxide again and goes back to work. "The truth?"

"Always," I grit out as she wipes off the slightly formed scab covering the wound on my eyebrow. It starts bleeding immediately.

"Oh God, I'm sorry but I had to clean it—"

"It's fine."

She rushes to cover it with gauze and opens the pack of

butterfly stitches. With gentle movements, she removes the gauze and applies the end of one stitch to my skin so she can pull the wound close together.

"Now, Kira."

Another sigh. "I shouldn't be here, Brayden."

"*What*?" After everything? After it all finally felt like it was falling into place? She was opening up to me like she used to back in the day, and now she's hitting me with this shit?

Kira finishes applying the butterfly stitch and begins cleaning the cut on my lip. I'm glaring at her and she glares right back, unafraid. "Things are bad right now."

"Because you want Austin?" I ask.

She flings the cotton ball across the coffee table. "You idiot, this isn't about him!" Huffing, she grabs another cotton ball and soaks it in alcohol instead of peroxide.

I'm so on edge I don't even notice what she's up to. "Seems like it is to me and your refusal to discuss the issue of him makes it more obvious."

Glowering at me with an adorable pout on her face, she presses the cotton ball to my face.

Right on the small but deep cut on my cheekbone.

I hiss through my teeth. "Goddamn it woman."

"You want to keep talking shit about my ex-lay, when it's *your* ex-cockslut that's the real problem?"

I've slept with many women. God help me, I have. But only one has ever inspired that much venom in Kira.

Only one ever deserved it as much as she does.

"What the fuck is Jennifer doing?"

She doesn't answer, instead placing a bandage on my cheek. Then, she stands and goes to where her small

51

overnight bag is so she can get her phone. She pulls something up on it and hands it to me.

"Why am I looking at Jennifer's timeline?"

"Scroll down a little."

I do and without thinking about it, I start reading the most popular post out loud. "Incest is disgu—" The rest of it registers. My first urge is to fling the phone in my hand across the room. I have to remind myself it's not my phone.

My second urge is to hunt down Jennifer's jealous, petty ass and hurt her.

I don't care what she does to me, but this is more a direct attack on Kira than anyone else. Jennifer just added herself to the list of people I'm going to ruin for fucking with my woman.

"You see?" Kira asks, arms crossed.

"Do you want to stop being with me because of this?"

"No!"

Her quick denial soothes the beast.

"But we have to be so damn careful now, Brayden."

I place her phone on the couch and move to stand. On my way up, I lift her up and she wraps her legs around my waist. "Don't worry about it. Don't worry about any of it. I'll take care of it."

Her arms wind around my neck. "How?"

I nuzzle her cheek and walk toward my room. "I told you not to worry about it, baby. Just know this: no one's going to fuck with you or what we have together. I won't let them."

"Brayden," she whispers. "Your tone . . . You're scaring me a little."

I should. Deep down, I know how far I'm willing to go to make sure everything is okay between us. I'm not a nice person when it comes to protecting Kira.

"I don't want you getting into any more problems because of me."

"Baby, stop. We're going to be fine." I'll destroy anyone in our way in order to ensure it.

And I won't give a fuck who that person is. My father, Jennifer, anyone that comes between us? They're going to meet a side of Brayden Hunt they'll wish they'd never seen.

FIVE

Kira

It was almost five in the morning by the time we got to Brayden's place, the sun was just cresting the horizon. When my eyes crack open, it's no wonder that his bedroom is lit up from the sun shining in. Morning passed right over into afternoon.

I don't know what time it is, and I don't care, because Brayden and I are tangled together. A mass of limbs carrying out the base need we share—the need for skin on skin. The need to be close. To be together.

In this small window of harmony when it's just us.

I can already tell his apartment is going to become our sanctuary. The place we can be without restricting those needs.

The last time I was here, I did the walk of shame out the door, but today is different. Turning my head, I place a kiss on his chest. The small touch stirs him and fingers begin to lightly caress my arm. He doesn't stop, doesn't deepen it, just relishes in the feeling. Drawing his hand up and down as he leans to kiss the top of my head while I trace the tattoo on his chest.

The atmosphere is different, but I can't put my finger on why.

"Morning," he says in that gravely tone that makes my knees go weak.

That is when I understand the difference.

Peace.

Because I've come to embrace what I fought against. Without my struggle against this, there's peace and tranquility. Even if it's just while I'm here, in his room.

Just me and him.

Just us.

None of the bullshit that's waiting outside the walls.

I let out a contented moan. "That feels good."

He mimics my sound. "That's my favorite thing."

"What is?" I ask.

"Making you feel good."

I roll my eyes and press against his chest to sit up.

I'm about to crack a joke, but my jaw drops instead.

His torso is sprinkled with colored marks, his face still swollen and crusted with dried blood, not to mention the bruises and black eyes.

Guilt floods back in. I'm the reason he looks like a human punching bag.

Granted, I'm certain Austin looks the same. They were both out for blood, trying to settle a score in a match I unwittingly set up.

"Do I really look like that much of a horror show?"

I can only nod, my eyes flittering around. Last night, he said it didn't hurt. I didn't believe him then, and I certainly won't if he says it again this morning.

Reaching up, his thumb smooths at the patch of skin between my brows.

"Stop."

"But it's my fault."

He blows out a breath and moves to get up. "It was going to happen sometime." I can hear him grunting and groaning, see his arm hugged against his side.

"Brayden . . ."

He holds out his hand, a strand of black hair falling into his face. "You're so worried about me? Help me clean up."

I lace my fingers in his as I slide off the bed. It's all surreal. Like a dream I'm about to wake from . . . minus the damage done to him.

But the heat of his hand in mine, that pulse that dances between us, reminds me that it's real.

I follow him into the bathroom and turn toward the sink as he turns on the water in the shower. A scan of my reflection shows smeared mascara, giving me a raccoon-like effect. Hair's a mess and there's a bite mark on his favorite spot, the bottom of my neck.

His arms wrap around my waist while we wait for the water to heat. I moan as his lips kiss up my neck.

It's a standard size tub and generic shower head, but as we get in he makes sure the water is shared. Though split between us, the warmth soothes the tension I woke up with, washing it away.

After splashing some water on my face, I look up only to find him staring at the ground.

"What?"

His brow scrunches. "I feel like I'm vibrating with anxiety waiting for you to run away from me."

Last night changed many things between us. Forced me to face things I've been avoiding, feelings I didn't want to have.

Because they're hard. Not the feelings themselves, but what goes along with having them.

Reaching up, I cup his cheek in both hands, pulling him down until his forehead is resting on mine. His hands move to my waist and I stare into his eyes.

"I'm not going anywhere."

I feel the tension leave him with a sigh, his body relaxing against mine.

With everything that has happened, his biggest fear is me leaving?

I really have been the biggest bitch, even if it was deserved.

Reaching to the side, I grab the soap from the dish and rub it between my hands to create a lather. Soap in hand, I press it against his chest and move it around. He lets out a small moan as I work my way over his skin.

It's soft and hard at the same time. Full of warmth and strength. A body full of love and tenacity.

Just thinking about it makes me want to be wrapped in his arms. Surrounded by him, letting his love soak into the core of my very being.

I want it. Him. All of it.

I always have.

Once done with his chest, he takes the soap from my hand and mimics my movements. Only this time I'm the one moaning from the feel of the way his fingers dance around, flexing against my skin, building the heat in the shower.

Trails of washed out red flow from the cuts on his face and scalp. Pulling him under the water, I gently run my thumbs across the dried patches of blood, rinsing them away.

An innocent, sensual shower takes a turn the second I feel his cock press against my skin. Just the feel of it sends a shiver through me. It's a feeling I force myself to ignore for multiple reasons, the biggest being the soreness between my legs. I need a break.

But I can't leave him like that.

I lather up my hands, my breath speeding up as I reach forward and wrap my fingers around him.

"Holy fuck." He lets out a gasp and jumps, his eyes popping open as his hand slams onto the tile to steady himself. "Kira . . ."

I say nothing, but glance down, my tongue peeking out to lick my lips at the sight. My fingers slide up and down in a slow motion, gaining speed as he steps forward, bracing his other hand against the shower wall.

I let out a hiss when my back hits the cool tile, forcing me to arch and a ripple of cold to circulate my skin, making my nipples harder.

Letting out a shaky breath, he reaches out and places a hand on my hip. Distracted by his mouth closing over my breast, I don't even notice his hand trail around and down until two fingers slip into my pussy causing me to gasp for air.

I slap at his hand. "Ah-ah."

Out, but then right back in, the palm of his hand digging into my clit. "You need to be cleaned here as well," he says as he releases my nipple. A flick to make me shake, then a nip with his teeth before switching to the other one.

It's a battle I'm losing, burning in the pyre created by his touch. He kisses up my chest and neck, his mouth right next to my ear. "Empty out any leftover come so I can fill you with fresh."

My head falls forward onto his chest, and my eyes flutter, threatening to close. He knows all my weak spots, his long fingers pressing, working me, pushing me until my legs begin to shake.

"No. Stop."

I let go of his dick and push him back. His hand slips from between my thighs. "I'm not coming without you," he growls.

Looking up, I'm met with a heavy-lidded, intense gaze, green eyes seeming to almost glow. His cock is so hard the head is red, bordering on purple.

I stare into his eyes as I grab hold again, one hand on his shaft, the other cupping his balls as I stroke him again. "Just let me do this for you."

His mouth drops open in hard breaths and pussy pulsing groans. I can see the strain in the tendons on his neck. It's difficult for him. Leaning forward, he presses his forehead to mine and rests both forearms against the tile, caging me in.

"Kira . . ." His chest expands and contracts, the tempo rising. "Kira, baby . . . Fuck!"

I squeeze down a little bit harder, twisting as I pump up and down. Silky, hot, and hard, and from the sounds he's making, ready to burst. His hips flex in tempo, straining to get closer.

His brow scrunches, muscles tense. "Baby, I'm gonna come. I'm gonna fucking come all over you."

My pussy fucking clenches and comes a little just from those words being said in his deep, breathy, sexy tone.

I'm no longer holding his balls. They're pulled so high, his cock harder than I've ever felt him, hotter than I ever imagined skin could be.

A roar leaves him, his expression a cross between bliss and agony. Hot, wet drops land on my stomach and breasts. Again and again with each explosive pulse. I watch in fascination and a perverted desire as he marks my skin with pearly drops of his being.

When I look back up, he's staring down at the same erotic paint job I was. His chest heaves with labored breaths, one hand moving from beside my head to the thick liquid slowly sliding down my skin.

"Mmm, you look so good covered in my come," he says between breaths as he slides it around.

I push against his chest. "Perv." Stepping forward, I get my first taste of the warm water in minutes. It falls over my back and hair as I give him one last look of his handiwork before turning in the spray, letting it all wash away.

He lets out a little groan behind me. "Baby, that was art you just destroyed."

I feel his fingers ghost around my hips, then around to caress my stomach.

"Guess you'll just have to create another masterpiece later."

Hums vibrate against my neck. "I like that idea."

"I thought you would."

"What do you want to do today?"

I lean my head back to look at him. "You mean this afternoon, since we slept through the morning?"

He rolls his eyes. "Whatever. We can order some food. Watch a movie."

"I'm going to have to head home some time." I point out.

He shakes his head against me. "No. Don't ever go back to that place, to that poison."

"I can't leave my mom alone with him."

He's silent, seeming to have no response. "She will be soon when you move up here."

I lean forward to shut the water off, completely struck by his words. Fuck. I hate that he's right. Me going to school leaves her without a buffer. I wish she would just leave Steve. I wish she wasn't so emotionally dependent on him, because he's not good for her, and I hate what he does to break her down.

"Fine. One more night, but then I have to go."

He smiles as he hands me a towel. One more night won't make a difference to Mom and Steven, but I know, after everything, it will with Brayden. There isn't a want in him for me to stay—it's a *need*.

It was hard to leave Brayden the next day. Forced myself out of his arms, kissing his half-awake lips before heading out and driving home.

Brayden won't be alone for long. Ryan is headed up with his car, Dana following behind.

There will only be a short, but very long day until I see him again.

"I'm home!" I call out as I enter.

"In here!" Mom answers from the other room.

Thankfully, I don't hear Steven, and I find Mom alone in the living room folding laundry.

"Hi, honey, did you have a good time with Jenna?" She smiles at me, but it doesn't seem genuine.

"Yeah, with everything that was going on . . . "

"It was good you weren't here."

I scrunch my brow and take a hard look at her. She looks drained. Completely emotionally and physically drained.

"Mom?"

"Hmm?" She looks up, a blank look in her eyes.

What did he do to her?

"What's wrong?"

She shakes her head. "Nothing. I'm just tired."

Stepping closer, I stand next to her. She's still taller than me, making me the forever midget of the family. Ryan always gives me shit about it, but I still love the idiot.

I watch as she swallows hard—her tell that tired isn't what's wrong and she wants to avoid the conversation, but I'm not going to let it slide anymore.

"What did he do, Mom?"

Something's wrong, off with her. This isn't the woman I know. She seems scared, and after the last few months and getting samplings of Steven's anger, I worry that he's crossed lines that I won't allow.

"We just got into it this weekend, honey. It's fine. Really."

"Fine? You know I hate that word, right? You're not *fine*, Mom. Why are you still with him?" It's not the first time I've asked her, but each time she looks more and more run down. I wonder how far he'll push her until she breaks.

Her brow furrows. "I can't leave him," she whispers.

"Can't or won't?"

Her arms drop back down into the laundry basket. "It's not that simple, Kira."

I continue to stare at her. "Okay, then figure out how to make it simpler. I'll help. Ryan will help. You have us to help you, so let us." For almost as long as I can remember it's been just the three of us. We were all we had. "You just have to talk to me."

She quirks her brow at me and I get a glimpse of just how large the bags under her eyes are. "Aren't these my lines? I'm the mother."

I shrug. "Doesn't mean you're Superwoman. Everyone needs help sometime."

"When did you get so wise?" she asks.

"The life of a teenage girl."

"Well, daughter of mine, I have a stack of clothing for your wise ass to put away."

I plaster a smile on my face as I take the basket from her outstretched arms. "Thank you, mother dear." I turn and head toward the staircase, smiling as I hear her chuckle. Hopefully, in the smallest of ways, I made her day just a tiny bit better.

I barely get to the top of the stairs when my phone starts going off. Not just one text message, but five before I even reach my room.

Dropping the basket to the floor, I pull my phone from my purse.

They're all from Jenna and they keep pouring in.

Oh, my God! I'm going to fucking kill her!

Where are you?

Are you home?

I'mma cut a bitch.

She's screwing with the wrong motherfucker.

CALL ME!

The blood in my veins runs cold. Such a strong reaction can only be the result of one person's actions.

My hands shake as I press the screen, the breath caught in my chest as the phone connects.

I don't even register that the ringing stops when a loud noise causes me to pull the phone from my ear.

Gibberish at supersonic speed and shrill tones has me lost. I can only make out one or two words, but it's enough to make the ground fall out from beneath my feet.

"Jenn" and "Facebook," are the most prevalent after "Bitch" and "Cunt rag."

I'm to my desk, waking up my computer while I continue to decipher Jenna's ranting. The minute it takes to boot up and login seems like an eternity. Each second hours, minutes as days.

Facebook up, and it's the first thing in my timeline, staring me in the face.

"You want what you can't have, little girl. Enjoy it while it lasts, because once your dirty secret is out, you'll never be able to show your face in town again. #DisgustingBitch"

My stomach turns and I can feel the bile rise in my throat.

The post is even more popular than her previous one. Hundreds of comments filled with people wanting to know who she's talking about. There's no response from her, no replies. Her silence riles the crowd even more.

But she doesn't want to look like a fool with no proof. That, and naming Brayden will only hurt her goal of having him all to herself.

"Tell us!"

"What's going on?"

"Damn, girl, you're such a gossip tease!"

Gossip tease . . . More like gossip bitch. Based on her posts, I'd bet money she's spreading rumors on the down low.

How many know?

My hands begin to shake, no longer able to hold the phone. How many people has she named us to?

I sit back, Jenna's voice barely in the background on the phone that's now sitting in my lap.

I want to tell Brayden, run into his arms. At the same time, I don't. So much is going on with him.

He knows about the first post, knows Jenn is doing this shit. This will throw him off the deep end, and his hot head will explode in a rampage that will only make things worse.

Maybe I'm predicting him overreacting, but with his history, it's not really a prediction, but what *will* happen.

If she keeps talking, they'll all know and everyone will know we're having sex.

I love Brayden, I do, but I don't know how to handle this. We aren't dating. We aren't boyfriend and girlfriend.

I don't know what we are, because loving him doesn't mean forgiving him.

What I do know is that this is only the beginning. Jenn won't stop, and we won't ever be able to go out or have a normal relationship.

Everything is still as complicated as before, maybe more so. A complicated mess we may never make it out of.

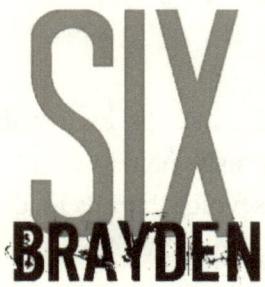

SIX
BRAYDEN

The reminder of why I was in front of a judge and meeting with lawyers is marked all over my face. The swelling has receded, but the bruises are still there along with a few gashes that are healing.

Austin was there, in the courtroom, his parents looking just as pissed off as my father who's in the car ahead of us.

I blow out a breath as we turn into the neighborhood. "Do we have to do this now?"

Mom gives me the side-eye. She's been stoic today and a buffer more than once between me and my father. "Brayden, my son, the light of my life . . . your ass is in trouble." *Fuck.* "You're twenty-one, very much an adult, and you need to get a handle on this anger inside you before you end up in some serious trouble."

Due to it being a first offence, neither of our lawyers has any belief there will be any jail time, for which I'm thankful, but we aren't going to come out of this ordeal completely unscathed. I'm very much aware that most of that damage will come from the man in front of us.

Community service, fines, probation; whatever the judge throws at me will be nothing compared to the shitstorm that's coming.

My whole body is poised for the fight, fists clenching on my thighs. I've been in defense mode ever since I parked in front of his house this morning.

Seeing Kira would really help, but I don't want her caught in the vile muck he's going to spit. One nasty word to her or about her and I will have him on the floor in seconds. He lost my respect long ago and I will *not* allow him to insult the woman I love.

The woman I love.

It's still a string of foreign words, strange to my own mind, but every time I say it my heart feels like it's going to explode. The energy that courses through me, giving me more strength than I ever thought possible, and it's all due to the connection I've had to her since we met.

I would give up everything I have, everything I am, my very life, for her.

Which often leads to less than rational thinking.

Mom pulls in behind my car in front of the house and puts it in park. "We're going to go in there and attempt to have an adult conversation." She reaches for my hand and I look at her when she squeezes down. "I don't want you to worry about anything. We'll figure it out. Just . . . don't hit him. He's going to bait you, it's what he does. Don't make it worse."

I nod, peering through the glass to the asshole staring us down. "I'll try, but he knows you and Kira are my weak spots."

She pats my hand and pulls the keys from the ignition. "Count to ten. I hear that helps. At least that's what our therapist used to say."

I can't help but let out a little chuckle at that as I climb out, which only makes my father's glare deepen before he turns to head inside.

It's still normal for me to walk in through the garage, but I glance back to my mom to check on her. Years have passed since she was last within these toxic walls. In fact, the last time I can remember was about six months after their divorce.

The house that they picked out together.

I know there's no lost love between them, but after everything, I'm left wondering what she feels.

Her eyes scan as she walks through, noting the differences, I'm certain, the changes.

When we enter the living room, the bastard and Sonia sit on the couch, on opposite ends, while Mom and I take the chairs facing them.

"A fucking misdemeanor," he says, wasting no time digging in. "You're damn lucky the judge went easy and didn't charge you with a felony." He looks at me like he's waiting for a response, but I have none for him. "Why the fuck you keep trying to ruin your life is beyond my comprehension."

One . . . Two . . . Three . . . Four . . .

"If you expect me to pay for this legal mess you've gotten yourself into, you can—"

"I'm going to stop you there," Mom cuts him off. "He will handle the fees."

"And how is he going to do that? It's my money he drains monthly."

Five . . . Six . . . Seven . . .

"He's been working a lot this summer, if you haven't noticed."

Dad scoffs and I start my counting back at one, nails digging into my palms.

Our eyes meet, his lip curling up into a sneer. "What I've seen him working isn't a job."

I'm to my feet before he can say another word, but my mom's hand around my wrist keeps me in place.

Same green eyes lock, boiling over with the same explosive energy. Then there's the sneer that only grows.

One, two, three, four, five, six.

"Stop baiting him, Steven," Sonia says, speaking for almost the first time in hours.

He sure has beaten her down—yet another reason to hate him. Another victim of his callous ways.

"Stay out of this, Sonia," he snaps.

She glares back at him. "We're here to talk about what's next, not to watch you try and prove you're the alpha."

"You'll fucking stay out of this. It's between me and *my* son."

Onetwothreefourfivesixseveneightnine.

"No, Steven," Mom says through gritted teeth, her grip on my wrist tightening as my body leans in to attack the asshole in the room. "It's between all of us and our son, you misogynistic bastard."

"Oh, Abigail, you're wrong on that word. I don't hate women. You more than anyone know how much I *love* women."

Sonia gasps and glares at him.

"I know how much your dick does. How many lovers do you have right now?" Mom asks.

He's on his feet, finger pointed at her with a look of murder on his face. "You zip your damn bitch lips."

"Make me."

He steps toward her and I move between them. "Fucking cunt. Always such a filthy, aggravating mouth spitting words, making me want to slap you."

I push against his chest, making him stumble back. "Shut the fuck up, you pathetic piece of shit!"

My anger is held on by only the smallest thread. Muscles so tense, ready to unload years of rage on him.

"So he can speak! Tell me, son, is the pussy worth all the trouble?"

Red. All I can see is him covered in red.

Counting to ten isn't going to cool me down. Only him bloody on the floor will.

"Enough!" Sonia pushes against us.

I resist, but it doesn't last long, and we both sit back down.

"Thank you, Sonia." Mom gives her a warm, genuine smile. I know she can see it, what he's done to her. "Brayden, why don't you go get a drink or something?"

My father shakes his head. "He's not going anywhere."

"He is, because we have a few things that have to be worked out."

"Like how he's not welcome here anymore?"

"Like how he will continue to have a room here for whenever he needs until he finishes school. How you will continue to comply with our divorce agreement and pay for college and his apartment."

Dad shakes his head. "No."

"Yes, or I'll sue you for contempt."

He mashes his teeth, glaring at her, while I dare him to say one more thing to her.

I haven't moved, waiting. Trying to hold everything down to get through this.

Where's Kira? Why isn't she coming down? Is she here? Fuck, I could use her presence right now, but at the same time not. Just him looking at her and he's dead. I can't even stand the fact that she has to share space with him.

"Fine, but per the decree, I'm only paying for the remainder of his undergrad. If he wants to pursue a Master's degree, that's on his dime. And I'm not paying for any of the legal fees for this shit."

Mom stares up at him, cool as can be. "We will split the bill."

"The hell we will!" He's practically snarling, but she refuses to back down.

"Do I need to remind you that *you owe me*, Steven?"

Everything stops and I turn to look at her. What is she talking about? And is it something I can use to bring him down? To free us all from him.

He's shooting daggers at my mom while Sonia's brow is scrunched. Whatever my mom is alluding to, Sonia is unaware of it.

"Half," he growls out, lips twitching.

His response is baffling and surprising on a level I wasn't expecting. Relenting to her not once, but twice?

My mom rocks. She's sitting across from him with an aura of confidence and a gotcha smirk.

"To recap, then. Brayden will continue to come back here

when he needs and you will welcome your child. You will continue to pay for his college expenses, including tuition and room and board. You will also pay half of his legal fees."

Everyone is staring at him in the strained silence. His response will dictate if he gets my fist to his face or if I will continue to behave for my mother's sake.

"Yes." It's a begrudging response, but clear.

I blow out a breath. At least some pressure and worry is taken off my shoulders.

He moves to stand, but Mom stops him. "One more thing, Steven." Her tone is sweet, but I know her. "Stop trying to bait him. This may be your house and your rules and whatnot, but try to remember he's your son. If you push him too far, I *will* be forced to dig up skeletons I know you want to remain buried."

His eyes widen, fists clenched so tight his arms are shaking. "I'm sure you remember where the door is, Abby."

She gives him a smile and moves to collect her purse before standing. "Sonia, if you ever need anyone to talk to, you know how to get ahold of me."

"Abigail! Get out. Now."

Sonia's gaze flickers between the two of them. "It was nice to see you again."

I follow behind Mom as she heads to the front door and away from the bomb. I'm still ticking, doing my count, but seeing her put him in his place is the only reason I'm still counting numbers and not the amount of times my fist met his face.

The second we're out the door and out of earshot the main question demanding to be let out pops. "What the hell happened back there?"

"I put your father in his place. He needs to remember his record isn't as spotless as he'd like."

"What did he do?"

She stops and turns to look at me. "I'm sure you know your father is far from perfect."

I nod. "But what do you have on him to make him relent to everything?"

"He may have relented only because I was there, so don't think he won't continue on fighting with you. Unfortunately, I may have just made your relationship worse."

"There's no way it could get worse," I say.

"Perhaps." She glances back at the house, then locks eyes with me. "I need you to promise me a few things."

I nod. "Anything."

"If he starts to come at you, leave."

"Okay."

"Oh, that's not all, my son." She shakes her head. "You've made a real mess. No more fighting. Period. You're a hothead, just like him, and you're passionate about those you love, just like me. Next thing is school. Kira will be there, but if your grades slide, even a little, my financial support of your Master's degree will slide, too."

My mouth drops open. "You can't afford that."

"You don't know my financial situation, and yes, I can. Though you will need to pitch in as well, even if it's just student loans that you will pay off."

"Thank you, Mom."

"Thank me by making this a one time thing and making it through the next ten months without engaging in battle with your dad. Oh, and also by not getting Kira knocked up."

"Mom!"

She holds her hands up. "I'm just saying. She's only eighteen and I hope you two are using protection. I want grandkids one day, but not yet. I'm only forty-three."

I sigh. "Yes, we are."

She gives me a smile, but it doesn't reach her eyes. Instead, her brow furrows. It's like she's warring with herself.

"What?" I ask, suddenly worried.

"Take a drive with me."

She turns back to her car and I follow. The curiosity is strong, but there's also an anxiety fueled vice tightening around my chest. My mom isn't like this.

We pull away in silence, but there's a definite tension in the air.

"Mom, you're scaring me."

As we turn onto the on ramp for the interstate she lets out a loud sigh.

"Baby, I need to tell you something, but it's not easy. It's not even something I can prove, but it is what stopped your father, which makes me believe even more that it's true."

"Okay . . ."

"You know your father cheated on me, just as I'm certain he's cheating on Sonia."

I mash my teeth. "Yeah, he's a fucking bastard."

"One time, at the last Hunt family reunion we went to as a family. When we left at the end of the night, I was pretty sure he'd been going at it with a woman there. I could smell her on him."

The blood in my veins freezes and I turn to look at her. The story has my full and complete attention. I see a trainwreck coming, but I'm not sure of the outcome.

"That was when the fighting got really bad. I tried to make

our marriage work, to keep us together as a family."

"I get it. You told me a few years ago."

"Anyway, a few months ago a woman and her daughter, who's about eleven, came into the office. She recognized me right away as Steven's wife, even though I don't think we were ever introduced. Turns out she is his first cousin, the daughter of your dad's Aunt Ellen."

My stomach drops and I have a feeling I know where this is going, but as my fingers tighten around the handle on the armrest, I plead that it won't be what I fear.

She glances to me and I can see how hard it is for her to say it.

"Just tell me," I grit out.

"When I looked at the little girl, she smiled at me, her eyes a beautiful, glowing green. The same color as yours. The same as your father's."

I'm shaking, trying to wrap my head around it all.

I swallow hard. "Do I have a sister?"

"I'm pretty sure you do."

I mash my teeth together, fists clenched. Fucking asshole. "Why didn't you tell me?"

"Brayden, I have no proof other than what your cousin told me."

Jesus, what she said hits my brain and finally connects. The woman he fucked was his cousin, which means the mother of my sister is also my cousin.

And the motherfucker tells me being with Kira is disgusting? I want to tell my mom to pull over so I can vomit.

"What did she say?"

"It was hard to find a tactful way to ask, but she did name

75

Steven as the father." She lets out a tense breath and I glance over. Her brow is scrunched, knuckles white around the steering wheel. "She was in tears as she told me. Her parents disowned her, threw her out. She said Steven refuses to acknowledge the child is his or to help in any way, and the poor woman is barely making it."

"Motherfucker." I want to beat his face in even more now. How could he? "But for months you've known and never mentioned it to me."

"Other than a stranger's word and your father's 'you don't have any proof' denial and refusal to take a paternity test, what do I have other than a theory?"

"But you believe her? You believe that the little girl is my sister?"

"Yes."

"Why?" I ask.

She lets out a sigh. "Because she looks just like him."

Just like him.

Just like him and he won't take responsibility? He fucked a girl, while married, and refused to acknowledge he had a kid with her.

How many others are there? Do I have more siblings hiding in his closet of secrets? He's fucked more women than I know, so there could be half a dozen others out there. Younger *and* older.

The high school flashes in the window and I realize we've turned around, only a few miles out from the house. Silence continues and I try to process it all. I need to see for myself, meet her.

My *sister*.

"Brayden, what are you thinking?" Mom asks as we pull

76

onto the street.

I shake my head. "I want to punch him, kick him in the nuts until he can't procreate anymore."

"Brayden . . ." she trails off as we pull up to the house. The car rocks to a stop and as she turns toward me I shake my head.

"I just . . . can't right now, Mom." I jump out of her car, slamming the door and not even looking back.

It's too much. All of it.

My brain is in overload, my emotions wild.

Thank fuck his car isn't here, probably went to work, because I would beat his face in. It's too fresh and nothing would stop my anger.

How could he fucking do that to any woman, let alone family? My brain keeps trying to think up different reasons on *how* the situation came about, because the reality of it makes me nauseous.

After entering the house, I close the front door and lean against it.

I have a sister.

A real, blood sister, and not the one by marriage that I hope is upstairs.

Two at a time until I'm at the top, five steps until I'm at her door. It's open and she's sitting at her computer.

"On the bed," I say. I'm so overwhelmed I feel like I'm about to start crying, which is very pussy, but I can't stand thinking about what he's done.

"Brayden!" Her hand flies to her chest. "You scared me. Are you all right?"

I shake my head and point across the room. "Get on the bed."

She stares at me, but complies, lying down. "Mom's still home."

"I don't care." I climb on to the bed and collapse down, my arms wrapping around her body, pulling her close, my face buried in her neck.

This. Her soft body in my arms is enough to calm me some, but not enough. I'm shaking, tearless sobs.

"Brayden? What's wrong?"

I can't even form words. All I know is what's *not* wrong with me and that's her.

SEVEN

Kira

I still haven't told Brayden about Jennifer's second post.

How can I? He's dealing with so much already. The arraignment yesterday, that bullshit family "reunion" right after. He was an emotional wreck afterwards. I've never seen him so distraught.

My stomach twists sickeningly. I still can't believe they want to charge him and Austin with a misdemeanor assault.

Will I ever get over the guilt?

I wrap the blanket tighter around me and continue surfing through the channels. A few minutes ago, I gave up on the idea of sleeping tonight.

The temptation to head across the hall to Brayden's room was strong, but I fought it. Why? Because one of us has to learn some self-control.

Two sane people would have stopped fucking each other already. Not only can we never be together but the situation is becoming more dangerous by the day.

We're not sane. That's a fact that was proven a long time

ago.

We need to stop. Brayden won't accept it; my body doesn't want to either. But if we don't stop soon, our dirty little secret is going to spill out and stain the lives of everyone we love.

Just thinking of letting him go makes me want to run up the stairs and fling myself on him so I can hold on tight.

Pathetic. Sad. Hopeless.

A sound from the second floor landing reaches me. Then another. I realize someone's coming down the stairs.

The master bedroom is closest to the stairs, but the room is right above where I'm sitting, and there's been no sound. Which means there's only one person it can be.

I tense, on edge, wary and so fucking excited that it disgusts me. I can't see the stairs from where I'm sitting, yet I turn my head in that direction anyway.

Waiting.

Yearning.

Obsessed.

It's never going to end, is it?

Brayden comes into view and he pauses at the entrance to the living room, looking between me and the television.

He's shirtless. His tattoos stare at me, art to signify me, branded into his skin.

Lord help me, he's also wearing tight, light gray boxer briefs.

His seemingly, forever-hard cock is pressed sideways along his hip bone.

It twitches.

"Stop looking at it like that, baby, unless you want me to fuck you right on the arm of that couch." His voice is rough and deep from sleep.

Oh. God. How can any woman ever let go of him when he does shit like that? "Brayden," I whisper, ripping my eyes away from that perfect dick. "You shouldn't be down here."

Obviously, he ignores me. Like he does every time I try to put any distance between us.

Making his way around the couch, he takes the remote from my hand and makes himself comfortable next to me.

Practically naked.

In the dark.

The only light is coming from the TV and a little pouring through the window from the streetlights.

Underneath this throw blanket, I'm wearing a large pajama T-shirt. Beneath that? Tiny underwear, as usual.

Fuck, it'd be so easy to just jump on his lap and—

Brayden tugs on the blanket. "Open that thing up, make room for me, and come here."

I hold the blanket tighter and shake my head. "They can come out any second and see us."

He sighs and runs his hand down his face. For a second, all I see is the weight of extreme stress in his eyes. "Kira, I can't right now. Don't push me away. We need each other. That's why we can't sleep."

And because we're both stressed the fuck out about what's happening to his life.

What's happening to his life because of *me.*

I hurry to slide across the couch. Brayden grabs me and lifts me onto his lap. I readjust the blanket so it's covering us both.

One arm around my waist, he brings me back so I'm leaning on his chest. It's such a compromising position, but it feels so good to have him close again.

Brayden nuzzles the side of my neck. "Hmm. Fuck, you smell good."

His cock is hard against my ass and I choke on the urge to rub on it. "How's your wounds?"

"Healing, as you can see." He places a soft kiss to my cheek.

Everything is forgotten and I spin around enough so that my lips meet his.

Perfect fucking bliss.

Brayden moans into my mouth, lips opening for me. Our tongues touch and in a single instant the air around us is on fire with need.

He tilts his head, licking my tongue in that lewd way of his, letting me know exactly where his mind is at.

Our parents are sleeping right above us. It's been days since I had him inside me and I won't be able to remain quiet once I feel his cock.

Out of breath, I pull back.

Eyes heavy-lidded and locked on my lips, he follows me, trying to bring me back.

I avoid his lips and press my forehead to his. My heart's racing so hard I wonder if he can hear it. The pulse is loud and powerful between my legs. "We can't." My voice is a hunger-filled whisper.

I know that look in his eyes. He's too far gone. Lost. Focused only on his need to fill me with his come. "Yeah we can, baby. We'll just be quiet." His hips shift under me.

One rub. Then, he loses control, as if the sensation was enough to set him off, and he starts grinding his dick into me nonstop.

"Brayden," I hiss.

His hand slides up my thigh and between my clenched legs. "Give it to me baby. I need to give you my come so badly."

"They'll hear us," I whimper, but open my legs anyway, powerless to resist.

He palms my pussy, grinding the palm of his hand into my clit. "They won't. Shit. You're soaked. I need that."

That hoarse whisper does me in.

He tugs my panties down and I lift my ass to let him. Leaving them around my thighs, he lets me go long enough to push his briefs down.

"We'll be quiet. Somehow. I'm just dying for that pussy. Want it wrapped around me. Squeezing tight. My balls are fucking aching for it." His low rambling almost rips a moan out of me.

He sounds out of his mind for me. Desperate. Obsessed with his desire to fuck me.

His hot dick slides between my legs. I mewl quietly and shift my hips back to help get him into position.

Brayden squeezes my tit with his other hand. "Give me that tongue when I slam my dick inside you."

I do. God, I do. I slam my lips on his, licking at his tongue frantically, and he forces his dick inside.

Painful, delicious stretching.

He holds me in position, making out with him and refusing to let me slide up and down his length.

I whimper into his mouth, rocking on his cock, so full of him I can barely breathe.

"Shh." He rains small kisses on my lips and sucks my bottom one. "Just take it however I give it to you."

I nip his lip. "I need more."

He rocks his dick back and forth, forcing me to feel the sheer size of him.

"Oh shit," I whisper on an exhale, my inner walls jumping uncontrollably. He's pressing against my g-spot with the thick head of his cock and every time he rolls his hips like that, I feel like I'm this close to squirting all over him.

"Don't fight it. Drench my dick. I want it dripping down my balls."

Squeezing my eyes close, I struggle to breathe. To remain quiet. To remain fucking *sane* as he continues fucking both my body and my mind.

That huge sword of a dick.

That deep, rough, husky voice.

The smell of him.

Brayden latches onto my jaw with one hand and squeezes down tight. "You look at me while I tear that pussy up."

I want to obey him, I do, but I'm overwhelmed. That tight sensation of having to pee is building in my womb. I know it's an earth-shattering orgasm building and I also know I'm going to scream my fucking head off when it hits.

Brayden rubs his finger into my swollen, soaked clit. They're gone before I can grind into them.

My eyes fly open and I open my mouth to beg.

He slides his other hand between my legs, finding my clit once more, and I feel the wet fingers of his other hand press between my ass cheeks from behind.

My heart explodes in my chest. Whimpering, I shake my head at him, silently begging.

He ignores me, as always, using my body however he wants. His index finger presses into my tight bud and slides straight inside my ass.

Using his other hand, he caresses my clit in slow maddening circles.

My head falls back on his shoulder. I stare up at the ceiling but I'm not registering what I'm seeing. I just feel.

Brayden growls behind me, his low, displeased warning growl, and thrusts up into me hard. "I told you to fucking look at me."

I lift my arms up and behind my head. Wrapping my hands around his neck, I spread my legs wide and take his next thrust.

"Oh fuck yeah." He nips my ear and curls his finger inside my ass. I'm full, so fucking full of him, and he starts working yet another finger into me. "You're such a needy little slut for it."

"Brayden. I'm going to—" I press my lips together, struggling to swallow the cry that's pushing its way up my throat.

"You want this so badly that I'm fucking tempted to give it to you right here. Imagine my dick in your ass baby, pumping you deep." He licks my neck frantically, thrusts up into me faster. "You'd let me fuck every one of your holes at the same time if I could, wouldn't you?"

Yes. Oh yes. I nod, my vision slowly bleeding white.

"You want me to fuck your ass with my cock and your sweet little pussy with a toy?"

I rock back into his thrusts, just like I did upstairs the day he fucked me next to my open bedroom door. Small, whispered cries leave my lips. I'm way past holding them back. Way past caring if I'm heard.

Let them come. His father, my mother. Anyone. I don't care. Couldn't give a flying fuck if they saw me like this, legs spread for his fingers and cock, hips churning frantically for more.

"Who's fucking you so good right now baby?"

"You are," I whimper, loving the sound of his cock rocking into my wet cunt.

"Say my fucking name."

"*Brayden*," I groan, fisting the hair at the back of his head.

"Next time I fuck you, I'm going to put the head inside you." His fingers slide in and out of my ass in time with his thrusts. "Right here."

I become nothing more than a pulsing, leaking, needy pussy as I fall headlong into an orgasm. My entire reality shatters, robbing my breath so I can't even cry out.

In retrospect, a blessing. Right now? It wouldn't have mattered to me if I'd screamed loud enough to be heard up and down the block.

Brayden shoves his fingers deep into my ass and pushes his dick into my pussy. His chest expands behind me, and the low, long groan echoing out of him is more animal than human.

I feel his dick get harder. Thicker.

His tight balls press into my clit.

His shaft gives one powerful kick as he starts coming. Then another. And another.

A high-pitched, shocked sound leaves me and I start coming all over again, squirting uncontrollably all over his dick.

My walls are clamping too tight. His come is forced out of me along with my own juices, and it's an utter mess of wetness between my legs.

Brayden bites down on my shoulder blade, cursing under

his breath. We sit here like this for a while—me slumped on him and him curled around me, our rushed, quiet breaths echoing in the silence.

He softens enough to slip out of my pussy on his own. Another gush leaves me. It's downright wet and messy between us but I can't bring myself to move. My legs are still numb from the power of those orgasms.

Every damn time. It doesn't matter how much we fuck, it's never enough. And each time is somehow even better than the last.

"I love having our juices all over me." Brayden pants softly against my back.

I bite back a giggle. "It's messy."

"Yeah. And it's perfect." He brings me back so he can kiss me. "I love smelling like us."

"I think I was too loud."

"Yeah, probably." At my horrified look, he smirks ruefully. "But no one came out to disturb us."

This is so sick. I'm fucking my stepbrother in secret and our parents might have heard us going at it. They also might have decided for some reason not to interrupt.

My pussy ripples.

Being with Brayden isn't sick. Not in my eyes.

But the fact that we have to hide it, that we're *this* close to getting caught, makes me want to fuck him all over again. My heart speeds up once more. My skin tingles with awareness.

I'm fucking excited *and* aroused and that's what's fucking sick about this whole situation.

What's wrong with me?

I think Brayden reads my facial expression because he

87

pulls me closer and kisses my cheek softly. "It turns me on, too."

Throat tight, I ask, "What does?"

"Knowing we have to be so careful. That we might get caught if we're not."

If I'm sick, that means he's far gone as well. Both of us are more than a little twisted because of each other.

I can't lie—I love it.

Brayden tucks the blanket around us once more and grabs the remote. He doesn't make any move to slide his boxers back up or to readjust my panties or clean up the mess. The tension from earlier seems to have melted out of him.

The volume on the TV is low. Low enough not to disturb our sleeping parents. Low enough that I know it did nothing to muffle the sounds of us fucking.

Brayden flips through the channels anyway, his sleepy eyes on the television.

"We should go upstairs." I fidget on his lap, slightly uncomfortable with all the wetness down there.

His eyes flicker in my direction and I see a flash of hurt. "Why didn't you come straight to my room?"

I don't have to answer that question. He knows.

"It happened anyway," he says, hugging me tighter with one arm.

I want to tell him it shouldn't have but the words won't leave my mouth.

As wrong as this all is, it also feels so right.

I have no interest in hurting him anymore.

I have no interest in hurting myself.

Letting him go is going to leave a hole in my being that I'll never be able to fill.

Which means I'm fucked regardless. Eventually, I won't have a choice but to live without him. Unless my mother leaves Steve by some miracle, there's nothing Brayden or I can do.

My mother won't leave him. I've seen her sick dependence on Steve over the last few weeks.

"Brayden, please. Let's go upstairs."

Emerald eyes focus on me in the dim lights, searching. I know what he's searching for, too. "Will you sleep with me tonight?"

"Yes." I'll go back to worrying about the rest tomorrow. We both need to be with each other and it's worth the risk.

I wonder how far that excuse will get us in the long run.

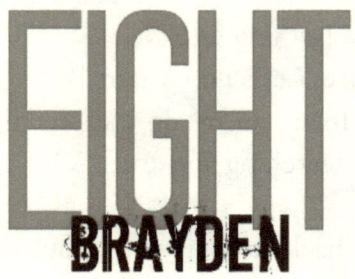

EIGHT

BRAYDEN

"Where the fuck are you going to put all this stuff?" Ryan asks, setting a box precariously on top of another against my living room wall.

It's official—all my shit is gone from my dad's house. All but Kira, that is.

I shrug. "Mom said I could store it at her house."

"Did you even go through it, or just shoved it in a box?"

"I just tossed shit. It was fastest." It took away from what little time I had with Kira between it and my last week of work.

"Damn."

"What?"

"I just . . . nostalgic, I guess." He picks up a framed photo sitting on top of an open box. "Eleven years we've been friends. It's going to be weird to go back into that house and that not be your room."

I look down at the photo in his hand—me, Ryan, and Kira.

We were at the edge of the pool, Kira between us. Her tiny arms were hiked up to reach around our shoulders.

Mom took it the summer before the divorce, in the period of time Ryan hit a growth spurt and was taller than me. Kira's all of ten or eleven, a shrimp by comparison, decked out in pink goggles and fins.

"I'll still sleep there when I need to, but I can't call that place home anymore." Not with my father there.

The entire week while I was packing, I kept a mental note of where he was. Not just that he was at work, but starting with what time he left the house to his lunch plans, to the time he arrived home.

In one day, any lasting grievance I had against my stepmother evaporated. She's another victim. It's too obvious.

Living with him for years between when Mom moved out and Sonia moved in, I knew his routine, even when he had a tart on the side. I didn't realize it at first, but once I found out he was cheating, the pattern became abundantly clear.

Even after years, it hasn't changed. What seems like a normal, average day to Sonia, I know to be him having an affair.

"Why did you move everything out if you're still going to stay there from time to time?"

"Because I don't trust that bastard not to just throw all my stuff out." I trust him with nothing and nobody. Before I graduate, things are going to change, and I plan to never see him again.

"True." His head shakes from side to side. "I can't imagine treating my child the way he does you, his only child."

I have to stop myself from correcting him, from letting my

bestfriend know the skeleton in my father's closet. There's more than just me walking around with his green eyes.

"Child? Is there something you need to tell me?" I quirk my brow, hoping his over perceptive nature didn't notice my pause.

"Fuck no."

"Sounds like you've got babies on the brain."

He glares at me. "Just because I like to come in my girl without a condom doesn't mean I'm in any way ready for kids."

I blow out a breath, my lips quirking as I try to not get hard as I think about being inside Kira without one. "I never knew bareback felt so fucking good. I praise whoever created birth control."

All humor drops from Ryan's face. "Dude . . . no. Shut the fuck up right now. We've talked about this. I don't want to know the perverted stuff you do to my little baby sister."

I laugh and shake my head. "I didn't even allude to her."

"Deduction. Your ass is so paranoid about VD's and girls who want your baby I *know* you've never fucked any without one. Which only leads to one conclusion of how you've made this rubber free discovery."

"You could just *not* always jump to her when we're talking about sex."

His gaze narrows on me. "Why the fuck would you ever talk about sex with another woman?"

I throw my hands up in the air and back away. Last thing I need is his fist on my still fucked up face. "I'm fucking damned if I do, damned if I don't here, man. Sex with all the women before her was just a way to get off. Sex with her is like ascending to the erotic heavens where all my dreams come true."

Ryan just stares at me before unfreezing and returning the photo to the box. "So Dana and I were thinking of going to Kings Island one last time before school starts back up, you in?"

"Way to segue."

"Hey, I let you be with my sister, but that doesn't mean I want to hear about it."

"I'm grateful and thankful for your approval. I didn't want to end our friendship, because I was going to be with her regardless of what you thought."

He shakes his head and smirks. "Dude, I came to terms with it years before you ever realized you were in love with her. Besides, it's not that easy to get rid of me." Just then his phone goes off, his face lighting up as he looks down at the screen. "Hey baby . . . yeah, we got everything in. Where are you? Yeah, I'll be right there." He hangs up the phone and looks up. "What?"

"Not that easy to get rid of, huh?"

He lifts his shoulders in a shrug. "I've had enough of your ass today, time to get some ass from my girl." One of his hands claps down on my arm. "If you need anything, I'm always here for you, bro. Just don't call me for the next hour."

I push his arm off and roll my eyes. "Get out of here, fucker."

He just laughs and heads to the door, waving as it shuts. The moment he's gone, the silence creeps in, almost suffocating and eerie.

Three hours. It's only been three hours since I kissed her goodbye and it kills me. I don't feel right, this place isn't right, nothing is right without her.

Girl has turned me into such a pussy. So much so, that I can't stop my fingers from texting her as I fall down to the couch.

I miss you.

Yeah, I'm that whipped. But I actually don't mind. If being like this means I have her in my life, then I don't give two fucks, because she's mine.

Kira is mine.

It was a long, hard fought battle where I lost old friends, but having her by my side is everything.

Maybe not *everything*, but it's a step toward the life I want to have with her.

It's strange. My life is calm and chaotic at the same time. While everything is exploding around me, Kira is there. Like the eye of a hurricane, she's the calm in the storm that is my life.

Every part of my being believes without a doubt that this shitstorm is necessary. That it will pass. There may be pieces to pick up after, but life will be the way it should be on the other end. We just have to weather the turbulence.

The phone goes off, pulling me from the melancholy attitude my mind had fallen into.

You just miss my pussy.

Her jab makes me laugh, but there's also an underlying worry there. One way to find out. I type out a response, something to lighten it and see which way she was going with her comment.

Damn typing leaves out all emotion in the words. I feel like we're still a bit on uneven ground, afraid she's going to turn back after it took so long for her to come around.

I take offense to that.

A few minutes of flipping through channels until my phone pings with her response.

Aren't you going to come back with some line like "Baby, I want you for more than just a lay." Or some crappy line like that.

Again, I laugh, but the doubt does creep in. I used to be that guy, just not with the cliché lines. I'm not some club guy looking to get off.

I continue with my light hearted banter.

I'm offended again! I'm not a thesaurus for cheesy lines and crappy comebacks.

Her response is even faster, and I know I've finally got her full attention.

All right, hit me then.

Performance anxiety is something I don't have an issue with, unless it's talking about feelings.

Roses are red, violets are blue, I want to fuck your pussy, and you want me too.

It's not smooth or eloquent or the slightest bit romantic, but they incite the intended reaction when I receive her next text.

Bwahahahaha! You aren't right. You also need some better material if you expect to get a pussy with that.

I blow out a breath and relax. There's my girl. Yeah, she was just playing with me, but being away from her amps up the insecurities that still linger.

Well, I don't want any pussy, I just want one, that happens to be part of this sassy chick that likes to insult me and I just can't get enough of her.

Not seconds later I get: *Masochist.*

Sad, but true. *Only for you, baby. Everything I am,*

everything I have, is only for you. I want to give you the world, make you happier than you have ever dreamed you could be. Spend every day of the rest of my existence by your side.

It takes her longer to respond. No longer quick quips, which lets me know that one got to her, so I decide to dig in a little more and draw from some older material.

When you're my girl, the sun will seem to have faded as it will be your light that guides me. When you're my girl, there's nothing I can't do. When you're my girl, our love will be told in history books as one of the greatest.

It's all sappy as fuck, and I'm no romance guru, but I can't deny the truth of the words. They are how I feel, in the gushiest, flowery way I can stomach to say them. She needs to see them, to be reminded that I'm here and I'm not going anywhere. That my track record does not define me. That I've always been hers.

Idiot.

At her response, I can imagine the pink spreading against her skin, maybe even hiding her face. Embarrassment taking over her brain.

I decide then to lay it all out. To tell her those feelings that are so hard for me to voice.

When you're my girl, I'll tell you every day how much I love you, how much I can't survive without you.

Silence.

I love you, Kira. Now and forever.

I don't expect her to respond, and even less so that she'll tell me she loves me. The past, our past, will stop her from saying the words, but I know them, even if she can't voice them.

So Ryan ditched you for Dana, huh?

Texting isn't going to work anymore. I need to hear her voice. She picks up before the first ring is even finished. "What makes you think that?" I ask.

"Because you're bothering me," she says.

"Am I really?"

A little laugh dances across the line. "No, but I was having dinner with Mom when you were texting."

"My dad was missing, I take it?"

"Of course."

"Fucker."

"Did you get everything unpacked?" she asks.

I glance over to the wall and the stack of boxes and plastic containers. "Out of the car, yes. I'm not really sure what I'm going to do with it all."

"What are you doing now? Since Ryan ditched you and all."

I'm half tempted to tell her my plan. Fill her in on what I'll be doing in the time I'm away from her. The urge is strong, but the want to protect her is stronger. The less she knows, the more evidence I can collect, the better her mom will be in the end.

"Are you okay?" she asks after I don't answer. Apparently I spaced out longer than I realized.

Okay? Her question throws me, her voice soft, full of that concern she always showed from almost the moment we met. The same voice I made disappear for a while. She has no idea how much I love to hear it directed at me again.

"Tell me you miss me." The words almost come out in a whisper. Hearing them will calm me. Hearing her say it will wipe away the doubt that's crawling around me. Help to center me.

"Brayden?"

"Just . . . Please."

She's silent for a beat or two. "I do. I miss you." Her voice is low, sad, and exactly what I needed. "The house is so empty without you here. I just want to get in the car and drive up. Lay on the couch with your arms around me and do nothing."

"Do it." I'll beg if I have to.

"You know I can't. There's so much to do before I move."

I rub my hands over my face.

This was the feeling I always avoided in the past. Getting close to anyone, having my life dictated by my emotions. Feelings that I never wanted to have.

Now, all I think about is Kira. There's an itch, an annoying, desperate need to have her in my arms. Skin touching skin, even in the most PG of ways. An ache where I don't feel complete unless she's close.

Maybe that's the feeling all those romantic movies she loves was trying to convey. Hollywood does a shit job showing just how crippling it is.

"Yeah."

"Besides, I'll be there all the time soon."

All the time.

Yes. All the time.

"And you'll stay with me, right?"

"Well, I'll have to spend *some* time in the dorms, or we won't get any work done, and remember what your mom said."

"Yeah, I know."

"As much as I can, I'll be there."

That's what I needed. Confirmation.

There's a commotion on the other end and I hear Sonia's voice in the background, though I can't make it out.

"Crap. I'm sorry, I have to go. I forgot we were going shopping after dinner. Someone kept distracting me."

My lip twitches. "Distracting? Who would do such a thing?"

"Don't play coy, you know you love creating distractions."

"I'd create one right now with your clit if you were here."

"There you go, trying to distract me again." Sonia's voice comes through again. "I really have to go."

"Have fun."

"I'll call you later." She makes a kissing sound and hangs up.

I miss her more now.

The void of her, of thinking that she's there, with that man, sends me on a rollercoaster of emotions. From depression to anger, and the need to punch something. That wouldn't be good.

Which reminds me, I have to call my lawyer in the morning. He called when we were unpacking the car. Probably has my hearing date.

Another thing I just can't stand to think about. It just reminds me of Austin, and the feelings I know she has for him, even if they aren't as strong as the ones she has for me.

There's a storm that rages within me, working in tandem with the one on the outside. It's black and violent. There's a darkness creeping in. I can feel it. It is what fuels my every decision—good and bad.

It's going to fuel the vindictive wave that wants to tear my father to pieces. I'm determined to watch his world crumble.

As an adult I've seen just what kind of vile he is and it makes me sick to be associated with him, let alone have half of my DNA be his.

There's nothing I can do about the latter, but help those who are the same. Make him pay for denying my sister recognition and support. He makes a shitty father, so she's not missing out there.

It's funny how I haven't even met the girl and already I'm sure she's my sister. Call it a gut feeling, whatever.

Mom is still working on arranging a meeting, but I'm sure in her belief that a little girl named Emily is my sister, and I'm going to make certain he owns up to what he did.

I open up my laptop and pull up the internet. My phone plan is with my mom, but it used to be with my dad, and knowing him, he hasn't changed any of the passwords.

His is the lead number on the account, so only he has access to all the detailed information on the account, including call records.

Sonia can't see who he's called, but a few strokes of the keys and I'm in.

The man really does need to change his passwords more often. Five years with one is too long.

Since his number is primary, all of his information is easy access, including his call log. I quickly pull up an Excel workbook and start inputting the numbers. Once done, I pull up the previous months bill.

After going through almost a year of bills, I have a starting point. There's only four numbers he seems to dial on a pretty steady basis outside of Sonia's, the rest appear to be one offs. A little Google search, and I tick off another number as his office.

Out of the last three, only one provides a name. I don't recognize it and it's female.

I stare at the screen, at my findings. Without calling them, there's no way to find out who they are and if they're anything more than someone he talks to.

If only I could track his movements to prove what I know. Evidence of where he is and going.

I tap my thumbs on my laptop.

Is there a GPS tracker I can somehow attach to his car?

The thought sends my fingers flying on the keyboard, bringing up Amazon and typing in my search.

A sense of elation comes over me as the perfect item comes up—a real time GPS tracker and it's only eighty bucks. It's a small fob like device with an app that tracks all movement. I can hide it in his car, maybe the glove box with all the other crap, and keep constant watch of when and where he's going.

Added to my cart and checked out using my bank card, not his credit card. Confirmation comes through with a delivery date by mid next week.

Perfect.

Excitement courses through me. A smile on my face and a lighter feeling than I've had in weeks. It's the break, the step I need to get Sonia away from him.

More than just a selfish want so I can be open with Kira, it's for Sonia. I've seen the damage the years with him have done to her. She's nothing to him, and she needs to be everything to someone, like Kira is to me.

She deserves better than his cheating ass, but she's stuck, afraid to break away, even though it's what she needs to do.

It hurts Kira to see her beaten down, and it angers Ryan

that she won't listen.

That's why I'm doing this, because she should be happy, too.

NINE

Kira

August 19th 2015

"Hang out?" Brayden asks.

I still can't believe I'm doing this, calling him.

"Yeah, hang out. Not sex." There's silence, and I wonder if the connection was lost. "Hello?"

"I'm heading down. Do you want to watch a movie? Play a game? I can bring my PS4." The eagerness in his voice catches me off guard. "We could go to Dave and Busters, or maybe Kings Island."

My heart hammers against my ribs. Why did I think this was a good idea?

"Whoa, slow down there, sparky." The crinkling on the other end of the phone stops. "Just come home, we'll figure it out when you get here."

"I'll be there soon."

I don't get another word out before he hangs up and reality settles in. He's coming over. Just me and him. Alone.

My hands begin to shake and I run upstairs. The pajamas I'm still wearing will not do. Hell, the most I've accomplished today is breakfast and brushing my teeth.

After stripping out of my clothes, I jump into the shower for a quick hose down. Just because I said no sex doesn't mean I shouldn't be at least presentable, is the lie I tell myself twenty minutes later as I work on my makeup.

There's a cute tank top hanging in my closet that catches my eye. I slip it on, leaving my bra off, since we're just going to be hanging out. The sight of my nipples poking at the fabric makes my pussy clench with visions of Brayden's fingers pinching them.

More of him yanking the neckline down, exposing it before attacking it, devouring my skin as he strips us both, ready to fill me.

This freaking Brayden fever is going to kill me.

Even telling myself I don't care what he thinks, my actions tell the truth—I want him to want me.

I want him as consumed with the same thoughts I'm having simply so that I'm not the only one suffering.

A car door slamming as I pull my shorts up surprises me and I glance at the clock. Time has flown by. I take a few deep breaths and head down the stairs, my feet hitting the landing at the same time the front door opens.

As soon as he steps through his lips are on mine and I have to force myself to push him back. Which really is a hard thing to do, especially when all I want is him all over me, around me. But I set the terms of today, and I have to stick by them.

"I said no sex."

He smirks at me, almost radiating with happiness,

practically bouncing with excitement. "That was just a hello kiss."

I roll my eyes at him, trying to hide how much it affected me, how much I want more. "Whatever."

He swings his arm around my shoulder, pulling me toward the basement. "Come on, brat. Time for a lesson in defeat."

Still smiling, happier than I've seen him in years. It's strange. That weird déjà vu that only comes with knowing someone for far too long, and the changes that time brings to a relationship.

I pop my elbow into his ribs. "Jerk face."

It's reminiscent of an easier time, and the simple teasing calms my nerves. I missed this, as much as I hate to admit it.

The basement is dark and with the house empty, it's a dangerous place to be. But instead of coming onto me, trying to touch me, kiss me, Brayden opens up a cabinet by the TV and pulls out one of the gaming consoles.

He's different. Pure happiness and calm. A lot like he was years ago.

It's a side of him I haven't seen in a long time. The usually overpowering sexual presence replaced with a childlike playfulness.

Maybe all the sex the other day has had a calming effect on him. No longer the tortured guy forcing himself to stay away from me. A relief from his soul.

Not that it's not there. Just like with me, the weight is always pressing down, twisting and pulling. Old battle wounds that refuse to heal.

His smile is infectious, and when he turns to me, holding up two games, I can't help but smile back.

"Lego Batman or Mario Kart?"

I quirk my brow at him. "Going old school?"

He shrugs. "No one uses the *Wii* anymore."

My lips twitch. No, Brayden doesn't use the *Wii* anymore, but I'm the reigning Mario Kart champ with my friends.

"Okay, Mario."

After sliding the disc in, he hands me a remote and plops down next to me.

"Prepare to eat my dust," he says with a grin.

I turn back to the screen. Brayden has chosen to be Diddy Kong, while I pick my favorite girl, Baby Peach.

"Of course you're a girl," he says with a roll of his eyes.

"Shut your mouth. Baby Peach is awesome." He's not going to disrespect my girl. Especially since she's going to kick his ass. "Do we do same teams or not?" I ask after we've set up our characters.

"Different. Whoever gets the most points wins and gets to pick what's next."

"Deal." We shake on it, binding our friendly bet, and start.

After four races, the Blue team, my team, squeaks by with a win, but I'm twenty-five points lower in the polls.

"Best two out of three?" I ask, needing to wipe the smirk off his face and the conniving thoughts from his mind.

He glances at me, then nods. "That will give me more time to come up with something spectacular to do."

"You're going to say anal, aren't you?"

He turns to me. "I thought this was a no sex day."

Shit. Now *I'm* the one corrupting the situation, contaminating the purity of our day. But it's an improbability that it could really stay that way. My skin crawls, itches with a base need. I'm high off his presence infecting every cell, simply by being near.

It's *me* that will break first, and I hate that.

"Just because it's a no sex day doesn't mean I don't think you'll try something."

"And you want to try anal?"

I squirm in my seat. "No."

"Then why did you mention it?" he asks.

Embarrassment floods in as I silently beg him to drop it. "Because it's something your perverted mind would come up with."

His fingers move down my arm and I'm almost hyperventilating. "Trust me, baby, with a body like yours, I'm always thinking about every one of your holes and sticking my dick in them."

"Such a charmer."

"Now you have me thinking about anal," he says, then licks his lips. "That's your fault. Keep it up, baby, and your no sex rule is out the window when I win."

"Who said you're gonna win?" I ask as I pull my controller up, ready to kick his ass.

Now I need to win.

"Your funeral."

And it was. He beat me every game, even on the areas I owned.

"Yes! Yes!" He's bouncing around, arms open, before falling back down on the couch.

"Are you proud of yourself for beating up on a poor helpless girl?" I ask as I fold my arms in front of me.

He turns to look at me like, *really?*

My eyes narrow at him. "Jerk."

He chuckles, still beaming from his victory. "Tell you what, as victor, I say we watch a movie and I'll let you pick which one."

"Any movie?"

"Anything."

"It's going to be girly," I say and wait for a groan or some complaint, but he shrugs.

"My penance for wiping the floor with you."

"It's a start," I grumble.

I get up and pluck *Pride and Prejudice*—the 2005 version—from the shelf. Not sure why, but I've been wanting to watch it lately. Maybe because the relationship between Elizabeth and Darcy reminds me a bit of me and Brayden.

When I sit back down, he throws his arm around my shoulder and pulls me in until my head is resting on his pec. I freeze for a moment, waiting for him to do more, but when he pulls back the recliner, I relax. My hand rests on his abs, and one of my legs hitches up over his.

It's an intimate position that scares me with how comfortable and right it feels.

If we could reset the last year, this would be an everyday thing. Just chilling, wrapped up in each other. Instead, so much happened.

I'm so distracted in the what-ifs, barely paying attention to the screen, that I don't even realize that my fingers are fisting and twisting his shirt.

We're only about half an hour in and question after question I've built up for months screams at me. I have him here, all of his attention, no interruptions, no distractions but each other.

"Why did you expect to get sex on my eighteenth birthday?" I ask, needing to know the answer to the most prominent one.

"Because you were legal then," he says without missing a beat, like it's the most obvious answer.

It's not the one I'm looking for.

I pull back and stare at him. "Eighteen isn't some magical number. If it happened last summer, it wouldn't have mattered."

He turns to me, his jaw flexing. Talking about his feelings like this is hard for him, but I'm going to make him. He owes me.

"No, it's not, but sometimes it's the lie you need to believe to protect the one you want the most. To keep yourself in check. But the lie doesn't always work."

"Why would you have to lie to yourself?" I ask, trying to piece together what he's saying.

He blows out a breath. "When I kissed you that first time, I wanted to do so much more, but I told myself I couldn't. You'd just turned fifteen and I was about to be eighteen. I wanted to wait . . . for you."

Freaking hell. It's . . . sweet.

"Realistically, I know I wouldn't have been able to wait nearly that long—you would have broken me down long before."

As much as I hate to admit it, he makes sense. Now that I'm older I can see how the logistics could hold him back.

My chest clenches from the sentiment alone, because I believe him. Because he was my best friend back then. Because I was innocent and I know he always cherished me.

"Okay, I get that. Even though I wouldn't have minded back then, I get it. I even . . . appreciate it. Why did it stop you later on?"

"Like that day when I was high?" he asks. I nod. He runs

his fingers through his hair, looking away before reaching down and adjusting his junk, then looking back to me. "If Sonia hadn't called for us, things would be different, but I don't know for good or bad. That day, once again, I used your age, but even then I knew it was a cover."

"For what?"

"For what I knew reality for us really was. Having you then would have complicated things for us even more. I was only home for a few weeks, then back to college."

Back to being away from me. School called, and it's not like he could stay behind just to go out with me, even if that was an option.

"Our age difference has fucked everything up for years. Not because of you being legal or not, but where we are in our lives."

"And now?"

"Now it's our time. Now, there's nothing holding us back."

"Except for you being my stepbrother." Except for me keeping him at a distance.

"Words on a paper. I don't give a shit about that anymore. It was just another stupid excuse. Another way to try to not hurt you that only ended up hurting you."

His words stop me. "So, you did it all for me."

He grimaces, jaw clenched. "The good, the bad, and the really ugly, and I'm not sure I can be proud of any of it."

There is some really ugly, painful stuff that happened. Choices he made that hurt both of us. But then there's the underlying reason why. "Yeah, you can."

Not all of it, though.

He was a whore long before that kiss and long after. I don't know if I'll even understand why, but I do know it will always hurt.

I feel like telling him that's the one thing I can never forgive him for, but I have a feeling he already knows.

"How so?" he asks.

That's when I realize what neither of us has seen in all of this. It's fucked up, but if he wanted to hurt me, use me, he easily could have. He could have destroyed me long ago. He could have indifference like I have with Austin and used me without remorse or feeling.

Instead he's here, telling me how he wanted me and kept himself away. Noble intentions that crumbled what we had to the ground.

Then there's my brother.

"Ryan hasn't told you to stay away. As much as he's your best friend, I know I come first. If he thought you were bad for me, we wouldn't be sitting here."

Even I can't explain why we're sitting here. Maybe I just missed the other connection, the one we used to have.

"He's always the voice of reason. When he found out, which was an unfortunate public display, I was such a fucking mess. He made me wait, to help me get my emotions straightened out. To pursue you with a clear mind instead of razing my way to you."

Sounds like him.

"Ryan pressed for it, with his fist I might add, because you're his baby sister. You know how protective he is. If we hadn't been at college, he'd be the cliché father figure with a shotgun, ready to shoot any male that came near you. His baby sis having sex before eighteen was unthinkable to him."

I giggle at the image. It's true, Ryan will always do what he thinks is best for me, just like Brayden. Only difference is that Ryan mulls over and uses his brain before acting.

"If I give up on this—give up on you, on us—I give up on any chance of ever being happy." His head falls forward, resting against mine. "And I don't want to live a miserable life."

Now I'm the fucked up one.

I reach up and stroke his cheek, soothing, giving us a small taste of that link to the past, to each other.

I'm not ready to give in, to trust him, to open the locked box in my heart, but I will give in to the nostalgia that calms me. Makes me remember when I didn't hate him.

But it also raises the question I'm afraid to ask myself—do I really hate him or am I just punishing him?

His head drops, lips pressing against mine. Light, sweet kisses. Many of them, fogging my mind. NO sex? Did I really say that?

He pulls back, only enough to detach his lips, and nuzzles my nose.

"I love you, Kira."

For the first time I have to catch myself, stop from responding in an almost automatic response.

I'm cracking and it scares me more than anything.

TEN
BRAYDEN

August 20th 2015

This isn't a good idea. At all. If it was up to me, Kira wouldn't be accompanying me to this party.

Accompanying *us*. Ryan and Dana are coming too.

I want to beg Kira to stay in with me. Nothing would make me happier than taking her to my apartment and spending the night with her.

It's Nick's birthday, though, and the last blowout of the summer. I feel guilty not showing up. And if I ask Kira to stay behind, I'm going to hurt her feelings. I know it.

I have enough secrets from her at the moment. She doesn't know what I'm planning to do to both Jenn and my father. I'm no fool. I know her finding out is inevitable.

And despite my good intentions—or bad ones, whatever—she's going to be hurt when she finds out I'm hiding this from her.

I don't want to add more instances of pain to our fucked up

113

relationship.

Ryan comes out of his old room. He, like me, still uses it from time to time, even though I moved everything out. We both decided to get ready here to save time.

He adjusts the collar on his dark blue button down and walks up to me. "Did you even try to convince her not to come?"

"Absolutely not." We both glance at Kira's closed door. She's getting ready behind there, possibly naked at this very moment.

My mouth waters like it does every time.

My dick twitches, preparing to die at the sight of her.

I know my girl. She's going to walk out of there in full vixen-mode, even though she knows damn well I won't be able to claim her in front of everyone.

She doesn't care. She wants to drive me crazy. Wants the beast to lose his mind until I have her alone and I devour her.

My girl is a sadist like that. And, as much as it kills me, I can't deny how much I masochistically love it.

"It's not a good idea for you guys to go. Jennifer is going to be there." Ryan, like the whole town at this point, knows about the two Facebook posts.

"Her friends are going to be there, too. I can't ask her to lock herself away from life because Jennifer is being a psychotic, vindictive bitch." Once upon a time, I wouldn't have spoken about Jennifer like that.

There was once a time that I'd thought her a friend of sorts. A friend with occasional benefits, of course, but someone I was cool with.

No longer. She's fucking with the thing I love the most in the world just because I could never bring myself to love her.

It wasn't personal. I could never force myself to love anyone, even when I tried, and that's because only one woman ever owned me like that.

But Jenn took it personal and now she's making it personal. Now, I see her as nothing but an enemy. An obstacle.

No one hurts Kira and she's going to learn that the hard way.

"Damn. You're right." Ryan sighs and pulls out his phone. No doubt to hit up Dana and see if she's ready. She went home yesterday to visit her mom.

I hear the knob on Kira's door turning. She walks out of there wearing a tiny cream top that almost resembles a bra.

The only reason I don't walk up to her and force her to change is because of the skirt. It's just as tight as the top, and begins two inches below where the top ends. It encases her entire, luscious body all the way down to her knees.

Her hair is pin straight. Her beautiful eyes are highlighted by black, smokey eye shadow, and her lips are coated in nude lipstick.

No earrings. No jewelry. She doesn't need any extras. She's going to kill every man at that party and she knows it.

I walk up to her and wrap an arm around her. "Why do you insist on dressing like this while knowing I can't let every fucker at that party know you're mine?"

Her hazel eyes seem to glow surrounded by that dark eye shadow. She looks me up and down, raising a perfect auburn eyebrow. "I'm sure it's for the same reason you insist on going out like that in front of the whole town—AKA your bevy of ex-sluts."

I lean down to run my nose along her cheek, then whisper in her ear, "I do this for you. Only for you. Even if you can't touch me until later tonight, you know this is going to be yours after."

She exhales and places a shaking hand on my chest, on my dark green button down. "Yeah, but none of the horny little cunts there will know I'm the one that gets to fuck you."

The most painful part of our relationship. Beyond all the still open wounds, and the hideous, tainted, yet beautiful history, this is the thing that causes us the most agony— having to hide who we are to each other.

I kiss her ear and suck on it lightly, aching to claim her. "God, I just want to rip that tight little outfit off you and take that pussy deep." I make sure to keep my voice low so only she can hear me.

She bites back a whimper.

"Dude, can you please not maul my sister in front of me? Thanks."

Kira and I laugh, but step back away from each other regardless.

"You might as well go ahead of me, bro, if you don't want to get traumatized." I motion for Ryan to go down the stairs first.

He groans under his breath, disgusted, and it's obvious he knows what I'm talking about.

Hey. It's not my fault his sister makes me hard simply by breathing.

Ryan jogs down the stairs. Our parents aren't home tonight, so I grab Kira's hand and hold it until we're down in the foyer.

I cup her chin and give her a kiss. She pulls back away from me before I can deepen it.

"Careful," she says while I scowl at her. She reaches up

and wipes at my lips. "You got some of my lipstick on you."

I wish I could tell her to just leave it. Having her mark on me in public wouldn't bother me one bit.

Fuck this hiding shit. I don't know how much longer I can do this.

We all get into Ryan's car, which is now Kira's. Ryan drives, Kira and I in the back, and he pulls out of the driveway to head to Dana's.

I reach for Kira's hand. She lets me grab it although her attention is on her phone. Must be texting with her friends.

After so much time of having her pull away from me every time I tried to get close, the fact that she doesn't think twice of holding my hand goes a long way.

Ryan parks in front of Dana's house. She comes running outside in a tight red dress and dark heels.

"Are you trying to kill me?" Ryan asks her in a rough tone when she gets in the car.

"Oh. Ew. Keep the porn voice to yourself. Thanks."

I laugh at Kira's snark.

Dana leans toward her man and drags his face to her for a kiss. His hand wraps around the back of her head, holding her still for his tongue.

"Keep that shit up, and I'll climb on Brayden's lap right here."

I tug on her hand. "Please do."

Dana ends her kiss with Ryan, laughing while he glares back at Kira. "Hey guys," she tells us in that sweet way of hers.

She's sweet when she wants to be. I've seen her dark side, though. I admit, both are equally alluring, just like Kira's are, and I can understand why my boy is so hooked on her.

"Hey," Kira responds just as sweetly, clearly forgetting whatever trauma her brother just dealt her.

I laugh again and nod at Dana.

She turns around and turns the radio on. "Girl, try this." She reaches back, handing a flask to Kira.

"Stop corrupting my underage sister."

"Baby shut the fuck up. Hypocrisy is not allowed in this relationship."

"I love her," is all Kira says, letting go of my hand to unscrew the cap.

I don't like her drinking, either, but it's not as bad as what Ryan and I were doing at that age so I can't really bitch.

Well, I can, but I already know from experience how well that would turn out.

She takes a few sips and hands the flask back to Dana.

Nick's house is only ten minutes by car. About three minutes away, Ryan turns to stare at mine and Kira's intertwined hands. "Don't take this the wrong way, but I think you two need to keep your distance from each other at the party."

"I'm taking it the wrong way," I grumble.

Kira lets go of my hand which only blackens my mood even more. "We just won't touch, duh."

I hate how matter-of-factly she says that.

"It's not enough. You guys have this pure fire between you. Even when you don't look at each other the chemistry is obvious," Dana says.

Kira's cheeks turn pink but she says nothing to that. Why? Is she embarrassed at our blatant attraction to each other?

Even more of a reason for me to want the right to blatantly claim her.

And I fucking can't.

"I'm not keeping my fucking distance. I'll behave, but no more than that."

"Your ex-skank whore is going to be there." Kira's mumbled statement makes me look in her direction. Her head is turned toward the window, away from me. "They might have a point about us being extra cautious."

She hates the idea as much as I do. I can tell. "Dude," I tell Ryan, my need to destroy Jennifer and separate my father from Sonia choking me. "We're not staying more than two hours."

"No problem."

His easy agreement does nothing to better my mood.

We arrive at Nick's house and the driveway is already packed, so we end up having to drive around the block to find parking.

Walking back to the house becomes an exercise in frustration. Dana loops her arm around Kira's and takes the lead, with Ryan and I trailing behind.

"It's not the end of the world. Try not to look so pissed off."

I glare at Ryan. "How would you feel if you had to keep your distance from her for appearances sake, while other guys flirted with her everywhere you went?" I motion with my head toward Dana.

He nods with a contemplative expression on his face. "I know. I'm not saying I don't understand how fucked up this is. But unfortunately it's how it has to be."

"Not for long." The comment is mumbled under my breath but he catches it anyway.

"What does that mean?"

I don't answer.

"I hope you're not thinking of doing something stupid."

Stupid? Yes. Necessary? Also yes.

I refuse to confirm or deny his suspicions.

Which Ryan takes as all the confirmation he needs.

We're already walking up the driveway so there isn't much he can say, aside from, "We're discussing this later."

We're absolutely not discussing anything. I'm not dragging anyone into my plans. This one's all on me.

The house is thumping with music and absolutely packed as we walk inside. Almost all male heads turn to watch my girl walk into the house.

I'm pretty sure just as many females have already honed in on me. It used to be me and Ryan, but it's been obvious he's been off the market for months now.

Whatever. I pay them no mind. I'm too busy trying to avoid staring down any of the assholes slobbering after my girl.

Dana and Kira head over to one of the tables lined up with drinks on the other side of the room.

Ryan leads me in the opposite direction.

"What are you doing?" I ask.

"Keeping you company, of course."

"Bro, you don't have to spend time away from your girl just to babysit me."

A drink is shoved in my hand and he simply shakes his head at me. "Do me a favor. Don't fight it. It's happening. Just go with it."

I can't help but laugh at his ridiculous ass. "That's just wrong. I feel like I'm going to get violated tonight and you're not giving me a choice in the matter."

He just rolls his eyes at me.

Craig comes up to us and slaps hands with us. "What up?" He nods at Ryan but doesn't wait for his response. He locks stares with me and I know what's coming before he even speaks. "Austin used to be your boy."

I stare straight ahead, jaw pulsing. Off in the corner, a group of people yell out and clap their hands. Some guy already has a girl up against the wall and is licking salt off her tits, preparing to take a shot.

"Yeah. He used to be."

"I get that he slept with your little sis when she was underage but come on man. He already paid for that. Both of you beat the shit out of him back then. Is it necessary to keep the war going?"

His intentions are good. I remind myself of that in a litany, hoping it'll calm this irritation down.

Damn, I really do have an anger problem. Especially as of late. Every little thing threatens to set me off.

"You don't know all of it," Ryan tells Craig calmly.

I don't look at them. Raising my drink to my lips, I pound back half of it in one shot. Yeah, I know drinking's bad for my temper but it's all I've got right now. "The fucker doesn't know when to take a hint."

"Yeah, I spoke to him about that part, but Kira's old enough to defend herself. She's a tough one. Besides, he'd never hurt her."

Like I have.

That reminder fucking kills me.

"Just let it go, dude. Brayden already understands that what happened can't happen again. Now let's just hope that Austin does."

Out of nowhere, a slim, tall blond sashays up to me, the tiny scrap of fabric she's wearing barely covering her tits.

I know her from somewhere. Can't remember her name. Can barely recall how I know her.

She stops in front of me and leans into me.

I jump back away from her but there isn't too much room. My back hits the table behind me. She doesn't even seem to notice how unbelievably averse I am to having her near me.

Shit.

She's one of them. One of my ex-sluts, as Kira likes to call them.

"Brayden Hunt," she murmurs in a voice I know is meant to be sexy, but in reality she sounds like a straight-up lush.

"Do me a favor. Step it back a few."

"Whoa," Craig mumbles.

To him, my reaction is a surprise. The old me would've already had her in a private area with that tiny little dress around her waist.

She giggles like I'm fucking joking or something. *Delusional.* "It's my birthday today. You know that?"

"I don't care to know."

She's either so drunk she doesn't hear me, or so desperate that she doesn't care.

"Well, I'm sure you know what I want for my birthday."

All right. That's it. I open my mouth to tell this chick to back the fuck off once and for all.

"I want the same thing you gave me two years ago for my birthday. This perfect cock." She steps right up to me and cups my dick over my jeans, squeezing tight.

ELEVEN
BRAYDEN

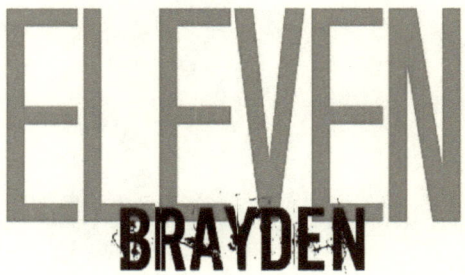

I barely restrain from sending her flying across the room. Wrapping my hand around her wrist, I fling her away from me and force her to finally step away.

"I didn't give you permission to touch me."

Her wide eyes actually flash with hurt.

Seriously?

I'm so fucking livid I can't even see straight. Looking at Kira isn't an option. I won't be able to handle the look on her face if I do.

"Since when do you turn down pussy?"

This bitch is loud enough to call everyone's attention.

She doesn't know it, but she's hurting my girl with her vile fucking existence. I'm beyond the point of caring about how she's going to take what I'm about to say. "I grew the fuck up, okay? Easy, used pussy isn't my thing anymore."

A hush falls over the entire living room.

Her lips open and close like a fish. Clearly, she doesn't

know how to respond.

A red head comes up to her and grabs her arms gently. "Come on, Renee. Let's just go get some air."

Good. Her friend is aware that *Renee* is out of control and needs to be removed from this situation before she makes it worse for herself.

Renee allows herself to be led out of the living room. I don't know where she and her friend are heading. Honestly don't fucking care.

I still barely remember tapping that.

An almost faceless, meaningless fuck from the past. That's why my girl is suffering.

"I barely recognize who you are now, dude." Craig shakes his head and takes his leave.

Good. He was pissing me off too.

Funny how I suddenly hate almost everyone at this party.

When I dare look at Kira, I see that she's facing away from me. Can't see her face or what's going on in those pretty eyes.

Dana's sneaking worried glances at her as they speak.

God damn it. I knew coming here would be a mistake.

"Look away. The way you stare at her makes it obvious."

"Makes what obvious?" I ask Ryan.

"Everything."

He doesn't need to expound on that. I'm very aware of what he means.

Just as I'm about to rip my stare away, a tall kid comes up to Kira. He's fucking gigantic, at least five inches taller than me, if not six.

He bends at the waist to get low enough to hug Kira. The smile on his face is too huge.

He's into her. *Really* fucking into her. His eyes say it all.

That's probably what I look like every time I smile at her. Like a besotted fool.

"Turn around. Walk away. *Now.*"

I have no idea how I manage to listen to Ryan, but thankfully I do. It feels like one moment I'm in that living room, seconds away from storming over to Kira and yanking that boy off her.

I blink, and the next moment I'm out in one of the halls, near a staircase.

Yeah. Upstairs. It's the last place I want to go, especially with that kid near Kira, but I need to put distance between me and them.

The amount of questioning glances thrown my way while I'm heading up the stairs makes me pause on the landing.

Shit, I know I probably look like an angry devil but I usually do. Why the hell are they looking at me like that?

A prickling suspicion arises in my mind.

If that bitch is spreading more rumors around . . .

Son of a bitch.

Another thing to worry about.

I go in search of a bathroom, because I have nowhere better to go until I cool down. Two bathrooms later, and I still haven't found an empty one to chill in for a few.

With no actual destination in mind, I roam the halls, heading deeper into the house. I make a right and see the end of the hallway.

No point going that way.

I'm about to turn and head back in the direction I came, when the slightly ajar door at the end catches my attention.

What sounds like a feminine moan reaches me.

Whatever. Someone's getting laid.

I turn to leave.

Another feminine moan, different in tone to the first, makes me pause.

Did I just hear what I think I heard?

Out of curiosity, I walk toward the door, stepping quietly and straining to hear.

Two women are moaning. No sign of a male with them. Maybe he's watching? Or maybe it's two girls getting it on.

But that's not what has me sneaking closer to the door. I think one of them moaned a certain name.

A few feet away from the door, I hear it again.

"Oh my God, baby, yes. Lick my nipple. Your tongue feels so good, Jenn."

My heart explodes into a racing, excited beat.

Holy fuck. Bingo. *Yes.*

I always suspected. Always. But she's been good all these years. Kept it under tight wraps, to the point that none of us really knew no matter how much we dug for information.

One thing is for the whole world to know she's slutting it around. That's bad, but excusable.

But everyone knows her dad's stance on any kind of homosexuality. Man on man. Girl on girl. It doesn't matter, he's utterly against it.

And daddy holds Jennifer's entire life in his hands.

I stop before the door. On the other side, the moans are escalating and I hear the wet sound of kissing.

Slowly, moving like a snail, I bring my phone out and open the camera. Just as slowly, I push the door open with my index finger, holding my breath. Praying. Waiting for a sound.

The door opens enough for me to see.

As soon as I do, I aim my camera at the scene before me and hit record.

Jennifer's on top of another blond girl. Their skirts are around their waists, panties gone. Shirts are pulled down, tits bared.

They're making out, messy, tongues glistening. Bodies writhing. Pussies grinding on a wet slide. Hard nipples brush against hard nipples.

It isn't until Jennifer stops kissing the girl and lowers her head to suck on her nipple that I recognize who she's rubbing pussies with.

Jesus. That's Megan. Nick's girl.

Nick is one of the only people I know that has been big on monogamy his whole life. He was raised to believe in that.

There's no way he okay'd this. No way he'll forgive Megan.

This is going to destroy my boy.

Yet, I can't disregard it. This is the thing I've been searching to get for weeks. I need to use this against Jennifer. It's the perfect revenge.

Plus, Nick deserves to know he's being cheated on even if it's with a girl. I wish I could tell him straight up, but once this gets out, I can't have this traced back to me in any way.

The goal isn't to make Jenn an even bigger enemy. It's to fuck up her life so bad she won't have the energy or time to focus on me and Kira.

Jennifer rises up and adjust her legs, so one is over Megan's and their pussies press together even more. She reaches down to play with Megan's rock hard nipples.

Megan reaches up to play with Jennifer's, their hips

circling faster and faster. Right as their moans escalate, and it's obvious both are about to come, Megan pulls Jennifer down and starts making out with her again.

God damn. These girls are *passionately* fucking the shit out of each other.

Back in the day, this would've had me drooling. Stepping into the room and offering them both cock.

Now, I'm drooling for an entire different reason. It's fucked up, but Jenn has this coming to her.

And I'm going to make sure this video ends up in the right hands.

Both girls cry out loudly as they come.

That's all I need. Before they come down off their high and notice me here, I end the recording and head back the way I came.

I can't fucking believe my luck. If I had never come up here, I would have never stumbled upon that little scene.

Shit, man. I guess it's true what they say. Sometimes things happen for a reason.

On that note, it's time I return downstairs and check on my girl.

As I jog down the steps, I make sure the video gets uploaded to my cloud drive. Don't want to risk losing it.

I bump into Ryan and Dana at the foot of the stairs. Where's Kira? I lower my voice and ask them just that.

"She said she was going to step outside for a bit. Someone was talking about how you once fucked them, and were betting they could succeed where Renee failed. She was really pissed."

Fucking shit. What the fuck is wrong with all these girls? I gave them dick once, a select few twice, and they think they now own a part of me or something?

Ryan shakes his head, jaw tense.

I pull out my phone to call Kira. "How the hell do you deal with the vindictiveness of these chicks?" I ask Dana, because I know she goes through the same thing when it comes to Ryan.

"I don't deal with it very well. But…" Dana lowers her voice so no one can hear her either "… at least I can claim my man publicly."

The need to separate my father from Sonia chokes me. I dial Kira's number and walk away from everyone.

She picks up on the second ring.

"Where are you?" I barely stop myself from adding *baby*.

"Outside."

Fuck. She's livid. That tight, controlled tone is one I know well. "I'll come to you."

"I'm seriously considering leaving."

"I'll come with you." Her silence tells me she just might not want me with her. Fuck that. I love her but distance is one thing I'm not giving her. "I'm coming out to search for you so you might as well tell me where you are."

"I already requested an Uber."

I walk out the front door. "Please. Where are you?"

She's silent for a second, then mumbles, "Two houses down to the right. I didn't want anyone to see me."

Because she's upset. I clear the driveway and make the right turn. "I'm coming, baby." I hang up the call with her and let Ryan know we're taking a cab home.

I find Kira right where she told me she would be. She's leaning against one of the trees at the end of a driveway.

There's an open bottle in her hand.

My girl and I share yet another unhealthy trait; we drink when we're pissed.

I stop next to her and rub my thumb across her cheek. When she doesn't pull away, I let out a silent sigh.

She holds up the bottle to me. "Want some?"

I take it from her with a smirk. "How far is the Uber?"

"Says ten minutes now."

Meaning: she's been out here waiting for it for a while. Probably the entire time I was recording Jenn and Megan.

I swallow a mouthful of Jack, wincing. Rum isn't my go-to. I'm usually a whiskey or vodka kind of guy. But I'm guessing she went with the first thing she found.

I watch her as she stares off into space. I'm next to her. For now, that's enough. I'll give her a few minutes to mentally deal with whatever she's dealing with before talking to her.

"We should know better than to go to parties together, huh?"

Her wry tone makes me chuckle. "We shouldn't go at all. Staying at my place from now on is the best option."

Her eyes flash with sadness and she finally looks at me. "It's your friend's birthday. Go back in there and spend the night with him. I'll be fine on my own."

"No." I hand her back the bottle, hoping she understands that this is one argument she will never win. Sure, I didn't even get to see Nick and wish him happy birthday, but Kira isn't leaving without me.

She rolls her eyes at me and tilts the bottle to her lips. "Where did you go off to?"

I want to tell her so badly, but I promised myself I'd keep her out of my fucked up plans as much as possible. Lying to her is fucked up and one of the last things I want to do.

The very last thing though? Drag her deeper into some twisted shit. She has enough of that to deal with while being with me.

"I had to cool down. That girl pissed me the fuck off." Not a lie.

"You?" She scoffs and hands me back the bottle.

I know she's being sarcastic, but I answer that anyway. "Yes, me. I didn't want her fucking hands on me. And I definitely didn't want you suffering because of a stupid mistake from the past."

Kira stares at me out of the corner of her eye. "Oh? So now it's a mistake?"

I know what she's really asking. Back then, I didn't consider my lifestyle to be a mistake. I was too busy having fun, using chicks, and running from my feelings for Kira.

But now I know the truth. "Had I never lived the life I lived, you wouldn't have more reasons to suffer today."

Her expression softens and it makes me want to kiss the breath out of her. "I've made my fair share of mistakes that have caused you pain, haven't I?"

Austin. Thinking about him burns as always. Will it ever not hurt? And he's only one. She has to deal with the many and I don't know how she does it. "You didn't make as many mistakes as me, baby."

She shrugs and we segue into silence. The bottle is passed between us a few more times and we manage to finish almost half of the liquid by the time the Uber car pulls up.

Kira twists the cap back on the bottle. The driver lowers the window and leans toward her. "Kira Roth?"

"Yup. That's me."

I open the door for her and she slides in. I get in after her and bring her in close to my side.

We sit like that the whole ride, exchanging the bottle for a few more drinks.

The car comes up to Kira's old house and I remember that the entire family that lives there is currently on vacation. "You can drop us off here."

Kira quirks her brow at me, questioning me.

The cab stops in front of the house and I urge her to exit.

"What are we doing?"

I grab her hand without answering and lead her up the driveway, toward the back of the house.

"Oh my God, Brayden!" Kira hisses, trying to pull her hand out of mine. "Are you crazy? You just finished getting arraigned for one offense! We can't get caught trespassing!"

TWELVE

BRAYDEN

I turn and yank her so she falls against my chest. Hugging her, I lower my head to lick and suckle her bottom lip. "They left on vacation. All of them."

She's fighting hard not to lean against me. I can tell. "But we still shouldn't take a chance. You can't get into any kind of legal trouble."

I remember the last time I was up there with her. How I was dying to slam her against the tree house floor and force her to choke on my cock. "Baby, no one's there. We'll be careful. Come."

"Fuck. You're hard."

I pull away before she can feel anymore of me. Not that she probably hasn't guessed at my intentions yet.

Yeah, I want to fuck her up there.

But, most importantly, I need to spend time with her in a place full of good memories for us. A place that will help her see why this is all worth it.

Everything is dark and fucked up between us. Nothing is normal. We pay with agony for every ounce of love we share with each other. That love is the only thing that makes all of the drama worth it.

"Fine. I'll go up there with you. But if we get caught, don't say I didn't warn you."

I laugh and pause where the driveway ends, turning to wait for her to take off her shoes.

Her lips twitch and she bends down to slip off one heel. Handing it to me, she steps onto the grass with her bare foot and takes off the other one.

She slaps it against my chest before walking ahead of me. "This is your crazy idea. So you can hold onto my shoes."

Laughing, I follow her to the tree house ladder. There, she pauses and looks at the shoes. "On second thought, just leave them down here."

"You sure?"

"My purse and the bottle are way more important. Especially the bottle. And we each need one hand free to get both things up there. That being said, can I trust you to not drop this *very* necessary bottle?"

I laugh again and place her shoes on the grass by the base of the tree. Fucking love how fun this girl is. "Baby, since you want this bottle so bad, you can bet your sexy little ass I'll protect it with my life on the way up there."

She gives me an adorable cheeky smile that makes me want to bite her and hands me the bottle.

Just like that, all the stress of the night melts out of me. This is exactly what we need. Why I'm risking yet another round of legal trouble to have this moment with her.

We climb up into the tree house, our pace slower than usual

due to us having to use one hand.

Once inside, she settles on the floor by the wall, leaving enough room for me to sit next to her.

I don't want to sit next to her. I want to bring her on my lap and let her feel what she's doing to me with that outfit.

Kira, however, has gone back to being distant. Her facial expression makes it obvious she has a lot on her mind.

I know what, too.

Settling next to her, I hand her the bottle and try to patiently wait until she's ready to talk to me.

"How long can we keep living like this?" she asks me quietly in the dark.

I bring out my phone and turn on the flashlight. I need to see her better. Laying it on the floor so the light reflects off the roof of the tree house, I accept the bottle from her and ponder how to respond.

I don't want to give away what I'm up to. Even if it kills me, I don't want her involved in this twisted shit I'm doing. Thinking about the video I now have on my phone, I honestly tell her, "It won't be forever."

She glances at me, eyes full of disbelief, then looks away. "You're right. It won't."

What does that tone mean?

I hate this distance between us. How we keep bouncing back and forth between it and that perfect intimacy we share.

"Talk to me, Kitty. What's going on in that head of yours?"

She giggles at my question and opens up her large clutch. Reaching inside it, she brings out her pair of black and pink kitty ears.

Putting them on, she turns and gives me that mischievous sneaky smile of hers.

My cheeks feel like they're going to split open, that's how wide my smile is. "You always rocked those ears like nobody else."

Laughing, she snatches the bottle from me.

I want to bask in this, in us being back to where we're meant to be. No negativity. No tension.

But it'll be back. If I don't address it, try to fix it, there's no avoiding its return. "Baby, talk to me."

"You know, it still surprises me that you're so into talking now."

"And it still surprises me that you're not."

Her raised eyebrow says it all: in a weird, twisted way, we've switched roles here. I'm the one constantly reaching out to her, while as she's the one shielding herself from me.

I took all of my love related hang ups and shoved them down into her. I morphed a once loving, openly affectionate girl, into a bitter, closed off woman.

She's better lately. At least, she's trying to be. But nights like this, when the seediness of my past rears its ugly head and reminds her, I know the pain returns.

"I'm sorry she thought she could come up to me and grab my crotch."

Kira shrugs, subdued once more. Fucking gorgeous with that smoky-eyed makeup, luscious nude lips, and those cat ears on her head. "It's not your fault."

Fuck that. We both know it is. This is *my* past coming back to haunt us.

"Brayden, stop." Her small, soft hand cups mine soothingly. "I know what you're doing. Just stop. Neither of us can change the past."

That's the most fucked up part of life. There's no going

back. No undoing what's been done.

And no erasing the scars our actions leave behind.

"Who was that kid that came up to you?" My head's starting to buzz from the alcohol, and my hot blood's still thrumming with that dark, psychotic possessiveness I feel for her.

"My friend." Her eyes are glazed, and I know her cheeks are probably pink by now. The liquor is hitting her, too.

"Your friend." I can't hide my dislike for that term. I have no right to begrudge her male friends, but I fucking hate every last one of them.

"Nothing's ever happened between us."

"But he wants it to."

Her silence is all the confirmation I need.

"I can't control who's attracted to me, Brayden. Just like you can't control who's attracted to you."

I let her take the bottle. It's more than halfway g one. I'm at the edge, right before being drunk, and my entire body feels hot.

Watching her bring it back up to her lips, I lean in close, running my nose along her jaw.

She chokes softly.

Smiling, I press my lips to the spot where her jaw meets her neck and lick the skin softly. When her skin breaks out in goosebumps, I smile wider.

"I know what you're doing."

Ah, fuck me. I love when her tone drops to that low, siren's tone. My balls tighten, my dick jumps once inside my jeans, and I lick her again. "What am I doing?"

She eases away and presses the bottle to my lips. "Mind-fucking me. As always."

I'm frustrated that she took her skin away from me, but I'll let her play her little game.

For now.

Her eyes flash seductively as she watches me swallow the rum.

"Do you like that? Having it in your blood?"

I feel precome gather at the tip of my dick from that tone alone. Swallowing, I nod, wondering where she's going with this.

I won't let her maintain control of this situation. Not for long. But damn, the curiosity of this moment is too delicious to ignore.

Kira places the drink on the wooden floor. Her purse follows. At first, I think she's going to come straight at me.

She doesn't. She leans her shoulder against the wall, facing me, her legs curled to the side on the floor.

Calm.

Unhurried.

Eyes shuttered.

While I'm on fucking fire and dying for her.

I start leaning toward her, eyes on her lips.

She has the nerve to press her index finger against my lips and push my head back. "How about me?"

I jerk my head away from her hand impatiently. "What about you?"

"Do you like having *me* in your blood?"

The question breaks something inside me. Growling, I move toward her.

Kira rises up on her knees and throws all her weight into pushing me back. The momentum sends me flying backwards onto the wooden floor.

Some of the wind is knocked out of me. I stay here, laying on my back, staring up at the ceiling in shock.

That wasn't a nice push. It wasn't a seductive one, either.

This girl means business.

I raise my head to stare at her.

Kira kneels next to my hips and reaches down to practically rip my zipper open. "Why do you always insist on believing that you're in control of this situation between us?"

I open my mouth to answer.

She yanks me out of my jeans and mounts me. In the low illumination of my phone light, I see her pull her skirt up to her hips.

When the fuck did she take off her panties?

My eyes widen dangerously as I realize.

She went to that fucking party commando.

Holding me in her fist, she positions herself and slams me into her.

A loud groan is ripped out of me. My back arches off the floor. Grinding my teeth, I throw my head back and try to hold on.

Shit. She feels even tighter today than ever.

Kira grabs my button down and tears it open. The rage in her movements should worry me.

Instead, I'm fucking on fire for her more than ever.

Grabbing my wrists, she places my arms on the floor, straight above my head. I know what she's doing before she even speaks.

One small hand wrapped around both my wrists, she reaches down with her other hand and caresses my pecs. "If you want this pussy, you're going to have to keep your hands there."

I circle my hips beneath her, feeling the silky wet suction of her cunt. "I can just take it, baby."

"I'll refuse." Her voice is so calm. Flat.

There's no denying how serious she is.

She wants this. Wants me at her control. More than that, she wants me to *willingly* submit to her.

As if I hadn't done that a long time ago.

I don't know for how long I'll be able to give her what she wants, but I clench my jaw and nod.

And she starts moving.

Hips rotating.

Ass bouncing.

Slow, torturous circles of her hips that tease my cock with the promise of more.

I moan, grinding my teeth so hard that pain shoots through my jaw.

"Do you remember when we used to play up here?" Kira asks me in a low, breathless voice.

I nod, hands opening and closing helplessly. Of course I remember. How could I forget? Especially with her wearing those cat ears while she rides me, reminding me of our past. I lose control of my hips. My legs rise up behind her, feet pressing flat on the floor.

Her eyes flash when I thrust up into her, but she can't hold back her high-pitched little moan. "Stop. Or I'll climb off."

"I'll fucking follow you."

Her expression hardens and I know I've crossed the line with her.

Heart pounding throughout my entire body, I lower my hips back onto the floor. Sweat gathers on my forehead and slides down my temple.

Appeased, she gives me a tight-lipped smile and resumes riding me in that slow, sensual pace that makes me want to rut like an animal.

"*Kira.*"

She moans for me, making my dick jump inside her. "Do you? Do you remember Brayden?"

"*Yes.*" Holy fuck. My balls fucking hurt. I'm so close to coming like this and yet, I know I won't be able to. Not without pounding into her like a beast.

She tightens her hold on my wrists and rakes her nails down my chest.

Hard.

Violent.

I cry out and raise my head to see welts of blood gathering on my chest.

Jesus. She's clawing into me. Marking me.

"How old were we the last time we were up here as kids?"

"I-I . . ." My words trail off, lips parted as I see the moonlight and my phone light hits the wetness on my cock. Her pussy lips.

She's fucking soaking me, our skin glistening from it.

Kira slams her hips down on me. Only once. Then she resumes her slow speed, as if she didn't just tease me with that one hard thrust.

"How. Old. Brayden?"

"I was sixteen. You were thirteen."

She nods, eyes heavy-lidded. She's slowly losing herself to the feeling of my cock. Just a little longer and she won't care if I take control. All that will matter to her is that I pump her full of my come.

"We were alone. Remember that?" She scrapes her nail

over my nipple.

My legs shake behind her. My abs clench. "Fuck, Kira. I need to come. *Now*."

She doesn't speed up. Doesn't acknowledge my statement. "Do you remember?"

"Yes, damn you!"

"I wanted you. Even then." Her hips rotate, walls sucking at my cock, and I almost don't understand what she's saying to me. "I was only thirteen but even then I wanted to have sex with you. Wanted you to fuck me."

A desperate sound leaves me and I slam my head against the wood beneath me.

What she's saying to me . . . it's so wrong.

It's so fucking hot.

I wanted her, too. Hadn't admitted it to myself that day, that my cock had been rock hard the entire time I was up here with her. I told myself I just wanted any random pussy.

But I wanted her little pussy and even with the denial, I'd almost died from not having it.

"I wanted you, Brayden. Kept mentally begging you to slam me on this floor and rip me apart with that beautiful cock of yours."

I snap.

Snarling, I shoot up off the floor, holding her to my cock.

One twist and I slam her under me, pussy still impaled on my dick.

It isn't nice.

I probably just hurt her.

Her thighs spread wider for me and I forget to care about any of that.

I tear the front of her small top open and her luscious tits spill out for me. Sliding one hand under her, I thrust two fingers into her tight ass.

Her legs seize on either side of my hips.

There's so much more that I want—*need*—to do to her but there's no time. One thrust, and I'll flood her insides. "When we're done here, I'm flipping you over and eating this sweet ass." I thrust my fingers into her, feeling her tightness, how full of my cock she is.

I can feel my dick through the thin barrier separating her ass and pussy.

She whimpers my name like she's fucking praying to me. Like I'm her motherfucking God and she's ready to sacrifice everything she is at the base of my altar.

I play with her nipples with my free hand, loving how she loses her voice and can't even speak. "That's right baby. Let that pussy worship my cock."

As if following my command, her pussy ripples around me, trying to rip the come out of me.

Always. Without fail. Her pussy demands and it takes everything in me to stop my dick from obeying.

Kira's hair is spread out on the wood around her head. In the darkness, it looks almost black. Her hazel eyes are glazed over, full of tears.

The cat ears fuck with me. Remind me of the sweet girl I started falling for all those years ago.

Her hands fist the material around my shoulders and I feel them shaking.

"One move, baby," I say hoarsely, emotionally battered from this connection with her and loving it. "One move and we're both going to come."

"G-give it . . . *Oh God*." Her hips rotate in circles beneath me, fucking my cock and my fingers with both her tight holes. Her teeth start chattering from the intensity of the pleasure. "*Give it to me, please.*"

I pull my hips and thrust back into her with all the strength in my body.

She can't even scream my name. Her beautiful eyes are wide, fear at the intensity of the pleasure shining in them.

I roar her name, pumping my hips. It hurts. My body begs me to stop as the orgasm burns through me.

I don't. Can't. This pain she causes in me is too addicting for me to stop.

Another wave. One more throb of my dick inside her. A shiver tears its way down my spine and I collapse on her, my cock and fingers still in her.

Her pussy and ass pound to the harsh beats of her heart. Obliterated by her, I lay my head on her chest and curl into her.

There's peace in the aftermath of that kind of pain and pleasure. These are the moments I've come to live for. When it's me and her, ruined by what we do to each other.

Nothing else matters. We work each other up to the point of no return and then crash back to Earth together, weak. Sated. Limp.

There's no fight left in her. She circles her arms around me and just melts into what's between us. Resentment. Anger. It's all gone for now.

I don't know how much time passes, but eventually I ease back away from her. She sits up, still breathless.

Her top is destroyed. There's no way it'll be able to cover her tits now.

I take off my shirt and hand it to her. "It won't close but

you can hold it together 'til we get in the house."

Shaking, she slides the kitty ears off her head and takes the shirt from me. "How about you? You can't walk to the house with me with your shirt off. Someone might see."

I don't know if she's talking more about my tattoos, or someone piecing it together if they see me shirtless and her in my shirt.

"You go first. I'll run after you once you're in the house. So if anyone sees me, they'll only see me."

She seems skeptical but goes with it.

Using my phone light, I go around the tree house, picking all the buttons of my shirt off the floor. I don't want to leave a trace that we were here. Not that anyone would really notice or care much, but still.

"It's leaking out of me," Kira says sheepishly.

I close my eyes. Fuck, that's hot. "Take your bag and go. I'll catch up."

She nods and heads for the entrance of the tree house.

I grab her arm before she can descend the ladder. "Leave the front door and your bedroom door open."

"Brayden, you can't keep sneaking into my room. If your father catches us—"

"Fuck him. Leave the door open." I stare into her eyes until she nods. Nothing is stopping me from sleeping with her in my arms tonight.

Fuck my father. Fuck the world.

Jennifer is going down pretty soon.

My father is next.

After that, I'll figure out what I do about what people will have to say. But none of them are going to stop me from being with her.

THIRTEEN

Kira

August 22nd 2015

You should have just moved in with me.

I press my lips together to hold back the giggle that wants to escape. Brayden's in his car, driving next to me, and even from here I can see the small, petulant scowl on his face.

My mom is in the car behind me, because she insisted on coming along this time. She wasn't there when Ryan moved into college, and since I'm "the baby," she is determined to be there when I settle in.

I raise my windows, turn off the music, and call Brayden through my car's Bluetooth. Out of the corner of my eye, I see him raise all his windows before picking up.

We can't chance my mom overhearing our conversation in any way, and we both know that.

"I'm serious, baby. You're barely going to be staying at that dorm and you know it."

I shake my head at his stubbornness. "Our parents…" God, I hate referring to Steve in such a way "expect me to be at the dorms and that's what my mom is paying for."

"Fine. But half the shit in there is going to my house eventually anyway, including that sexy little ass of yours."

I squirm in my seat. Fuck. All it takes is a few words from him and my pussy hollows out with need. "Maybe," I say, teasing him.

"There's no maybe about it," he murmurs in a deep, serious tone that makes me even hornier. "The exit is coming up."

Flipping the signal, I merge over to the right, keeping an eye on my mom's car and making sure she's doing the same.

Brayden lets her pass him, then merges behind her, and we drive down the ramp off the highway.

We couldn't speed as we usually do, due to my mom being with us, but after an hour and a half drive, I'm more than anxious to arrive.

Five minutes later, we pull up in front of Lincoln Towers on the school grounds. It's utter mayhem, with cars struggling to find a spot to pull over so other students can unload their things.

Ryan and Dana are standing in front of two open spots. They wave us over the moment they see us.

Brayden pulls over next to me and lowers his window. I do the same and lean closer to hear him. "You and your mom can park here. I'll go find parking and come back."

I nod at him, my heart in my throat. The last few weeks, I've been nothing but a ball of excitement at the prospect of being out of the house on my own. *Finally*.

But now that the moment has arrived, I feel an odd fear clawing up from my chest.

Brayden drives off and I have no choice but to push it down. Once Mom and I are parked near the curb, Ryan flings my door open and all but drags me out.

"You're under my mercy now!"

I elbow him in the stomach while Dana laughs. "As if, dumbass."

"You see?" He scoffs at my mother as she comes up to hug him and give him a kiss. "She's cursing already. I told you she would need my *adult* supervision now that you won't be around."

Taking advantage of my mom's turned back, I flip Ryan off and give him a cheeky smile.

Dana laughs again and comes up to me to say hi. A small group of girls passing by stop near us, staring at my brother with blatant interest and whispering among themselves.

Ew. Gross. Seriously.

Dana's brow furrows. Raising an eyebrow at the girls, she goes up to my brother and loops her arm in his. The look in her eyes makes one thing very clear: had my mom not been here, she'd be laying a claim on him in a very different way.

A fissure of dread goes through me.

If history is anything to go by, I'll be dealing with this for God knows how long. And, unlike Dana, I won't be able to lay a claim on the man I'm sleeping with.

Fuck. I just got here and already my mood is ruined.

"You guys start taking things up and I'll stay here with the car," Dana offers.

The dorm rooms are smaller than my bedroom, but that doesn't mean I haven't loaded down my car and Mom's. Still, with three to four people, it shouldn't take us too long to get it all up.

Brayden comes running up to us and leans into my car to pick up a box.

Almost two hours later, due to having to take an elevator up to the seventeenth floor with each load and having to wait with hundreds of other people, we bring the last of my things into my small room.

The floors are covered in a brown carpet. The set up is odd compared to most dorm rooms. The "room" area is small and long. Twin size beds are on opposite sides, up against the walls. In front of the beds, on either sides of the door, are two small closets. Two personal-sized dressers finish it all off, placed next to each other between the beds.

Thank God there's a small study area right outside the rooms. I'd be utterly claustrophobic.

My mom places my laptop bag on top of one of the two desks in the study area.

The door leading outside opens. "Ah! I can't believe we're roommates!" Jenna drops the box she was holding on the floor, uncaring, and rushes toward me with open arms.

We hug each other as her parents say hello to my mom and Ryan. "Well, duh, we asked to be," I say with a laugh.

Her father shakes hands with Brayden. "And you are?" he asks with a friendly smile on his face.

"Brayden Hunt. Nice to meet you."

Recognition flashes in Jenna's father's eyes.

"He's Kira's stepbrother," my mom says, smiling.

Jenna's father doesn't say anything but I can see the censure in his eyes. He clearly remembers the phone call Jenna made to get me into the holding cells to see Brayden faster.

The atmosphere changes after that, becoming heavy and tense. Suddenly, all I want to do is get out of here.

No. What I really want is everyone to go away and for it to be just Brayden and me. The look in his eyes bothers me. The itch to comfort him leaves me antsy.

Jenna and her parents move into the small room area to drop off her stuff.

Ryan comes up to me and hugs me one more time. "See you later tonight."

Dana is right behind him and she hugs me with a sympathetic smile on her face. She can see what I'm dealing with and the concern in her eyes touches me. "We'll be around if you need anything. Just give one of us a call."

I nod and say goodbye to my mom next. The tears she's holding back make my throat tighten and my eyes burn. She hugs me tight for the longest, almost as if she's afraid to let me go.

My mom's been through this already. When Ryan went off to college, I remember how sad she was the weeks following that.

But this is different. Although both me and my brother are now at this school and it's only an hour and a half away, me leaving the house leaves her utterly alone.

I hug her tighter. "Mom, promise me you'll call me if anything goes wrong over there." The thought of leaving her in that house with Steve frightens me. He's never put his hands on her, but I can't shake the feeling that she's going to be in danger with him.

My eyes cut to Brayden and I see him staring at us with a worried look. I'm sure he's thinking the same thing I am.

Mom pulls back. Laughing, she wipes the tears off her cheeks. "Honey. Don't worry about me. Everything is going to be fine."

No, it's not and deep down I know she knows that. I can see how forced her smile is.

"She's right, Sonia. You can call us, either one of us, at anytime if something goes down," Brayden says softly.

My mother gives him a small smile. "It's fine. Don't worry about me. Either one of you. And, Brayden, please. Take care of my daughter."

Something about the way she says that fills me with anxiety.

Brayden studies her as well, searching her expression for God knows what. "Always, Sonia. But I think you know that already."

Something passes between them.

What the hell is going on? What do the looks on their faces mean?

My mom says goodbye to me one last time and then she's gone.

Brayden remains standing where he is, his eyes turbulent. He starts taking a step toward me, then stops abruptly, his eyes flickering toward the room area where I can hear Jenna and her parents.

I want to leave. My things can be set up later. I don't want to be here at all.

Brayden's jaw twitches. He pulls his phone out of his pocket and starts texting.

My phone vibrates two seconds later and I pull it out to see his text.

Stay with me tonight?

The question mark at the end makes my heart clench. Lately, he'd gone back to being more sure of himself. More confident. More of his usual, cocky demanding self.

I think about it for a second. My roommate is Jenna, and I doubt anyone else on my floor will pay attention if I don't come back tonight. Even if they do, no one is going to guess I'm with Brayden.

Of course, I text back, even though this is probably a bad idea.

Every day, I'm falling in deeper.

So is he.

Our situation is just as complicated as always.

I put away my phone and stare up at him. He's smiling at me, this small happy smile that makes it impossible to regret anything.

For the first time in a long time, I truly want to see him happy.

But we can't be together.

Even if we could, do I want to? This isn't about me being vindictive anymore. It's only been five months since he came back to me with the intention of finally doing right by me.

Five months compared to years of almost constant pain.

Maybe it should've been enough to heal me by now.

It isn't. Sometimes, when I look at him, everything he did still hurts so fucking much. Like a huge scar that will always be tender to the touch.

The smile drops off his face. In two strides he's in front of me, grabbing my chin.

Heart racing, I try to pull back. If Jenna's parents come out and see how close he is to me...

Brayden tightens his hold, eyes boring into mine.

"What are you doing?" I hiss quietly.

"What's wrong?" he whispers.

Damn this man for being so in tune with me.

"Nothing," I whisper back. "Brayden, step back before they see us."

"It's not 'nothing,' Kitty. I know you."

He does. So well.

Against my will, my heart melts, and I can't help but nuzzle his palm.

He hums low in his throat, that pleased, sexy hum he gives me when I've made him happy, and some of the worry melts from his face.

"I'm fine, Brayden. But we need to be careful."

He swallows, the hunger in his eyes making my heart race faster. "You're coming over tonight, right?"

"I already said yes."

Suddenly, he drops his hand from my face and bends down to pretend he's tying his shoe.

He's still close but at least it doesn't look as bad now.

Jenna and her parents exit our room. Her dad's eyes flash with disapproval when he sees Brayden still here with me.

That's all it takes for me to dislike the man. Yes, he did me a favor getting me in to see Brayden. And yes, I get it. Brayden got arrested and Jenna's father is a judge.

I get that he's worried me and Jenna are associating with the wrong sort. Not that I have any choice since Brayden and I are related by marriage.

Still. Who the hell is Jenna's father to dislike Brayden without having all the facts? Protectiveness rises up from my chest. Brayden didn't get arrested for stealing or for another type of violent crime.

No, he got arrested for being in a fight because of me.

It takes all of my willpower not to snap at Jenna's dad and set him straight about the facts.

Brayden stands. "Call me or your brother if you need anything."

It's an innocent enough statement, but it makes me nervous because other people are here. Shit, everything about our situation makes me nervous.

It isn't about me, either. I don't give a damn what anyone would ever have to say about me. But if we're found out, this will be another stain on Brayden's reputation because of me.

And my brother. I haven't spoken to him about it, but what would he do living in a town where everyone is constantly talking shit to him about his stepbrother and little sister fucking?

I don't want that for either of them.

Nodding at Brayden, I give him what I hope is a friendly smile.

He nods back at me, says goodbye to everyone else in the room, and heads out.

Deciding to play nice, I turn to say goodbye to Jenna's parents.

"You two should try to limit your time with that young man," Jenna's father says.

My lips part.

"Daddy! How could you say something like that?" Jenna cries out, outraged on my behalf, I'm sure.

"Honey, he's just trying to watch out for the two of you," her mom tells her softly.

Through clenched teeth, I grit out, "It was a single fight, and with all due respect, although I appreciate the favor you did for me, I would also appreciate it if you didn't insult him in front of me."

Everyone falls silent.

I bid both of Jenna's parents a safe trip back home and head into our small room.

"Daddy, you're being unfair and you know it."

"I get that that's her stepbrother and that they love each other like siblings, but that doesn't mean I'm wrong about him. Keep your distance, Jenna."

I want to slam the door shut in a fit of anger but somehow refrain.

Stepbrother.

Love each other like siblings.

Keep your distance, Jenna.

Groaning under my breath, I push the box on my bed to the side and collapse on it, my face in my hands.

I hear Jenna angrily telling her dad to let it go and then saying goodbye to both her parents.

First day at college. It's supposed to be an exciting time for everyone.

For me, this is what I get. And all because the stupid world has to always attack Brayden in some way.

Always has to stand between us, too.

Then again, if this is as bad as it gets, I suppose I can't complain too much. Right?

Then I remember that Jennifer is in this school as well, along with a ton of other people from our high school, and I realize that this is probably only the beginning.

Knowing Jenn, things are probably going to get much worse at some point.

FOURTEEN

BRAYDEN

Meet me by the oval after class.

My leg bounces with impatience. I'm frustrated. More anxious than I've been in a few weeks now.

I see Kira almost every night, sleep with her in my arms.

But it doesn't ease what I feel. I think some part of me, back in the far corners of my mind, had foolishly hoped that things would be easier once we came to college together.

They aren't. There is a large number of people from our school here. They know us.

And I'm more convinced than ever that Jennifer managed to start rumors among them. No one has said anything. The actual rumors haven't reached my ears, or that of anyone we know, but the questioning looks are always there.

I can't hang out with Kira without it seeming like there's someone analyzing our behavior toward each other.

I wouldn't care so much if I didn't see how it's affecting my Kitty.

Worse than that, it's starting to affect Ryan, too. I don't know if it's because he's frustrated at the whole situation, or because he's worried about how he'll deal with the backlash of everyone finding out.

I make a mental note to have a serious talk with him about it. I need to know where my best friend stands as I move forward.

Fuck. This would all be so much easier if it only had to do with me and Kira. If our families weren't in danger of also being punished for what we feel for each other.

I think a part of me needs Ryan to tell me he doesn't care what people would say. Kira still might, but as long as Ryan doesn't, then that's one last thing we need to worry about.

Kira's response finally comes through. *I need to rush back and get ready for tonight.*

One of the fraternities is throwing a party tonight and we were all invited.

I, for one, would rather not go. What I need is to be at home with my girl. A selfish thought, I know, which is why I haven't voiced it. I had my college experiences, went to my fair share of parties. Who am I to take that from her?

Just for 5 minutes baby. I need to see you.

Her response is almost instantaneous. *Ok. I'll be there <3*

The anxiousness literally melts from me. That heart means everything. Most guys wouldn't pay attention to shit like that. I, however, know what it means.

Kira hasn't confessed that she still loves me. I tell her I love her all the time, but she doesn't say it back.

That doesn't mean I haven't noticed her softening toward me. The walls around her heart coming down.

159

Fifteen minutes later, I'm rushing across campus, hellbent on making it to the oval in time. I catch sight of Craig on the way there. He waves me over. I shake my head and just wave hi, indicating that I'm in a hurry.

Kira's waiting for me by the Thompson statue, looking absolutely fuckable in a pair of tight, dark blue skinny jeans. Her back is facing me, that long auburn hair flowing down to the top of her ass.

I come up behind her and roughly grab her ass before I can think better of it.

She jumps almost a foot in the air, whirling around with rage burning in those beautiful eyes. When she sees it's me, the rage morphs into panic. "Brayden," she hisses, her eyes darting all over the place.

I know. I know. That was absolutely careless on my part and I should be more careful. But . . . "I couldn't help myself," I mumble, eating up the sight of her in those jeans and her cute pink T-shirt.

Her expression softens but I still see the fear of discovery in her eyes.

And I fucking *hate* it.

Next weekend, I'll have a chance to drive back to my dad's house, and I'm taking it. We might not be able to escape the public censure of being together *after* having been stepsiblings, but I need to at least get that legal title bullshit out the way.

I'll figure out what we're going to do about everything else later.

"I'm sorry," I apologize in a low voice.

She tries to smile at me. "It's okay."

But we both know it's not. "Come. I'll walk you back so you can start getting ready for tonight."

We start walking side-by-side, the tension thick between us. Three girls turn to watch us pass by, and Kira tenses even more.

"What is it?" I ask her.

"They went to school with me."

Meaning: they know us.

The looks on their faces say that they know *of* us.

"Jennifer," Kira growls under her breath bitterly.

My vision has clouded over with red. My thoughts turn to the video I have saved in my cloud drive. The pictures I screenshot off it.

"Maybe we're imagining it," Kira mumbles to herself, but her tone says that she doesn't believe it.

Neither do I. But I want to. Because if what I believe is true . . .

Kira finishes my thought for me. "That little bitch actually found a way to get between us."

I'll destroy Jennifer for that.

"I hate this fucking hiding shit." I'm grinding my teeth so hard my jaw is starting to ache.

"We wouldn't have to hide if . . ." Kira trails off but it's too late.

My heart's already fucking breaking because of her unfinished thought.

We wouldn't have to hide if we weren't together.

Clenching my jaw harder, I hold back my remark. Five minutes later, we're standing outside her dorm hall.

I can't go up with her. There's no telling who's watching us.

Holy fuck. We're literally being stalked by all of the nosey motherfuckers we went to school with.

"I'll drive us to the party tonight," I say, preparing to leave. Without hugging her. Kissing her.

"Come up with me really quick."

Surprised, I stare into her eyes. Is she serious? She's willing to risk fanning the suspicions? "You sure?"

She nods but I can tell she really isn't. At the same time, I can tell she's being earnest. She wants me to come up with her.

I motion for her to lead and school my expression. The ride up is hell. She stands next to me like we're nothing more than friends while people get on and off.

Once we're on her floor, she starts talking. "You'll be able to give it to Ryan for me?"

More deceit. Ignoring the bitterness that causes, I play along. "Yeah. I already told him I would." We're pretending for the sake of the girls in the hallway. The ones lounging by the open doorways.

I don't think we know any of them, but we have to be ridiculously careful regardless.

Kira pulls out the key to her dorm and lets us in. "Jenna?" she calls. There's no answer but she walks back toward the small bedroom and peeks in.

I start walking to her, but I don't get far. Kira spins around and rushes back in my direction. No more than ten feet away from the front door, she pushes me back against the wall.

My book bag falls on the floor.

Her's follows.

I can't even take a proper breath before she's on me, hands fisting my hair, hungry little tongue in my mouth.

162

She presses in to me, her body shaking with urgency.

That's all it takes. In the span of a single breath, I shoot hard, my cock swelling unbearably.

I squeeze her ass and lift her off her feet. Turning, I place her down and pull my lips away from hers. She starts yanking on the button of my jeans and I almost rip hers wide open in my haste to get them down.

She gets my jeans open enough to pull out my cock. The feel of her soft hand playing with the sensitive tip makes my hips jerk.

I push her jeans and panties down to her hips. Spinning her around, I press her to the wall.

She whimpers my name.

I slide into her soaked pussy. It's so wet I don't even have to prime her.

What feels like weeks of frustration snap free inside me. Using all my strength, I start fucking her, ramming my cock into her like I haven't fucked her in months.

Like I didn't have her last night.

Biting down on the urge to scream my goddamn head off, I fuck her like it's the last time.

One of my hands is braced against the wall by her head. Kira bites down on it to muffle her cries. I hiss at the sharp sting.

I'm lost in her. The hunger to possess her grows more vicious with every moment I have to hide what she means to me. I've already gone mad for her.

At the rate I'm going, it won't be long before I become utterly psychotic in the name of the love I feel for her.

Kira bites my hand harder, rocking those sexy hips back in circles against me, urging my clock deeper.

Balls tight, I push into her with all my strength.

The door opens behind us.

"Holy shit!"

Hissing, I jerk out of Kira's wet, pulsating cunt, my heart hammering. Adrenaline pumping. I see a flash of blond hair whipping around, a thin body rushing back out the door before it closes.

"Oh God," Kira whimpers behind me, and there's no missing the embarrassment in her tone. A second later, her phone starts vibrating inside her bag at our feet.

Trembling, she lifts her jeans up and bends to get her phone.

I force my stiff dick back into my jeans although it's the last thing I want to do. What I really want is to force Kira up against the wall again and finish what we started.

As I watch Kira's eyes widen with panic, I realize that not doing so is the best idea. "What is it?"

"She's with someone!" she whispers frantically, her pupils enlarged with fear. Her fingers fly across the screen as I register what she just said.

Whoever is with Jenna probably—*hopefully*—didn't see it was me fucking Kira. But they most likely heard.

And now they're standing outside with Jenna, blocking the only escape route, so there's no me leaving here without being seen by that person.

Fuck.

Fuck.

"She's going to head back to the lounge area with her friend for a few minutes."

Heading back to the elevators means walking past the lounge. Still a chance I might be seen, but fuck it. It's better than being caught in here.

Kira gets to her feet and I walk to her to give her a quick kiss. "Tonight," I promise both her and me. "You're staying with me. I want you in my bed."

Her small nod makes my chest clench.

After buttoning my jeans and grabbing my backpack, I follow her to the door. She peeks out, checking the hallway, and then steps back so I can exit.

Thank fucking God there's no one out here at the moment.

I rush back toward the lounge. Right before it, I spot the door to the stairs. I hadn't seen it on my way in.

Luck seems to be on my side again. I slam my way into the stairwell, anger and frustration a tight band around my neck.

I won't live like this for much longer.

We won't.

Kira is finally starting to open up to me, to forgive me, and I'll be damned if I let anything else get in the way of us much longer.

Kira

I want to hate Brayden at this moment, but I can't. Not anymore. Yes, he's the reason I'm miserable instead of enjoying my first college party, but I also understand it isn't truly his fault.

I can't be with him like Dana is with Ryan.

Instead, I have to keep my distance while other girls keep trying to throw themselves at him. To his credit, he seems annoyed and disgusted by their inability to comprehend that he isn't interested.

No. He's actually livid. More than once, some drunk frat boy has come up to me, misguided in his belief that I'm his ticket to getting laid.

And more than once, I've seen my brother quietly reminding Brayden that homicide isn't an option.

Dana, bless her soul, has tried to keep me company, although I can tell all she wants is to be with my brother.

I just walked away, supposedly to use the bathroom, giving her an excuse to be by his side again. I don't want to be the thing that comes between them enjoying themselves together.

Every room I try to go into is occupied. I hear moaning and grunting from behind more than one closed door. Always at these fucking parties, man. Shaking my head, I step away from the last door I tried.

It's pretty quiet on this side of the frat house. Well, except for the two people fucking each other's brains out in that room.

Whatever. I didn't have to go anyway. I just needed an excuse to give Dana a break.

Jenna and the other girls should be here any time now anyway so I might as well head back.

I turn to walk in the direction I came from.

My body jerks to a stop.

Jennifer is standing before me, her phone raised to her chest and a smirk on her face. "Needed some privacy?"

Images of my fist connecting with her face invade my mind and almost hijack my control centers.

166

Nothing would make me happier than ruining her. Nothing.

However, I can't. It isn't the smartest move.

Lord help me, though, because if she doesn't move out of my way soon, I'm going to forget about what's smart and lay into her.

"I don't have time for you. Get out of my way."

She giggles at that and the gleam in her eye gives me pause.

This bitch is up to something.

"I needed a moment alone, too. Was feeling *nostalgic*."

I scowl at her, confused. Is she fucking crazy? What is she talking about?

She moves closer to me and I tense. "Jennifer, you don't want to get too close. Trust me."

"But Kira," she says in a mocking tone. "Don't you want to see what I'm reminiscing about?"

My eyes dart to her phone and dread slithers up my spine. Whatever she's up to, it's going to cut me. The sadistic, gleeful look in her eyes is too blatant.

"No. I don't. Now *move*." I shove her away, self-preservation warning me to get the hell out of dodge.

Fuck it if it looks like I'm running. I don't care.

A sound I don't want to recognize starts playing behind me and against my will, my body freezes in place.

"You like how I'm sucking this dick, baby?" Jennifer's voice plays from what's obviously a recording on her phone.

"Yeah, Jenn. Of course I do. Now less talking and suck it deeper."

My heart shatters in a way I hadn't felt in a while.

A way I remember too well.

167

I know that raspy voice. He sounds intoxicated, but I know his voice with every fiber of my being.

Jennifer walks around me, taking advantage of my frozen shock, and her phone is facing me now.

My eyes focus on it before I can tell myself not to, and I see the video in all its detail.

Jennifer is clearly the one holding the phone, pointing it her direction while she slobbers all over a dick.

A dick I know even more intimately than this pitiful bitch does. I don't need the camera pointed at his face to know it's him.

Jennifer looks younger in this video. It was probably taken years ago.

It. Doesn't. Fucking. Matter.

Brayden fists her hair in the video and holds her still as he starts thrusting hard into her mouth. He barely makes a sound, but almost at the end he groans in a low voice, "That's it. Right there. I'm coming."

The camera is shaking from Jennifer's efforts to keep it steady but I still see clearly when he tenses and shoots his load into her throat.

"God," Jennifer groans in front of me, rolling her eyes back. "I come every damn time I watch this vid—"

She doesn't get to finish.

The sound of my fist connecting with her face echoes loudly down the hall.

BRAYDEN

I hear the screech first—a hellish sound of pure indignation.

Then everyone's rushing to the source of the sound.

Immediately, I'm looking around for Kira, my eyes bouncing off faces. She went to the bathroom a little while ago and Dana rejoined us.

People are gathering at the entrance to the hallway, where it leads to the rest of the house.

Someone pushes through the bodies and I hear a small, feminine grunt.

"Excuse me!"

Kira bursts out of the crowd. Her face is red. Her eyes are *on fire* with an unholy rage I haven't seen in a while.

I start following after her. I don't care who sees me. What they'll think.

She storms out the front door.

Behind me, Jennifer screams, "That fucking bitch almost broke my nose!"

I stop momentarily, torn between following Kira and choking the shit out of Jennifer for whatever she did to Kira.

Of course, the pull to my Kitty is stronger than my need for violence.

Blithely, I realize that Ryan and Dana are on my heels.

We all hit the lawn outside.

Kira takes off at a run.

I'm after her before I can process that I've started running, and the pounding footsteps behind me tell me that Ryan and Dana are running after her, too.

My heart beats like a war drum. Concern suffocates me. What did Jennifer do to her?

What the fuck did she do?

It takes me less than a block to catch up to Kira. I call her name and grab her arm.

She jerks away from me with enough force to send her stumbling backwards on the sidewalk.

"Baby," I rasp, completely forgetting about who might be watching. Who might hear.

She's so frantic to get away from me that she scrambles backwards across the concrete. Her eyes are downcast but I swear I see the shimmer of tears in them.

"Kira—"

"Leave me alone. *Please.*" Her voice is broken. Hoarse. She jumps up to her feet.

I reach for her again.

Ryan and Dana stop next to us, panting.

Kira takes off running again, and just like before, I'm after her.

It doesn't take me long to gain on her once more, but I still feel it.

Cold. Unyielding. Expanding.

It's a pain so fucking familiar.

Distance. It's a twisted virus spreading between us, undoing all the happiness we'd begun to form together.

Kira's dorm is feet away. At this time of night, I can't follow her upstairs. If she gets in there, I've pretty much lost her.

Lunging off my feet, I catch her around the waist with both arms. Turning, I take the impact on my back, shielding her from the concrete. I feel the skin of my back scrape open.

Kira's panting. Disoriented. Ryan comes up behind her and lifts her off me despite the animalistic growl I aim at him.

His eyes flash dangerously at me. "Stop." One word. A calm order.

One I don't feel like obeying at all.

But I have some rationality left. People are all over the place. Watching.

Ryan wraps his arms around his struggling sister.

"Get the fuck off me, Ryan!" She pushes him away with enough force to break his hold.

Small, dry sobs leave her, and her rage-filled eyes lock with mine. "You fucking let her record you," she hisses, only loud enough for our little group to hear.

I'm on my feet, my mind reeling, so damn confused.

More than that, I feel pure panic. The kind I haven't felt since the day I found out she slept with Austin. That insidious fear that screams I'm losing her.

"What are you talking about, baby?" I ask her in as gentle of a tone as I can muster. She's a feral, injured animal right now. I have to proceed carefully.

The last thing I want is for her to bolt away from me.

For a brief second, the fury overcomes her and transforms her entire facial expression. She opens her mouth to yell at me. Seeming to force herself, she looks away and takes a deep breath before responding in a low, cold tone, "You know exactly what the fuck I'm talking about."

I do.

God fucking help me—no, God help *us*.

I can't even begin to fathom which time Jennifer recorded us. All I know is that there was more than once.

And she wasn't the only one.

I just didn't give a fuck back then, had been too focused on getting my nut off each time to care if any of those girls took a video or not.

I just remember being fucked up at some of those parties, doing my thing, and not caring about anything else. I'd been trapped in the mad rush to numb myself from the ache in my soul that kept demanding the one person I couldn't have.

The one person I keep hurting with the sins of my past.

I want to apologize for whatever she saw, but the words won't leave my mouth.

How many apologies have I thrown at her? How many of them did I mean? All of them. Were they able to undo any of the pain I dealt her? Not a single one.

That's the problem with those two little words. *I'm sorry*, no matter how much it's meant, doesn't do shit to erase the memories trapped in someone's mind. The phantom, sharp ache of the emotions.

All I can think, over and over, is that I've lost her again.

This is it.

The end.

I'll never break through her guard now.

I'll never manage to erase the monolithic mountain of shit she's gone through because of me.

This is our point of no return.

"Baby, please." Hand out, I beg to her. It's all I can do.

"I might have slept with Austin, but at least you'll never have to *see* it."

She's right.

I wouldn't handle it.

I'd want to kill him.

And, as much as I adore her, I'd want to kill her, too.

"Kira—"

She spins and rushes away from me without another word.

I start to follow but Ryan grabs my arm. "Bro, let me fucking go."

"People are watching, you dumbass."

Does he not understand how much I don't give a fuck?

"Don't make this worse for her. We'll help you get through to her."

"How?" I grumble.

"Me and Dana . . ." His eyes flash to his girl. She's standing near us, arms crossed, scowling at the ground. Ryan's facial expression melts with concern. "We went through something like this."

Dana's expression tightens even more.

Surprise shocks away my turmoil. I stare between the two of them, wondering . . . Then again, they were on again, off

173

again for years and the whole time, Ryan was partying his ass off right next to me.

"How did you forgive him?" I ask Dana.

Wrong question.

Her furious, light blue eyes focus on me. "I haven't. Not fully. But I, unlike Kira, did give him a good tit for tat all those years, and now we're both just focused on making it all up to each other."

Ryan squeezes my arm and lets go. "So for now, give her space. Go home. Call her in a few hours and see if she's up to talk to you. Focus on just being there for her. But for the love of God, don't make this worse for her."

Don't make this worse for her by letting the whole world know we're involved. That's what he means.

I'm always being forced to give Kira space even when it's the last thing I want to do.

But it's my fault, so I won't be a little bitch about it. I'll take this hit like I've taken all the others, because I'm man enough to know I fucked up here.

And Jennifer?

My blood pressure sky rockets at the thought of her.

She has no idea the line she just crossed. This was the last hit. As soon as I can, I'm doing what I have to do to ruin her life.

Kira

My phone keeps vibrating in my back pocket.

I keep ignoring it.

I feel bad for doing so. Of course I do.

It doesn't change anything. Whatever guilt I feel for what Brayden's going through isn't more powerful than the mindfuck I'm dealing with.

I spoke to him last night. It was brief. I couldn't stay on the phone, hear his voice. That need for healing distance is back and it's starting to seem like it's stronger than ever.

We haven't spoken since. It's almost one in the afternoon and I'm on my way to class. I shouldn't bother going since I know my brain won't function for shit, but skipping this early isn't an option.

I slept very little last night and every time I did catch some sleep, I had nightmares of that video.

Nightmares of that night, so many years ago, when I climbed that tree and saw Brayden fucking her on his bed.

Oh God. It never occurred to me before. That's the same bed he's fucked me in.

Maybe most girls wouldn't think about that, or care, but *I* do. I feel so sick that I can't deal with it.

I rush into the building and almost bump into a group of girls that are by the door. "Sorry," I say as I start to rush past them.

"Wait up. Aren't you Kira Roth?"

I turn to see who spoke and if I know anyone in the group.

Nope. If they went to my high school, I never saw them before. "Yeah…"

There's three of them and they share a nervous look with the one in the middle. She shrugs at them and steps forward with a weird look in her eye.

"I know we don't know each other, but I just have to ask. I mean, you don't know me, and have no right to trust me. I swear I won't tell though."

A cold shiver races through me.

"Chelsea, leave it alone," one of her friends hiss at her and tug her arm.

"It's just a question. Come on!" Chelsea shrugs her friend's hand off and steps closer to me. In a conspiratorial tone, she says, "What's it like getting to sleep with that sexy as hell stepbrother of yours?"

I swear my gasp bounces up and down the halls, so loud *everyone* hears.

"Oh, my God," Chelsea's other friend whimpers and comes up to me while pushing Chelsea back. "Ignore her. She believes every stupid rumor and—"

"You don't know for sure it's a rumor, and everyone saw them arguing last night!"

I'm going to throw up.

Last night, I knew I'd crossed a line when I punched Jennifer. That there would be retribution.

This is just the excuse the skank needed to come at me.

A hand lands on my shoulder and I jump up with another gasp.

It's Ashley, and her eyes are narrowed, snapping fire at the three girls in front of us. "Are you all fucking stupid?"

They take a step back collectively, clearly shocked.

"Jennifer is a dirty, slutty psychopath that got some of Brayden's dick *years* ago and is now jealous of any girl who spends time with him. You idiots seriously believe the garbage that leaves her mouth?"

"You see?" one of Chelsea's friends whisper to her. "I told you it was probably rumors."

"Yeah." Ashley sneers at them. "And even if it wasn't, next time mind your own damn business." She grabs me by the arm and begins leading me down the hall.

"I'm sorry!" one of the girls calls out to me.

"Fuck off," Ashley growls under her breath.

I'm shaking. The world around me is covered in a haze.

"Hold on," Ash tells me.

It's too late. I'm falling apart.

What is this going to do to Brayden? To my family?

Ashley reaches into my back pocket and pulls out my iPhone. "Unlock it."

All I hear is the blood rushing in my ears. I stare at her cluelessly, trying to make sense of what she asked me.

She pushes me into one of the bathrooms. After checking around to make sure it's empty, she returns to me and repeats her request. "Unlock your phone."

I swallow in an effort to wet my dry mouth. "Why?"

"Because I'm calling Brayden to come get you."

She hadn't even finished her sentence and I'm already shaking my head. "No." I take the phone from her hand.

Her eyes soften. "Kira . . . Are you thinking of pushing him away again?"

Yes.

No.

Honest to God, I don't know.

I want him more than ever.

I hate him all over again.

It's not his fault that Jennifer is obsessed with him—no wait. That is his fault. Had Jennifer been like the others, a one night stand only, maybe she wouldn't be this hooked.

But she was his first.

She was the only girl, until he got a girlfriend, who got him more than once throughout the years.

No wonder she feels special. Entitled.

It's illogical, but look at how crazy *I've* gone over him.

It's not his fault that she decided to show me the video.

It *is* his fault that he allowed her to record it in the first place.

What the fuck was he thinking letting a girl who wasn't his girlfriend record him?

I know what he was thinking. Brayden is into freaky sex. All he cared about was the exhibitionism of it. Coming in her mouth.

Tears spring to my eyes.

"Kira?"

"I am not missing this class." Subtext: I am not ruining my life for Brayden Hunt anymore.

I don't care what this costs me. Somehow, I'm going to get through this without having an emotional breakdown.

"Kira, I'm sure you can get excused."

I shake my head. "Thanks for standing up for me, Ash." I give her a small smile and start heading for the door.

She follows me and I feel her stare on my face the whole time. "Are you going to tell Brayden about this?"

I want to ask her to please not mention his name, but it's a bitchy comment and I decide it's best to keep it to myself.

"What are you going to do about all of this?"

178

I'm hurting and not thinking clearly. In the back of my mind, I know this. Even so, it doesn't stop me from saying the first thing that comes to mind. "What else?" I ask her as we turn a corner in the hallway. "There's nothing else I can do except not see Brayden anymore."

Ashley slams to a stop and inhales sharply.

I stop next to her but it isn't until I look up that I see her reason for stopping.

Brayden.

SIXTEEN

BRAYDEN

Kira's going to leave me.

Those are the only words bouncing around my head and shredding apart my heart.

I'm frozen in place, staring into her wide eyes. I know my expression's emotionless. I'm still as a statue. Can't speak. Can't move.

"Brayden," Kira whispers, her eyes darting all over the place. "Please. People are watching."

She's thinking of leaving me and all she can focus on is that people might catch onto what's between us?

"Brayden, Jennifer told people. Like, *really* told them. It's not a rumor this time."

Ashley's low whisper finally pierces through my apathy. I look at her then look at Kira.

Kira bites her lip and nods. There are tears shining in her eyes.

Murderous rage nearly obliterates my common sense.

Jennifer did what?

If I could kill that petty bitch and get away with it, I really would.

I'm still furious at Kira that she's thinking of walking away from me, but between what happened last night and this, her renewed panic makes sense.

"I'll walk you to class," I tell her, striving for calm.

"I'll go with you guys."

I smile gratefully at Ashley. Having her around makes it less suspicious in the eyes of everyone around.

Kira stares at the floor as she walks by.

I fall in step beside her, my mind torn between her and something I now want just as bad—Vengeance.

I waited too long to get that payback on Jennifer. Left Kira and myself open to this attack. Had I done what I had to do by now, she would have gotten the hint to back the fuck off.

Or at the very least, her life would have been seriously fucked up enough for her to lose focus on us.

I look down at Kira next to me, at her hunched shoulders, the defeated expression on her face.

We arrive at Kira's class. She pauses at the door, but doesn't look at me. There's something she wants to say to me, I can tell. I watch her, waiting.

Shaking her head, she opens the door and walks into the room, leaving me here, staring at her through the small window.

Aching.

Worried.

More enraged than ever.

That woman is out of her fucking mind if she thinks I'm letting her go.

I'll be back for her.

But first, I have a package to mail out.

Deciding to skip class, I nod at Ashley and head straight out the building. It's time to go home and set my plan to destroy Jennifer in motion once and for all.

After today, that bitch will never fuck with us again.

Kira

The next day

Stop distancing yourself from me. I know this is all so fucked up but we both know that living without each other isn't an option.

I'm sitting on the grass at the Oval, staring at my phone.

More like glaring at it.

If I could disintegrate it with my stare alone, it would have melted by now.

How the fuck do I even respond to that? Aside from the obvious—people watching us like hawks wherever we go—my emotions are all over the place.

Supposedly, Brayden spoke to Ryan last night. Asked him how he would deal with the world finding out about us.

My brother, the half saint, half devil that he is, simply told him that as long as I'm happy, he wouldn't kill Brayden.

He'll deal with the criticism of the world.

That's the issue though. Living without Brayden doesn't equal happiness. And what people have to say doesn't matter if my family is okay with it.

That being *my mom* as well. Not just Ryan.

But the main issue is that being with Brayden right now isn't making me happy, either.

Sometimes it feels like no matter what we do, a piece of his past will always rear its ugly head to fuck with us.

I want to go back in time, beat the shit out of his younger self, and chain him somewhere so that he'll stop being such a fucking whore.

The past is only the past *if it can be kept in the past.*

His won't stay where it belongs. It's always staining the present, and I can't help but wonder if it'll always stain the future as well.

Speaking of pasts, mine decides to appear out of nowhere and plop himself in the grass next to me.

I stare at Austin, surprised and speechless. It's been two weeks since we started school and I haven't seen him at all.

I have this odd feeling that he's been purposely staying out of my way.

But can I blame him?

I did to him what Brayden did to me—tore his heart out of his chest.

And because I can't control who my heart wants, there's nothing I can do or say to make this better for Austin.

He smiles at me, this sad little smile that makes his bright blue eyes shine and it tugs at my heart. "Hey you," he says, chucking me softly under the chin.

I'm so sensitive that his behavior is making me want to cry. "Hey," I whisper, throat tight. "How have you been?"

His smile somehow turns sadder. "Do you really want to know?"

Jesus, I can't be around him at this moment. The guilt of

what I've done to him is killing me and I'm too emotionally volatile to deal.

"Hey, no." He reaches up and catches my stray tear with the tip of his finger. "I know you didn't mean to hurt me on purpose. I'm not mad at you."

He never has been.

Dear God, he's a better person than I could ever hope to be.

"This isn't just about me, is it?" Austin leans back on the grass and stares off into space. "Jennifer is fucking with everything."

I don't say anything. What can I say?

"I warned her to stop hurting you."

My lips fall open. "You did what?"

"Yeah." He shrugs and looks back at me, his expression deadly serious. "I don't care if you're not mine. I made it very clear to her she needs to stop her shit."

"I—" I choke on a sob and have to take a few seconds to try and compose myself. "I don't deserve that from you. She's your friend." And his ex-lover.

"Not so much anymore. I don't like what I'm seeing in her. And like I said, no one hurts you." He pauses, jaw twitching. "How's he treating you, by the way?"

He wants the answer to that question to see if I'm all right with Brayden. To make sure I'm happy.

But at the same time, he doesn't want to know the answer because it's going to hurt him either way.

"Do you really want to know?" I ask.

He laughs a mirthless laugh. "Yeah. It's going to burn, but I kinda have to know."

"He's been real good to me. I can't lie. But…"

"Jennifer showed you that stupid video."

184

My eyes widen. "She told you that?"

"Kira, she told everyone. That's how she convinced everyone her rumor is true. Told the whole world she showed you that video and you attacked her in a jealous rage."

"I'm going to fucking kill her."

Austin's eyes shoot wide at my unholy growl. "Easy there, Satan. She has to be around for you to kill her. Her parents came and picked her up this morning."

"Why?"

"I don't know, but damn, she was sobbing in front of the Union and everyone standing outside. Her father was pissed like there's no tomorrow."

What could have happened?

Do I care? Hell no. But as petty as it sounds, I would like some confirmation that karma has finally found the bitch.

"She should've never showed you that video."

"Brayden shouldn't have let her record that video in the first place," I mumble angrily.

Austin grimaces. "You don't think about things like consequences at the time."

What the fuck?

Did he just defend Brayden?

Wait a minute . . . "Are you telling me you did something equally as stupid?"

Another sheepish grimace. He won't meet my stare.

"*With her*?" I almost shriek, not believing this shit.

"Shhh. Jesus, woman."

Their mutual desire to fuck Jennifer in kinky ways is ridiculously disturbing. Especially because both men are also attracted to me.

Are me and that hoe so similar?

"Stop," Austin chastises. "I can tell what you're thinking."

"And I have good reason for it, don't I?" I clench my jaw stubbornly.

"Kira, Brayden and I fucked Jenn, yeah. But we both fell in love with you. It's not the same."

Whatever he says. "So I guess even if I had picked you, and that bitch ended up jealous, or any of your ex-fucks for the matter, I was still going to suffer." It's a twisted thing to say but I can't help it.

Austin exhales slowly and grinds his teeth. "Maybe. But I would have never done to you the things he did."

I know he wouldn't have. Austin isn't as emotionally fucked up as Brayden. He grew up with parents who liked each other, unlike Brayden's who were constantly at each other's throats, and for good reason.

It's why my sympathy for him is so large. Not forgetting that he's been a good friend to me, as well.

Austin's head turns. I'm too busy looking at his profile, lost in thought, to turn my head and see what he's looking at.

"You're going to kill Jennifer and this bastard is going to end up killing me. The entire school is going to love it," Austin says wryly.

Oh God.

I instantly know who he's talking about.

Heart pounding, I turn and see Brayden storming across the grass toward us.

There's no denying it. That murder Austin talked about is shining clear in Brayden's eyes.

Grabbing my bag, I jump to my feet.

Austin slowly stands.

When Brayden stops next to us, he's breathing deep and

186

steady.

I know his tells. He's trying to control his temper.

"I was just seeing how she is. Relax."

Brayden narrows his eyes at Austin. "While staring at her like a starving man."

"Can't control that part. Now, calm the fuck down or I'll have to leave, and considering how things are right now, you don't want to be alone with her in public. Do you?"

Brayden growls low at him, like a coiled, dangerous animal about to attack.

"I have a few hours before my next class. I'm going back to my room to take a nap." I slip the strap of my bag over my shoulder and turn to leave.

"I'll walk you," two voices say at once.

Oh, no.

"Are you trying to *die*?" Brayden snaps.

I turn back around. "Brayden, relax."

"I'm not making any moves on your girl."

Brayden bares his teeth in a totally feral way. "Just by looking at her you're making moves on *my* girl."

Austin looks like he's praying for patience and it's obvious it's a matter of time before he snaps. "If you walk her back, it'll look suspicious. Don't be dumb."

"I'm walking by myself," I say firmly, my heart aching from how hard it's beating.

"Actually, I'm walking her. And you two better not kill each other while we're gone." Dana, seemingly appears out of thin air, and loops her arm with mine, tugging me away from both guys.

"They're going to kill each other." I look over my shoulder and see Brayden and Austin staring after us.

"Girl, they're more likely to do that with you still around."
Dana smiles ruefully at me. "Are you and Brayden still
having issues?"

"What do you think?" I sigh.

"You don't want to know what I think."

We cross the street. "No. I do."

"Kira, I'm a vindictive bitch that has put your brother
through hell. You don't want my advice. Trust me."

Now she has my full attention. "Considering my brother is
best friends with Brayden, and I know how they've spent a
good portion of their lives, I'm pretty sure he had it coming."
He's my brother, but it's true.

Dana laughs and it makes her eyes literally sparkle. She's a
gorgeous girl with that coloring. Aqua eyes and dirty blond
and brown hair. "You're my kind of girl."

I smile at her.

She sobers and looks at me with this sad look that reminds
me of the way Austin stared at me.

It's heartbreak. I know it very well.

"He tore me apart first. I came back with a vengeance. It
made his guard rise up. He became defensive and callous. I
got more vindictive. The only thing that made us keep
coming back to each other is this crazy, intense addiction that
neither of us can kill."

Holy shit, they sound almost like Brayden and I.

Which is kind of disturbing, I'll admit.

Come to think of it, they sound slightly worse. I didn't
become vindictive toward Brayden until later on. Dana
started hitting back from moment one.

"You guys seem so happy now."

"Most of the time," she says. "We also don't have that

188

major obstacle standing between us like you two do."

The hopelessness of it all is something I should be used to by now.

I'm not. I'm constantly stressed. Finding a way out of this situation is my number one priority.

But I don't know if that means being with Brayden or not.

Unbidden, the memory of that video hijacks my mind. "Did you ever see my brother fucking someone else?" Even more disturbing, but I have no one else to ask about this.

"Yeah."

My head flies around in her direction. "On video?"

She momentarily closes her eyes. "In person."

I'm so shocked I slam to a halt and end up pulling her back. "*What*?"

"Ugh. I shouldn't be telling you things like this about your brother."

I shake my head and try to control my shocked expression. "No. It's okay. I'm not judging him." I might be judging him just a little.

Okay. A lot. *What the fuck Ryan?*

Dana's actually blushing as she tugs me along. "I really shouldn't talk to you about this."

"Please. I literally don't know anyone else who's been in a similar situation as me, especially not one I can talk to about Brayden. I don't know what to do."

She sighs as if this is the last thing she wants to do. "Fine."

"So he did it on purpose?" Silently I'm praying he didn't. It'll change my entire opinion of him if he did. I can't help it.

"Well, he flirted with her in front of me. Went off somewhere with her while I was watching. But I walked in on them accidentally."

189

It wouldn't change her level of heartbreak. I know. "I saw Brayden fucking Jennifer when he was seventeen."

We share a look of female solidarity.

"And you didn't get revenge?" she asks me.

I shake my head. "Not for a long time."

"Girl, you're a better person than me."

"How did you get back at my brother?" We stop in front of my dorm building.

"Well . . ."

"Oh my God." Ryan's my brother. I shouldn't want to laugh.

But I kind of do.

"You totally fucked someone else in front of him."

She closes her eyes and there's no mistaking her shame. "His wasn't on purpose. Mine was. Sometimes I don't understand how he forgave me for that."

I want to hug her but I'm too shy to do so. "You forgave him too, you know?"

"Sometimes I still want to strangle him, although I have no right."

"It's too late for me to get any vengeance on Brayden for that video." I don't want to hurt him anymore.

"But you can't forget it, either."

I nod sadly. "Do you think I'll ever be able to move forward from this?"

"Do *you*?"

No. I don't think so.

And that breaks my heart more than ever.

It's not just the video. It's all the memories this one event has dredged up. I feel like I'm reliving all of it once more.

"Thanks for walking me and talking to me, Dana."

She gives me a small hug. "Any time girl. Feel free to call me."

I might just take her up on that. I have a feeling the next few days are going to get even harder for me.

SEVENTEEN
BRAYDEN

Why the fuck is Kira at this party?

Stupid question.

I have no right to begrudge her this. She should be here, having fun, experiencing college to the fullest.

It just burns that she came here without telling me. That she didn't even think of inviting me.

That she's pushing me away while making time to sit on the grass with Austin.

If Dana hadn't told Ryan to call me, I wouldn't have known Kira was here.

This party is taking place in one of the student's homes—a mansion so fucking big, it's bordering on ridiculous.

I'm never going to find Kira here, and according to what Dana told Ryan, Kira's shitfaced. Drunk out of her mind.

And Dana lost her. That was almost an hour ago.

Growling under my breath, I push past the crowd, ignoring

every drunk girl who tries to grope me.

Sometimes I wonder how I ever got high off this kind of attention. How my ego fed on it. It's annoying as fuck.

I've already checked the large ass kitchen. Two of the sitting rooms. The foyer. The pool room. And almost every room upstairs.

I get a text from Dana. *Marilyn just spotted her going into the movie theater on the first floor. OMW there now.*

Of course this place has a movie theater, too.

Fucking ridiculous, as I said.

I about-face and practically fly down the stairs. I have no idea where the hell the movie theater is, so I grab a few people as I walk and ask them.

All of them are as clueless as I am.

They look at me as if I'm crazy.

To them, I probably look like I am.

Finally, I find one person who knows. Don't know who he is, don't care. He points me in the right direction, and I rush away without even thanking him.

The theater is all the way in the back of the house, in an area that's actually empty. I get there in time to see Dana opening the door and rushing in.

Man, she's an awesome girl. I can never thank her enough for caring for Kira the way she obviously does.

I go inside and find the small theater empty, except for Dana, Marilyn . . .

And Kira.

My breath whooshes out of me at the sight of her. I'm instantly hard, aching, furious, and possessive.

We haven't fucked in days and I'd be lying if I said my balls aren't full to bursting. I need sex like a fiend and she's the only person to give it to me.

But she came here, in that tiny, dark purple dress.

I have no right to tell her how to dress. *What the fuck is she doing coming to a party dressed like that without me?*

Kira's leaning against one of the chairs all the way at the front of the theater, refusing to move despite Marilyn urging her.

It's obvious she really is drunk as a motherfucker.

"I just want to be alone, guys," she says, almost whining.

I refuse to be amused. Now's not the time. I'm too pissed at her.

But, fuck me. She's sexy, adorable, and those lips are begging for my cock.

"I know, sweetie. But it's not good for you to be alone right now."

Kira swats Marilyn away. "Stop your shit, girl. You're not my mother."

Even Dana laughs at that one.

"She's not. But I'm your man. And I say you're not going to be alone."

They all turn to stare at me as I walk down the short steps toward them.

Kira's eyes flare with resentment.

With lust.

She rakes me with a cold stare that still manages to burn my entire body with how hungry it is.

Damn. If any of these girls just happen to look down a bit, they're going to get an eyeful of how hard my dick is.

"I don't want you here, either." She swats me away like an imperious little queen.

"Girls. Leave us."

Marilyn and Dana hesitate at my tone.

I don't have time for this shit. *"Now."*

Dana snaps to action first and leads Marilyn up the stairs and out of the theater.

Kira's still looking at me with that rebellious hunger, a lust-filled sneer on her face.

I have no qualms about reaching down and palming my dick in front of her.

Her eyes flare with even more hunger.

"We're leaving, Kitty. Now." I can't fuck her until she sobers up considering how angry at me she is, but I'm getting her home.

Kira steps toward me and stumbles at bit.

I rush forward and catch her, pulling her up against me.

Contact. Searing, torturous contact. I have my arms wrapped around her, my hands on her ass, before I realize what I'm doing. As always, it's an instant reaction. Absolutely zero control over my own body.

Kira pushes at my chest and that sexy small growl she gives me turns me on so much. "Don't touch me."

My barely leashed temper snaps free. "Like hell. You're mine."

She struggles against me, her body sliding along mine. "Excuse me if I don't want to go back to fucking the dick I've seen inside Jennifer two too many times."

She's hurting. I get it. Shit, I'd be even more feral in her shoes.

But I'll be damned if I let her pretend she doesn't want me anymore.

Fisting her hair, I slide my other hand under her dress and roughly shove her panties to the side.

Kira lets out a broken gasp at the feel of my fingers slipping inside her.

I move them around on purpose so she can hear how wet she is. "Lie to me again. Tell me you don't want me," I growl in her face.

Her arms wind around my neck and she slams her lips against mine. Growling at me like she hates me and wants to eat me at the same time, she kisses me with everything she has.

Owning me.

Trying to control me.

I want nothing more than to show her who's fucking in charge here, but she's licking my tongue like it's the tip of my dick, and her hips are thrusting up and down, fucking my fingers.

Using me for her pleasure.

Her body locks up, her plump pussy swelling around my fingers. A throb, a rush of liquid, and she's drenching my hand, her sexy moans echoing between our lips.

God damn.

I manhandle her, my mind cracking under the pressure of so much need. Spinning, I fall to my knees on the short steps and place her beneath me.

The steps are short but they're huge. Enough to accommodate her lower body on one.

Kira leans back with her elbows on the step behind her. Head thrown back, gorgeous throat exposed, she struggles to pull in air.

I lean back on my haunches and yank my belt open.

The sound makes her raise her head. By the time her eyes are on my crotch, I already have my cock out in my hand.

She whispers my name like a prayer.

Finally.

This is what I need. No more distance. No more pain. Just her and her nearly demonic need to have me.

And I need this even more.

I grab her thighs and tug her toward me. Kira says my name again. Her hands land on my shoulders, fisting my shirt.

I spread her legs wide, wider than I probably should, and slide that juicy cunt right onto my dick.

Her body arches off the stairs like she's being possessed.

She is.

If I haven't left enough of me inside her for her to understand—for her to *accept*—that I own her and always will . . .

I'm going to remedy that.

And there's nothing she can do about it.

I pull my hips back, slow, hissing at the slick feel of her pussy walls tightening. Trying to keep me in.

Kira whimpers, clenching me even harder.

Wanting to let me go and powerless to do anything but keep me.

Using all my strength, I slam back into her.

One hard, vicious thrust.

She cries out and comes all over me.

Again.

Just like that.

I crack my neck, a growl purring through my chest, and lay into her. No mercy. No thought.

I'm close. Just a few more pumps into that slick cunt.

Kira fists my hair, her moans bouncing off the walls around

197

us. I lower myself down and brace my elbows on either side of her head.

She tries to tug me down and kiss me.

I slide one hand beneath her head, fisting that beautiful hair, and drag her up to me. "Who told you that you could come here dressed like that?"

She bites my lip hard enough to make my vision snap white. I think I taste blood. "Fuck you. You don't own m—" She chokes on her words with my next thrust.

I can't stop groaning, yet somehow I'm laughing in her face at the ridiculousness of her statement. "You want to keep fucking lying to yourself, Kitty?"

She hisses like the wild cat she is and leans up to lick across my bottom lip. When she pulls back, I see it.

Her lips are stained with the blood she drew from me.

I press my lips to hers, our tongues dueling. We're nothing but a mindless mass of sex, and I can feel the come rising up my shaft.

In the back of my head, it registers that I hear people speaking.

Drawing closer.

On the other side of the door.

"That bitch ruined my life!"

"First off, don't ever call her a bitch in front of me. Got it? Secondly, you have no proof it was her that sent your parents that video. Third, back the fuck off, or I'm going to forget we were ever—"

The door opens.

I raise my head enough to look up. For a split second, the fact that we've been caught freezes me.

Then I see two pairs of familiar blue eyes locked on us.

Jennifer.

Austin.

A sick insanity takes over. A raw need for both vengeance and possession that drives me to do one of the stupidest things I could ever do.

Rearing up over Kira, I wrap my hand around her neck, pumping my cock quick and deep into her.

She looks up and sees them standing there. I glance down at her long enough to make sure she's not looking at *him*.

No. Her eyes are on Jennifer. There's fear in them.

Gloating.

Vindictiveness.

I look back at Jennifer and see that she's staring at *me* with tears in her eyes.

Smirking coldly at her, I lean down and kiss my girl with everything I have.

And Kira comes. Loud. Violent. Un-fucking-deniable. There's no way our little audience won't know what just happened.

I laugh into our kiss, my balls so tight they've almost crawled into my body. They haven't left.

Probably too shocked to do so.

This is evil of me to admit, but I hope they're both too pained to react.

I nip Kira's chin and fuck her like there aren't people watching us. "My little sex kitten wants to be filled up with my come?"

She can't even nod, she's so far gone. Tears streak down the sides of her face. Her nails are clawing at any part of me she can find.

I'm about to come. There's no way I'll be able to hold

back.

Locking eyes with Jennifer, I let it roll over me, and make one thing very clear. "I love you, Kira. I fucking love you."

Jennifer's eyes snap with hatred and she reaches for her phone right as I start to come.

The orgasm is so powerful I get trapped in each wave, even as my mind screams that this bitch is about to record us.

Austin snatches the phone out of her hand and lifts her up, kicking and screaming in rage, out of the room.

I can hear Jennifer trying to scream something and then all of a sudden her voice is muffled, as if someone put their hand over her mouth. What sounds like a struggle takes place outside for a few seconds.

Then silence.

I fall on Kira.

She sobs, pushing me off her.

For a moment I think she wants me away from her.

She rolls over, choking for air and I realize I was pressing her into the step completely. I'd cut off her air.

"Baby." I reach for her.

She slaps my arm, a dangerous sound leaving her right before she starts crying. "You just had to come for me, didn't you?" Another slap to my arm.

There's no heat in her words. No power to her hits. She's frustrated with me, but she isn't angry.

She drags herself to a sitting position and wipes at her cheeks. "We have to get everybody prepared for the backlash. That bitch is going to let the whole world know."

Fuck. Fuck. *Fuck*. She's right. God, I'm so stupid. "And Austin was with her."

Kira shakes her head. "Austin won't tell."

Her quick defense of him pisses me off. "He wants you. He's jealous—"

Her phone starts ringing.

Kira looks around for it and spots it on the floor by the first row of seats. Scrambling toward it, she picks it up in her hand. She hesitates before answering, her eyes cutting in my direction.

"Who is it?" I ask, moving closer.

She jumps to her feet and moves away from me, stumbling a bit. Her torn panties are hanging limply around one thigh.

When the fuck did I rip those off her?

I was so crazed I can't even remember.

"Hey," she says into the phone, turning her back on me. "I know it was stupid, it just happened . . . I-I'm sorry you had to see that."

Austin.

I can't take this shit. I don't care if I'm being irrational when it comes to him, but I can't take another second of his presence in her life anymore.

I start walking down the steps toward her.

"What? Why would you do that for us?" She sees me coming and presses her hand to my chest to hold me back. She gives me an ugly, evil glare that tells me what'll happen if I reach for her phone.

Biting down on the inside of my cheek, I struggle to control myself.

Her eyes widen and she starts shaking. "He tried to get Jennifer out of here. She got away from him at the end of the driveway. She's running back here to tell everyone we're in here."

All right, Austin can wait. We need to go. *Now.*

201

I slide Kira's ruined thong down her leg. She lifts it and lets me slip it off her. After tucking it in my pocket, I grab her hand and start rushing up the stairs.

I pause at the door long enough to make sure the hallway outside is empty. It isn't until we're out of the theaters that I realize I have no clue which way to go.

We can't leave out the front and be seen together.

We can still be spotted trying to find another way out.

Fuck. We're going to have to separate.

It's the last thing I want to do.

"Come." Kira tugs on my hand. "Austin said the way out through the side entrance is empty."

She's still on the phone with him?

I look at her, and yeah. She is.

Deciding not to argue, I let her lead while Austin gives her directions through the phone. It takes no time for us to find the exit at the side of the house. It leads out to the side garden.

I'm still surprised no one's out here.

We jog quietly through the side garden, heading across it to the stretch of woods flanking this side of the grounds.

Hidden by the trees, is a small path that seems to lead back to the front of the house.

Austin must confirm that this is the way because Kira pulls me to it.

"Okay. We'll meet you there." She *finally* hangs up.

"What do you mean *we'll* meet him?" And where?

"Brayden don't start. He's *helping* us. And you parked your car near the front of the house. How did you even find parking there? It's packed."

"Someone pulled out as I drove up the driveway."

"Well, there's a ton of people there and Jennifer went that way. She's probably standing there right now and telling anyone within hearing distance about us."

"She wouldn't dare." She better not. Have I not done enough to prove to her how far I'll go to destroy her?

Something I heard Austin say comes back to me.

She thinks Kira's responsible for that video.

Fuck.

"What do you mean she wouldn't dare? Of course she would!"

I say nothing. I can't. Kira doesn't know about my plan and I want her to stay as far away from it as possible.

She stops and turns to me, her eyes questioning. "Brayden, answer me. Do you know something I don't?"

I can't stand to outright lie to her, so I choose omission instead. Taking the lead, I silently pull her behind me until we exit all the way at the end of the driveway.

The entire time I ignore that little voice that whispers omission is a form of lying.

"Brayden?"

I ignore her again, my eyes on the car waiting for us a few feet down. We approach it and Austin exits.

There's no mistaking the tortured look in his eyes, but he doesn't say anything. I'm surprised he decides to keep his eyes on me instead of staring at Kira.

"You're not going to like this—"

I interrupt him. "Then don't say it."

He shakes his head at me and continues anyway. "I can drive her to a meet up point while you get your car."

"Oh, hell no."

Kira steps next to me and glares up at me. "Brayden."

I scowl at her chiding tone. "Would you like it if I went on a car ride alone with one of the girls I've slept with in the past?"

The annoyance leaks out of her eyes and in its place is understanding. "You're right."

Austin scoffs and throws his keys at me. "Both of you take my car. That way no one sees you leave together in yours. Give me your keys."

I'm so shocked I don't move to comply.

Kira reaches into my pocket and takes them out to give them to him.

He takes off to head back to the driveway without another word.

Holy shit. Kira was right. He really is helping us.

She rolls her eyes at me, as if to silently say *I told you*, and we head to Austin's car. Once inside, I wait until she has her seat belt in place before hitting the gas.

"I guess you're not that drunk anymore," I say playfully.

Kira gives me the finger.

I laugh at how cute she is.

She gasps out of nowhere and covers her face with her hands. I hear her groaning.

"What?"

"It's starting to leak out," she mumbles behind her hands.

My brow scrunches . . . *Oh*.

A little glow of pleasure sparks in me at the thought that she's leaking *my* come out of her pussy and all over Austin's seats.

She lowers her hands and sees the smile on my face. "Oh my God!" Slapping my arm, she squirms uncomfortably and whimpers miserably.

204

"Fine. Fine." I pull over to the side of the road and take my seat belt off. Reaching behind my head, I pull my T-shirt off and hand it to her.

She takes it from me gingerly. "You sure?"

"It's all we've got."

She lifts herself up, wipes the seat, then folds my shirt neatly and sits on it.

I can't help but chuckle.

Kira glares at me again. "Shut it."

It hits me that I'm driving Austin's car. This is a new one but years ago us driving each other's cars wouldn't have been so out of place.

"We didn't agree with Austin where we're going to meet up," Kira says and starts dialing on her phone.

"I'll call him."

"Brayden . . ."

"Kira, please. Understand."

"Fine. You're right. But he's being nice to us. So please try and be nice to him."

"I'll do my best," I mumble, clipping my phone on the dashboard and dialing his number.

He answers on the second ring. "Wouldn't let her call me, huh?"

"Be honest. Would you let her call you if you were me?"

"Absolutely not."

There's amusement in his tone and for a split second I'm pulled back into the past. Back when we were friends. Not as close as Ryan and me, but I'd still counted him as one of my best friends.

I grind my teeth at the memory. "Why'd you have to go and fall in love with her, you asshole?"

"Like I fucking did it on purpose. If anyone should understand that I couldn't fight it, it's you."

"Hello? I'm right here," Kira says sarcastically.

I'm too focused on Austin's comment to reply to her. I get it. Trust me, I do. "It's not what you feel for her, so much as the fact that you keep trying to take her from me."

"Wouldn't you?" he asks.

I'm taken back to another memory—me in that bathroom, my world ripped apart. Ryan behind me, watching me lose my shit.

That final decision I made that no one would have her but me. Fuck the consequences, fuck the price.

"While I do like the idea of you two getting close again, this isn't a conversation I want to be witness to. Austin, where should we meet you?" she asks.

He tells us to just pull over and wait for him by the side of the road right before the highway.

We get there and I turn off the car. Kira checks that the seat is clean one more time.

Austin pulls up behind me in my car seconds later.

We exit his car and he exits mine. Immediately, his eyes are drawn to my bare chest, locked onto the scripted black *K* over my heart, the auburn haired mermaid wrapped around the sailor on my side. His eyes land on the hazel-eyed kitten on my inner wrist and a breath hisses out from his clenched teeth. "Shit. No wonder you won."

My chest puffs up with pride. "There's more of them."

He stares at me like I'm crazy. "For a girl you weren't sure would ever be yours?"

"Who said I wasn't sure?" I wasn't, there were moments of extreme doubt, but he doesn't need to know that.

He then sees the shirt in Kira's hand.

The look on his face is part devastated, part disgusted. "Don't tell me you guys started getting freaky in my car."

"Does it look like we had time for that?" I ask him.

Kira's blushing bright red.

Austin stares at me unbelievingly. "So then why is your shirt off?"

I can't help but smirk at that. "Do you really want to kn—"

Kira shoves me. "Leave him alone. Austin, thank you so freaking much. It's more than we deserve."

Is she serious? "Excuse me?"

She raises her hand in front of my face.

Austin inhales deep then exhales slowly. "This isn't fucking easy, but . . ." He hesitates and looks down at the ground. "So yeah." His eyes snap up to me and I see the resentment in them loud and clear. "You ever hurt her again, I don't give a fuck if I go to jail."

My hackles rise like a motherfucker at that.

"Austin," Kira says softly. "Don't."

"I'm serious, Brayden. Don't ever do anything stupid to hurt this girl again."

He means well. *He means well.* I keep repeating it to myself like the adult I am. "I fucking love her. Yeah I fucked up in the past but trust me, those days are long gone."

He nods, as if making his mind up about something. "Jennifer is out for blood. Someone sent her parents a video of her getting her freak on with a girl and they *flipped.* Credit cards canceled. Car taken away. She's threatened with no tuition for school either. And she thinks it was Kira."

I can feel Kira's questioning stare but I focus on Austin's instead and remain quiet.

"You two need to start being more careful if you don't want this whole thing getting out. And . . ." Whatever the hell he has to say, it's *burning* him to say it. I can tell. "Ah fuck it. If you two need my help for anything, let me know."

And he's gone, yanking his keys out of my hand, flinging me my own, and rushing back to his car like his ass is on fire.

Holy shit.

Did Austin just offer to help us hide our secret?

Fuck me sideways, I think he did.

EIGHTEEN

Kira

September 24, 2015

Brayden's lips run up my neck, igniting every nerve and sending shiver inducing pleasure through me. It's not an unfamiliar feeling. Even after months of fooling around with him, it's still there, turning me on a little faster each time.

"I haven't even been here five minutes and you're trying to get in my pants."

He chuckles against my skin, a feeling that turns me on even more. I'll combust one day if he doesn't slow down.

"That's what happens on Wednesday's when our schedules clash and I don't see you for over twenty-four hours." He paws at my shirt, pushing it up as his suckable lips press against mine.

"Horny motherfucker," I say against his mouth as I grab hold of his cock that's so hard, it's filling his jeans.

I haven't seen him since lunch yesterday, and touching wasn't possible. A project from one of my classes kept me late in the library and I crashed in my dorm.

If I had to admit it, the truth is I hate not being able to touch him, but I love his primal need that comes out after. It's a beast that overtakes us both.

He chuckles and dips down, grabbing my legs and wrapping them around his waist as he presses me against the wall. "I could have gotten off by myself, but I know how much you like to watch."

The dampness of my panties grows as he grinds into me and I let out a small moan. "Fuck, yes."

I do. Dirty, perverted, watching his body tense, face screwed up, mouth open as his cock fires off. A cock I'm dying to have pounding the shit out of me, right now.

"Through every class I kept thinking of every motherfucker looking at you, wanting you. I didn't even notice this girl come on to me."

I love his jealousy, but my mood is soured by the mention of some chick on his dick. "Yeah?"

He pulls back, eyes meeting mine, noticing the change. "I told her 'Sorry, my girlfriend owns all of me.'"

I blink at him and push back against his chest. "Girlfriend?"

His brow scrunches, lip twitching like I'm playing with him. "Yeah. You."

Two things happen simultaneously when he says that—an explosion of happiness that he called me his girlfriend and the overwhelming need to get away from him.

I wiggle out of his arms, getting my feet back on the floor and step away from him. The vibe in the room is off. I push my hair back from my face before turning to him. There's a confused look on his face as he watches me.

"I'm not your girlfriend," I say.

I can't be.

We aren't in a defined relationship. I never agreed to it.

We simply *can't* be.

The change in his demeanor is noticeable. All the playfulness leaves him, and the testosterone powerhouse takes over, bracing himself for a fight. It's a reaction I've watched many times over the years.

"The last month . . ." He clenches his jaw and looks down before back up to me. "What is this to you?"

My mind is blank. This is unexpected. His reaction . . . but it is what I've let it be. "Sex."

"And that's it?" His hands begin to shake, while my own fidget in front of me.

I hadn't thought about it, about what we are. We just . . . are. We wanted and took it.

He calls me his, and I know deep down that I am, but we can't label this. Not with the way things are.

I'm still hurting from seeing that video, for fuck's sake! It's only been a week in a half.

"Friends." My voice is barely above a whisper.

It's the only answer I can come up with. I love him, more than anyone, but there's too much stacked against us. Not to mention I still can't stop thinking about the video of Jenn sucking his cock, reminding me of all the shit he used to do, the girls he used to fuck. The wound is still too fresh there.

A loud, demented laugh springs from him and he threads his fingers through his hair. "I love you, have done everything for you, and it's still not enough for you to give me a chance?"

A burning pain knots in my chest. "Brayden . . ."

"What else do I have to do?" His voice rises and I jump in surprise. "Who do I have to . . ." He trails off, his head shaking.

Agony claws at my insides like something is ripping at me. Why do I feel like this? After all he's done. "Brayden . . ."

I know why. Hurting him is unbearable to me. I'm being honest with him about where I stand because he deserves it, but doing this to him is *killing* me.

Before I can say another word, he's out the bedroom door, storming away. I stare for a second, then go after him. A loud crash echoes off the kitchen walls and into the living room. There's glass all over the floor and Brayden is leaning over the sink, gripping the edge so hard his knuckles are white.

"You're mad at me," I say.

There's silence, all but the harsh breaths coming from him. "No." His voice is low and deep, and he refuses to look at me. "I'm mad at myself."

It's not the response I'm expecting. "Why?"

He stands straight, but continues to look at the wall, every muscle stiff, coiled like he's waiting for something. "You should go."

It's my turn to stare in surprise. My whole body has turned cold as fear creeps in. "Wait, why?"

When he turns around, his jaw is so tight I worry he's going to crack his teeth. His green eyes are dark, but almost glowing in the low light. "Because I can't fucking break down with you here."

Break down? I can't take my eyes off him, the words not computing. The knot in my chest grows tighter, almost unbearable. The pain coming off him is almost crippling.

His lip twitches. "Get the fuck out of here!"

I recoil like I've been hit, then turn and run to the door, picking up my bag as I dash out. The stairs go by too fast as I run down them and out to the sidewalk. I don't stop, and before I realize it, I'm a few buildings down, in front of Ryan's door, banging on it, because I have absolutely no clue what to do.

A minute goes by before I hear the lock click and the door swings open.

"Hey, baby sis!" Ryan smiles, but it quickly fades as he looks me over. "Kira, are you okay?"

"I don't know," I say honestly, because I have no idea.

My whole body is shaking, reeling from what just happened. Ryan pulls me in and I take a few steps before flopping down on his couch, my bag forgotten somewhere on the ground.

"What's going on?" Dana says as she comes into the room, her eyes wide as she looks at me.

By her hastened dressing and messed up hair, I can tell I've interrupted them having sex, which is what I should be doing right now. Letting Brayden make me feel the way only he can.

"I'm not his girlfriend."

I'm not.

I can't be that to him. *We* can't be anything more, it just isn't in the cards for us.

Ryan freezes for a moment, then falls to the ground in front of me. "What happened with Brayden?"

My head rises and I look at him, my vision warped by something. What? I don't know. Shit. Maybe tears? "I'm not his girlfriend. I love him . . . but I can't do it."

Dana and Ryan are the only people I've admitted that out loud to.

I feel it then. Hot tears start to slide down my cheeks and I drop down to the floor and into my brother's arms.

"Kira, I don't understand."

I pull back to stare into my matching eyes. "He called me his girlfriend, but I'm not."

"What are you then?"

My head shakes, almost without direction from me, shoulders shrugging. "Friends with benefits?"

Dana sits next to us on the floor and takes my hand in hers. "Hun, I don't think that's true."

"What other definition is there?"

"I know there's been a lot of crap lately, but I also don't think you see that everything you two do is what couples do. You may not have had a formal asking to be his girlfriend or the ability to go out on dates or show affection in public, but your actions show that you are."

"Since the fight with Austin, you've acted differently," Ryan says. "You two have been so close, to the point that you live with him well over half of the time."

"I just . . . want to be near him."

Ryan's fingers tap my chin, making me look up at him. "Kira, baby sister, I'd do anything for you, which includes telling you hard truths—you are in a romantic relationship with Brayden. Maybe you can't go out like a normal couple, but he is your boyfriend."

"You've always been on his side." I shake my head and push against his chest.

Men who fuck up seem to try everything under the sun to justify shit. It doesn't matter that we weren't together, I just can't freaking stand that bitch having done things with him, but also have it on video.

Twice I've seen it, and that makes two times I can't scrub from my memory.

"Don't pull that shit because you're upset. I told you before, I'm on your side, but if you're not serious for him, I've got to ask . . . how long are you going to keep stringing him along?"

"Excuse me?"

"He's right," Dana says.

I turn to look at her. "You too, Dana?"

"Sweetie, if you really don't want to be with him more than just as a fuck toy, you need to tell him. I'm not saying things are going to be rainbows and sunshine, because we both know it's not going to be easy, but being with someone is a lot of work and also means moving on from their past. You may not forget, but you can accept that it is a part of his history."

As much as I idolize my brother, as much as he's taken care of me and Mom all these years. I also know the past she's talking about. It's not much different from Brayden, but the two of them have one monumental difference that doesn't stand in their way.

"I *can't* be with him. All that other shit aside, which is a whole other issue, society says I *can't*." But if that wasn't there, if he wasn't my stepbrother, could I handle being his girlfriend knowing everything that I do?

"Whether you think that or not, you have been with him for the last month." Dana brushes some of my tears away. "To Brayden you are the sun. If he's your sun, then you have a lot to think about."

I scrunch my brow at her. "What does that mean?"

"It means it's time to do what we did. It's time to make up your mind. How much longer is he logically going to be able to stand you pushing him away before he gives in and lets you? There's no going back when that happens, Kira. When he's gone, that's it. You'll officially have broken him, and you'll have proved him right that the only thing that comes from love is pain."

He's pursued me with such determination that the idea of him not doing so had never crossed my mind.

I don't want him to go. I want to be with him. But how do we even do that? He comes with so much baggage.

"He broke me." My voice is barely over a whisper, but I know the strain in it is telling of the pain.

"And he's the only one who can fix you."

I hate that Ryan says that again, because just as Dana described, they were on the same level as fucked up as we are. Like Dana's payback, I got back at Brayden by sleeping with Austin. But unlike Dana, I hurt an innocent guy. An innocent guy who is in love with me, but I just couldn't feel that in return.

Because I can't seem to care about any guy other than Brayden. He's the one that makes my heart pound like it's trying to beat its way out of my chest. The one that sets me on fire.

He's also the one I want to literally set on fire sometimes, he makes me so angry.

"Can you give me a ride back to the dorm?"

Ryan's lips form a thin line as he nods. "Whenever you're ready."

He stands, heading to their bedroom, leaving me on the floor with Dana. Her lips are still in a thin line as well, brow scrunched.

"I have to ask . . . what do you think is keeping you from accepting him? Is it just because of the stigma?" she asks after a moment.

It takes me a minute to nod. Then there's the other part, the thing that brought my guard back up. "I refuse to be some gossip fodder. Seventy percent of our school goes here, and that's a lot of mouths running. Mouths that can ruin and hurt my family, and that includes you. Then there's Jenn. Fucking bitch showed me that video to hurt me, to hurt him, and she succeeded."

"First, don't worry about your relationship and what some assfuck *might* say to me, because I'll kick their ass. Second . . . Kira, that was years old. Like, probably before your parents got married. Things were different back then. *He* was different."

Logically, I can accept that, but emotionally? It's another thing that reminds me of all the girls he's slept with or fooled around with. Girls that he says were just a way to get off.

Doesn't that make me the same?

"I know, and maybe if it'd been another girl it might not be so bad, but it's *her*."

Having the actual act shoved in my face brought it all to life as well as inflaming pain and doubts I've been fighting for months.

217

An hour later, Ryan drops me off outside the dorms and I stumble into my room, dropping my bag down on the floor.

"Hey, girl. I wasn't expecting y—" Jenna's eyes widen as she looks at me. "Kira?"

"Is Brayden my boyfriend?"

Her brow scrunches before she rushes to the door that connects to our study room. "Well . . . yeah." Fuck. Even my best friend thinks it. "I mean, isn't he? Does he not think he is? Do we need shovels and plastic?"

I fall down onto my bed. "Apparently only if you're going to bury me, because I'm the one who doesn't think he is."

"Seriously? I mean, I assumed, you know."

"Why?" I need to know what everyone else seems to know. What about us gave off the impression we're an item?

Her eyes are wide, hands spread out in front of her, like what I'm asking her is obvious. "Because you spend half the week at his place. Because he's all you talk about. Because you love him. Because even after all that shit with the slut, you still spend almost every free minute with him. Do I need to continue? I can, if you need more examples of your utter life dependency on the guy."

Life dependency? That couldn't be.

Life without Brayden?

It only takes a second for a searing pain to flood my chest. No, it's not possible. She's right, her words are an accurate description of us. But how did I not notice the change?

Maybe that's it. Giving in to my feelings, when I stopped resisting, we flowed seamlessly into something I hadn't agreed to. Even with the explosion of shit two weeks ago, I couldn't stay away from him. As mad as I was and still am, it didn't take long to fall back into him.

It's like I'm some sick addict.

I let my head fall into my hands. "God, Jenna, I've never seen him like that before. He looked completely destroyed."

She moves to sit next to me. "What happened?"

I fill her in, taking note of her look of utter concentration. It's like I'm under inspection, or that my actions are, but I know that's just Jenna making sure she gets every detail.

When I'm done, her lips are set in a thin line, a look I'm getting a lot tonight. "Don't take me wrong when I say this, but I'm your best friend and roommate, and we haven't hung out since the second day of school. You are completely on cloud Brayden lately, and I've been so happy for you because for the first time in our friendship, you seem truly happy. Am I wrong?"

No, she isn't, but that doesn't mean our situation is even feasible.

I've had a taste of Brayden, a small piece of a relationship with him, but can I handle fully trusting him with my heart? Past that, is there any way to truly be together?

NINETEEN
Kira

September 25, 2015

The night was filled with nothing but bad dreams and a lot of tossing and turning. My gaze is locked on the ceiling, unable to attempt sleeping anymore. The knot in my chest won't let me now that the sun is coming through the windows.

Nothing in particular is on the ceiling, a bland patch of white, but still, I'm just staring. My first class isn't until ten, leaving me two hours to get my ass moving, but I can't find the energy to even think about going.

It's not the first time I've contemplated skipping, but every other time I was being persuaded by the ultimate of bad influences—sex with Brayden.

There's no messages waiting for me when I wake. No missed calls. It leaves me staring at the phone, finger hovering over the call button. I want to call him, but have no idea what to say.

What do I have to tell him? Last night's epiphany took us both by surprise and I don't know where that leaves us.

Is there an *us*?

It seems like it's always one step forward, ten steps back. Every week tumbling back to insecurities and hurts that were starting to heal. Mostly it's me, trying to cope with his past and sometimes failing.

The vile poison that Jenn spreads is tangled all around us. Her video was a power play, her rumors meant to set me off. We might be able to handle hiding, or at least handle it a lot better, if that bitch wasn't running her mouth. Always trying to find an angle to hurt me to get Brayden.

After an hour of nothing, I drag my ass out of bed, doing the minimal to get ready. Wash my face, brush teeth, throw my hair into a ponytail, put on clothes that hopefully aren't dirty. Pick up my backpack, and head out the door.

My first class I share with Marilyn and she always waits for me on the bench outside her dorm hall, which is the twin of mine, and just across a walkway.

"How's the morning treating you?" she asks as I approach.

I let out a groan. "I just want to be snuggled in bed."

Standing, she grabs onto my arm. "What happened?"

"Brayden called me his girlfriend."

"Yeah, well, aren't you?" she asks as we head down the walkway to our W131 class.

"Huh?" Again, it seems everyone who knows about us thought I was his girlfriend but me.

"I'm confused why this is a surprise, girl."

"What do you mean?"

She cocks an eyebrow at me. "Well, first off, you spend almost every free minute with him. Oh, and you're fucking

221

like bunnies." She stares at me, waiting for some response, but I have none. "You spend most nights at his place, according to Jenna. And this thing between you two was happening long before we moved to Columbus."

"I'm stupid for ever even entertaining the fantasy that this was just sex. We had a huge blowout yesterday because I wouldn't admit I'm his girl."

Marilyn stares at me, her eyes wide. "Have you heard from him after it?"

I shake my head. "No, and that just . . . worries me."

"Worries you, how?"

"I don't know how to describe it. There's just this lump in the pit of my stomach."

"Fear that he doesn't want you?"

I shrug. "I'm such a confused mess that I don't know what I want." I'm to the point I don't know what to say, what to do. I'm almost afraid to see him.

I hate this. All of it. I just want to go somewhere that nobody knows us. Somewhere that we can have a fresh start. No reminders of the past. Just him and me.

But that's fantasy, a dream, and not the reality we live in.

The radio silence continues all day, leaving me staring at my reflection in the dark window. I can't bring myself to break the silence because my insides are in turmoil, my heart and mind battling it out.

His Thursday is just about as booked as mine, but they're early out days.

What is he doing?

Normally, or as normal as the third week of college can get, we'd be studying and doing homework. Something so simple as hanging out. There's sex as well, along with the acquiring of food, but also cuddling and watching TV before falling asleep in his arms.

Something so innocuous that seems to imply so much.

Maybe that's another reason I had a hard time sleeping last night. I wasn't wrapped up in Brayden. Being in his arms is like being home. It's like I'm cocooned in comfort and love. Last night was cold and I can't help wonder if it's the same for him.

Doubt creeps in and I wonder if he's with another girl. Some other chick sucking on his dick, touching what should have always been mine.

It should have. *He* should have. From the beginning, or at least from the first time he kissed me. Maybe I could forget all the girls before then, because I was in Junior High for most of it while he was in High School.

Instead our parents got married and I caught him fucking Jenn. Everything went downhill from there. The implosion of my dreams and the harsh reality of what a whore he was. The pain of that day crippled me, changed me, but even that couldn't crush the feelings I had for him.

He did that. All in an attempt for us both to move on. It didn't work and made us both even more miserable. Lashing out at the injustice of our situation and all the bad choices he made.

Even now, I'm not sure I really trust him. Sometimes I find him on his computer which he suddenly closes, like he's hiding something from me.

"Jesus, Kira, just make up your freaking mind," I say to myself, but it's no help.

The war inside me . . . how do I call peace? What is the right answer?

Do I break both of our hearts, or do I put mine back on the line?

The next morning the struggle to get moving is as rough as the day before. My phone has no messages or missed calls again. My vision blurs and I wipe away a threatening tear before it multiplies.

When I head out to my one and only Friday class, which is a 9:00 a.m. lecture, there's a familiar car sitting at the base of the steps. My heart hammers in my chest as I approach, the profile of his head hanging making the tightness around my ribs worse.

At the same time, there's a lightness in my chest and it keeps growing brighter.

Is this what Dana was talking about?

"Hi," I say as I slide in.

There are dark circles under his eyes and no energy coming off him. It's a jarring version of him. I expected his usual persistence, but it's gone.

A completely defeated man.

He gives me a tight smile, then peels away from the curb and onto the street. Music plays softly in the background, but it's not enough to cover the awkward silence. It's only about a mile before he's pulling into a parking spot and reaching down between my legs to grab my bag. He swings it over his shoulder as he stands and shuts the car door.

It's an action of a boyfriend, not a brother. He's making a statement, which is dangerous with how things have been lately.

There's still about half a mile walk to my class, across the Oval and past another building, and I begin to wonder if the silence is going to accompany us as we walk.

Looking around, the Oval is empty with the exception of the random jogger. Early morning Friday classes are rare, and I happened to hit the lottery on that one. Yay.

"I love you, so I'll wait," he says when we're over halfway across the green expanse. The knot in my chest loosens some, and I can breathe a bit easier. "I fucked up, a lot, and this is my penance. I'm not a patient motherfucker, and I want you to be mine now. I just need to know you can even stand to be with me."

He turns to look at me and there's so much pain etched into his features. The feeling to nurture him scratches at me, and I desperately want to, but I can't given where we are.

My hand flinches at the feel of his fingers, but then quickly relaxes, letting him slide his fingers between mine. I glance around, fear filling me. There's just a couple of students, people I don't recognize, milling around, and we're almost out of the broad opening.

Jesus Christ, this is too dangerous.

But I can't bring myself to let his hand go.

It's a foreign feeling—his hand in mine in public—but not a bad one. Very good. Very *right*.

"Let me love you, Kira. Let me show you that you're my everything. You're all I've ever wanted. Please don't let my past influence our future."

In other words: don't let my whoring ways and that bitch come between us.

Tears sting in my eyes. "What do we do?"

"I'll do whatever you want. If you want to transfer, go where nobody knows us, I'll get it done." He looks down to our hands, his thumb caressing mine. "I can't live without you anymore. I'll back off if you need, but please . . . don't leave me." His voice breaks on the last words and I can't hold the tears back.

He's so afraid that we're breaking up and here I am so afraid I didn't know I was with him.

I focus on the feeling of our hands together. This was how it was always supposed to be, I get it. I'm scared, but I can't let that stop me anymore.

I take a deep breath, and then jump.

"Brayden Hunt, if you break my heart again I *will* fucking kill you with my own bare hands."

Tension falls from his body and he slumps against me. His hand cups my cheek, forehead resting on mine. It's too dangerous of a position, but one I need as much as he does.

Nobody is around. Just need his touch, for a few seconds.

"You own all of me."

Everything becomes clear, and as much as part of me rebels, all of me knows it's the truth and a truth I want. "I better. I'm your girlfriend, after all."

He smiles and there's a sparkle back in his eyes. "And my girlfriend deserves the best."

"Well, yeah, I have to put up with your idiotic ass," I say as I tug on his hand to get him moving again. "I better be getting something out of the deal."

A small chuckle leaves him. "Kitty, I'll give you whatever you want."

"I'll hold you to that."

We start walking again, our fingers still tangled together.

"When I pick you up, do you want to get . . ." He trails off, his hand tearing away from mine. Shock runs through me, but when I look up, I understand as the familiar vision of his friend Craig stands not twenty feet from us.

"Hey, Craig," Brayden says, stepping toward him.

Craig takes a few cautious steps in our direction. "Brayden." His eyes flash over to me, his jaw ticking as he looks back to Brayden. "What's up?"

Craig stares at Brayden, waiting for something. The fear that he knows creeps in, but not as much as the realization that Craig is Austin's best friend.

That Craig probably already knows.

Austin could have confided in him what happened, what sparked the fighting between them.

The answer is always me. Only not in the way most people reason, and the look in Craig's eyes tells me he's not in the same circle as most people.

"Just walking Kira to class." Brayden tenses and I start to reach out to him, but pull back before either of them notice.

Craig nods. "What a good brother you are."

Is that sarcasm in his tone?

Brayden's eyes narrow and he gives him a tight smile. "You know I'm always there to protect her."

227

The conversation is stiff, lacking the fluidity of decade-old friends.

Craig leans forward and I can barely hear the words he whispers in Brayden's ear. "Who's going to protect her from you?"

Brayden's jaw tightens. "Don't start this, Craig."

"You're the one alienating your friends, Brayden. I feel like I don't even know who you are anymore, man."

"I'm the same as I've always been, only with my priorities straightened out."

"And she's your priority?" Craig shakes his head back and forth. "She was someone else's, your friend, but you just couldn't fucking handle that, could you?"

Brayden's fist clenches at his side and I have the sickening feeling things are about to explode. "Kira, get to class."

I shake my head. "No." Grabbing onto his arm, I pull on him. "You can't get into another fight."

He promised his Mom, and it would cause a fist fight between him and Steven. I have no doubt Steven would press charges, he's that wonderful of a father, and that would spiral Brayden's current situation into a tailspin that would probably result in jail time.

"I'm not looking for a fight, Kira," Craig says as he steps back with his hands up. "I was looking for my friend, but I don't see him anywhere."

"Craig—"

"See you around." Craig turns and walks away, Brayden staring after him.

He doesn't move, seemingly lost in his thoughts. I worry about many things, but I also hurt to see relationships with his longtime friends crumble.

"Brayden?"

His head snaps to the side. Sad, tortured eyes stare back at me. "Anything, Kira. I will do anything for you."

My mouth drops open. He's ended so many friendships, he would've even ended his relationship with Ryan, I know that. All to be with me.

And in the end, we can be together, as long as it's in the shadows, hidden from the world. For now. Pariahs if people knew, and all because our parents got married.

Because my mom was lonely.

If only she'd met someone else, then we wouldn't be in this situation.

In the distance the bells of a nearby church chime. Panic shoots through me and I pull out my phone.

"Shit! I'm late."

He sighs and runs his hand through his hair. "I'm sorry. It's my fault."

I shake my head. "Don't worry about it. Let's just go get some food and take it back to your place." Fuck class. He's what I want anyway.

His lips twitch into a smile that doesn't meet his eyes. "We can start season three of *American Horror Story*."

"Which season is that?" I ask as we start walking back across the Oval.

This time there's no touching, and more space between us to help resist the temptation. It's an awful empty void filled with nothing but longing to be with him.

"Witches, I think."

It's hard not to wrap my arm around his, to lay claim to him, to show everyone that we are together. A united front.

A couple.

I, Kira Roth, am in a romantic relationship with Brayden Hunt—my neighbor, my best friend, my first love, my stepbrother.

TWENTY
BRAYDEN

October 3rd 2015

I love lazy Saturday's. Kira's in my apartment. We're sitting on the couch together, taking a much needed break from studying, her sexy legs stretched out across my lap. It's relaxation central. Just me and her.

She pulls another *M&M* in between those fucking suckable lips of hers, drawing my attention away from the current episode of *American Horror Story*. It's been a week since Kira officially, known to both of us, became my girlfriend.

No sweeter words were spoken then the first time she said she was my girlfriend. A milestone that gave me hope that things will work out. That we can make it past all the obstacles that still lay before us.

"You know what we haven't done in years?" I open my mouth and Kira tosses one of the candies in.

She quirks her brow while she crunches on the coated chocolate. "What?"

"Tom's Maze."

"I went last year with the girls."

I tickle under her knee, making her squirm. "Well, it wasn't with me, so it doesn't count."

She glances to the clock. "It's only seven."

My lips draw up on one side. "It's only probably what, an hour, hour and a half there? Doing it in the dark is best."

She shrugs. "Should we call Ryan and Dana?"

"Sure." I kinda want to go on our own, just the two of us, but if we're going with anyone, they're who I want. It's one of the safest places we can go and actually act like a couple. There's a chance that people from our hometown could be there, but between the dark, and them knowing her as my stepsister, holding her hand won't be an issue.

While she calls, I go rummaging through some of the boxes that are still lined up against the wall. I'm going to Indianapolis next weekend and plan to take some with me, because there just isn't room for them here.

In one box I find bits of my camping gear and locate two working flashlights.

Kira's arms wrap around my waist and I let out a low humming sound. I never knew such a simple show of affection could completely disarm me. I turn into fucking goo every time she does it.

"They're occupied." She chuckles against my back.

"Oh, are they?"

"Yeah. I used your phone and all I got was 'I'm fucking getting head, piss off' before he hung up. Which is something I *really* didn't need to know."

I shake my head. "Bro says he has my back, whenever I need. I'm surprised he answered."

"I think it was an accident. If he called while we were having sex, would you be all friendly?"

My lip curls up and I turn around. "Oh, yeah. I'd tell him all about how his little sister's pussy is milking me before asking him what he wants."

Her mouth pops open and she slaps my stomach. "Oh, my God. No. Don't you freaking dare!"

"What? It's not like he doesn't know."

"It's my *brother*. That's just weird and wrong on so many levels." Her sour face morphs into wide-eyed horror. "Please don't tell me you talk to him about sex with me, because that's just weird."

I laugh and shake my head. "Shit, I can't even mention anything sex related without getting crap about either how he doesn't want to hear about our sex life or him being pissed if he thinks I'm talking about another chick. And before you start in, it's always about you."

She gives me a side-eyed look, her hand running down my chest. Fingers flatten out when she hits the waist of my shorts before moving a little further and curling around my dick and balls.

I draw in a stunted breath, my dick beginning to stir in her hand.

"Better be."

I clear my throat before turning on as much charm as I can muster with her holding my goods hostage. "Baby, my dick is yours and only yours for the rest of my life."

Her lips curl up into a smile and she begins to massage my fear-filled flesh. "Good boy."

"Do I get a treat?"

"Maybe on the ride home I'll give you a blowjob."

Fuck me. Road head.

"Yes, please."

A giggle springs from her and she reaches up to pull my head down to press her lips to mine. "Come on, I need to hit the dorm to grab some jeans and sneakers."

"You've got both of those in the bedroom."

She blinks at me, then steps closer and wraps her arms around my waist. "Oh, yeah. Kinda forgot how much of my stuff has migrated over here."

"Have I told you how much I love that?" I lean down and kiss her nose.

She gives me the happy little smile, the one from when we were kids. Genuine and pure and makes me want to do whatever put that look on her face over and over again.

Kira's been lounging in nothing but my T-shirt, which looks fucking sexy on her, since we got up. It takes a lot of willpower to not just grab her when she's changing, naked except those fucking cheekies she loves teasing me with. They make her ass look somehow even more biteable.

I prevail, moving on to the task of locating my boots and throwing on some jeans.

Ten minutes later, we're on the road, my hand on its usual resting spot on her thigh. Right where it should always be.

The trip is filled with music, some singing along, and calm. Just being with each other and I fucking love it.

The drive isn't much longer than from my dad's house, but it's still over an hour and totally worth it. *Tom's Maze* is a fall favorite and has been since my mom took me when I was about ten. The owner takes almost ten acres and every year, carves a new intricate maze and drawing out of the corn stalks. This year is a cannon, above it written "Have a blast."

It's more than just a maze. It's also a puzzle, with a goal to fill in all the pieces of a map found in mailboxes hidden in the passages. A grid of twelve, it usually takes at least an hour and a half to make our way out, especially in the dark, with a flashlight as the only source of light.

Daytime isn't bad, but night is so much more fun and challenging.

When else are you going to see a green glowing pumpkin that was shot from a cannon streak through the sky?

"When was the last time we went together?" I ask as soon as we're past Dayton.

She lets out a little hum as she thinks about it. "Your senior year."

"Oh yeah, your freshman year." The age gap that made things so difficult. Being older, our three years doesn't seem like a lot, but back then it was huge. Hell, I didn't stop growing until that year. "Remember the first time you went at night? You were such a wimp. You had my arm in a choke hold."

Her mouth drops open and she stares at me. "I was twelve and you and Ryan told me for weeks that it was haunted."

I can't help but chuckle at the memory of her wide, scared eyes and how she was glued to me. "And you believed us."

"Two freaking biggest jerks on the planet," she mumbles.

"You'd been there before, gullible."

She swats at my arm, but it only makes me laugh.

"But never at night, dumbass. Mom wouldn't let me. I was sidelined, resigned to daylight hours only until Ryan convinced her I'd be fine with you two."

I slide my hand into hers, linking our fingers. "You'll always be fine with us. I'll always protect you, even from the fictional and imaginary things."

"This is our exit," she says.

It takes the focus from her back to the road and off the subject of her scaredy cat freak out. Another fifteen minutes down some dark roads and we arrive. The parking lot is packed, but there's no line, meaning everyone is already in the maze.

It also means that as soon as she's out of the car, I've got her hand in mine.

We walk up to the ticket booth and a woman who gives us a warm smile. "Evening."

"Hi. Can I get two tickets?"

Kira makes a sound next to me and I look to find her wallet in hand. I shake my head and bring her hand up to my lips.

Taking our change, tickets, and guide map, we step away. "This is our first official date. If you think you're paying for anything, think again."

She pulls her bottom lip between her teeth, then releases it, her lips drawing up into a shy smile. "My first date with Brayden Hunt." She squeezes my hand. "Gotta say, not what I was imagining four years ago."

I hand our tickets to the person at the entrance and pull my flashlight out.

"Blame my father for that."

As soon as we enter, there is a definite problem. The first acre looks decimated, the corn unable to grow. It appears to improve further back, but finding the mailboxes with the puzzle pieces in this part of the maze is going to be easier than normal. "Looks like the summer was hard on the corn."

"I don't think I've ever seen it this bad."

A giant light in one corner shines, lighting up that area and the entry path.

"Back to dates," she says as she swings our arms. "What would we have done back then?"

I shrug and shine the flashlight down the pathway, looking out for the first hiding mailbox. "Honestly, there were only two things I was thinking about. One was not getting killed by your brother and the other was keeping my dick out of you."

"Seriously?" She pulls at my hand, turning us left.

"You'd just turned fifteen, so I devised all sorts of reasons to not have sex with you, and your age was the main reason. I wanted you to hold onto that for just a little longer."

"But you still wanted to."

"Fuck yes. I did, but you were also so special to me. The last thing I wanted to do was go to fast and end up hurting you." Boy did I end up doing that in the worst possible ways. "Now, if you'd been my prom date as I'd planned, I can't exactly say if I would've ended up being as noble as my intentions."

Kira's head falls back in laughter before her free hand sweeps around to pat my jeans over my dick. "I was definitely up to give him some love back then." She heaves a sigh and leans into my arm. "I would've loved being your prom date. You know, if you hadn't stuck your dick in that slut."

I cringe. "Way to burn, baby."

She doesn't say any more, dropping the subject, thankfully, but it still dampened the carefree mood we were in and cooled the air between us.

The last thing I want to do is start into a conversation about that bitch again. If we're going to have a future, we have to move on from the past. I made some monumental mistakes, and I learned from them.

Another thing I learned was that I will never love another woman other than Kira. It's almost a biological impossibility. I will do anything to keep her and make her happy.

"There it is," Kira whisper yells, her arm pointing across my body.

Sure enough, barely poking out from the corn stalks is the first mailbox, complete with a littering of map pieces on the ground.

"About time. We were almost in another section."

I turn my flashlight off, so not to give away our position. It takes only a second for my vision to adjust and I slowly open the mailbox to keep it from creaking. Inside is a few tape dispensers. I grab a map piece and hand it to Kira before ripping off a few pieces of tape.

Voices come from nearby and I grab Kira's hand, running away so not to give away our findings. The hunt loses its fun when other people signal the locations.

Once we're clear, Kira turns around and I use the pieces of tape to secure our first piece to the map. One quadrant down, eleven to go. Creating separation between sections is different colored plastic ribbon draped on the edges of the corn rows and I look at the guide to determine which way to head.

Kira flips on her flashlight and looks down at the paper. "Okay, we're in purple polka dots. Do you want to go down the length?"

My lip twitches up into a smirk and I wrap my arms around her. "I don't know. Do *you* want to go down the length?" I press my hips forward and place open mouthed kisses down the side of her neck.

"Brayden, not here!" she hisses, but she can't hide the flash of excitement as her ass pushes back. "Come on, we're looking for yellow and white stripes."

It takes almost twenty minutes to find the next three mailboxes in the row, then another twenty for the next two. The entire time I can't keep my hands off her. It doesn't matter what part of her, any part of her. Whatever to keep her close, to freely touch her.

In that time my dick has also gotten so fucking hard in my jeans that I'm practically rutting against her.

"Jesus!" Kira smacks her hand on my chest and pushes.

I can't help but look at her in confusion. We were walking, searching out the next mailbox. "What?"

She blows out a little huff, then steps closer, her little fingers tangling in my shirt. "You're getting a little too handsy."

I can't see her skin in the low light, and we stopped using our flashlights most of the time. It's a full moon anyway. But if I could see her, I'm certain her cheeks would be bright red. What I can see a little bit of is her face, and her eyes are heavy, lips parted.

Dipping down, I flick my tongue out across her lips. A groan leaves me when her mouth follows me back, her whole body leaning toward me. I reach out and brush a lock of hair over her shoulder.

"Something you want, baby?"

She blinks at me and stares. It doesn't last long, seconds until she's pushing off my chest and stomping away. A few of my long strides and I'm back on her. I wrap my arm around her waist and pull her back against me, her feet barely touching the ground.

I've never fucked anyone in the maze, and I'm suddenly dying to try it out with Kira. The thrill of it with so many people close by. Hidden but not.

And I know the perfect place.

We have almost half the map done, and there's a section where the maze doesn't intersect.

I latch my teeth onto her neck, nipping at the skin, loving the way she tilts her head to give me more access. It makes the urge to rock my hips into her an actual action.

"Come on, Kitty." I somehow peel myself from her tempting little body, and grab hold of her hand.

"W-What?"

She follows behind me. It takes more than a few twist and turns before I find the right place, the outer wall of the letters Tom has carved out at the farthest end. The only way in is through the corn stalks, which are at least ten feet tall in this area, a stark contrast to where we came in.

I start to break a path between two of the giant plants, but Kira yanks on my hand, forcing my attention back to her.

"We can't."

I step back to her and wrap my arm around her waist. "Don't you want it, baby?" I kiss down her neck, moaning against her skin. "My cock all the way inside you." I nip at her ear. "Right now."

Her breathing picks up and I know I've got her. "Damn you."

I lean down to kiss her before continuing on my path through the corn. It's only about five stalks deep of a wall, but with no light, we'll be hidden. Once we're through to the open area, we look around it to find we're in the carved out letter T.

No time is wasted. I slip one hand down the front of her jeans, the other up her shirt. Pussy in one hand, perky tit in the other, and luscious skin to devour. She tastes like the sweetest wine beneath my tongue, and I'm dying for a drink.

I rock my hips into her, making sure she can feel how hard I am. She reaches back and fists my hair as her back arches, pressing her perfect ass against my aching dick.

Slick, wet heat coats my fingers as I press in, then slide back up against her clit. Teasing her, making her as mad with want as I am.

Loud laughing, followed by some yells and screams and beams of light bounces through the leaves. I know they can't see us, their vision dimmed by the use of the flashlights and the obscurity of the corn.

Kira begins tearing at my arms, trying to pry me off. "Brayden, people will see us!" she hisses.

"No they won't, the maze doesn't come through this section."

It doesn't settle her panic. "They can see us from the bridge."

It's only fear of being caught behind her protests, because her pussy has my fingers soaked and is clenched around them. She's just as dirty as I am. Kira might not have had much experience when we started, but I couldn't even tell, because her hunger matches mine.

"Kitty, it's pitch black out here and that damn bridge is over an acre away." I run my teeth up her neck. A sweet little moan crawls out of her mouth as her back arches again. "Besides, it says to 'Have a blast' and I intend to."

"Gonna blast all your come into my pussy?"

Fuck yes.

I let out a groan and flex my hips forward, holding them against her. "Baby, if you keep that dirty talk up I don't know where it's gonna blast."

Her hands grab onto her waistband and undo her jeans. "Inside me, that's where."

Her words in that breathy, desperate tone, telling me to come inside her, make all thought leave me, drowning in nothing but the mindless need to do exactly that.

I lower my zipper and pull my dick through the opening, making sure to get my balls through as well. There's not a lot of time and there are a lot of people, so the more of my clothes that are on, the better.

Pushing on the edge of her jeans, I get them just enough over her ass to get my dick into her pussy. I lick my fingers, running it over the tip of my dick before finding the right angle to get in.

I bend my legs, but I can't get low enough. Without her fuck-me heels or the lack of *anything* steady to grab onto, as well as the constriction of our clothes, our near foot height difference is causing problems.

"Fuck."

"Brayden?"

"Get on your knees."

"No," she says.

"No?"

"Both of us going out there with dirty knees will tell everyone what we were doing in here."

I hate that she's right, because the only thoughts in my head are about how my dick needs to be inside her right this second. The drive to have her tight pussy wrapped around

242

me, stroking my come from my balls.

The vision of her riding me gives me an idea and I drop to my knees. I sit back on my haunches, my dick sticking straight up.

"Fuck," she groans.

"Come here."

Leaning back, I help her get one leg of her jeans off, pull her forward to straddle my legs, then help her to sink down on me.

Warm, wet, and so tight, her pussy makes my eyes roll back and a moan to crawl out from deep in my chest when she hits the base.

It's a little awkward, but also possibly one of the most intimate positions I've ever been in. Almost like she's riding me, but I also have a lot of room to stroke deep into her. Legs clenched around my hips and torso but her feet firmly planted on the ground.

She wraps her hands around my neck and pulls me to her, that tasty tongue of hers slipping between my lips.

My hands splay out, moving up her back, pulling her closer as we both begin moving. Slow, shallow thrusts and her moans at my ear are torture and I don't know if I can hold on to the last bit of rationality left in me.

In the background we hear kids laughing and running, adults talking. Flashlights send small beams of light between the cornstalks, but I know we're hidden.

That doesn't lessen the excitement.

In the moonlight, I can see that Kira's eyes are heavy-lidded as she bounces on me. She lets out a shuddering breath and a long, low moan.

Each thrust up, each connect, drives us further into

madness.

Our love *is* madness.

A sane love can't compare to the depth of our connection, our need for each other on a cellular level.

I'd rather have five minutes of this kind of love than a lifetime of any other.

It's real and hard and not for the weak.

In risky moments like this, with my cock buried inside her, racing to paint her with my come, I don't care about anything or anyone outside.

Only Kira. She gives me life. Without her I'm dead. A despicable guy.

I move one hand around her waist and up her side until I'm cupping her face. In the quiet all I hear is our heavy breaths along with the wet squelch of my dick spearing her pussy.

The open mouthed, empty expression on her face probably matches my own and tells me one thing—she's just as close as I am.

Moving the hand on her back to her waist, I take control. Holding her against my chest, giving me leverage to stroke into her as long and deep as I can.

A low keening sounds leaves her, lips ghosting across my own. Her fingers fist into my jacket, twisting and pulling as she tries to stay quiet, to keep from screaming. From letting everyone know the ecstasy I'm giving to her.

That she's giving me.

My mind is blank from the overwhelming pleasure of her tight pussy, my body's need to come driving my hips in a manic pace. In and out. In and out. Muscles locked down to only this one motion.

Teeth clamp down on my neck and send an electric pulse

all the way through my body.

Fuck. I'm coming.

It's pain, it's pleasure. It's every muscle simultaneously clenching and releasing. My cock pulsing as it fires off in the most explosive way in the most perfect of places.

I can feel her walls flutter around me, pulling my come out of my balls.

It's when I've relaxed back down on my haunches that the others sounds come crashing in, mixing in with our pants. Kira freezes, which makes her clamp down and me to groan into her neck.

"Ssh, they're just walking through the maze. They can't see us."

She pulls back when the voices leave and cups my face. "You're such a freaking kinky asshole."

I chuckle at her and nip at her lower lip. "Uh-huh. You don't know how much I love the idea of us trying to find our way out of here and you're stuffed with my come."

She pushes against my shoulders and I grab her waist to help her up. Almost to the top of my shaft and my dick wants to slide back into her. It's warm inside her and fucking cold out.

As soon as she's off some of the come falls back down onto me. Looks like a shower and laundry are in order when we get home.

I love watching her shimmy to get her jeans over her hips and ass, her tits giving a nice little jiggle. She just rolls her eyes at me.

I tuck my softening dick away and take her hand, listening for more voices before making a path between the stalks.

"So, do you want to finish the map?" I ask as we begin

walking down a path.

If she doesn't want to there's a way to find the exit without the map.

She shrugs. "It's not like another half hour or so is going to change anything because it's still an hour drive back."

I pull her close and lean down to kiss her. "There's still six quadrants left."

"We better get moving then." She smirks at me before pulling away and running, a giggle leaving her lips.

I smirk, watching her run before taking off after her. She's not getting away from me. Not now and not ever.

TWENTY ONE

BRAYDEN

October 9th 2015

I should be reading. I should be absorbing the material. Instead, I'm tapping my pen against my book at a staccato pace.

Kira lets out a huff and draws her legs off mine, pulling my eyes up to her.

"Learning anything over there, other than how many times you can tap that pen in a minute?"

I stop moving my fingers, silencing the sound which I now realize was probably annoying. Can't help it though. I've got nervous energy to burn and it's my only outlet.

"What are we doing this weekend?" She asks as she stands, then stretches her arms up into the air. A small squeak leaves her, but I can't take my gaze off the smooth skin her raised shirt reveals.

I'm a few more ticks from pouncing her, my body searching out another outlet even though we had sex an hour or two ago.

"I've got to go to my Mom's tomorrow."

Then hopefully my nerves will calm down.

It's finally time. I get to meet the girl, to see if it's true, to gain evidence to prove she's my sister.

"Yeah? Okay, I'll go with you."

"No." The word jumps from my mouth before I can stop it.

Words before thought are never good. My heart hammers in my chest at both fear of her going with me and fear of her reaction from one little word.

Her brow furrows. "No?"

I blow out a breath and reach out to pull her back down. I place my hands on her thighs, but it doesn't lessen her laser glare. The lack of relaxation and tense muscles makes me curse myself for not anticipating her response.

"We've got to talk over court stuff and I'm taking a bunch of shit over. It's not that I don't want to take you, but next time and every time after that, baby."

"Oh, now you're going to 'baby' me? What's going on, Brayden?"

Shit. Shit. Fuck.

Lying to Kira is something I *really* don't want to do, even one that in the end will help everyone in our family. Just a little longer. I need more. The phone records and conversations, the GPS tracker info, I have aren't enough. I need to nail his ass.

Sure, he wasn't with Sonia when he fucked his cousin, resulting in my sister, but I know the information along with the rest will be what I need to convince her to get away from him.

"Nothing. I just have some personal stuff to go over with

248

my mom."

"Personal stuff."

"I'll be back Sunday morning."

"Sunday?"

There's a tone to her voice I don't like and need to diffuse. "I can probably come back the same day."

"What were you planning on doing Saturday night? Or who?"

"What the fuck, Kira? Who? That's insecure fucked up shit there."

"I'm just saying, it's a little weird."

"I can't just spend some time with my mom, who is helping me out a fuck ton because of that fucking fight over you?"

She crosses her arms over her chest. Fuck. "So it's my fault?"

"Jesus. I can't fucking not upset you right now. I've got stuff to go over with my mom, legal stuff, court dates. I need this shit behind me. Pay my debt to society or what the fuck ever and move on. The sooner this shit is done, the sooner we can leave."

"Where are we going?"

"I don't know, baby, but think about it and we'll talk about it more when I get back."

She doesn't respond more than just a humming sound that makes my skin crawl. It's not a good sign, but I can't worry about that right now.

I'll fill her in, tell her everything, when the time is right.

My gut is twisted the entire drive from Columbus to my mom's in Indianapolis. It would be anyway at the impending meeting of a little girl who could be my sister, but even more so thanks to the way I left things with Kira.

She's pissed, and I get why, because I did lie to her. I just hate that she actually thought the reason might be because of another girl.

Well, it technically is, but she's twelve and shares half my DNA.

I pull into Mom's driveway and get out. The house is at the end of row of townhomes that are three stories high, and overlooks a pond. The front door is unlocked, and I curse internally, making a mental note to talk to her about that. She lives in a safe area, but she needs to make sure the door stays locked. I have a key, she doesn't need to unlock it for me.

I take the steps up two at a time to the second floor, the first mostly occupied by the garage. She's standing at the kitchen island, sipping on a cup of what is probably her third cup of coffee for the day.

"Hey, Mom." I wrap my arms around her and kiss the top of her head.

"Hi, my baby."

It feels so good to hug her. Mom is my constant comfort and companion. She knows a lot of my secrets and how to get them out of me. The only person who I can talk freely with about my feelings. About the ones I have trouble admitting to myself, let alone anyone else.

"How's school going?" She asks as we move to the family room. It's open concept, so about ten feet from where she was standing.

I plop down on her couch and nod. "Going good."

"Keeping your grades up?"

I shake my head and try to keep a straight face. "Nope, failing everything."

"So, you're on the Dean's list?"

I shrug. "The semester isn't over, but it looks like it."

"Good. How's Kira?"

"She's good. We had a small hiccup, but things are good."

She raises a brow. "A hiccup?"

"A misunderstanding of what she is to me, what type of relationship we're in."

"I'm sure it's difficult for her. She's more sensitive to the situation than you are."

"Are you calling me an insensitive jerk?" I ask.

She lets out a chuckle as she takes another sip. "No, I'm calling you a man. You want what you want, when you want it, and don't give a crap what other people think."

"True."

"But your love for her alters that, and that's where you're different from your father."

Comparisons to my father are pretty standard for my life, but considering how many of his traits I possess, I've gotten used to it. It's nice when the attribute is in contrast to his.

"How so?"

"Your father only cares about himself. He puts himself first and everyone else second. Whereas you put Kira first. You always have, even when it wasn't necessarily the right move for her."

I nod, and stare down at my hands. "So where are we meeting them?"

"We're going to their apartment."

"Where is that?"

"It's close. Carrie wanted Emily to go to a good school."

Carrie. It's not surprising that I don't remember her, but I'll admit I'm nervous as fuck to see her.

"Cookies?" I ask.

Her lip twitches. "Nerves or do you just want a cookie?"

"Nerves."

"Is it that bad?" she asks.

"Because if Emily is my sister, how many other children has that asshole fathered and denied? And how do I find them?"

She smiles at me. "You have such compassion. You have no idea how proud that makes me."

"It's a trait I thankfully got from you."

Once done with her coffee, Mom moves to the kitchen to rinse her mug off. My leg is bouncing and my gaze locked on nothing, but my mind is. A cyclone of thoughts and what-ifs and possible outcomes.

Color moves in front of my vision, forcing my eyes to focus again. It's a dark brown cookie that I greedily snatch from her.

"My precious cookie."

She laughs. "Of course I made you some."

Molasses cookies. Mom's molasses cookies. They're my crack. I would say they're my kryptonite, but that's Kira. Though we were *Marvel* lovers, who didn't love *DC's Superman*?

I nibble on the edge of the cookie in both a nervous gesture and as a way to savor the flavor. Crumbling it away until there's nothing but a bite left, and pop that into my mouth.

"Can I have a dozen more?"

"No, but when we get back I'll send some home with you."

She's got her keys in hand, purse on her shoulder, signaling she's ready to go. I blow out a breath and stand.

When we get down to the garage, I run over to my car and pull out my backpack. We take her car, and my leg bounces the entire time.

"Did Dan call you?" Mom asks once we're out of her development.

I nod. "Yeah. He seems hopeful. I've already talked to my teachers. I just hate that this takes so long."

I'm thankful that my legal issues will be settled soon. One less stress on me.

"I know I don't need to reiterate it, but . . ."

"No more fuck-ups. Got it."

"Well, I suppose that's a good way of saying stay out of trouble."

While driving we move through newer developments, fading into older, until we reach the center of the small city and its much older section.

It's here, in one of the side streets, that Mom pulls up to a small two story brick building. It's not a house, but a small apartment building with a few units that looks like it's sitting on the lot of an older home that may have burned down.

The brick building is plain with no exterior detail. Basic.

I blow out another breath as I climb out of the car and toss my bag over my shoulder.

"1A," Mom says as she glances around for the numbers.

Rusted with the A upside-down, we head down the broken and heaved concrete. Mom reaches out and knocks on the door and my heart begins to fly in my chest.

Seconds later the handle twists and the door swings open.

Time stops. My eyes go wide, locked on to the exact same

shade as my own.

"Hello," she says, a big smile lighting up her face.

His smile.

"Emily, who's there?"

"It's nurse Abby and a cute boy!"

A short brunette appears behind her. "Abby! Oh, jeez, is it noon already? Please, come in." Emily's mom, Carrie, ushers us with a rag in her hand.

She's not what I expect, but even I'm not sure what that is. Petite with brown eyes and matching her hair. I study her, trying to see any familial resemblance, but it's difficult.

Her face is round, not square, lips in the classic cupid's bow. She's pretty, but plain, and I can see the years of hardship etched into her features.

Stepping into their home is like a gut punch. It's a minimalistic style, but I have a feeling not by choice. None of the furniture matches, every piece looking like garage sale leftovers. It's the basics: couch, coffee table, small dining room table with four mismatched chairs.

I glance at Mom who plasters a smile on her face. Does it bother her to be here? Standing with a woman my father fucked while they were married?

A woman who's his cousin.

How could this woman sleep with her own cousin?

I try my best to refrain judgement, because I have a sinking suspicion it might not have been a choice.

I stare at my mother again. It's more likely she genuinely wants to help them and screw my father over at the same time.

Maybe I got my vindictiveness from her. Compassion is her core, but you don't piss my mom off.

"Wow, Brayden, you've grown so much since the last time I saw you," Carrie says. Her posture is stiff and she holds out her hand, then drops it, seemingly unsure how to welcome me in this mess.

My mouth opens to ask when that was, but I immediately shut it. About thirteen years ago, when Emily was created.

Emily's arms wrap around my waist with a force that jostles me from the unexpected attack.

"Emily! You don't do that to strangers." Carrie chastises.

"But he's not a stranger. He's my brother, isn't he?"

I ruffle her hair and smile down at her. "I hope so."

She beams back at me and when I glance back up to Carrie, she's got her hand over her mouth and tears filling her eyes. "I didn't tell her that. I told her she might have a brother, but I didn't tell her your name or that you were Abby's, I swear."

There's a panic filling her. Almost like she's trying to diffuse an accusatory situation.

Looking back to Emily, who's still locked on to me, I tickle her side, making her squeak. "It's the eyes, isn't it?"

She nods, the ear-to-ear grin still lighting up her face. "They're like emeralds."

"I may be your brother, is that okay?"

The nod picks up in speed. "It would be awesome! I've always wanted a sibling."

Carrie pulls one of the dining table chairs over and motions for us to sit on the couch. Emily plops down between us, her thin body like a rail.

"Where to start?" Carrie says with a nervous laugh.

The whole situation is a bit awkward and I'm doing everything I can to relieve the tension I know we're all feeling. I know what it's like for me, but what has she been through?

"How about the beginning?"

"Right. The beginning. That's a good place." She blows out a steadying breath. "Well, I'm the youngest child from the youngest sibling, whereas your father is the second oldest of all of us." She gives a small smile. "I was only twenty when Emily was born."

The math flies through my mind and I curse under my breath. She's only thirty-two.

"You're younger than my father was when he . . ." My hands start shaking and I have to lace my fingers together to get it to stop. He was thirty-five at the time. "How?"

"Everyone has their own version of what happened that day."

"Everyone?" I ask.

She nods. "Your father. My parents. Me."

"What's your version?"

She glances to Emily whose brow is scrunched up in another facial characteristic of my father. "Baby, why don't you go play in your room for a little while?"

"But I don't want to. I wanna stay here."

Her small hand grabs onto my arm and I wonder how much she knows or understands of what's going on. She's not a small child, she's in seventh grade.

"Just for a few minutes, sweetie, then we can go get some lunch," Mom says to her with a warm smile.

"Okay." Emily gets up and trudges to her room.

When she hears the click, Carrie starts in with the story. "It started with me trying to sneak some booze from behind the bar at the family reunion in 2002. Steve had been watching me the whole night."

"You weren't the only one. With so many people, I don't even remember you being there," Mom says.

Carrie nods. "He made sure we didn't interact, but I think he forgot we'd been introduced the year before, and I knew right away who you were. Anyway, I was trying to sneak that drink and he noticed. He pulled me into an empty room and handed me his drink. Being one of my older cousins, I trusted him, completely."

I don't like the way her tone dips or the fact that she had to point out that she trusted him.

"Two drinks later, the world was spinning and I felt so weak. He starts getting a little touchy feely. He rubbed his hands up my arms, telling me how I'd blossomed into such a beautiful woman."

I almost can't remain in my seat. My heart pounds with disgust and rage. "He *drugged* you?"

She nods her head, her face twisted in what I can only guess as a mixture between embarrassment and pain. "When he kissed me, I managed to pull back and asked him if he was crazy. Told him we couldn't do that, we were cousins and he was married. But he was persistent and I . . . I just didn't have the strength to fight him back."

Out of the corner of my eye, I see my mom cover her mouth with her hand. Her eyes are shining with horrified tears.

"He drugged you and raped you," I whisper, trembling from head to fucking toe.

I shouldn't be surprised.

I shouldn't.

I am. I'm shocked.

Heartbroken.

"Is it really rape when I didn't really fight back?" Carrie whispers tearfully.

"It is. It fucking is," I hiss under my breath. I have my fingers laced together so tight that my knuckles crack from the pressure. This is a story I don't want to hear but need to, and then go find something heavy to bash his skull in with.

"The most I could do was beg him to please pull out once he was finished. He swore he would."

Of course, *he lied.*

My stomach turns. Even in my time using girls to get off, I never did anything like that. Shit like that is fucked up.

"I wish I could say that I hated it, that he raped me, but no matter what anyone says, I can't fully go with that version of the story. I just lay back and let him. And even worse, I didn't feel disgust until later on."

"When the drug left your system, Carrie," my mom says softly.

"He drugged and assaulted you, Carrie, and it wasn't right." The words are strained, hissing out from between my clenched teeth. "You couldn't stop him. He made sure you were drunk and high. He was probably drunk too and was looking to nut off and you became his target."

Fuck. How many girls has he roofied? Assaulted?

I have to believe this is an isolated case. I have to. If I don't, I'm going to go mad at the reality of who my father is.

Besides, someone would have reported him if there had been more. Right?

"And you fit his type perfectly." Mom's gaze, which had locked on the coffee table, moves to Carrie. "Young, pretty, and not to sound mean, but were probably putting off a desperate for attention vibe."

I nod in agreement. "His M.O. He preys on the weak and lonely. You can't blame yourself for what happened."

Carrie reaches up and swipes a few tears from her face. "I wish it was that easy. The problem is, everything that happened after that. When I found out I was pregnant . . . my parents threw me out. The rumors flew after that. People called me a whore, even people I didn't know. I had to get out of the area."

"Is that when you moved here?" I ask.

Carrie nods. "No money, college drop out, and no support. It's been hard, but I've managed."

"Brayden?" Mom reaches out to me but I jump up from the couch. I know she can tell just how close to the edge I am.

Would I kill my own father if it wasn't against the law?

Hell. Fucking. Yes.

Guess we're both monsters.

My lip curls up in a fight to rein my anger in. "I want to make sure he pays for it, monetarily as well as his beloved reputation."

Carrie shakes her head. "I don't want him to ever see her. He hasn't in twelve years."

Mom leans forward and takes Carrie's hand. "With the results showing paternity you'll be able to get some financial support you desperately need to give Emily what she deserves, but there is the chance the court could grant him visitation. Whether he chooses to use that visitation or not is unknown."

"He won't."

Mom turns to me and quirks her brow. "And you know this?"

"I lived with him for two years in high school and he didn't

259

give a shit about me or what I was doing. He just cared about the next woman he was going to fuck. That bastard doesn't give two shits about anyone but himself, just like you said."

"Jesus, Brayden. Language."

Carrie's eyes are wide as she looks at me. "I take it things aren't good between you two."

I shake my head. "You have no idea how many fist fights were narrowly avoided over the last few years. Once all this is done, once he's divorced from Sonia, I will never speak to him again."

"He doesn't sound like the type of man I want anywhere near my daughter, even if she is his."

"Have you talked to him at all?" I ask. There's no doubt in my mind Emily is my sister, the physical evidence is strong. Even with Carrie and my father being blood relations, Carrie and I have very little resemblance.

I'm convinced Emily got her looks directly from my father.

She nods. "It's been over a decade. I called him when I found out I was pregnant, but he said he didn't care, that she was my 'problem' to deal with. When she was born, I called him again and let him know I was putting him down as the father. He got angry, said it wasn't him, called me a slut. I tried to get him to take a paternity test so I could prove it to him, but he refused to consent."

Which is why I'm here. "I guess he thought we'd never meet."

She nodded. "He threatened me that if I continued to pursue it he'd have Emily taken from me."

I grind my teeth together, anything to keep the anger at bay. Carrie's place is sparse but clean and I don't need to be making any messes for her by fucking up the walls with my fists.

"And without a support system or money, I couldn't risk it. Emily is all I have."

She has support now and I'm going to make sure she buries him.

"I think it's time."

Carrie nods. "I'll go get—"

"No, I'll get her," I say, interrupting her.

There's a small hallway that separates the living spaces with the bedrooms. The two rooms are then separated by a bathroom.

I glance to the left and through the open door to one of the bedrooms. It's just a mattress on the floor with a dresser. No decorations and only a few small knickknacks on the top of the dresser.

With a small push the door to the other bedroom swings open. I see then where any of Carrie's extra money goes. Emily's room doesn't have a lot, but it has the only matching furniture in the house. There's also some toys and games and a small television, along with the dozen stuffed animals on the pink covered bed.

Emily is Carrie's whole life. Everything she does is for her.

The only thing that stops me from falling to my knees and breaking down in front of this little girl is that I'm her older brother. The grown up.

She's never had a dad. The least I can do is remain strong for her.

"Hi," Emily says, her bright smile beaming at me from the floor.

It's contagious and I find myself smiling back as I kneel down next to her.

"What are you doing?"

She flips the pages of a very large book and it takes me a second to realize it's a photo album.

"I wanted to show you what you've missed."

What I've missed.

Damn, talk about ruthless. She doesn't mean anything about it, she's excited to show me her past, but it is just another thing glaring at me, screaming at me *this is what he denied you.*

Not just me, but her as well. He denied us, denied family.

"You know what? Why don't we wait on this for next time? Then I can bring my book and we can share."

She nods. "I'd like that. I especially like that it means I'll see you again."

"Me too."

Her excitement over me, an essential stranger, kills me. A fucking knife in my chest and a pang of guilt that I don't understand.

I hope I'm not leading her on. I hope the test shows what I know in my gut to be the truth.

Especially because while I look at her, I'm understanding more and more what Ryan feels for Kira. The emotion is a tight band around my throat and chest.

"Come on," I stand and hold both of my hands out.

She slips hers in and I pull, rocketing her off the floor with all my strength.

The high pitched laugh that comes out of her is almost lyrical, and she's still giggling when we go back out to the living room.

"What were you two doing?" Carrie asks with a smile as she pulls Emily to her side.

Mom's smiling at me as I sit back down, her hand patting my knee in a very "good boy" gesture.

"It's a secret," I say

"Oh really?" Carrie's lip twitches.

Emily nods. "It's a sibling thing."

"Speaking of . . ." I pull my bag in front of me and pull at the zippers. From inside I retrieve the package that arrived a week ago. "Sibling paternity test from an accredited lab that is trusted in court."

In my hand is the way to get help for them. In my hand is more proof and another step to get Sonia to leave him. In my hand is the key to ending one family and opening up to another.

Mom takes the box from me and pulls out the contents. She studies the instructions just to make sure we get it right, even though I know she knows what to do. Leave no room for debate due to a contaminated or incorrectly processed test.

I even put the charge on the bastard's credit card. He was paying for this just like he's going to pay for everything else.

A swap of Emily's cheek, then mine, and for extra measure and clearer results, Mom and Carrie, and it's done.

Something so simple. A little bit of DNA taken in the most innocuous way, is all that's needed for something so momentous.

"Once the results are in and show that Brayden and Emily share a father, I have a family lawyer friend who is also willing to help you out pro-bono," Mom says as she packages the tubes containing our swabs into the box provided.

Carrie blinks at her. "What?"

Mom smiles. "Steven has already made things financially challenging on you and this shouldn't add to it."

"I don't know, Abby. You've done so much for us and now this? After what happened?"

"You weren't a mistress, knowingly and with purpose pursuing my husband. You were taken advantage of, raped." Mom stands and picks up her purse. "I think it's time for lunch."

"I can't thank you enough. All of this, being accepted versus us shunned." Tears begin to roll down Carrie's cheeks. "It means so much that you believe me."

"It's pretty obvious," I say as I stand. "I *know* what the test is going to say, and it means so much to me as well." I look over at Emily. "I want to know all of my family, and he's refused me that."

Carrie stares at me, her brow crinkled. "You think there are more, don't you?"

I nod. "Before Emily I had no clue I had any siblings, but after hearing your story and knowing his ways, I'm pretty sure there are more. The hard part is finding them, if they exist. I don't know if it will ever happen, but I'll keep looking."

"Do you hate him that much?" she asks.

My brow furrows as I stare at her. "I do, but that's not why. I was the lucky one, because I grew up with the support you desperately needed for Emily. I can't stand thinking about how I may have other siblings and not knowing them. Screwing my father over more is just icing on the cake. Making him own up to what he's done, to the lives he's harmed."

"But . . . he gave me Emily."

I shake my head. "Don't build him up to be anything more than a conniving sperm donor. He had one focus, Carrie, and

264

he had absolutely not a care for you or your wellbeing. And he harmed Emily by denying her a better life and most of all by denying her me. Because unlike him, I will be there for her. Unlike him, I will protect her."

Carrie jumps up and wraps her arms around me, nearly knocking me down. Her body shakes with sobs as she cries against my neck.

"Thank you, Brayden."

I pat her back for a minute, then pull away. "I'll get this sent out on Monday. The instructions say it'll take a couple of weeks to get back. I'll come back when they do."

She smiles at me and nods as we move to walk out the door.

It was an emotion filled hour and I'm drained. We still have lunch, and I may have to crash at Mom's before I head home.

"So who is this lawyer you know?" I ask Mom after we drop Carrie and Emily back at home.

Mom is silent for a few beats too long. "He's a friend."

I turn in the seat. "What kind of friend?"

She ignores me again, pretending she's concentrating on driving. "He's a friendly friend."

"Is he your boyfriend?"

"Brayden, I don't think—"

"No." I interrupt her. "It's an easy answer, Mom."

She sighs. "I suppose he is."

"Suppose?" What kind of answer is that?

"We went on our first date a few weeks ago. Our schedules clash a lot, so we haven't gone out that much."

"How did you meet?"

"A common friend's party last year," she says.

"And you just now went out on a date?"

"We were friends for a while, and things just changed."

"Uh-huh."

"Why are you giving me the third degree on this?" she asks. "I'm an adult and can date a man."

"Yes, you can, but I want to meet him."

She shakes her head and smiles. "Heaven help if you ever have a daughter. Poor girl will never get a date."

"Damn right."

It is an automatic response, and one that stuns me.

Kids were never a thought because I made it that I was never going to fall in love. That things like relationships and marriage were for other people.

But things have changed. Things that were once a never are becoming my new ideal future.

Kira is my future. I want to be cemented to her forever. For the first time in my life marriage isn't a never. My own family isn't a never.

I want a life with Kira. I want everything with her.

Now to make it happen.

TWENTY TWO

Kira

Everyone I need is busy right now.

Everyone.

Ashley and Marilyn are both on dates. And I'm happy for them. I really am.

Jenna? She's getting laid. She hasn't responded to my text but I know her. There's no way she isn't.

My heart races. My hands are sweating. I'm pacing back in forth in the small lounge area of my dorm room, my body thrumming with violence.

And it's violence. I won't deny it.

I'm fucking *pissed.*

I tried to be cool. Tried to go on about my day as if Brayden leaving the way he did doesn't matter.

Why is he treating me like this? Does he think I'm stupid? That I wasn't going to notice he's hiding something?

I've known for a while now that he is. And I ignored it long enough. At first, the signs were few and far between.

Now? The red flags are all up in my face, telling me I'm six different types of fool for trusting him.

I tug on my hair. That's not fair to him. He's been trying so hard to change. I know he has. I give him all the credit in the world for it.

But is it fair to me that I have to live knowing how he once was and now I have to deal with him lying to me about things?

I need to talk to someone about this. It's too much to keep locked up inside myself. I can't sift through all this on my own.

There's only one person that might be available right now.

If she isn't giving my brother head at the moment.

I cringe at my own stupid thought. What a way to traumatize myself. I head back into the room area to text Dana.

Picking up my phone, I can't help the way my stomach drops at the lack of text notifications.

Brayden text me once this morning to tell me he was pulling up to his mom's. I replied. After that, he didn't.

All day. It's been nine hours since he last text me.

Any other girlfriend would be blowing up his phone by now. It's my right as his girl.

I don't feel like his girl. I'm not being treated as such. If ignoring the girl he's with is the way a boyfriend acts, I don't want part in any of this.

So I haven't reached out to him. I've left it alone. If I'm not important enough for him to keep in mind during his trip, then I won't bother him. I'll give him his space.

It's better than blowing up on him. I'll just deal with my shit on my own.

Dear God, this *hurts*. I don't mean to be untrusting of him, I really don't. He isn't making trusting him easy, though.

Dana responds to my text. ***Hey! No, I'm not busy. What's up?***

Maybe it's wrong to reach out to my brother's girl for relationship advice but what choice do I have? I have no one at this moment, and besides, she's been there for me before.

I was wondering if you have time to go out for some drinks. I kind of need someone to talk to.

Her next text comes through within seconds of me sending mine. *I'll take the car and will be there in less than 30.*

Damn, man. Even if she did slice my brother up in her quest for vengeance against him, the girl has a side to her that is just too awesome.

I hurry to change my clothes and make myself look at least semi-human.

"So . . . He's hiding his laptop when you walk into the room. Set up a pin on it *and* on his phone?"

I stare into my beer and nod. "The only reason I found out is when I went to use both. The phone pin is recent. It happened right before he left. The computer? That was two weeks ago."

Dana runs her hand through her hair. "Did you ask him about it?"

"Why should I? He locked me out of his devices. I doubt he's going to tell me why."

She pounds back her drink like a pro. "God damn it, Brayden. What are you doing?"

At least now I know I'm not going crazy. I've asked myself that question at least fifty times since he left yesterday morning.

"Text him." Dana waves the waitress back over to us.

"What? No!"

Dana ignores me and orders us shots of tequila.

My eyes go wide. "No to that as well woman!"

She waves me away like my two refusals are ridiculous. "Trust me. You need them. Now text him."

I finish my beer and resign myself to the shots. The text, however? "No. He hasn't reached out to me all day. Why should I bother him?" I can't hide the bitterness in my tone.

"I want to see how long it takes him to get back to you."

"What if he doesn't get back to me at all?" I ask in a small voice. Fuck, I'm pathetic and weak, but I'm pretty sure I'll cry in the middle of this bar.

Dana raises her eyebrow and for the first time, I see that merciless, vindictive side of her shining through. "I hope the boy isn't actually that stupid. Especially since you and I are starting to get close."

Our shots arrive.

I slam mine back for courage and send him that text. I tell myself before typing it out not to come off as bitchy or petty.

I fail.

I guess you've been too busy to call or text.

"Let me see."

I turn the phone around so Dana can read it. "Was it wrong of me to say that?"

She scoffs. "Girl, you were *so* much nicer than I would've been. How does this sound? 'Useless motherfucker, get back to me now or you can kiss my fine ass on its way to the next dick.'"

I want to both laugh and cry at that. "I don't know what to do. I feel guilty for not trusting him. What if he's just hanging with his mom as he said?" I place the phone face up on the table so I won't miss his text if it comes through.

"Well, has he ignored you like this while with his mom before?"

My response is quick. "Never."

Her eyebrows raise high. "Combine that with his recent behavior . . . Listen, I'm praying with you. *Hard*. And there's a part of me that keeps insisting Brayden adores you and he wouldn't do anything stupid to ruin what you two have."

I nod because there's a big part of me that feels the same way.

"But it's not your fault you're panicking. Kira, you're human, and he hoe'd his ass all over the place back in the day. That's not something you forget. How you feel is understandable." She reaches across the table and grabs my hand.

I smile at her although I feel like going home and curling into a ball. Stupid, since the last thing I needed was to be alone, and that's why I called her.

"He hasn't gotten back to you, yet. Has he?"

I would have seen my phone light up if he had. Still, I pick it up and double check.

Nothing.

The urge to call him chokes me.

If I do, I'm going to end up cursing him out. I know myself. I might go ahead and use Dana's line after all.

"We need more drinks." Dana twists around in her seat, looking for the waitress.

"Are you sure that's a good idea? I tend to get stupid when I drink."

"I won't let you get to that point, trust me."

So I do. She orders us one more round of shots and after that we go back to drinking beers.

Mixing different types of alcohol is a recipe for disaster, but we aren't planning on having too many more.

To her credit, she drops the Brayden subject and tries to distract me talking about other things.

Obviously, it doesn't work.

My life has become mostly about him lately. What more do I have to talk about? "Um, I hate that I even have to ask you this, but can you please not tell my brother? I don't want to cause a rift between him and Brayden."

"Of course. I mean, if Brayden ends up really fucking this up, I won't have a choice but to tell him. However, we're going to stick on the side of faith and believe that he has a perfectly rational explanation for this."

I rub my face with my hands. "Now I feel like a huge bitch all over again." How could I doubt Brayden? He's been busting his ass to do right by me.

"Stop chastising yourself, you're human, and you're utterly in love with him. It's normal."

"It's still not right. I owe him more faith than that."

But an hour later, he still hasn't responded.

"Okay. I'd be officially freaking out by now. Text him. Something along the lines of 'Austin is coming to pick me up in five minutes. Talk to you later.'"

I laugh at Dana's comment. She's so bad. What the hell was my brother thinking ever going up against someone like her? I'm sure he lived to regret it. "He's also driving back super early in the morning, so he's probably in bed early for that."

She nods, but the look on her face is disbelieving.

It's only 8:30pm. Therefore, I don't blame her for the disbelief. I'm grasping at straws here and I know it.

"Well, we agreed we weren't going to get drunk, but . . ."

It's a bad idea but I'm right there with her. "Another round?"

She smiles and slams her hand on the table. "My kind of girl."

I somehow managed to shower without slipping and breaking my neck.

I've gotten so used to showering at Brayden's, that using the shared showers here sucks for me now.

Jenna still isn't back yet. I suspect she won't be back until late tomorrow. Just in case I send her a text to make sure she's all right.

Yeah, I'm aware I'm not her mom but I can't help worrying for her regardless.

I almost trip getting into my bed. My promise to not get drunk went down the shitter after that last round of shots. Somehow, that turned into another three rounds.

I fall face first into the bed and within an instant I'm passed out.

My phone's ringing incessantly. I can feel it vibrating against my face.

The last thing I want to do is wake up. Why can't they just leave me alone?

I roll over and shut my eyes tight, determined to ignore it. Happiness floods me when the phone stops ringing seconds later. Sighing, I curl back up and go back to sleep.

It's ringing again.

Actually, I think I heard it ringing in my dreams. Non-stop. Annoying.

Groaning, I roll onto my back. The world is pounding. My mouth is so fucking dry.

That phone won't shut the fuck up.

I think I feel it vibrating under my pillow. Whoever is calling isn't going to leave me alone until I answer.

I search blindly under my pillow until I find my phone and answer without looking at who's calling.

"What?"

"Kira where have you been?"

A wave of equal parts giddiness and anger flow inside me at the sound of Brayden's voice.

"Home. In bed." Jesus. My voice sounds like shit.

Brayden's silent for a few seconds. "Are you okay?"

I try swallowing to help ease the dryness in my mouth. All it does is make it worse. "I'm trying to sleep."

"I've been trying to call you."

I pull the phone away from my ear. Squinting at it, I pull up my call records to see when his calls began. "Yeah," I say, bringing the phone back to my ear. "*Three* hours after I text you and over twelve hours since I last heard from you. Sorry I didn't stay up waiting by the phone."

"You're angry at me. I get it."

No. I don't think he does. "I really need to go back to bed, if you don't mind. My head's pounding."

"What were you doing?"

"Are you going to honestly answer that question if I ask you?"

"Kira . . ."

Dear God, he's annoyingly persistent when he wants to be. "I have an issue, okay?"

"An issue?"

"Yeah. I've developed a bad habit of drinking my problems away."

"Your problems . . . You're drunk."

I don't like the condemnation in his tone. "I was," I snap. "I'm coming down off it and I would like to sleep through most of it."

"Kitty, I'm going to tell you. You know that right? When the time is right, I'll tell you everything."

My heart speeds up, which does nothing to help my headache. "Tell me what? Why can't you tell me now? What's going on Brayden?"

"I can't tell you, yet. But I promise I will soon. As soon as it's all sorted out."

"You're hurting me with your secrecy," I whisper.

He curses softly. "I'll hurt you a lot worse if I drag you into this."

Despite how shitty I feel, I sit up at that, alarmed. "Are you in some kind of trouble?"

"No. Nothing like that. Just . . . You know I love you, right?"

I chew on the inside of my cheek.

"Tell me you know I love you, Kira."

Thinking back on everything he's done for me the last few months, all the emotional hits he endured, how hard he's tried to change his ways, there's only one answer I can give him. "Yes."

"Then trust me. Please, baby. I know this isn't easy on you, but *please* trust me."

"I miss you," I say instead, because the tone of his voice is slicing me up and all I want is to be in his arms.

"I fucking miss you so much it's killing me."

Yet he went twelve hours without even texting me a single word.

I bite back that comment. I'm stuck between righteous anger and guilt for not trusting him.

"Kira, please tell me you'll trust me."

I can't promise that. I'd be lying. But I can promise something else truthfully. "I'll try, Brayden. I promise I'll try my absolute best."

TWENTY THREE
BRAYDEN

I love coming home to find Kira on my couch. It makes my day better, just seeing her sitting there, studying. All because of what it means. After all the years of pain, she's finally mine. We've fallen back into old habits, like friends reuniting after years apart. In some ways, it feels like no time has passed at all, so when the reminders come, they hit hard.

"Hey, baby," she says as she looks up from her books.

Fuck.

Baby.

I set my bag down, along with the groceries I picked up on my way home, and walk over to her. She's smiling up at me and that, in combination with her simply being here, turns me on.

"What are you up to?"

"I'm *almost* done with this paper."

I lean down and press my lips to hers. It's more than the quick peck she was thinking when I lean in as she tries to pull away.

"How close?"

She blinks at me and looks down to her laptop, then back at me. "Umm, an hour?"

I run my fingers across my lips as I look down at her. My cock started to get hard the second I saw her, and it's already pressing against my jeans. When she breaks my stare, her eyes drift down and I can see pink start to spread across her cheeks.

Spreading my legs, I straddle hers and lean forward, hands gripping the back of the couch, caging her in with my body. My crotch is inches from her face. A groan slips out as I stare down at her biting her lip and looking up at me from under her lashes.

"You can't wait an hour?" she asks even as she reaches to undo my belt.

Her hands are cool against my skin and I let out a shuddering breath as she pulls me out. Two seconds and I'm a panting fucking mess, her tongue lapping at the tip, lips wrapping around the head.

I wasn't fully hard, but the second she reached for me, all the blood moved to my dick.

Maybe if she can suck me off real quick, I can get my brain back with the program. There's a plan I've been brewing for days, and I'm ready to unleash it on her.

Problem is, she won't be finishing her paper tonight and I don't care, because her fucking hot, wet mouth is almost down to the base of my shaft, hitting a new record.

"Jesus, baby, fuck."

Her lips are the best. I've gotten head lots in the past, but nothing compares to her.

My grip on the couch is so hard my knuckles are white. A shudder runs through me. One of her hands cups my balls, the other wraps around my shaft while her head moves back and forth. It takes everything in me not to grab onto her hair and fuck her face, to stay still, but I need her to suck me dry on her own.

I need her to take it from me like I'm going to take it from her.

Her lips are stretched around me, creating the most erotic view. My mouth's hanging open and I can feel my balls draw up.

"That's it, baby."

In and out. Swallowing me. Watching inch by inch disappear between her lips.

I can't think. Can hardly speak as my muscles lock down.

I stop breathing, every nerve in my body exploding. She's still fucking sucking, swallowing each blast I empty into her mouth.

When my cock stops twitching, she takes in as much as she can and pulls off, her tongue wiping off every inch until her lips pop off with a smack. My legs give out, knees crash down to the couch on either side of her.

"Feel better?" she asks, her hands resting on my hips.

I shake my head, still panting. "No."

"No?"

I drop my arms down as my head falls to her neck. Reaching between us, I press against the seam of her jeans, driving it against her clit and making her gasp. I lick her neck before biting down while I press harder.

"Not until you come, and then I fill you."

"I have to finish my paper." It's a weak protest. She's too turned on, rocking her hips against my hand.

"Later."

She lets out a little mewling protest that only spurs me on. Lips on hers, my tongue opens her mouth, giving her a sample of what I'm going to do to her pussy in a few short minutes. I want her naked and spread for me.

"Come on, Kitty." I stand up, and pull her with me.

I can't keep my hands off her as we walk the short distance back to the bedroom. She's sucking on my tongue like she did my dick. My girl's more than excited, and hopefully she still will be when she sees what I've got planned.

Fuck, it's been days since I've had her pussy in my mouth. Tasted her on my tongue. Too fucking long since I ate her out.

Between school and all the other shit, it's been hard to get more than a quickie in over the past few weeks. But now it's time. I've carved out this space of time for a specific purpose, and I intend to spend it trapped between her thighs in one way or another.

I'm tearing at her clothes, pulling off each piece between desperate kisses. Littering the floor, creating a trail as we go. She reaches back as I tug at her jeans, popping her bra off and setting free the most perfect breasts I've ever seen.

Maybe that's because I'm biased toward her. Whatever. All I know is I want to bite her tit, suck on her nipple until she pushes me off.

Almost there. I've got her flat on her back as I tug her jeans down her legs.

"Fuck, where are your panties?"

She bites her lip as she smiles down at me. "I took a shower after class, only to find I had no clean panties here."

We've been so busy that the laundry has piled up to the point of overflowing.

I step forward and nudge her knees apart. "Lucky me." Her pussy lips are shiny, her skin puffing up and begging me to spread her open.

Leaning down, I wrap my lips around one of her nipples and suck. She bucks beneath me, drawing in a sharp breath. I trail my hand down, slipping over her mound, across her clit to her slick slit.

"Mmm, Kitty, we're going to have so much fun."

I dive down between her thighs, throwing her legs over my shoulders. The first lick gets my cock stirring again. My tongue explodes with her flavor and I moan, licking, pushing my tongue inside her to get more.

Her chest rises and falls, the back of her hand against her mouth. I can't take my eyes off her and when her heavy eyes open and look down, her face scrunches up in the most beautiful torture.

It makes me want to do more, to not just have her panting, but screaming my name with her hands fisting my hair, pushing my face into her.

There will be more, but I'll start with my fingers so I don't freak her out. I move up to suck on her clit, flick it with my tongue. She bucks under me, and I waste no time slamming two fingers deep into her pussy.

"Fuck!" she cries, my name coming out in a broken breath.

Her pussy is so hot and wet my dick is jealous of my fingers, especially when she squeezes down, tightening like her whole body is. My fingers are soaked as I lean over her, fucking her with them, pressing against her G-spot.

I'm practically dripping with her juices. I pull out of her pussy and the whine that stutters from her makes my raging dick twitch.

"Nooo! Please."

I lean down and flick my tongue against her clit and suck it between my lips. Her hands pull at my hair while I slide my fingers down and press them against her tight puckered hole.

She squirms beneath me, but tries to relax like we've practiced, and I get one fingertip in, then the other. My teeth scrape against her clit as my tongue laps at her pussy. A shuddering moan leaves her and she tries to flex her hips up, but I'm in charge today. She can ride my face later.

I time the lashing of my tongue with the thrusts of my fingers. Fucking her ass, working her open each time I push in and open my fingers as I pull out.

"Baby, please . . . oh fuck."

She stops breathing, her muscles tensing, thighs shaking. Her scream echoes around the room and I keep going until she pushes against me, her body jerking as aftershocks rock her.

I lick my lips as I pull my fingers out, sucking in more of her sweetness. She's naked, boneless, and laid out on my bed, exhausted from a body crippling orgasm.

Fuck, that makes me feel like a king.

I did that to her. Turned her into a pile of spent flesh.

Me.

Only I can do it and I will be the only one for the rest of her life.

I grab a bag out from under the bedside table, and pull out the dildo I bought the other day. It's perfect, good for pussy and ass with a finger loop to help drive it in and out of her. The size is smaller than my dick, but not by a lot and it's bigger than the other toys we've been using.

"What is that?" Kira asks. Her eyes are wide, almost horrified.

She knows.

I've been slowly working her ass open, getting her used to it a little bit at a time. Prepping her for my cock. This is the final step before her fucking tight ass is going to stretch around me. No more toys or plugs.

"Have you ever thought about DP?"

"DP . . ." Her eyes widen further and she shakes her head. "That *and* you? No way. It'll never work."

She's worried, but I know it will be okay.

"Oh, baby, we've watched enough porn together to know it will work."

She pulls in a breath and it shudders. Proof that she's just as fucking excited about it as I am, she just doesn't want to admit it.

But I'm going to make her. Have her tell me exactly how badly she needs my cock in her. Tease her until she can't stop coming. As much as my cock is begging for her pussy, I have to do this first.

"Do you want my cock?"

She nods.

"Where?" I ask

"Brayden."

"Where?"

"In my pussy," she answers.

284

It's what I knew she was going to say.

"Then what about this?"

She lets out a little whimper. I smirk down at her and rub the tip of the dildo against her slit, getting it wet from her flooded pussy. She rocks against it, but I place an open hand against her abdomen, holding her down.

My lip twitches and I push it forward, all the way. Kira's entire body arches, her mouth open wide in a silent scream. There's no breath in her body, I've taken it away.

"Look at that, you got your new toy all wet," I say as I slowly pull it out.

The desire to see the black silicone spreading her ass works me up even more. It takes all the strength I have to not just throw it to the side and shove my cock in instead.

Kira whimpers, her hand reaching for me, her eyes drawing me in. She claws at me, wanting me to give it to her, to bury myself deep inside her. A growl rips from me and I slam one of her legs down to the bed, opening her up to me.

Reaching back to the bedside table, I grab the lube and drip some on her puckered ass. Even though the dildo is still wet with her juices, I drizzle some of the lube on the tip is well.

"Relax," I say as I press the bulbous tip against her tight, pink skin and push.

My dick twitches, watching her spread around the silicone, just imagining how tight it would feel around me. Shallow pants make Kira's chest bounce, her hands fisting the sheets.

And I can't tear my eyes away from the erotic view of her ass swallowing each inch all the way to the finger loop.

"Oh, fuck!" she cries out. Her thighs try to close, forcing me to press harder, keep her down.

Pulling on the dildo, I watch it slide slowly back out almost all the way before pushing it back in. My cock twitches, precome leaking from the tip, crying with the need to fuck her.

Once more, in and out.

Her pussy's leaking, glistening, begging and she's thrashing on the bed, her fingers crawling down her stomach and ghosting across her clit.

I shove the dildo all the way to the hilt and rub the head of my cock at her entrance and push in. My head spins, cock aching as Kira convulses beneath me. Her eyes roll back and a guttural moan rips from her as she shakes.

I can feel the dildo filling her ass, pressing against my dick through the thin barrier. She's never been this tight.

"Fuck." I shake my head from side to side, holding back the urge, the *need* to come.

Kira's eyes are barely open, but her mouth is, and I bend over to lick her lips. Summoning strength, she flings her arms around my neck, her tongue slipping against mine.

My dick pounds, demanding friction. I hook my hand under her knee and place it on my shoulder. Grabbing onto the dildo, I pull it out slowly at the same time as my cock. Just a little bit, then shove them back in.

Her mouth falls open, slack, and her body rocks against mine. I feel the bite of her nails digging into my back and arm, the heat of blood welling up.

And I don't care.

I pull out again and thrust in, driving both the dildo and my dick in at a steady pace. The wet squelch of her pussy is fucking heaven.

"Do you like it, baby? Do you like both your holes filled?"

"Fuck, yes," she groans.

It's a struggle for her to say anything, and I'm right there with her. She's so fucking tight, ready to come all over again, all over me. There's a desperate drive in me to get her there, to hold on until she does.

But I can't fucking take it.

Mind blank.

Eyes unfocused.

Hips driven by sheer need.

So far gone, I can barely hear her screams, but I do feel the pulsing of her pussy. It's so intense, I let go of the dildo, hips jerking, every muscle tensed, screaming.

I'm coming so hard, firing off almost painful eruptions of come as deep as I can inside her.

I can't breathe. Consumed by the fire that is incinerating me from the inside.

Drained, I make sure to fall beside her, my dick so sensitive I hiss as I slip out of her. We're both panting, unable to move or say anything.

"Take . . . it . . . out," she says between breaths.

Turning onto my side, I reach between her legs and slowly pull the dildo out, tossing it to the floor for now. I'll clean it later.

"Did you like it?" I ask, flopping back down, my arm lying across her stomach.

"No."

"Liar."

"Yes."

I chuckle and kiss her shoulder. "Next time, it's my dick."

She nods, eyes drifting close. "I'm ready."

I can't hold my eyes open any longer. "Good."

TWENTY FOUR

BRAYDEN

October 19th 2015

"Be good, drive safe, and give Kira a hug for me," Mom says and she gives me one last squeeze.

"I will. And the same for you. Text me when you get home."

"Don't forget to go on that website and get it all scheduled out."

I nod. "As soon as I get home."

"No, as soon as you get home you're going to be distracted by Kira."

My lips twitch up. "True, but I promise I will do it later today."

"Good boy." Another hug and she steps away. "Love you."

"Love you, too."

My feet are glued to the concrete, waiting to make sure her car starts before heading to my own and climbing in.

It's almost noon and I swing into a drive-thru before heading back up to Columbus.

Today was my trial, and my lawyer, Dan, said it went pretty well. The judge went light on me, being a first offense, but not too light to help avoid a free pass. There are still repercussions from the fight that I'm going to have to suffer through, but it could be so much worse.

I'm dying to tell Kira all about it, but more than that, I'm dying to have her in my arms. Dying for our connection to calm my fried nerves.

I've been away from Kira for almost twenty-four hours and that's way too long under normal circumstances. Meaning my lead foot is in full force, speeding my way up the interstate.

The trial was a good excuse to stay at my father's house and charge up the GPS tracker I put in his car. It died a few days ago, and I couldn't find an excuse to come down before now.

We avoided each other, which was good. After meeting Carrie and Emily, I was itching to put my fist in his face. Even more so when I saw Sonia.

It took everything in me to stop from picking up one of the kitchen chairs and hitting him with it.

Without another person in the house, he's sucking the life out of her at a faster rate.

I started the night out in my stark bedroom, but it didn't take long until I was across the hall and in the comforting zone that still felt like Kira.

Fifty minutes of driving later and I'm parking outside Kira's dorm.

She gets out of class any minute, so I walk up to the benches to sit and wait, texting her where I am. The sun is out, which helps with the cool October air that forces me to zip up my jacket.

I surf Facebook while I wait, which is something I haven't done much of lately. Mainly because I don't want to see any more of the shit Jennifer has been spewing. She'd calmed down for a while after I sent the video to her dad, but after I stared her down while I was balls deep in Kira, I set her off again.

Not much is going on, but I am happy to see pictures of Kira with her girls. I'll admit, I monopolize her free time, because I'm possessive like that. I want her next to me all the time, but I do like seeing her sitting in her dorm room with Marilyn, Ashley, and Jenna, hanging out.

No party, just friends. Probably gossiping, and I'm more than certain I was a topic of conversation.

"You a free man?" Kira's voice pulls me from my phone and I jump to my feet.

I smirk at her and reach out to run my fingers down her arm. "Six months' probation and fifty hours of community service. But if I have any more trouble with the law, my ass will be spending time behind the shiny bars."

"That's nothing to joke about, baby." Her voice lowers on the last word. A slip that I needed to hear.

"No, but as soon as my probation is over, we can go."

"Go?"

I wanted to talk more about our options later, when we were alone. So I glance around and lower my voice. "Get away from the whispers and the rumors and the stigma. We'll

291

leave, find another school in another state where they don't know us."

"I don't know about that, Brayden."

The urge to grab her, to reach out and cup her face, to make her look up at me in a way that doesn't look platonic, but like she loves me. But I resist, my voice lowering again. "I want to act like a normal couple in public, not just private."

"So do I."

"I want to show my girl off, let everyone know how much I'm hers."

"Transfer schools?"

I glance around. "Why don't we go home and talk about it more?"

"Wise idea. Away from eavesdroppers."

"That and I need to touch you so badly right now. You don't know how much I wished you were there."

Her brow scrunches and she nods. "Okay, I just gotta go switch out some books."

"I'll stay here."

"You don't want to come up?"

I shake my head. "No, because I'm sure everyone's around and this'll give me a minute to get ahold of myself."

She nods again, and I wonder if she can see just how tightly wound I am. It doesn't help that she unknowingly turns me on as I stare at the sexy sway of her hips as she walks away.

Five, maybe ten minutes pass. It feels more like a half an hour, but I know she wouldn't take that long. It's just that it feels like an eternity every moment I'm not with her.

I people-watch while I wait, and the hackles stand up on my neck when I spot two familiar people walking toward me.

"Hey." I nod to Austin and Craig.

"Hey." Austin's hands are stuffed in his pockets. "How'd it go?"

It takes less than a second to understand his question. Between my clothing and Ryan running his mouth, they know. "Probation and community service. You?"

"Mine was last Friday and the same."

The silence that stretches between us is awkward as fuck, and it's Craig that breaks it.

"Can we go somewhere and talk?"

My gaze bounces between them and then back to the door leading to Kira's dorm. "I'm not sure right now is good."

Kira chooses that moment to step out, bag on her shoulder, and my eyes can't seem to look away from her. Austin and Craig both notice and turn to watch Kira, who's eyes widen and her pace slows as she approaches.

"Hi," she says as she tucks her hair behind her ear. "How's it going?"

"Good." Austin reaches out and pushes against her shoulder.

I watch some of the tension leave her, but not all as she looks between us. There's not going to be any fighting, at least physical, but I think she may be afraid there will be.

"My place?" I ask.

They nod in agreement and we all head to my car. It's a strained seven minute drive from her dorm to my apartment.

Once the door is unlocked, the buzzing in my veins kicks up in intensity. Austin closes the door behind him. The signal I need that it's safe to touch her.

I know they're here, but I can't stop myself. Grabbing onto Kira's arm, I pull her to me. She lets out a squeak, but wraps

293

her arms around my waist. I blow out a breath and sag in to her, nuzzling the top of her head.

My fix. A small hit to stop the vibrations consuming me.

It's not a show of ownership or to rub it in Austin's face. It's the need of her warmth, her skin to soothe me. To steady my rocky nerves.

Okay, maybe it is a small show of ownership.

There's so much going on, a delicate balance of so many pieces. So much at stake I can't make a single mistake, and the toll it takes on me and us only grows.

"Ssh, calm down," she whispers, her hand running up and down my back.

Did she know I was about to break in an opposing mixture of relief and panic?

I take a few deep breaths, then straighten out. There's a strand of hair attached to her lipgloss and I reach out to swipe it back. Her brow is furrowed, but relaxes as I caress her cheek.

"Thank you, baby."

The worried look doesn't entirely leave her facial features as she reaches up to my neck, tugging me down to her lips, which I'm all too happy to oblige. It's a light kiss, just a spark to get us through until later when we're alone.

But it's not, because I need more. I cup her face and part my lips. Force her mouth open with the same need I have and taste her, my tongue against hers. Devouring her for too brief a time before parting.

When I look up, they're both staring at us. I set my arm on her shoulders and pull her against my side.

After everything that happened between them and us, I can feel Kira's nervousness seeping into me. She's even having trouble looking at them after our display of affection. Not me. The history as well as the stigma doesn't affect me like it does her, which is why I'll do whatever she wants. I want her happy and comfortable.

The situation in front of us is neither.

"What did you want to talk about?"

Craig blows out a breath and walks over to my couch and sits. He looks more relaxed, but Austin's jaw ticks and he does a short little pace before sitting on the other end.

"This," he waves his hand at us, "is hard to see. I crushed on Kira for years, but I had no clue there was something going on between you two. Blinded by my own feelings, I never picked up on the undercurrent which is more than obvious now."

"None of us did," Craig says.

"That first fight . . . ." Austin trails off and shakes his head. "I thought you were just being protective, like I saw you do time and time again in school."

It's a fight I remember, but not very well. Red fury blinded me, drove each hit I pounded into his face. I walked away with a couple of bruises and some fucked up fingers, minor compared to the second beating I gave a guy who'd been one of my best friends.

"And?"

"Then I walked in on you two with Jenn." His eyes lock with mine.

Kira draws in a sharp breath at the memory, her eyes wide as she looks him straight on.

"And then you helped us get out, for some reason."

"Because I knew what was about to happen. You baited Jenn, fucking put a knife through her heart and twisted."

"There's no heart in that demented bitch." If she hadn't done all that she had, I might not be calling her that, but she chose to do it all. Chose to go head to head with me.

"I'm beginning to agree with you on that. I already filled Kira in on some of what happened after that, but there's more."

I glance down to Kira at this news. She didn't mention anything to me about it, but the last time I know that she saw Austin she wasn't really speaking to me. It shouldn't bug me, because she's standing with me in front of him, but it still does.

I'll always be a jealous motherfucker, especially when it comes to the only other guy she's had sex with.

"Jenn's more than just a jilted ex-plaything." Austin blows out a breath. "I don't know what happened, but she's become twisted and mental. I went back and stayed within earshot of her, listening as she spread rumors, both true and false, and all painting you both in a bad light. But what really got me was when she gushed to one girl about how you were going to be hers again soon."

"He wasn't the only one." Craig shifts in his seat. "She's gone completely deranged in this obsession of hers."

"Well, yeah, I knew that. I haven't touched her in years, but that hasn't stopped her from coming after me every time I've been within a hundred feet of her."

Kira's fingers dig into my side. "And this isn't anything new, so why are you here?"

"She's not the only one that's been watching you two. I have as well. Waiting for my opening, for you to fuck it up, and ready to console Kira with open arms when you did." Austin smirks and shrugs his shoulders.

"But?" I knew he was lying in wait.

"But that's not what we saw," Craig says.

"Shit, man, those tattoos alone tell me you're serious. And I kept my mouth shut about you two out of my own feelings for Kira. I don't ever want to hurt you," Austin says with his gaze locked on Kira. "And after the last few months I finally get it. There's this magnetism between you. And damn, man, you're lucky. I wish Kira looked at me with half the emotion she has in her eyes when she looks at you."

For the first time, I can't even fucking imagine that. Loving someone and watching them love someone else, being able to see it in their eyes.

"Brayden, I've only ever known you to be the womanizing, fuck all the girls who gives a shit kinda guy, and I was pissed at you." Craig leans forward and glances between me and Austin. "After what went down, I'd written you off, dead to me. Austin kept me from hunting you down. But then I saw you that day, and I watched you from the shade of that tree. You didn't see me, but I saw it all."

I wish they'd just get to the fucking point and get out. "Okay, you know about us. That was kind of obvious."

Austin jumps up from the couch. "Stop being a defensive fucker. We didn't come here to argue or fight."

"What did you come here for then?" Because now I'm really fucking curious.

"To let you know we're on your side," Austin says.

Kira's eyes widen as she stares at him. "What?"

"This is our olive branch, dude." Craig stands up and steps forward. "Put the shit behind us and leave it in the past. Get our friendship back. We've got you. You can rely on us."

"Seriously?"

"People will always talk shit, but that's all it is. Garbage."

It was only a few years ago they were like my brothers. The shit we got into was legendary and we always had each other's back.

I pushed them away. It was all me. Caught up in my own shit, drowning in my feelings for Kira. Not coming home for almost two years, all because I couldn't stand the void between us and the inability to have her as mine. A state away was easier.

In doing that, all of my friendships but Ryan fell into ruin. It wasn't the same, because I wasn't the same. All I cared about was dulling the ache in my chest with weed, booze, and girls on my dick.

I raise my arm and extend my hand out. Austin looks at it for a moment, then slides his in. We give a hard shake.

"Thanks, man."

I do the same to Craig. He takes a second to look between me and Kira and shakes his head. "I gotta ask . . . How long?"

The question is open, but I know what he means. I look down at Kira and run the back of my fingers down her cheek. "From the moment I saw her."

A grin spreads across his face and he nods. "Now that's something worth fighting for." He holds out his hand and I slap mine in.

"I've got a date, so I need to get going," Austin says as he makes his way to the door.

"A date?" Kira asks as she quirks her brow at him. A little smirk plays on her lips.

"Not that kind. It's with my project partner. Eighteen hours left until it's due, and we're really behind, so she's meeting me in the library."

"Damn, that's not a lot of time," Kira says.

"Yeah, she's hot, but useless, and I refuse to get a shit grade because she thinks she can fucking skate by with me doing all the work."

I swing my arm out and clamp my hand on his shoulder. "Put her ass to work."

I mean it in the sexual way and suddenly it feels like old times.

Craig pulls Austin back, a scowl on his face, but his lips are twitching up into a smirk. "Don't put fucking ideas into his head. He'll fucking trade a joy ride for work and end up doing it all himself."

Austin's face turns beet red and he glances at Kira. He shrugs. "It might happen. Until I find the next perfect girl, I gotta get off somehow."

Kira smiles back at him. "Wrap it up. Who knows how many other guys she's traded it for."

Craig's head tilts back, a loud bark of laughter bouncing off the walls. "Oh, Kira, damn girl."

I'm laughing as well, trying to hold it in at the look of utter shock on Austin's face.

Austin turns to me. "Got any condoms?"

I have to release Kira to pull out my wallet and search for the emergency rubber I always keep on me. Though I haven't needed one in a long ass time, it's just habit. I toss the foil package at him, which earns me a sharp elbow in the ribs.

"What the fuck?" Kira asks, her brow scrunched up in a scowl.

"Habit. And that's been in my wallet since January."

"And to avoid learning why it's been since January, I'm out." Austin waves to us and is out the door.

"Give us a call if you need anything or want to hang sometime," Craig says, following behind Austin.

Once the door is closed, I walk over and flip the lock, then turn back to Kira. "That was . . ."

"Yeah."

"But good."

She nods in agreement. "Allies are good."

I step in front of her and place my hands on her hips. "You know what?"

Her arms lace around my neck and draw me down. "What?"

"It's time to put *your* ass to work."

"Is it?" She runs her lips down my jaw. "What are you thinking?"

My heart is pounding against my chest, pumping blood through my body and making my dick rock hard.

"A little sixty-nine action. Those sweet lips wrapped around my cock and me eating the fuck out of your pussy."

"Mmm, that sounds good." Her hands move down my waist and pull my belt through the loop on my pants. "Then what?"

I'm kneading her ass cheeks. Pushing and pulling at them. Sliding my fingers between her cheeks, I push the seam of her jeans against her pussy.

"I'm going to fuck you."

Meet me at the library.

I stare down at my phone, fixated on the time.

Shit.

She sent the message over half an hour ago. My fingers fly over the keys, like each second counts.

Just got out of the shower, be there soon.

When I got home from the gym, I'd thrown my phone on the bed and jumped in the shower. It was longer than normal because I busted a nut thinking about the way Kira squeezed my cock when she came three times in a row yesterday.

It was fucking erotic as hell and caused a semi to pop halfway through my workout.

Studying didn't happen last night, which is where I'm certain her library idea came from.

It takes less than five minutes to throw on some clothes, but another five to try and figure out what's in my eye before ripping out my contacts.

In the living room, I pick up the books I need from the floor and coffee table, stuffing them into my bag and heading out.

After parking the car I shoot her another text to find out where she is. The library is huge. Four floors of a massive building with an open atrium.

She's on the top floor and I watch as the amount of people lessens with each floor I climb.

There's a long bank of tables, probably thirty or forty feet long. One guy at the end close to the stairs and Kira on the other end, hunched over a textbook, highlighter in hand.

"Hey," I say as I pull out the chair next to her and sit.

She blinks up at me. "You're wearing your glasses?"

I nod. "Contacts were bugging me. I think there's something stuck in my eye."

I can feel her eyes still on me as I unpack my bag. Book, notebook, pen, highlighter; ready to get my study on.

She continues to stare at me, but I return to my book and find where I left off. Twenty pages down earlier today, thirty to go, then I have a project from another class to work on.

Two pages in and I jump, startled at the feel of a hand on my leg. Slowly, I turn my head to look at Kira. She's focused on the book in front of her, highlighting a passage, but her left hand is under the table's edge and making circles on my thigh.

I say nothing, and return to my reading. I'm loving that she's unable to resist touching me. Scribbling notes and reading become more difficult though as she slowly works her way higher, making my dick twitch and grow in anticipation of her final destination.

It's fucking with my concentration and my writing. I look down to find my handwriting has gotten worse and apparently that my notes have moved in a direction I wasn't expecting. Scribbled in the last sentence is some gibberish of "cock in cunt."

There's a small smirk on her lips when I glance over again and her hand grazes against my now raging hard-on. I'm breathing heavier than I should be, but having to stay still while she touches me, to not react, is fucking torture.

Fuck, I got off in the shower to help keep me from immediately pulling her into a secluded corner of the library, and now she's begging me to.

And there are places. I scouted them out the first time I visited.

My gaze bounces all over the library to anywhere and anyone I can see. There aren't a lot of people on this level, and most are too absorbed in their own work to care that my girl is stroking my cock through my pants. There's a guy at the other end of the row of tables we're sitting at, but he's about twenty feet away and I've never seen him before.

Jaw locked down, trying to keep my breathing steady. My fists clench and unclench.

"Kira," I hiss between my teeth.

"Yeah?" Her voice is light, playful.

"You're going to make me come."

She moves her head to look at me and I let out a small groan at the fucking want pouring out of her eyes. "Good."

I shake my head. "Oh, no, you misunderstand." I turn and slip my hand between her thighs, grinding my fingers against her clit. She lets out a gasp. "I'm going to fucking drag your teasing ass over there and make a large deposit inside you. I'll let you choose pussy or mouth, but whichever way, you're going to make me come and you're going to take it all."

Now I'm not the only one breathing heavy and she hasn't stopped stroking me. A shudder runs through me, sparking a rush packing of my bag.

"Get your shit together." I groan when her hand leaves, immediately missing her touch.

My hands are all over her as I move us through the shelves. It's like a maze, but I know where I'm headed. In the back corner, the last shelf doesn't lean against the wall, creating a small nook in the corner of the building.

One more corner and as soon as I'm around I stop in my tracks, Kira bumping into me.

"Damn," I whisper as I find the spot I was dragging Kira to is occupied.

Not only is it occupied, but I can see Ryan's cock driving into Dana, pinning her into the wall with it.

"Oh, my God." Kira's eyes are wide as she sees a side of her brother I've seen too many times to count, but probably not for his sister's eyes. "I-I can't unsee this."

"Dude, they catch us and they're never going to let us come back."

"Brayden!" Kira swings her arm out, smacking me in the stomach.

That catches Ryan's attention and he flips us off.

I smirk down at Kira, my arm circling around her waist, grabbing her ass as I go. "See, baby, we're not the only ones."

Kira covers her eyes and turns, walking as fast as she can away from the low groans and pants of her brother and his girl. The shock of it all may have changed her mind, but that pussy of mine asked for it.

A few steps and I catch up to her and slip my fingers between hers and make a sharp right, dragging her with me.

She lets out a surprised squeak and tries to pull back. "Brayden?"

My lips twitches up into a smirk. "That's not the only place, little tease."

The perfect O shape her mouth makes tells me exactly how she's going to get what she asked for. Right between those full lips and down her throat.

Now to find the other spot on this floor.

TWENTY FIVE

BRAYDEN

October 26th 2015

Most of the time parking space is limited on campus or way out in the boonies where the distance is the same as if I walked from my apartment. Which is when the bus comes in handy. It picks up outside my complex and drops off at multiple places, including right in front of the lecture hall.

On Monday's, Kira and I both have a class there. Hers is in one of the giant rooms with five hundred seats while mine is in one of the smaller rooms with less than a hundred. It's probably less than fifty, but I haven't bothered to count. The great thing is they both begin and end at almost the same time, meaning I have thirty minutes to read while I wait for her to get out.

I rub at my eyes, blinking down at the text. It's only three in the afternoon and I could use a nap. Being our last class of the day, I'm hoping she's down for a siesta with maybe a little afternoon delight.

The workload for the night is as heavy as my backpack and I can use the recharge.

I hear it as I sit here. The whispered words. The school is huge, but the circle we run in is as well. There were hundreds of people at that party where Jenn showed Kira the video. Near a thousand, or at least close, where Jenn walked in on us.

It is a little bit of justice in my eyes. Fucking Kira like that, making it absolutely clear I am never going to be with Jenn. However, it had the added effect of people staring at us. People who don't know who we are, but know by sight thanks to Jennifer.

Even with Jenn slowing down as she's lost friend after friend, the gossip is already out there.

"If he was my stepbrother, I'd be fucking him as well," a girl whispers, though not as low as she thinks in the echoing hall.

"Erika! That's disgusting." The second girl's face scrunches up and she gives me a dirty look.

"Can you mind your own fucking business? Or are you that big of gossip whores? Because I don't even fucking know who you are and you're talking like you know shit when you don't."

I'm fucking tired and they're rubbing me wrong, souring my mood.

The girl, who I think is named Erika, blushes, her eyes wide.

"I-I'm sorry," Erika stammers. "She didn't mean anything . . ."

I stand from my seat on the floor and Erika's eyes wander up my body. It's a look I'm familiar with.

"That girl you're talking about is my best friend and has been since I was ten, which was long before she became my step sister. Jealous bitches who want my dick again make up all kinds of shit when they're clawing at one tiny little thread to get me in their bed."

The other girl is staring at me, seemingly unconvinced. "Then why is she saying this stuff if it hurts you as well?"

"She doesn't look at it that way. She sees it as taking out competition that she doesn't even have." There is no competition, there is only Kira. "Rumors are a trap. I can spread one right now that you two are lesbians. How the fuck would you feel about that?"

"It's bullshit."

I press harder. "Or how your Daddy gives it to you good when you go home."

"Shut up!"

"Doesn't feel good, does it?" I ask.

They both shake their head. "No."

"Then think twice about the gossip mill. It's filled with shit and all it does is cover you with shit. No guy wants a shitty girl."

"Hey." Kira's voice drifts over, causing me to look at her at her.

She's smirking and lifting brow, but there's a bit of a furrow and a cautious edge to her expression. "My brother is demanding my presence. Can you give me a lift?"

I smile down at her. "Sure." I wave at the girls one last time. "Don't be gossip girls. It's not a good look."

Leaving the building, it takes everything in me to keep from mauling Kira, because I know they're watching. All I want to do is fuck her right here all caveman style to show everyone the truth, that she's mine and I don't want any other.

"What was that all about?" she asks.

"Fucking bullshit Jenn rumors."

"I had a feeling. You did a good job dispelling them with those girls."

I scoff. "They were more interested in if it meant I was a free agent or not."

"Big fat no."

"And besides, I never said that the rumors were lies. I said they shouldn't listen to rumors. So what if some of Jenn's rumors are correct, she's a fucking cunt."

She lets out a little chuckle. "So wrong."

I nod in agreement. "Does Ryan really need you?"

"Nah, but it was a great excuse to be leaving with you."

I blow out a breath. "Good, because I need you."

"Do you now?"

I nod, my eyes scanning the bus schedule as I look down at my watch. There's a bus arriving any minute.

"I need a nap. Followed up by some Netflix and chill. Only no Netflix, just chill. And from the bed in the spooning position."

She lets out a sigh and shakes her head. "Just say sex."

"I like my way of saying it just fine."

"Idiot."

I smirk down at her. "Hey, I'm your idiot."

She shakes her head. "You're not right in the head, I swear."

The bus arrives and we get on. It's a quick ride, maybe ten minutes, and drops us right at the entrance of my apartment complex.

My apartment is in the back, and we make our way along with one or two of my neighbors. The mailboxes are grouped together, and I pull out my keys to check to see if there's anything. I've been checking it religiously every day since about day four after I sent the tests in. The wait is killer.

"What's your load tonight?" Kira asks.

"You mean besides the one I'm leaving in you?"

She swats at my arm. "Yeah, besides that one. Or two or three or whenever you collapse."

"High sex drive, baby. You get to reap all the benefits of my studness."

"Oh, my God, you did not just say that."

I pull her chin up. "Do you want this stud to breed you, Kitty?"

"You're so wrong in the head."

"You need more material. You already said that." I stop in front of the mailboxes and turn to her. "Or is it that I've gotten to you and your brain has stopped working because all you can think about is my cock in that cunt of yours making you scream out."

"Shut up!" Her face has flushed to a bright pink. "Freaking perv. People can hear you."

I glance around. "Who? There's nobody here."

"As I was asking that you had to turn dirty, what is your homework load?"

"Oh, homework." Turning the key, I open the door and pull out more pieces than I expected. Did I check the mail yesterday?

Her eyelids drop, her mouth as well, giving me that *really?* look.

I shut the metal door and return to our path as I finger through each piece.

"I've got about fifty pages to read tonight and . . ." I trail off. In the stack of mail is an envelope from a lab. From *the* lab that I sent the DNA test off to.

It's here. Finally.

"Brayden?"

I blink up at Kira before hastily shoving the envelope back between the rest of the mail. "Sorry. What were you saying?"

"It's not what I was saying, you were telling me about your homework."

I nod. "Right. So, nap, sex, food, then read fifty pages of boring. You?"

"I have a report due on Tuesday, so I'm going to have to spend some time at the library."

I groan. "Seriously?"

"Sorry, but you're kinda distraction central."

I throw my arm over her shoulder as we begin the rest of the walk down to my apartment. "Pot, this is kettle calling."

"Hey! You're always the one to start the shenanigans."

"Me? So last night when I was falling asleep on the couch and you pulled my cock out and woke me up by sucking me to attention, that was me?"

She purses her lips and refuses to look at me.

"Or last week at the library when your hand kept riding up my leg until you were practically jerking me off through my jeans."

"You started that one."

My mouth pops open. "I was innocently reading."

"Innocent my ass, you were wearing your glasses."

I smirk and scrunch my brow. "How was that starting it?"

She quirks her eyebrow at me before turning away. "You know."

"I do?"

"Yes."

"What? Because I really don't know."

She let out a little huff, her cheeks darkening. "Because you're sexiness triples when you wear them."

My lips twitch up into a smirk. "Really?"

She rolls her eyes and huffs. "Idiot."

"No, seriously, tell me more about my sexiness," I say as I slip the key leading into the building into the lock.

"You already have a huge ego, I'm not going to inflate it more."

"You're my girlfriend, isn't that something you're supposed to do?"

"I'll inflate your dick, but your ego needs no help from me," she says as we step inside and head up the stairs.

"You're not going to tell me how big I am? How you don't think it will fit?"

She rolls her eyes. "We had sex this morning, but that seems to be all you have on your mind."

I shrug. "I'm a guy with a dick that's always hard for you, what do you expect?"

"A little breather for my pussy to recover."

"So, you're ready for anal." I wag my brows at her.

She purses her lips, which is not the physical reaction I'm expecting. No swats or name calling. Just a flush of her cheeks and biting her lower lip.

Fuck, yes.

A first for both of us. The only one we have, and I'm more than ready.

October 30th 2015

"Again?" Kira asks in one of the most annoyed tones I've ever heard, clearly upset by my announcement of going to Indianapolis. "What happened to all that stuff about taking me with you each and every time after?"

"You just said you have a huge project you have to work on."

Kira huffs as she stands, her arms crossing over her chest. "That doesn't matter. It's Halloween tomorrow. What are you really doing, Brayden?"

"Mom's got a new boyfriend." It's not a lie. "And I'm going to meet him, size him up, but I'll be home in time for the party."

"Not meeting up with some girl you were doing at Purdue?"

"Jesus, Kira. Do you really think I'd fucking cheat on you?" How the fuck did we get back on this subject? I know she's trying to trust me and isn't fully there. Doesn't help that I keep hiding shit from her, but I don't want her involved in case something goes bad.

"You've cheated before."

I open my mouth to deny it, but then it hits me, like a punch in the gut. We didn't have sex, but I fooled around with Kira when I was dating Amanda. It didn't seem like cheating on Amanda, because the whole time I was with her, I felt like I was cheating on Kira.

Oh, fuck. "I never looked at it like that." My stomach turns. "How did you look at it?"

I stand, but that doesn't make the nausea any better. "Like I was in hell, being tortured by having the one person in the whole world I need so close, but unable to be with her."

My voice is strained, head spinning. I hate cheating. It's a horrible thing to do to someone you claim to love. It's one of the reasons I never wanted to fall in love, never be in a relationship.

As a child, I watched it destroy my family. I watched *him* destroy it. I vowed to never do it. Death was a better alternative. I gave my friends shit about it if they even thought of cheating on their girls. They looked at me weird, but they listened.

"Brayden, you're pale."

All strength leaves my legs and I fall down to my knees, my head shaking almost violently from side to side. Kira's in front of me, her hands burning as they run across my shoulders. She's speaking, but I can't understand her.

I grab onto her face with both hands. My vision is warped. Harsh breaths expel from between my lips.

She's worried. Not angry.

That doesn't help.

"Never."

"What?"

"I'll *never* cheat on you, Kira."

"Okay." Her response is only to placate me, to calm the panic attack that's taking over.

That's not what I want and need. She has to understand how much it is the truth.

"No. Not okay."

She nods. "Then tell me."

"Never. Never. I felt like I was cheating on *you* when I was with Amanda." I take her face in my hands, making sure she's looking into my eyes. "I was using her to make me forget you, but there is no forgetting you. There never will be. I'm yours forever. Completely devoted to you."

She blinks a few tears from her eyes as she nods. "I get it."

My muscles relax. There's no strength in me and my head falls down to her shoulder, hands to her thighs.

Jesus, this love shit is rough.

I thought she knew, understood, but I broke her so badly, I have to keep reminding her that she is all I want, all I've ever wanted.

"I still don't like all the secrecy."

I nod against her. "I'll tell you, soon. I promise. Everything."

I have to. The stress is too much and causing me way too many physical and emotional issues.

I could tell Kira was still a little leery when I left. She knows I'm hiding something, I told her as much, but hopefully my breakdown convinced her I wasn't cheating on her.

It really surprised me when she said that and the epiphany that ensued. She of all people knows my stance on cheating. When my parents were going through their divorce, Kira was the one I confided a lot of my inner feelings and fears in. She knew what I wanted from my life and knew why.

I never knew at that time that I was waiting for the perfect woman. She still had some growing to do.

How was I to know the seventh grader sitting next to me would become my whole world? I should have, because she was from the moment I first saw her.

When I pull up to Mom's house, she's standing outside waiting for me.

"Everything okay?" I ask as I jump out of my car.

She nods. "Yes. I just need you to drive."

"Okay. Why?" My gaze narrows on her.

"Because my car is in the shop."

I lean a little closer. "Because?"

Her return gaze is hard, before she gives up, realizing she's never going to win against me. "I was T-boned yesterday."

My eyes pop open. "What?"

"I'm fine." She waves her hand in front of me. "Really, just a little jolted."

"Don't you have a rental?" I ask as I look over her shoulder to the empty garage.

She shakes her head. "No. Tom's been driving me around."

I tense. "Tom?"

She rolls her eyes. "My boyfriend."

I don't like that she's dating a guy I haven't met. It's not that I don't trust her judgement, it's that I don't trust any man with my Mom. She deserves the world after being married to my prick of a father for so long.

"And when am I meeting him?"

She lets out a sigh. "Later. Come on, we have to get going."

As she climbs into my car, I see that it wasn't as small of an accident as she said. On her left hand is gauze, wrapped tightly around and moving up her wrist.

"What's that?"

She purses her lips. "It's just tweaked. I'll be fine in a few days."

"And the car?"

I back out of the driveway and make my way out of her neighborhood. She drove last time, but I've gotten to know my way around the area and it was a pretty easy path to Carrie's.

"It'll be back in a few days."

"And when is your next shift?" I ask.

"They gave me the weekend and Monday off."

I nod. "I should stay with you this weekend."

"Brayden, I'm fine."

"I'm not sure I believe that. How do I know you're not just placating me so I don't worry."

Her hand lands on mine and she squeezes. "So many years, and you were the only man who ever cared about me."

"I only have one mom, and she's kinda awesome and is one of two women I love."

"I know you two have had your ups and downs, and I'm also kind of biased here, but she's lucky to have a man who is as devoted as you are."

"If only that was enough," I say with a sigh. It's a fucking uphill battle for Kira to even consider looking at me like that.

She still hasn't told me she loves me, which causes me more anxiety than it should. I know she does, even if she doesn't say it. In the way she looks at me, the way she touches me, and in the way she wants to be around me as much as I want to be around her.

"The past is the past. It's part of you, but not who you are. You learn from mistakes and move on. Forgiveness and trust are hard to gain, but quickly lost."

"You've gone all spiritual kumbaya. It's like those sayings people have on painted wood hanging around their houses."

"Hey, I'm trying to impart valid words of wisdom here."

"You're a fortune cookie."

She gasps and swats me with her wrapped hand, then cries out in pain.

"That'll teach you to hit your child," I say

"Pain in my ass," she grumbles.

"I thought I was the light of your life."

"You are, but you're also a royal pain in my ass sometimes."

We pull up to Carrie's and I turn to her. "You ready?"

"It's not my life that's about to change. I'm just here for support."

We walk up and I reach out to knock. On the other side I can hear footsteps just before the door swings open. Carrie stands in front of us, and there are dark circles around her eyes and her smile doesn't quite reach them.

"Abby, Brayden, come in."

"Are you okay?" I ask.

She nods. "I took a second job a few weeks ago and it's third shift."

My eyes go wide. "What?"

"It's only fifteen hours a week, but it's from eleven to four in the morning."

"Are things that tight?" And how can I help.

318

She shakes her head. "Christmas is coming up and I want to start saving for it now. It's the only time I can spoil Emily, but it takes a toll on me for a few months. I've also got some car bills that popped up to pay off."

It irks me that she has to work so hard because of the asshole.

"Brayden!" Emily practically screams when she sees me. She runs full force for the ten feet that separate us before jumping and wrapping her arms around my neck.

A chuckle leaves me. I love her enthusiasm. "You should try out for volleyball with that kinda ground clearance."

We all sit, Mom, Emily, and I on the couch, Carrie on one of the sad dining table chairs. There's no need to drag it out. We all know why I'm here, and I can almost feel the nervous energy rolling off Carrie.

"I haven't opened it, I was waiting until I got here."

I know the results. They're obvious every time I even glance at Emily, but there's still that small thread of doubt in the back of my mind. What if Carrie slept with other guys around the same time? What if the story she told was a lie?

But she didn't start this process, Mom did. Carrie would have remained in this sad state, and I never would have known what my father did.

"Emily," I start as I pull the envelope from my jacket pocket, "do you want to read the results?"

Her head bobs up and down furiously as she rips the envelope from my hand. It's a struggle for her to get it open, and the face she makes with her tongue sticking out lightens the mood a little.

Papers out, she looks them over. It's hard not to peer over her shoulder and sneak a peek.

Her brow scrunches and she looks up at me. "I don't understand it."

My heart is hammering against my ribs as I turn the paper toward me. It takes me a few times of scanning over the words to process them.

"Well, Carrie, you are Emily's mother, and Mom, you're my mom."

"Tell us something we don't know," Mom says with a small smirk and a shake of her head.

"Hey, that's just the order they put it in."

And there it is. Weeks of worry, months of wondering, and I can actually feel tears burning my eyes.

"Brayden, please . . ." Carrie's practically shaking.

"There is a ninety-nine percent match."

A wail springs from Carrie as she falls to the floor, sobbing. Emily's brow is scrunched, her chest rising and falling with deep breaths as she looks at her mother breaking down.

"What does that mean?" Emily asks.

I remember reading the paperwork. Anything below ninety percent is deemed inconclusive and inadmissible in court. Meaning anything under ninety won't help us and it is all a waste.

But we're ninety-nine.

No room for him to debate.

"It means you're a Hunt."

"A Hunt?"

I turn to her, relief and disbelief and so many other things exploding inside me. "You *are* my sister."

A blinding smile covers her face as she leaps into my arms again. I wrap my arms around her and hold her tight.

My sister.

My baby *sister.*

Emily is my sister and now I have the proof.

TWENTY SIX

BRAYDEN

I tried my absolute best to text Kira while in Indianapolis. Time flew while at Carrie's house. The whirlwind of the results set us all into a tailspin and the next thing I knew, we'd been there for six hours.

When it was time to head out to meet mom's boyfriend, I texted Kira to let her know.

I also text her a few more times while out to dinner with mom and her new boyfriend.

I wanted to focus more of my attention on getting a read on him.

Kira was taking her sweet time responding to my messages and I immediately knew what it meant.

I can't blame the girl for not trusting me. I'm convinced she loves me, but every time I see her near Austin I want to knock them both upside the head for being close to each other.

My past isn't one that I'm proud of. I wish I could say I had my fun, and in a way I did, but the whole time I was running.

Consumed with an ache that followed me wherever I went.

There's only so much fun you can have under those circumstances. So the reality is simple: I did what I did, caused her and others an untold amount of pain, left one mentally unstable bitch obsessed with me, and carry the stains of my past with me.

In the end, it was all for nothing.

Nothing.

I just wish there was a way that Kira could see inside me. Then she wouldn't have to live with this mistrust.

I know I'm not helping the situation with my secrecy. She'll know eventually. All of it. Just when it's over. When all the cards are on the table.

I had dinner with my mom and her boyfriend staring mostly at my phone the whole time. Like the junkie I am, my leg bounced under the table, my body vibrating with the anxiety of no contact.

How the hell did I ever go a year without speaking to her?

Each reply took her nearly an hour to send.

When I tried to call her, she didn't pick up.

So here I am, driving home at two in the morning, when I know damn well that I'm not going to be able to get into her dorm at this time.

If Kira doesn't answer my calls, I won't be able to get her to come down.

And that's *if* she's even home.

I'm already at my exit coming up on the school, when an idea hits me.

I drive past campus to my complex and pull into the closest spot to Ryan's apartment I can find at this time of night and take off running to his door. He lives on the first floor with Dana. Dialing him, I start ringing his doorbell like a maniac at the same time.

"That better not fucking be you ringing my doorbell like that."

"Get out here," I say, tapping my foot impatiently on the floor. *Tap. Tap. Tap. Taptaptaptaptaptaptaptap.*

A perfect echo of my rampant heartbeat.

Ryan flings his door open in a pair of shorts he probably pulled on when I started knocking. His hair is a hot mess. There are claw marks down his chest. A huge bite mark on his neck.

I envy him that. My Kitty has to be careful where she marks me. They can't be visible, because people have to be judgmental and can't mind their own goddamn business.

"Give me that." I snatch his cell out of his hand.

"What the—"

I hold my finger up to silence him, hang up the call with me, and dial Kira's number.

She picks up on the first ring.

And I hear what sounds like traffic and people laughing in the background.

"Hey Ryan, what's—"

"Where are you?" I ask.

She falls silent on the other end.

"Kira, don't make me look for you. Because I will."

"Oh, my God. *Fuck you.* You don't get to talk to me like that after how you've been acting."

She wants to fight.

Okay. Fine. But we're doing it face to face. "I'll track you down. I swear to fucking God I will."

She hangs up on me.

I let my head fall back and take a few deep breaths. Breaths that sound more like growls.

"What the fuck is going on?"

I ignore Ryan's question. "Please ask Dana to find out where Jenna is. She's probably with Kira."

It's a long shot, but it's also a start.

Ryan takes his phone from me. Shaking his head, he heads back into his apartment. I stay out here, keys in hand, ready to fly like a bat out of hell to that woman.

He comes back less than five minutes later. "Dick's Den. And you're going to tell me what the fuck is going on between you two. I'm not blind!"

He's calling after me from the doorway because at this point I'm already at my car.

The only reason I don't speed? Nothing in this world is going to get between me and Kira. Especially not some cop.

Kira's standing outside the bar with Jenna when I pull up. Jenna sees me first and her eyes widen at the sight of me.

Kira turns to see what she's looking at just as I slam out of my car. The outrage on her face is almost comical. "What the fuck? You don't control me!" She stomps her foot to emphasize her point.

"You're done drinking," I snap, partially because it's true, but also for show.

She takes a few steps backward away from me. "I'm not going anywhere with you, you asshole! And fuck Ryan for telling you where I am."

I bend down and lift her up unto my shoulder.

Kicking, hissing, and screaming, but I get her on there.

Jenna steps forward. "Brayden, maybe you should chill with the *big brother* display."

She's trying to hint that we're making a scene and people are watching.

As if I'm not aware.

"Good night, Jenna." I open the back of my car, throw Kira into it, and close the door before she can scramble out.

She tries to open the door.

I'm already holding down the button to keep the doors locked.

Glaring at me like she hates me, she slaps on the window.

I ignore it and head back to the driver's side. Using one hand to hold the key and the other to continue pressing on the button, I open the driver side door and hop in.

Kira tries to open the door.

I take off without even putting on my seat belt. *Now* I'm speeding. I have my cargo and I don't give a fuck about anything but keeping her in the back.

She might want to kill me, but she's not jumping out of a car going full speed.

"I should fucking slap you!" She kicks the back of my seat.

"Yeah? I should fucking spank the shit out of you. Now calm the fuck down."

She kicks the back of my seat again. "You're such a typical man. You can do whatever the hell you want. Lie to me. Leave me hanging. But when you want me to heel like a fucking dog, I'm supposed to just give in."

"That's not what this is about!"

"Open this goddamn door!"

"No!" I need to calm the hell down. I know that. But she isn't going anywhere and she better start understanding that.

All the stress of the last few months is thrumming through my veins. The tension is too much. The last thing I need is to fight with her.

"Let me out of this car, Brayden."

That deceptively calm tone isn't fooling me. "No."

She tries swinging at me.

I catch her arm mid-air without turning my eyes from the road. "I'm not fucking cheating on you."

Her foot presses to the back of my seat and she uses the leverage to try and get her arm out of my hand. "I wish I could believe you!"

I tighten my hold on her arm, driving with one hand. "It breaks my fucking heart that you don't."

"Do you think you can just lie to me? Hide things from me? That you can leave me behind whenever you feel like it and it's not going to be suspicious?"

"What you really mean is that a whore like me can't change his ways." We're almost at the house at this point. I just need to get her in there. Everything else can be figured out once I've secured her by my side.

"Who the hell told you to be such a whore then? Oh, wait. Your cock had complete control back then." She pulls with all her might and I have no choice but to let her go. Either that or hurt her arm.

"Not as much as it has now." Stay calm. I remind myself. I'm already hurting. With the whole shit about Emily, my mind is fucked up.

Now Kira doesn't trust me and although I don't blame her, she's killing me with this.

"Like I'm supposed to believe that?"

"Are you fucking kidding me?" I yell back at her, my temper hanging on by a leash. I'm not really angry at her; I'm just pissed at this entire stupid situation.

At the travesty of who my father is.

"Have you not noticed how insatiable I am when it comes to you?" I ask her in a calmer tone.

"You've always been insatiable when it comes to sex!"

Now I know the girl is drunk.

Drunk and spoiling for a fight.

And if she doesn't stop and listen to me, I'm going to end up giving it to her.

God help us.

I park back in the same spot I'd taken twenty minutes ago. As soon as I'm out the car, Kira is out the car as well.

Only she's not walking toward me.

She's walking in the direction of her dorm.

"This is the last time you'll ever try to leave me," I vow to her and myself in a low voice.

Then I'm running.

By the time Kira hears my pounding footsteps, it's too late.

I've got her. "Enough. You love me. I love you. Stop this shit."

She falls limp at my comment.

I sigh with relief and head inside. She's over my shoulder again, and I can't see her expression.

I open the door to my apartment and walk inside.

Kira starts crying, small almost silent sobs.

The sound of them kills me every time. And *I'm* the one responsible for them almost every damn time I hear them. My chest tight, I put her on her feet.

She shoves me back hard enough that I stumble backwards into the door. "How dare you throw me loving you in my face after lying to me for weeks?"

It's the closest she's come to admitting out loud that she loves me.

Whatever elation bubbles up is killed by her next words.

"Maybe you're not cheating on me, fine, but the mere fact that you're shutting me out and lying to me about things shows me that you're never going to change."

I stare at her, jaw unhinged, disbelief scrambling my brain.

She starts walking away from me, farther into the apartment.

I push off the door and follow.

Kira stops near the couch and starts pacing, as if working off extra energy. "Why am I even bothering to build something with you and change my beliefs about you, when you're still engaging in the same behavior that tore us apart in the first place?"

"*Are you fucking kidding me?*" Now I'm yelling. At the top of my motherfucking lungs.

My neighbors are going to hear this fight and I don't give a damn.

My yell startles her and she freezes mid step.

"You know I've changed for you! I've done everything to regain your trust!"

She snaps out of her stupor and comes up to me, slamming her finger into my chest. "You're such a fucking liar!"

"What is wrong with you?" I snap in her face. "Are you looking for an excuse to leave me?"

"You're giving me those all on your own!"

My hand snaps around her wrist, and I hold her so tight I know it's hurting her. "You're not fucking leaving me again. Do you hear me? I love you too fucking much to let you go."

"Oh really? Then why the secrecy? Why the lies?"

"I told you I would tell you—"

"Why the fuck did you suddenly lock me out of your phone?"

Her shrill yell pierces some of the angry haze covering my vision.

That's what set her off.

Why she's full-blown paranoid now.

Kira moves faster than I can keep up. In what seems like one smooth move, she yanks her wrist out of my loosened grip and manages to get my cell out of my pocket.

Everything slows down.

The phone is still locked and she doesn't have the code, but I never changed the notification preview on the lock screen.

And it's lighting up.

Something's coming through.

I try to reach for her and the phone. She runs away, stopping by the other side of the couch, and I see the fury in her eyes multiply.

"When can I see you again? *Emily*?" Her voice is shaking. She's shaking. Her entire body is a maelstrom of vibrating pain, so potent that it reaches me all the way over here.

Emily.

My little sister.

The one my mom and I chipped in money to buy a phone for and put it under my mom's plan.

The need to yell those words at Kira is drowned out by a brutal reality.

She truly does think I would cheat on her.

Someway, somehow, I've failed to show her how obsessed with her I am. That there would never be anyone but her.

Either that, or her wounds are too deep to ever heal. To ever allow her to truly trust me again.

The stress of the last few weeks explodes inside me. Every fucked up aspect of my life roars into my heart at once, igniting a rage that frightens the shit out of me.

"Who. Is. Emily? Answer me." Kira let's my phone drop onto the couch.

I glare at her, and I'm aware that I'm probably staring at her like I hate her.

Right now, I think I kind of do.

"What the fuck else does a man have to do to prove to you his love?" I whisper to her and even to my own ears the words sound menacing.

Kira grabs the lamp off the end table and flings it into the wall. "WHO THE FUCK IS EMILY?"

"MY FUCKING SISTER!"

She gasps.

I don't care. Fuck her shock. Stomping up to her, I grab her and pull her to me as I sit on the couch, laying her across my lap, her groin just above mine.

"Your *what*?" She tries to lift her body off the couch.

I refuse to let her, already reaching under her to pop the button on her jeans.

Kira squirms in my grip, trying to get off.

I lower her zipper, slam one hand down on her ass, and grind my fully swollen dick up into her.

Another gasp.

Just like that, the anger melts out of her.

Good for her. I'm still raging.

I pull her pants roughly down over her hips and take her panties with them.

"Wait a second—Brayden! What are you doing?"

What we've been both dying for me to do. The only thing that can hopefully calm me the fuck down.

I slap one perfectly round ass cheek, hard enough to make it sting.

Kira inhales sharply. "What the fuck?"

As pissed as I am, I still take my time rubbing the cheek I just spanked, making sure the sting melts into pure heat.

One deep breath and I have to let my head fall back with a groan.

I *smell* her. Rising up from that juicy pussy. Getting wetter with every second I rub her.

Fucking hell, this girl's scent is powerful. Drugging. I've never been with another girl whose pussy smelled this good or whose scent could be smelled from this far.

I spank her other cheek just as hard.

This time, she can't hold back a little moan.

"Yeah. This is what you fucking want." I still sound angry—I am *beyond* livid with her. With everything. Tone harsh, I growl, "You want me to punish your annoying little ass for doubting how much I love you."

"Br-Brayden. Wait."

I spank her again in another spot. I've been researching for weeks. Learning the best way to spank someone so they don't end up bruising. Distributing the spanks in different areas of her ass is the key.

I land another three spanks. Don't know if she's shocked, horny, or both, but she's utterly still, the only movements are those that come from her gasps and her round butt jiggling with each spank.

Pausing to let her ass adjust, I caress the bright pink flesh and admire how fucking sexy that looks.

Kira whimpers, her hips rotating. "What are you doing?"

"I told you. What you want me to do." I slide two of my fingers down to rub her hot, slick pussy lips, collecting all that sweet honey.

She cries out, trying to get me to fuck her with my fingers.

I'm going to.

Without warning, I slide my fingers up her crack and slide two of them straight into her tight ass.

TWENTY SEVEN
BRAYDEN

She comes.

Instantly.

No friction on her pussy.

Just two of my fingers deep in her throbbing ass.

Head thrown back, she mewls, her fingers digging into the couch.

Everything throbs.

I can feel her pussy squeezing, calling for my cock, through the thin barrier of skin separating it from her ass.

My dick jumps, trying to push through my jeans.

I don't remember sliding my fingers out of her. Standing up. All I know is that right now, I'm practically ripping her jeans off her. Her shoes.

Her shirt is still on but I don't care.

My pants land on the floor. My shoes are already gone but I don't remember taking those off either.

Kira lifts herself up onto her knees on the couch and tries to turn.

I grab her hips, holding her still, and sink down on the couch behind her. One pull and she's positioned over my jutting cock, reverse cowgirl.

"Brayden—*fuck*! Wh-what?"

I spit down on her ass and rub the head of my dick into that tight, pink asshole, prepping it. "It's time. You're giving me this."

"But—"

I line up with her pussy and slide in, cutting her off as I wet my shaft, lubing it up. I've been using toys on her for weeks. Dildos close to my size.

She's so fucking wet my dick is shining when I press against her puckered ass. I pull her down and thrust up in one move.

Despite her protests, she relaxes and bares down to take me in, just like we've practiced.

A desperate cry leaves me as my cock slides halfway in.

It's the tightest fucking grip I've ever felt.

Her thighs are shaking, her ass clenching, choking the ever living fuck out of my dick. "*Oh God.*"

"Mm-hm," I groan, rotating my hips in circles, watching that perfect, peach of an ass stretch around me and take me deeper. Jesus. I'm not going to last. It's too good. Too tight.

Kira rotates her hips to take more of me, like the perfect little cock whore. Her pussy's so wet it's dripping onto my balls. "That feels. Oh fuck. I can't. Yes, baby. Yes. Fuck my ass."

I growl like a motherfucking psychopath behind her, my balls drawing up into my body.

335

Too fast. The come's rising up my dick. I have no control over it. "It's mine. No one's had this. Only me. Always me." I'm rambling. Shaking beneath her. Frantic.

Kira nods, her gorgeous hair sliding up and down her back.

"Ride me faster, baby. Take what's yours."

She does.

Holy . . . *fuck me* . . . she does.

I don't know if it was all the preparation we've been doing the last few months, or if she's just that desperate for my dick, but she bounces on my dick like a fucking pro, taking me into that sweet ass over and over.

I shake beneath her. Fist her hair in both my hands. Try to regain control of this.

Struggle to fucking breathe.

But I'm lost in her. "You're not giving me a fucking choice." I spank her ass hard, loving how it jiggles around my dick. "Taking my come from me so fucking hard."

Kira mewls, sinking her hand between her legs and playing with her cunt. "Yes. Yes. Fuck me, *yes*!"

I do. Faster. Harder. The only thing that's stopping me from coming is my ego. The need to dominate her. Make her come before I do. "Say my name." I push my dick deep into her ass and stay still for a few seconds, letting her feel it throb inside her.

Her hips move in impatient circles, no doubt to the same rhythm she's strumming her swollen clit. "Brayden."

I reward her with a thrust. She quivers all around me. "Say my fucking name again."

She does, her high-pitched moan ripping a groan out of me.

I lift her off my dick, hissing when her tight ass almost refuses to let me go.

She cries out, sounding heartbroken that I've taken this cock away from her.

Chuckling, I ease her forward and rise up on my knees on the couch. Then, I'm sliding back in, working past the tight ring of muscles until half of my dick is in.

"Yes. Fuck yes. I'm right there. Oh my God, it's amazing!"

I slap her hand away from her clit and slide two of my fingers into her cunt.

Kira seizes, entire body locking up, on the edge of coming.

So I refuse to move, leaving both my dick and my fingers inside her, letting her feel how full of me she is. "Say my name again."

"Fuck you!" she cries, tearless sobs of mind numbing frustration jumping out of her.

"Bad girl." I spank her ass with my other hand, watching the blood rush to the surface.

Her back bows, her body milking my dick and fingers. "Please. Why did you stop? Oh God, *please.*"

"This pretty ass wants to come all over my dick?" My eyes are locked on her pink, juicy skin stretched around my engorged dick. I wish I could see what her pussy looks like, full of my fingers while I stretch her ass with my cock.

"Yes!"

I slide out slowly, seeing how swollen all the veins on my shaft are. "How bad?"

Kira tries to thrust back, recapture me before I can slide out. "Bad!"

"Whose ass is this?"

"Yours, you asshole!"

"And whose pussy is this?" I vibrate the palm of my hand against her clit.

337

"Yo-yours."

"And who does this dick belong to?" I thrust the tip shallowly into her, teasing her sensitive opening.

"Mine. Fuck, it's all mine."

"And you know that now, don't you? You'll never have the nerve to doubt it again, will you?" I growl, wrapping her hair around my fist.

"Mine. All mine. Mine," she mumbles mindlessly, thighs shaking.

"Then scream my fucking name. Scream it loud enough for the neighbors to hear you!" I thrust my dick into her, the movement forcing her to ride my fingers, and yank her hair back until her entire back curves.

My name starts leaving her on a scream—then she chokes, coming. Coming so fucking hard that all sound gets stuck in her throat.

I feel it.

Holy shit, I *feel* everything.

Her ass.

Her pussy.

All that wetness.

My voice cracks, and pure fucking pain explodes through every nerve ending in my body.

Come shoots hard out of my dick, flooding that sexy ass, and all I feel is that wetness growing, her ass squeezing tighter.

"I love you. Oh God, *I fucking love you*!" I scream, pushing her down into the couch with my hips, rutting against her ass like a madman.

It's good. So good. I never want it to end. Need more of this. My balls are beyond empty, but my dick is still hard.

Feels like I'm still coming. My come covers my dick, her ass, I see its stickiness with every thrust.

"Brayden—I'm—shit, coming again. Coming, baby."

"*Ahhh, fuck*, woman." I let my head fall back, still fucking her, feeling pressure building. Building.

Shit. Again?

What seems like a mini-orgasm pulses through my dick, and I fall on her, hips churning, lungs burning.

I can't breathe.

Worse, it sounds like she can't either.

Somehow, I find the strength to slide out of her and roll over—

Right off the couch.

What little bit of air is in my lungs whooshes out of me on impact.

"Oh my God, Brayden!" Kira sounds exhausted and drunk. She rushes to lean over the couch, staring at me worriedly.

All I can do is lay here, on my back, my wet dick laying across my thigh, and pant up at her.

Her worry melts away and suddenly she's laughing down at me, her eyes shining with love. "Are you okay?"

"Are—are *you*?" I wheeze, realizing what I've just done.

Namely? Fuck my girl in the ass like a barbarian, even though it was her first time.

She struggles to stand, her legs shaking. Halfway through she gives up and just sinks down to the carpet next to me. "I'm fine. I think. My legs don't seem to be working." She smooths the hair away from my forehead. "Brayden . . . I'm sorry."

"You better be." I glower at her, still hurt and angry that she'd thought I was cheating on her.

"Your sister?" she asks, the worry returning to her eyes. "What do you mean your sister?"

I just fucked her in the ass, and now she wants to talk about Emily. That's so wrong, yet I have no choice but to come clean. At this point, not doing so is going to cause even more problems for us.

Struggling to catch my breath, I sit up. "My father had a daughter twelve years ago that no one knew about until her mom walked into the hospital my mom works at and Mom saw her resemblance to me."

Kira's jaw unhinges and she just stares at me in shock.

"I've been following him for weeks. Trying to catch him cheating on your mom. That's where I've been going. And also to visit Emily and her mother so we could do a DNA test and prove she's my sister."

She covers her open mouth with her hand, horror dawning in her expression.

"It gets worse." I really want to get up, drag her to the bathroom, clean us both up, and crawl into bed with her. Finish the conversation there. But now that I'm confessing, it's like a floodgate's opened and I can't shut the fuck up. "Emily's mother . . . she's my dad's cousin. He roofied her and raped her at a family event."

Kira drops her hand. "No. No, no. My mom. No." Her head shakes back and forth, and she stands up suddenly.

I follow her and grab her by the arms before she can pick up her phone. "Kitty, what are you doing?"

"My mom. I have to be the one to tell her. She's going to be ruined."

"You can't, Kira."

Her eyes snap to mine. "What?"

I take a deep breath, praying she isn't so caught up in her worry for her mom that she won't see reason. "Emily is twelve. It happened a long time ago. No police report was ever filed against my father for the rape. It's his cousin's word against his. Your mom is obsessed with my dad. She's dependent. This won't be enough to get her to let him go."

Kira steps back away from me, her eyes searching mine. "That's why you've been stalking him. To catch him cheating. It's the only thing that's truly unforgivable in my mom's book."

Even though she was my father's mistress. I'm not stupid. I see the hypocrisy in Sonia's thinking.

But it is what it is.

I swallow nervously and nod. This is it. The moment I'm forced to face her censure for the path I've gone down.

"Brayden . . . I need you to tell me the truth now. All of it."

I nod again eagerly. I'll do anything as long as she doesn't turn away from me.

"I'm going to ask you something."

"Anything," I say.

"Were you the one that sent that video to Jennifer's parents?"

Fuck.

My girl's smart.

Too smart.

Why the hell did I ever think I could hide anything from her?

"She kept fucking with you—with *us*."

She exhales slowly. "So you've been on this vendetta against Jennifer, a mission to get your father out of my mom's life, and had to deal with learning of your sister."

341

What is she thinking? I hate when I can't read her. "Yeah .
. ."

"And you just decided to hide this from me? Oh my God, did Ryan know this whole time?"

"No! I was trying to protect the both of you."

"Protect us?"

I pull my jeans back on and walk to her. "Yes. Some of what I'm doing is technically illegal—"

"Yeah, I know. It's called *stalking*."

Is she ashamed of me? Disgusted? I can't fucking tell. "Exactly. And I didn't want to drag either one of you into it."

"You're fresh off legal trouble and you undertook this on your own? *Are you crazy*?" She pushes at my chest, her face flushing.

Wait. That's what she's worried about? She's not disgusted at my behavior?

Kira hits my chest again. "How many fucking times in our lives am I going to tell you not to shut Ryan or me out?" She walks away from me and starts pacing, as usual when she's agitated. "We're your fucking family. I don't understand why you always, *always*, have to try to handle everything by yourself."

I fucking love this girl. Intent on kissing the breath out of her, I start walking toward her.

She doesn't even see me coming. "I mean, I know you think you're Superman and shit. The almighty, invincible Brayden, but I—"

Smiling, I grab her and lift her up into my arms. "I'm not almighty. Not when it comes to you."

She pouts up at me and suddenly I'm very aware that she's still naked from the waist down. "We can't be in a relationship if you're constantly hiding things from me."

"You're right." I pause mid step to the bathroom, shocked at how much I mean that. "Shit. You're right. All I do is push people away every time I try to deal with something on my own."

"Exactly!" Kira slaps my shoulder and crosses her arms with a huff. "I know I need to bust my ass to learn to trust you, but you're not helping matters hiding things. And it's not good for a relationship. I mean, you're my first one . . ."

I smile down at her and if she had been looking, she would've seen the stupid lovestruck look on my face. "And you're my first one, too."

Her wet eyes stare ahead. "No I'm not."

"My first *real* one, Kira? Yeah. You are. That shit with Amanda was a farce."

She clearly doesn't believe me, but she moves on. "Anyway, I'm pretty sure hiding secrets from each other isn't healthy for our relationship."

I resume walking to the bathroom. "You're right and I'm so fucking sorry. God, Kitty, sometimes I think you're a better person than I can ever be."

Another huff. "That's right and don't you forget it."

I chuckle at her pissiness. She's adorable when she's like this. "I promise to never hide anything again." It goes against my self-defensive mechanisms, but I'll find a way.

"Seriously Brayden. Swear it. And bust your ass to keep that vow."

"I will, Kitty. I will. I swear it."

TWENTY EIGHT
BRAYDEN

I follow the car in front of me in my rental. I'm probably tailing him too close. Fuck it. I won't run the risk of losing him. I have the GPS tracking him, but I'm not thinking clearly.

The fight with Kira really fucked me up.

She was right. God help me, I'm an idiot that keeps fucking things up with my good intentions. She's my girl. As much as I want to protect her, my first obligation is to be honest with her.

Our relationship won't survive if I'm not.

But now she knows. She's in on it. She's being eaten alive by the possibility that, after everything he's already done, my father is also now cheating on her mother.

She knows that my little sister is also my cousin. First cousin once removed.

All this twisted shit is in her head, doing to her what it's been doing to me for weeks.

344

I didn't want that for her. I wanted to shield her until the end, at least. Once I had sent the proof of his infidelity to her mother and he was on his way out of the picture.

If Sonia actually leaves him.

It's not the first time the thought occurs to me. I refuse to entertain it for more than a few seconds, because her not leaving him isn't an option.

Even if Kira and I move somewhere no one knows us, barring changing our legal names, it's only a matter of time before the truth gets out. And if we have to live with the stigma of being together and being stepsiblings, we might as well stay here and deal with it on the home front.

Kira reassured me that her mother has made it clear— everything is forgivable but infidelity. Yes, he cheated on my mom with her, but I think Sonia was convinced he was the great love of her life. But if my father cheats on *her*, it's done.

Let's hope she's strong enough to stick to that.

My father takes a right turn. I slow down and let him get more of a lead. I've followed him twice before.

The first time, he went into a corporate building and I couldn't follow him in. Not without alerting him to my presence.

The second time he went to a hotel. The Crowne Plaza in downtown Cincinnati. I hurried to park so I could follow him in, but by the time I did he was nowhere in sight.

No way to find out where in the hotel he'd gone. I staked out the exit of that hotel for hours. When he finally came out, he'd exited on his own.

I know he was with another woman in there. I *know*. But I need photos of him with that woman. Without that concrete proof, the sneaky bastard might talk his way out of any accusation.

Just in case, I still took those photos of him leaving the hotel.

Don't think it's lost on me how sick my life has become.

I have a little sister I didn't know about, that's lived a life of struggle because my father wouldn't acknowledge and provide for her.

A little sister that is the daughter of my first cousin once removed. My father's cousin.

I'm stalking my father, breaking at least five different laws to do it.

I'm also desperately trying to hide from the world that my step sister is my girlfriend.

My life has always been dysfunctional, but fuck.

Although I've already made up my mind. If Sonia doesn't leave my father, and Kira tells me she can handle it, we're going to openly be together. Whether that means moving or not.

My father makes a left turn up ahead. I'm praying at this point. I'm not a religious person. It's hard to be one when you grow up the way I did, but I don't completely refute the existence of something out there.

If it is, I implore it to listen now. I'm not an innocent motherfucker by nature, but Kira and I *are* innocents in this. I've done my wrong, way more than she's done hers, yet our parents getting married is something neither of us should have had to go through.

For what? My father was going to fuck that marriage up anyway.

So I pray, and I pray some more, hoping against hope that this time I'll catch him red-handed. That I'll get what I need.

My father makes the turn into the parking lot of the Deerfield Town Center, and my heart starts drumming with hopeful excitement.

There's no hotel here. No corporate building. There's just a bunch of stores here, and a ton of restaurants. *The Rusty Bucket. Firebirds.*

Open places. Nowhere to hide.

It could just be that he's here to buy something.

I squash that pessimistic thought down. This has to be my moment to catch him. It *has* to be.

I pull into a parking spot the moment I see one, letting my father drive ahead so he won't see me. He parks right in front of *Firebirds.*

I scramble to get my Nikon ready just in case. Holding it up to my eyes, I squint through the lens and zoom in on him.

He exits the car.

In his hands is the largest, most ridiculous bouquet of flowers I've ever seen.

I start taking pictures instantly. Then, I turn my car back on and hurry to find a parking spot that's closer to him.

I don't want to miss a single thing.

As soon as I'm once again parked, no more than thirty seconds later, I have the camera back in my hand.

He walks to *Firebirds* with that cocky swagger of his, the bouquet held at his side.

We're so close to home. Close enough that someone who knows him can see him. Please tell me he isn't this arrogant.

Actually, scratch that. I need him to be. This is the kind of stupid ass mistake I've been waiting for.

He approaches the outside tables, seeming to head to one in particular.

A pretty, young looking brunette lights up at the sight of him.

My stomach turns. She doesn't seem much older than Kira.

Her hair is more toward the brown side, and from here her eyes look brown or hazel.

But the resemblance . . .

THAT PIECE OF FUCKING SHIT.

I remind myself to breathe.

To not slam out of this car.

To not walk up to him and use the very heavy camera in my hand to end his life.

To not drive my car straight into him.

That sick, twisted, worthless waste of skin!

Oh God. He's fucking a young girl who looks like *my* Kira.

There's no outlet for my anger. It rises up my throat, unvented, choking me. I swallow back wave after wave of acidic bile, feeling like a snake swallowing its own poison.

I shouldn't be surprised, and I desperately need him to fuck up right now.

Doesn't change that there's a voice in my head begging him not to be *that* low. He's in his late forties. That girl looks no older than twenty.

She looks like my girl. The stepdaughter he judged me for sleeping with. The stepdaughter that lived for years under his roof.

She stands up, eyes glittering at my father with all the foolish, young adoration of a naive little girl who has no idea she's inviting Satan into her bed.

He swoops down on her, crushing her to him, and devours her mouth in plain sight.

My finger abuses the button, taking shot after shot.

I'm on autopilot. A sickened spectator to this man's utter depravity. My hands are sweating and I'm struggling not to shake as it occurs to me what this is going to do to Sonia.

He's not just cheating. He's doing it with a girl young enough to be his daughter. A girl that looks like *her* daughter.

Sonia is about to find out he had a daughter with his cousin.

She deserves a life without him, free to hopefully find the right man for her.

But this? I wouldn't wish this on anyone. And I also wish I didn't have to do this. That she'd gotten out of the marriage on her own long before now.

No one gets between me and Kira anymore. If there is a God, may it forgive me because this has to be done.

My father sits to have his meal with his pretty young thing. Flirting. Caressing her. Making out with her in public like he's also a young, horny teenager.

I'm still taking shots. So many that my finger is cramping up.

I don't stop. Fuck that.

At one point I switch over to recording mode and record them for a few minutes. When my father gropes her, tonguing her mouth like he wants to fuck her right on that table, I want to throw up.

They enjoy their meal for almost two hours before they stand up to leave. I push my chair all the way back and lower it, struggling to hide my large frame.

It's not necessary. My father is too engrossed in that girl to realize anything around him. They get into his car together and I'm tailing him almost immediately, too reckless in my haste to be patient.

Less than five minutes later he pulls into the back parking lot of the Hyatt.

I slam the car into a spot right across the street, not caring anymore if I'm spotted. I just need one shot. One picture of him going in there with that girl.

It occurs to me he might go in through the back entrance.

Shit. Shit. Shit!

I hurry to drive around to the back parking lot and get in there in time.

Such a stupid mistake. I could be losing my chance.

I grab the first spot I see, luckily with a view of the doors leading inside. My hands are so sweaty that I almost drop the camera.

My father doesn't disappoint. Hand in hand with the girl, he walks to the entrance. Once there, he turns around to swoop her up against him again. I can't hear them from this far, obviously, but I can tell she's giggling.

Without even thinking about it, I switch the camera back to record mode and hit the button.

And then they're making out again. My father is groping her ass. Grinding his hips into her.

That's it. I got all I need. I don't have to be here anymore, the bile choking me.

I can't tell if I'm having some weird version of a panic attack or a suppressed anger attack.

All I know is that he's literally about to fuck that girl first chance she gets, and *she looks like my Kira.*

They finally break apart and head inside.

I drop the camera into the passenger seat and cover my face with my sweating, cold hands.

I got it. After almost two months of planning and stalking him, I finally got what I need.

All I have to do is go home, upload this onto a USB, print the pictures, and slip all of it, along with the DNA results of the paternity test in an envelope.

There's no feeling of triumph to be found. I want to kill that man. Honest to God, I want to storm in there, while he's probably mid-fuck with that Kira lookalike, and remove him from the face of this Earth.

In the back of my head, I realize that this shit isn't healthy. He deserves what I feel, but it's not normal for anyone to walk around their whole life despising one of their parents this much.

Eventually, I'm going to probably have to see someone about this.

Eventually.

Right now, I have a really fucked up phone call to make. I have to warn Kira. My girl needs to be prepared for what her mother is about to go through.

So does Ryan.

Heart heavy and a sick feeling in my veins, I turn the ignition and head out of the parking lot, aching over what this information is going to do to my girl.

TWENTY NINE
BRAYDEN

I've calmed down.

I've calmed down.

If I repeat it enough to myself, I will calm the fuck down.

I'm in my apartment, pacing back and forth, waiting for Kira and Ryan to come.

Because I'm about to show them those pictures.

The video.

Shame chokes me. You would think I'd be used to it by now. That years of my father's bullshit would be the norm. I should be inured to this.

I'm not.

Disgust sits heavy in my stomach.

Destructive rage messes with my impulses.

Hunt him down.

Break his face.

End him and his nasty existence once and for all.

I'm angry he's cheating on Sonia like he did to my mom. I am.

But that girl? The young one he's cheating with? The one with the brown hair?

Her eyes aren't gray like Sonia's.

I zoomed in on the images. Was able to see enough of her to know—her eyes are definitely hazel. Not the golden-green mix my girl and Ryan share, but fucking close enough.

It's a for sure thing. My father isn't sleeping with that girl because she reminds him of his wife when she was young.

He's sleeping with her because she reminds him of *my Kira.*

I already punched several holes in the wall. It's a miracle my neighbors didn't hear. Either that, or I got lucky and they weren't home at the time.

They're there now. I heard them come home an hour ago.

I have to remind myself not to decimate that wall anymore.

He wants my woman. Somehow, he hid it all this time. But for years Kira lived there, under his roof, without the protection of either me or Ryan.

He could've done anything to my girl.

Anything.

I was so busy running from Kira that I left her alone with that monster.

The doorbell rings, pulling me from the shit in my head. I head straight to the door, wishing there was some way to spare both of them this.

Kira's standing outside with Ryan. She was hanging out with Dana and her friends, and Ryan volunteered to pick her up.

Something about my expression makes both of them frown.

353

"How bad?" Ryan asks.

I shake my head. "You have no idea." This is going to hit him the hardest. I know it is. He's extremely overprotective of his baby sister.

If I had been anyone but me, I would have never been allowed to date her so easily.

They both walk inside.

I grab Kira and press her to me. Kissing her is the only thing I can think about. The only thing that centers me.

It isn't anything more than a sweet, close-mouthed kiss but I needed it anyway.

Not that I don't want to devour her. I do. But how do I do that when she's about to see my father mauling a girl that looks like her?

I pull away from Kira. She cups my cheek, looking at me worriedly.

Reading me.

Like she always does.

Like she's always been able to.

"What's wrong?" she asks.

"It's bad," is all I can say.

"He's definitely cheating on my mom."

I nod.

"With who?"

This time I shake my head. I can't answer that. It's better to just let her see it for herself.

Well, not better. But necessary. I promised not to hide things from her anymore. To be completely open about everything.

Grabbing her hand, I silently lead her in. My body revolts with the force of my shame. Self-disgust. Not for the first time in my life, I wish I could reach inside me and rip out the half of his DNA I inherited.

I urge Kira and Ryan to sit on the couch.

The camera is connected to the TV. It's on. All I have to do is press a button on the camera and the video will play.

I lift the camera off the TV stand.

And freeze.

I can't do it. Can't do this to them. It's bad enough that man is my father. How can I, his son, bring something this heinous to their attention?

"Brayden?"

The sweet way Kira says my name makes me look over my shoulder at her.

One look. That's all it takes. A single reminder of why her mother needs to leave my father. Of why this is needed for us to ever be truly together.

"It's bad," I repeat, eyes bouncing between her and Ryan.

"Play it," Ryan says in that infinitely calm tone of his.

Swallowing, I step aside so I'm not blocking the screen, and do as he asks.

I started recording as soon as my father exited his car. And it's a short walk to the outside seating.

It doesn't take long for the girl to come into view.

Ryan's foul curse hisses through the room.

I can't look at him. I can't. He's my best friend. He's been better than any best friend could ever be. Forgave me for hurting his sister. Forgave me for lusting after her.

Forgave me for being with her.

Now my father does *this*.

Kira takes longer than him to react, but when I hear her sharp intake of breath, I instantly seek her out.

Her mouth is hanging open. Her eyes are glazed with tears. Furious tears. I know her well enough to know the difference.

I drop the camera on the carpet. Didn't even notice. Don't care. I kneel on the floor before her and place my hands on her knees.

The video dies out behind me.

Kira's eyes are still glued to the screen.

"Son of a bitch!"

My brand new lamp goes flying into the wall.

For a second, this is so out of my depth of experience that I think I've imagined it.

"THAT FUCKING SICK BASTARD, I'LL END HIM!"

My end table flies across the room next.

Kira jumps to her feet. "Ryan!"

Ryan is no longer Ryan. He's nothing like the guy I grew up with.

A tornado of pure murderous rage barrels down on my flat screen.

In seconds, it will be nothing more than broken pieces on the floor. A poor stand-in for my father.

Kira slams into Ryan, her feet dragging across the carpet. "Ryan, stop!"

He almost doesn't listen.

And that's what finally slaps me out of my apathy. He's far gone. Lost. Turned into something I never expected or recognize.

I rush to them.

He comes too suddenly, blinking down at his sister.

There are tears streaming down her face. She begs at him wordlessly. Shakes her head once.

"I'm going to kill him." His voice vibrates with the force of his barely leashed fury.

Kira cries harder. "Oh God. You mean that."

"I do."

The scariest part of that statement? Ryan sounds like himself when he says it. Calm. Collected.

Decisive.

I approach him and put my hand on his shoulder. It's a sad fact that I expect him to jerk away from my touch.

My touch. The touch of my father's son.

He doesn't. Turning his head, he stares at me with a calm facial expression and blazing eyes. "How can you stand it?"

"What?" I ask.

"Being his son?"

"I don't. Sometimes I can't breathe. It disgusts me," I say in a low tone.

More tears fall down Kira's cheeks.

"We need to get your mom away from this," I tell Ryan.

He's breathing slow, trying to calm himself down. "Yeah. Let me call her."

"No," Kira and I say together.

"What?" *Now* Ryan shrugs out of my hold, his agitation returning. "I thought the whole point of this is to get my mom out of that asshole's life!"

"It is. But Steve can't find out Brayden is involved with this. We don't trust him. Some of what Brayden did is illegal. If Steve wants, he can press charges on him," Kira says.

Ryan runs a hand down his face. "Shit. Didn't think about that."

I did. For months, that knowledge followed me. My freedom was on the line with every move I made.

It's still on the line now.

Ryan goes to sit back on my couch. "So how are we doing this? And how fast?"

"Have to plan it right—"

He interrupts me. "Brayden, get that man out of my mother and sister's life before I fucking kill him."

It's chilling hearing him say that in such a calm, assured tone.

"I have to anonymously mail this video and the pics to your mom. I'll have to go outside the city, maybe Lima, and send it from there." Wearing a hoodie and glasses and praying that's enough to hide my identity.

Just like I did it the first time, when I mailed that video to Jennifer's parents.

Ryan shakes his head. "Whatever post office you go to, there'll be cameras."

I divulge the hoodie and sunglasses part of my plan.

"Not good enough. Let me do it."

Kira and I gape at him.

"Absolutely not." He glares at me but I continue regardless. "I'm not letting you put yourself in danger to do this."

"I'm not the one with a recent arrest on my record."

Damn it, he has a point, but him or Kira putting themselves in any kind of legal danger was never part of the plan. "I don't like the idea. When I came up with this plan, my intention was to keep you both out of it. *Safe.*"

Ryan and Kira shake their heads at me, their stubborn expressions identical.

It's times like this that they seem more like twins than regular siblings.

"Either Ryan does it, or I do."

I glare at her. "The hell you will. You are definitely staying out of this."

"Then my brother does it and that's final."

I want to kiss that raised, stubborn chin as much as I want to spank her.

Ryan stands back up and stops in front of me. "Get everything ready. We're leaving. Now."

Jesus. He's in even more of a hurry than I am.

And that's saying something.

Not that I blame him. "Fine."

He rushes out of my house while I unplug the camera from the TV.

"Going to get a hat and hoodie. Meet you back here with Dana. I'll have her get her car."

We're taking Dana's car instead, too.

Shit. I don't want him involved with this. *I don't.*

Kira comes up to me. I didn't even realize I'd frozen in the middle of disconnecting the camera. She must read my facial expression because she caresses my cheek lovingly. "It's the only way, Brayden."

"If something happens . . . if my father decides to investigate who followed him . . . if he presses charges—"

"It'll fall on Ryan. We both know that. It's a chance we have to take. And Ryan won't get hit as hard as you. You already have a recent prior. A prior that's all *my* fault."

It's mine, actually. I will never condone her sleeping with Austin, but I've come to realize that him caring for her the way he does must have helped her get through what I did somehow.

She should have picked someone else.

A selfish part of me wishes she had never picked anyone at all. That she'd waited for me.

But the entire thing went down because of one person—*me*.

I pushed her away.

I left her hurt and vulnerable.

I left her open to Austin's advances.

He couldn't help but fall in love with her. I of all people know that better than most.

And it was I who couldn't deal with the reality of both of them together.

Shit, I can't even blame him for not backing off right away. Look at me. An entire world seems to be standing between us, and even that's not strong enough to keep me away.

"What happened between you and Austin, and what happened later on between me and him, is all my fault. I'm also not ready to stand back and let you or Ryan put yourselves in legal jeopardy."

Kira stares at me with a tender but almost shocked expression. "Jesus, Brayden. You really . . ."

"I really what?"

Blushing, she drops her hand from my cheek and blushes. "Nothing. You just grew up into the man I always knew you'd be. You were always such a wise little fucker, even when we were kids."

I can't help but laugh and bring her closer. Inhaling her hair, I hold her to me, scared as hell of what's about to happen once this video makes it into her mother's hands. "You mean I grew up, period."

She shakes her head against my chest. "You always had such a big, good heart. Aside from your dad, you really did

360

see the best in everyone sometimes. Even the people you shouldn't have given chances to."

She means Jennifer. I'd considered her a friend for a while there. Not my best friend of course. That role was already taken by Kira and Ryan. But Jenn? Yeah. I'd cared for her. As a human being and nothing more. I shouldn't have fucked her again after our first time together.

Fuck. I'm probably to blame for the road she's taken. I thought being friends with benefits with her from time to time was cool.

"I disagree with what you said, though." Kira pulls back to stare up at me. "The Austin thing is my fault. Stop shaking your head at me. It's true. And the other part? About protecting us? We're a motherfucking team. We always have been. Stop with this flying solo crap. Every time you try to do that, it backfires. Want to know why? Because it's not meant to be that way. It's meant to be all of us. You, me, Ryan—"

"I hope I count in there, too."

We turn toward the door at the sound of Dana's voice.

Ryan must have left the door open.

She smiles sheepishly at us. "Just saying. I'm down for whatever as well."

"Dana," Kira says in a serious tone. "Said it before. I'll say it again. I think I fucking love you."

Dana does this goofy little dance and fist pumps. "Score! I'm in."

I turn to Kira and pinch her chin so she'll look at me. "And *I* love *you*. More than anything. For-fucking-ever."

Her eyes water but she smiles at me. "And I love you, you stubborn, sometimes irrational man."

361

I've waited so long to hear that I go weak. Cupping her face, I try to control my breaths and stare into her eyes. "Say it again," I whisper in a hoarse voice.

She gives me a teary smile. "I love you."

Closing my eyes, I let that sink in for a moment. "Again."

Giggling, she complies. "I love you, Brayden Hunt."

I crush her to me and kiss her like I want to eat her. Don't give a fuck if Dana's watching. Hearing that just made every problem in my life so much easier to bare.

I don't think it's ever going to be enough. "I'm going to need you to tell me that like fifty times a day, baby."

Kira giggles again against my lips.

"I love seeing the two of you happy, but we have to fucking go. Mom needs to be free of that bastard." Ryan is at the door, zippering up a black hoodie and adjusting a black ball cap on his head.

"Give me a few minutes. I need to burn this onto a DVD." I rush to my laptop and do just that, making sure to drop the pictures into it as well.

"Type up something for her. Tell her to please play it, or something like that."

I almost jump at the sound of Ryan behind. "Jesus, fucker."

"Do it." He has no patience, those hazel-green eyes focused on my laptop screen.

I do as he said and hand him the DVD once it's done. We exchange a silent, tense look, almost an acknowledgement of sorts, and head outside.

Kira comes up to me and holds my hand the entire way out.

She holds my hand on the hour-long drive to the post office we picked to send this from.

No one says anything.

No one can.

The heaviness of our purpose is almost suffocating.

And when Ryan slips on a pair of sunglasses and heads out to mail the package, we can't do anything but watch him go.

THIRTY
BRAYDEN

Kira's fingers are wrapped in my hair, tugging and pulling as she holds a molasses cookie in front of my mouth, just out of reach.

"Yes, Kira, that's how you get him to do whatever you want," Mom says in the background where a phone rings.

We're at her house.

I think.

It's also my Dad's house, at least the pool.

Kira's on my lap, wearing nothing but a skimpy little pink bikini and grinding down on my cock. I push my hips up into her, but it's not close enough.

The phone rings again.

My eyes snap open. *Shit. I was dreaming.* Groggy, I reach over Kira for my phone that's lit up on the night stand.

"Hello?" My voice is gruff and I rub my eyes before looking at the clock. It's 1:27 a.m.

"Brayden, it's Mom."

I shoot up into a sitting position. The move tosses Kira off my arm and onto her back, waking her with a confused start.

"Are you okay?" I ask into the receiver.

"What's going on?" Kira asks as she sits up next to me.

"I'm fine. Is that Kira?" Mom asks.

I nod, my mind still sleepy even with my adrenaline spiked jolt of panic. "Yeah, she's here."

"Good. I need you to grab her and Ryan and get down here as soon as possible."

"What is it?" My blood runs cold.

"It's an emergency. Just get in the car and call me once you're on your way down."

"Down where?"

"Bethesda North at Arrow Springs. The hospital in South Lebanon."

The adrenaline spikes back up and I know. Suddenly I know.

I'm halfway off the bed and flip on the light. Kira cringes as I throw clothes at her. "We're on our way." I hang up the phone and turn to her. "Get dressed."

"What's going on?"

"I don't know, but we need to get Ryan."

The mention of needing Ryan sends Kira into the same panic I'm in. It takes two minutes to put on whatever clothes we can find, slip on some shoes, grab our coats, and lock the door.

There is only a block down to Ryan's, but his apartment is on the way out.

I'm shaking, because I know what happened. Almost a week has passed since Ryan mailed out all the information to

Sonia. A week of all of us waiting on pins and needles for a call from her or some way of knowing she received it.

And this is it. A worried, frantic call, but not from Sonia, from my mother.

That tells me everything, because my worst fear came to fruition. The same darkness, the anger, which is in my father is in me. It's not hard for me to imagine what he's done.

He hurt Sonia.

And it's my fucking fault.

He's been sitting on the edge, holding it back for years, and I've been waiting for the explosion since I was a kid. I just didn't even think about the consequence of him unleashing it on her.

Back out of the car, I start slamming my fist on Ryan and Dana's door while Kira presses on the doorbell.

"Motherfucker!" Ryan yells when he swings the door open, but the anger evaporates when he sees the serious expressions on our faces. "What's wrong?"

"Get dressed, we have to go. Now. Get Dana and let's go."

"Babe?" Dana walks out of the bedroom wearing one of Ryan's shirts.

He glances between her and us. A pained look crosses his features and I can almost see the gears working in his brain. "You have your presentation at eight, right?"

Her brow scrunches and she nods. "Yes. What's going on?"

Leaving the door open, he rushes past her and into the bedroom, coming out thirty seconds later dressed and hopping on one foot while he puts a shoe on the other.

"Family emergency. You stay and do your presentation, and I'll give you a call when I know what's going on."

"I'll go with you."

He shakes his head and reaches out to cup her face in his hands. "It may be nothing while that presentation is seventy percent of your grade."

Dana's arms fold over her chest. "Ryan, don't do that. We're talking about family. I'm part of your family, right?"

"Baby, you're one of my three favorite women in the world, the three members of my family."

"Ouch, man, way to burn."

Ryan rolls his eyes. "And the dipshit over there." He pulls her closer and kisses her. "I'll call you as soon as I know anything. Just make sure you get your presentation done, okay?"

Her mouth forms a thin line and she relents, nodding in acceptance. "Drive safe."

Fifteen minutes from the time my mom called, we're loaded in my car and peeling out of the complex.

"She could have come with us, you didn't have to stop her," I say as I turn onto the road that leads to the interstate.

"No." He shakes his head. "If we're about to commit murder, I don't want her associated with that."

Ryan is thinking the same thing I am. It's the only reason all of us would be going.

And if we're right, then he means what he says.

After his reaction to the video, the beating my father is about to receive might not be one he can walk away from. Who knows what that means for us, but there's no going back now.

"What did your mom say?" Kira asks from the backseat. I hand my phone back to her. "What's the password?"

I never got around to changing it. "My favorite number."

367

In the rearview mirror she's giving me that "really?" expression. If it wasn't such a high strung moment, I'd tease her, but it's not the time.

"4-13-97."

She types them in as I say each number, but looks back up in the mirror. "My birthday?"

I swear tears start to form in her eyes, but it's hard to tell from the dim reflection in the mirror.

Wasting no time, she pulls up the call history and seconds later, the phone starts ringing.

"Brayden?"

"Hi, Mom."

"Do you have them?"

"Yeah, we just got onto I71."

"Abby, what's going on?" Kira asks, the anxiety of the situation leaking out into her voice by a little wobble.

There's a sigh through the speaker. "I'm at the hospital with your mom."

"What happened? Where's Steven?" Ryan asks and I can feel the anger start vibrating off him.

"I don't know where he is. Your mom called me at eight and asked me to come out. It took just over two hours to get to the house, and when I got there I found her on the living room floor."

Kira's face crumples up, tears streaming down her face. My knuckles are white on the steering wheel and I want to pull over to comfort her, but there's no time to waste and by the murderous look on Ryan's face, I don't want him driving.

"Is she okay?" Kira asks.

"I had to call 9-1-1. It . . . she was struck. Multiple times."

A sob breaks from Kira's chest, her free hand covering her mouth.

"She's awake now and they're doing some tests, but I can't go in with her for a lot of them because I'm not family."

"Was it *him*?" Ryan hisses between clenched teeth.

"I don't know."

"How do you not know?" He explodes, making us all jump.

"Calm down, man," I say to myself as much as him. Nothing would please me more right now than beating in my father's face with my fist.

"Don't fucking tell me to calm down. You know it was him, just as much as I do."

I glance from the road to Ryan. Never in all the years I've known him have I ever seen him as angry as he's been these past two weeks. Not even in the times he exploded on me was it this strong.

Kira's hand slips between us on the armrest, reaching for her brother. "Ryan, please."

That calms him. Seeing the distress of his sister drains the anger out of him to a manageable state for now and he takes her hand in his.

"Steven wasn't in the house when I got there."

I freeze and stare out the window watching the stripes on the road swish by. "Was his car there?"

"No."

Which means he's in his car. The car that I haven't taken the GPS tracker out of yet. I hope it stills has some battery left.

"Kitty, pull up the Optimus app."

"The tracker you put on his car?" Ryan asks.

I nod. "It's still in there."

Kira's reflection shakes back and forth. "It hasn't moved in four days."

I slam my hand on the steering wheel. "Damn."

"You're not going after him, Brayden," Mom says.

"Not right now, but that doesn't mean I can't sick the cops on him."

There's commotion in the background, a bunch of voices, and one familiar one. It's not her usual tone, but it's unmistakably Sonia.

Both Ryan and Kira let out a hard sigh, their bodies slumping in the seats with relief.

"How close are you?"

The interstate is three lanes, and we just passed the outlet malls. "About twenty minutes." It's actually thirty, but I'm going to get us there in twenty.

"Okay, we're still in the emergency room area. They might transfer her to the main campus."

"Thank you, Abby," Kira says with tears shining in her eyes.

"Oh, sweetie, I'm just happy I can help."

Kira hangs up the phone as I press down harder on the accelerator until we're past ninety. At this time of night, the road is empty, nothing but semi trucks and farmland.

The Arrow Springs location is a small hospital, but is the closest emergency room in the county to the house. From past experiences I know they can't handle severe trauma, which is a good sign for Sonia's condition. However, Mom did mention they may transfer her.

As soon as we're out of the car, Ryan and Kira are running through the automatic doors. When I catch up, Ryan's already at the intake desk.

He's impatient. Kira, too.

"What was the last name?" the woman behind the desk asks, not even fazed by the panic of the three of us.

"Roth. Sonia Roth."

I wind my fingers in with Kira's. She doesn't look at me, but her grip is crushing. Fear and anxiety ripping her apart. Hearing her mother's voice helped for the remainder of our drive, but amped up when we got off the exit.

The woman picks up a phone and calls back. "The family of Sonia Roth is here . . . uh-huh . . . okay." She hangs up the phone and hits a button, a loud click sounds from the double doors. "Go through there and take a right. Someone will be waiting for you."

Kira pulls on my hand and we break through the doors into a wide hallway. Thirty feet later, Mom appears in front of us.

"This way," she directs us, wasting no time.

We follow behind, walking past a line of draped-off areas and into a hall with doors lining either side. At the fourth door on the left, she turns, and Kira lets go of me to run to her mother's side.

"Mom!" Kira cries, throwing her arms around Sonia's shoulders. Ryan follows, swallowing the two of them up.

It was just a glimpse before she was covered up, but I saw. Sonia's arm is wrapped up from hand to elbow, and there's a patch of gauze taped to the side of her forehead. Multiple bruises are forming on her face and neck and beneath her eyes.

I feel like an outsider, like I shouldn't be here, because it's my fault this happened, but a huge sigh of relief leaves me when I see her awake and alert.

"Don't blame yourself, Brayden," Mom says beside me, her arms circling my waist.

Somehow, she knew exactly how I'm feeling. Her words don't hold any comfort, though. My stomach is still tangled in knots.

"Are you okay?" Kira asks Sonia as she smooths out the hair around her face, inspecting her damage.

It's then they notice her arm.

"What happened?" Ryan asks.

I step closer to hear until I'm at the foot of the bed.

"I . . . I'm not really sure."

Mom steps forward. "She suffered a pretty severe blow to the head that caused a concussion. Memory of the attack is often foggy, but there's a chance it will come back."

Sonia looks up at Kira and Ryan, who are both sitting on either side of her on the bed. "I don't remember what happened, but I do know I was having a fight with Steven."

"What about?"

She shakes her head, her brow scrunched as she attempts to recall the memory. "I received a file this week, evidence of so many wrongs. Illegitimate children, affairs, and lies. And . . ." she looks at Kira and reaches out to cup her face. "I couldn't believe the twisted things I saw. I called Abby after I went over it all. Steven wasn't home, late again per usual, and I knew this time, the fight was going to be bad."

"Why did you call Abby?" Ryan asks. "If you knew it was going to be bad, why didn't you call me or Kira? We're your children, not your husband's ex-wife."

I want to jump to my mom's defense, but I understand what he means. Why someone you're not even friends with over your own family?

372

"Because I needed a witness, someone who's been in my position and could give me the strength I needed to confront him and not back down. Ryan, if you were there you would have gone to jail, and I wasn't going to let that happen."

Ryan gets up and paces. "It's too fucking late for that, Mom. He fucking raised a hand to you, and I can't stand for it." He stops in front of me, his hazel eyes alight with destructive energy, staring at me as he holds out his hand. "Give me your keys."

I shake my head as I stuff my hand in my pocket and wrap my fingers around them. "No, man. You're too worked up." Odd that I'm the calm one right now, but I think that's the guilt weighing me down. "Stay here, your mom needs you and you haven't even talked to the doctor yet." We're face to face, his jaw locked down, nostrils flaring. I shake my head. "Don't make me shut you down."

"Like you'd be able to fucking stop me right now."

A hand presses against my chest, pushing me away from Ryan. I let Kira toss me back, taking my place as her small fists pound against her brother's chest.

"Stop it! Just stop it, please!"

She's shaking, sobbing against him, and I watch his face morph into a tortured mess.

"I need some air," he says as he cups her chin and kisses the top of her forehead before storming out of the room and down the hall.

Kira's still crying, her fists clenched over her eyes as she experiences what I went through for years. Something I never wanted her to even witness let alone experience in her family.

"Ssh, baby, it's okay." I fold my arms around her and pull her close. I don't even care that it's in front of Sonia, because I suspect she's known for a while. Glancing up at her and the forlorn expression on her face tells me I'm right.

Ryan comes back half an hour later, calmer and in control. His gaze bounces over me and Kira, who's in my lap as we sit on one side of Sonia's bed, then to his mother. He takes a seat on the other side of her and wraps his hand around hers.

"How are you feeling? What hurts?"

Seems he's returned to some semblance of rationality.

Before Sonia can answer, the doctor comes in. "Ah, I see your family has arrived. Good, good." His gaze bounces around. "Unfortunately, I need only family right now."

I nod and move to stand, putting Kira on the ground when Sonia's hand clamps down on my arm.

"This is my stepson."

The doctor looks between me and Kira and nods in acceptance, and we return to our position.

"I'll be right back," Mom says. I hate that she's being excluded from this.

"Abby, wait," the doctor calls out, stopping her. "You're her nurse, aren't you?"

She smiles up at him and places her hand on his arm. "Thank you, Robert."

"So, I have some good news and some bad results. First, your arm isn't broken, but there is a possibility of a torn tendon that will need an MRI to determine and a possible surgery to fix."

"Was that good news or bad?" Kira asks.

"A bit of both. The bad is whoever attacked you gave you a nasty concussion and we're going to transfer you down to Bethesda North for observation and that MRI. Depending on how it goes and what your results come back with will determine the next course and when you might be able to go home."

The word home drops a heavy weight on the room.

That house is not a place she should spend another night.

It isn't a home. It's a prison created by my father.

A control measure.

It's time Sonia broke out.

The sun is cresting over the horizon by the time Mom and I get to the main campus of the hospital where Sonia is being transferred. We followed behind the ambulance that houses Sonia, Kira, and Ryan the entire way, but we're forced to break off, heading to visitor parking while the ambulance moves to the entrance.

"I need you to promise me something," Mom says as we walk into the hospital, linking her arm around mine.

I don't want to promise her anything, because I know what she's going to ask of me and I don't know if I can keep any agreement.

"You know I can't do that."

"Okay, then at least promise me you'll try hard not to kill your father and to keep Ryan from doing it as well."

"I'll try, and I'll try to keep Ryan out of trouble, but I've never seen him like this. He's always been super protective of his family and seeing everything my father has done . . ."

"Just try. And I also want you to stop blaming yourself. I expected to see you fuming with anger, but instead I can almost see the weight of your guilt resting on your shoulders. Sonia will be fine."

"She will be, but what if he didn't stop? What if he left her there hoping he hit her hard enough to kill her?"

"Your father is a son of a bitch, but the last thing he wants to do is to go to jail. He probably left right after to form an alibi."

"Did he know you were coming?"

She shakes her head. "I doubt it." Her mouth opens wide, a loud yawn escaping.

"You should get some sleep."

"I'm fine, and the same could be said about you three."

We get to the doors right after they've wheeled Sonia in.

Dad's insurance must be good, because she gets her own room, complete with a reclining chair for guests which I plan to take advantage of soon with Kira. There are a few other chairs, and once she's settled in, we wait for her new doctor.

Before we left the Arrow Springs location, the police came by to get a statement from Sonia and Mom after detailing the crime scene.

Kira, Ryan, and I left the room, or rather, I forced Ryan out of the room before he exploded again, and we went to find some coffee.

The adrenaline wore off long ago, and the need to sleep is creeping in. While there is a place we can crash for a few, it also isn't a place any of us want to go. In fact, I plan to ask Kira to pack up the rest of her stuff and we can store it in my apartment, or at my mom's, just so she never has to go back.

Sonia is awake, though just as tired looking as the rest of us. The new nurses take her vitals and are gone almost as quickly as they came.

"We need to get you moved out of that house," Ryan says.

It's something I'm sure we were all thinking, but the room had been so silent, it almost felt like he yelled it.

Sonia nods. "Abby and I were talking about that before you arrived and, after speaking with the police, she's offered me a place to stay for a little while."

We all turn to stare at her in surprise

Kira sits on the bed next to her. "In Indianapolis?"

"It's far, but safe, and she can look after me, take me to doctors' appointments for the next week or so until the doctor clears me to drive."

Sonia wasn't going to press charges, because she didn't remember anything and was afraid. However, Ryan insisted it and my mom was able to explain to her in a calmer way that it would be best for her. The police haven't been able to locate him yet.

Who knows whose pussy he spent the night in?

I look over to Ryan and he's got that lock on his face, the contemplative one. Weighing the options and using that ever-reasoning brain of his, he sighs and nods in agreement.

"We'll go get your stuff packed up." Kira says.

I nod as I sit down. "We can rent a truck and a storage place and get it all out, just tell us what you want where."

377

I'm trying to let the guilt go, but that leaves room for the anger to seep back in, and I can feel it taking control again. I keep clenching my teeth, my jaw locked down, my free hand wrapped around the armrest, squeezing it.

There's a storage center off 741 and 42 that's twenty-four hours and climate controlled. I pull out my phone, looking up the nearest U-Haul location. A small truck should do us.

Sonia's brow scrunches. "Is all that necessary? I was thinking just a suitcase for a week or two."

Ryan shakes his head. "Brayden's right. We need to get all your stuff out of there so you aren't near him alone ever again."

"We can get all of Kira's out as well." There, I got it out for her to hear.

Kira looks back at me, her mouth pops open to say something, but stops as she takes in my agitated state.

It's happening. Everything I wanted. Sonia away from him. Kira away from him.

But the price was too high.

And I'm going to make him pay even more now.

THIRTY ONE
BRAYDEN

"Why are we leaving her there?" Kira asks as we pull out of the U-Haul rental.

Ryan's behind us, driving a truck. We loaded it with packing boxes and cloth to protect the furniture, everything we need to store things.

I place my hand on her thigh and rub circles with my thumb. "Because the crisis is over and we need to handle this for her. To make sure she's safe."

Kira bites at her thumbnail, her brow furrowed.

It took Sonia practically throwing her out to get Kira to come with us. We need her though, we need all three of us, but especially her.

She's the only one that can calm us down if we lose it—our clarity.

I don't know what's waiting for us at the house. What evidence of the attack. What the police left behind.

"Okay," Ryan starts as he slams the door to the truck. "This is going to be fast and dirty. We'll clear Mom's furniture and boxes out of the basement and anything that's on the main floor. Kira, you need to empty out all your stuff so we can get your furniture in the truck with that. Just throw everything in boxes, but don't forget to label. I also need you to pack up Mom's clothes and jewelry."

She nods. "I'll grab her suitcases and pack those first. We can send those with her."

"After that's done, we need to scour the house for anything that was hers before they got married."

Walking in through the unlocked front door, we're confronted with not only the evidence of the police having been there, but also the remains of their fight.

The coffee table is tossed, papers everywhere—the pictures we sent her. There's dark red smudges on the carpet and we all stop.

Another wave of guilt washes over me. If only one of us had been here.

"Do you think he's been back?" Kira asks.

I shake my head. "I don't know. It is a work day, so unless he took clothes with him, I'm sure he came back."

"Maybe the police found him." There's a hopeful edge to her voice, but I think we all know we'd have heard something.

"Better them than us," Ryan says.

Kira grabs a handful of boxes and some tape and heads upstairs to get started. "Can one of you bring the suitcases up for me?"

Her eyes are blank, her mood somber. I step forward and cup her cheeks, pressing my lips to hers.

"I'll bring them up in a few."

She nods before turning and making her way up.

Ryan doesn't say anything as we head to the basement where a lot of Sonia's stuff was stored when she moved in. The scene in the living room affected us all.

"It's not your fault, you know?" he finally says after we've brought a dozen boxes up along with a dresser and multiple other pieces of furniture.

I blow out a hard, short breath. "How do you figure that?"

"He was a ticking time bomb." Ryan waves me toward the kitchen.

"That I detonated on your mother."

None of us have eaten, and we're both thirsty from all the trips up and down. There's nothing in the fridge to drink besides some wine and a couple of beers, neither of which would be good right now, leaving us with pulling out some glasses for water.

Ryan tilts the glass back, taking in huge gulps of water. "But that wasn't your intent."

"Good intentions don't fix the fact that the information I sent her was so damaging to him that there's no way he wouldn't react." I look up at him and lock eyes. "It wasn't just selfish intent, I promise you." Ryan's brow scrunches. "I couldn't stand to see what he's done to her, couldn't let him destroy her further."

"I know."

"Do you?"

He lets out a sigh. "You're not a malicious guy, you never have been. Your fucking fault is that you try to do what's best on your own, but don't always think about the consequences of your decision. But this? This was necessary.

This was you saving my mom by making her see what he hides. Make her wake up, because I sure as shit couldn't convince her."

"You tried?"

He nods. "The last year, every time I talked to Kira she filled me in on what was going down. How Mom was slowly losing herself. All summer, I tried to convince her, but he'd managed to take my strong, single mother and turn her into a woman with battered wife syndrome, only he'd never laid a hand on her."

"He's a master manipulator."

Ryan nods. "And exactly why you got so fucked up."

He looks at me, daring me to object, but he's right. My parent's relationship royally fucked me up, and in turn, I fucked up Kira.

A long, loud, thudding sound grabs our attention and we stare at each other for a fraction of a second before running toward the noise. We both blow out a breath at the source—a large suitcase that Kira slid down the stairs.

"That one goes in the car," she says from the top landing. "And I'll have another one ready in a minute."

"Hey, baby sis, want to go grab some food when you're done with that one?"

"Good idea, I'm starving and we have a ways to go." The basement is almost cleaned out, but there's still Ryan's room and Kira's, plus I'm sure a ton of other stuff.

She nods. "Sure, but can you help me for a second, Ry?"

"I'll go down for the next round," I say as Ryan makes his way up the stairs.

A few minutes later, I'm thankful to be grabbing the last box that's tucked away in the basement. From what I can tell, the downstairs family room has remained untouched by anything of hers. At least after this I won't be carrying anything *up* the stairs.

"What are you doing here?" my father's voice booms out.

I stop in my tracks and turn to look for him. He's dressed normally, acting like he's stopping home for lunch, like he hasn't committed some heinous crime and his wife isn't lying in a hospital bed he put her in.

"I asked you a fucking question," he snarls.

And I snap.

I drop the box, not caring if there's anything breakable and storm across the room to him.

"You motherfucker!"

He's so stunned by my reaction that I'm able to get my hands around his lapels, but I'm only able to push him back a few feet before he digs his heels into the floor. It's enough to throw me off balance so when his fists hit my chest, I'm forced back.

"How could you?"

"How could I what?"

"Don't fucking play stupid. Don't you even fucking try! Sonia's lying in a hospital bed because of you."

No flashes of surprise on his face, just his lip curling up in disgust. In the background I hear feet stomping on the stairs, running to us.

"People try and threaten me, but you'll never fucking touch me."

I'm running on little sleep and a lot of anger. My fingers wrap around his throat, my grip tight, precise, and I push on him until his back slams against the wall.

"You motherfucking piece of shit. I should fucking end you right here and now."

"Brayden!" Kira calls out.

I can feel her and Ryan behind me. Ryan says nothing, just waiting his turn.

There's surprise in my father's eyes, but that trademark sneer comes out, his lip twitches up. "What are you going to do? Nothing but a sniveling boy."

My grip tightens and I lean forward, inches from his face. "I'm not a boy anymore." I push against the wall, focus all my anger into my arm as I use the pressure to lift him up by the neck until his toes are all that's left touching the ground. Panic begins to fill his eyes as his fingers dig at my arm. "You're not the alpha anymore. I'm bigger than you, stronger than you."

I feel manic. My fingers squeeze tighter and I wonder how much pressure I need to stop him from breathing. The desire to end him is so strong, but it won't help anyone, it won't help Emily.

"Ryan, stop him!" Kira screams. I can hear her talking to someone else, and Ryan does nothing to stop me.

"My turn," is hissed out next to my ear and the panic in my father's face doubles.

It takes everything in me to release him, to let his body drop down to the ground and not fucking plant my foot up into his stomach.

But that doesn't stop Ryan from doing it. Kira grabs onto my arm, the phone at her ear.

"The police are on their way."

She then looks to Ryan, her eyes beseeching me to stop him, but I can't.

He needs this.

"You fucking piece of shit!" He pulls my father up by his jacket before he can catch his breath and defend himself. Hazel eyes are burning with anger. "I fucking trusted you to take care of my mother." His right arm flies back and then forward, his fist colliding with my father's face. It's hard enough that my father falls limp, forcing Ryan to drop him down to the floor. "Think you're so fucking tough now?"

Ryan's whole body shakes, vibrating with anger and the need to continue bashing in his skull, but he won't hit on someone who's out cold. He wants him awake so he will feel every hit.

We look at each other, both breathing hard, both ruled by the anger pumping viciously through our veins. A tiny hand grabs onto my shirt and pulls, doing the same to Ryan, until we're mashed together in a triangle, with Kira's head buried in the center, an arm around our waists.

She's shaking, crying, and exactly what we both need to calm down.

The three of us, like it used to be, protecting each other from everything, including from ourselves.

Flashes of blue and red show up a few minutes later and we let them in, directing them toward my father, who is waking back up. I don't know what Kira said to them on the phone, but two of the officers go immediately to him.

"I can do it!" my father says to them. "I'm not some fucking invalid."

"Settle down, Mr. Hunt."

"Settle down? You should be arresting those two animals, not helping me up. They attacked me." He's pointing to us, but we're all silent.

Another officer steps forward. "I'm not so sure I believe that, seeing as they've spent all night at the hospital with your wife." The cop pulls out his handcuffs. "Turn around."

"The hell?" My father steps back and glares at him.

"Sir, I asked you to turn around."

"What for?"

"Because once they're on I'm going to Mirandize you." He grabs onto my father's shoulders and flips him around, pressing his chest against the wall.

"You're arresting me? On what grounds?"

I love hearing the snap of the cuffs, the ratcheting sound as they are locked down tight.

"Assault," the officer says.

"But I didn't do anything."

"That's not what the evidence says," the officer growls in his face as he grabs his arm and pulls him out the door.

"Are you all right?" Another man asks Kira.

She nods and swallows hard. "Yes."

I pull her to me, wrapping my arm around her as I kiss the top of her head.

"You're his son, Brayden, correct?"

I nod.

"And you two are?"

"His wife's children," Ryan says.

The officer thumbs through his notes. "Sonia Roth?"

We all nod.

"So, what happened here?"

"We left our Mom in the hospital while they're running more tests to move her out of here so she didn't have to see him alone again. He surprised us when he suddenly showed up," Ryan said in his clear and calm tone.

"I was trying to hold him until you arrived, but he tried to get away. After what he did, we just couldn't let him," I tell the officer. It's the truth, though I did use more force than I'm letting on.

"There's been an APB out for him since this morning. It's good you were able to keep him here." The officer takes notes and looks between me and Ryan. "He's got a pretty nasty welt on his cheek, which one of you put it there?"

We glance at each other quickly before Ryan nods. "Me."

The officer nods and puts away his notes. "Nice. If you ever need to blow off some steam, I do a boxing class three nights a week." He holds out his hand and Ryan takes it. "But I have a feeling this was a onetime thing."

Ryan nods. "My mom didn't deserve what he did to her."

"No, and we're going to make sure he pays for it, okay? No vigilante justice, got it?"

We both nod and he gives us a smile before turning and heading for the door.

"Ryan!" Dana appears on the other side of the officer, and runs around him straight to Ryan and flings her arms around his neck. "Thank God! I saw the cop cars and started freaking out."

"It's okay, baby, everything's going to be okay."

Looking at them, then down at Kira, and all that's happened in the last twelve hours, I actually believe that.

Everything is going to be okay.

Once Dana arrived the packing went even faster and we were able to load up and unload at the storage site and get the truck back to the rental place before they closed. Kira packed up a bunch of essentials and favorites of her Mom's, which we promptly put in my mom's car as soon as we got back to the hospital.

Dana and I ran to get some food for everyone while Kira and Ryan spent time with their mom. When we got back, Dana called Ryan out and they went to find some drinks while I took the rest to the room.

I'm a few feet out from the door when I hear Sonia's voice out in the hall.

"We separated you two, you and Brayden, when we got married, didn't we?"

I peer in from the doorway enough that I can see and hear them, but they aren't looking my way.

Kira nods slowly. "Yeah."

"I'm so sorry, baby. I had no idea. I hate to admit that at the time I was stuck in my own little bubble, and I didn't see for a long time the change between you two."

"When did you finally notice?" Kira asks.

Sonia purses her lips. "It's been adding up, slowly over the last year or two. Much more so this year."

"He's my boyfriend, now," Kira says, her hand in Sonia's. "You marrying Steven messed us both up, but I think we've finally worked past it."

Fuck yeah, we have, and I can't wait to prove that to everyone.

"I'm so sorry, baby." Tears stream down Sonia's face and she pulls Kira closer. "I was alone for so long. So lonely. Steven saw that and took advantage of it. And in that, I took away your chance to be together."

I knock on the door, and both their heads pop up, fingers moving to eyes and swiping away tears.

"Anyone order some orange chicken?" I ask with a smile as I hold up the bag.

"Panda?" Kira asks, her eyes wide. My lip twitches up into a smirk and I nod. She reaches up and throws her arms around my neck, pulling me down to press her lips to mine. "Thank you, baby."

I pull the four containers out, one for the three of us and one for my mom. Kira and Sonia use the little table for the bed while I take a seat on the chair right next to them.

Dana and Ryan show up after a few minutes, passing out water bottles and a tea for Kira, before sitting down and eating as well.

"You four really should be heading back home soon. You missed a whole day of classes and have barely slept."

"You're more important than a day of classes," Kira says, squeezing Sonia's hand.

"Oh, everyone's here," my mom says as she enters the room. "Good, then you all can help me convince Sonia to not drop the charges against Steven."

Drop the charges? Hell no.

Ryan stares at her. "You *are* pressing charges. Mom, after what he did, you can't let him get away with it."

"What if he wins because I don't remember?"

"Sonia, they've arrested him," I say bluntly. "They have evidence even if you can't remember and that alone is a huge

389

power over him. He'll give you whatever you want just to keep you quiet."

She blinks at me, her mouth hanging open. Tears fill her eyes. "I'm just so confused on what to do."

"It's okay, Mom," Kira says as she strokes her hand. "We're here. We'll help you through everything."

She nods and looks to my mom. "I know I am the last person to ask this of you, after our history and especially after all you've already done, but please, will you please help me."

Mom's lips form a straight line and she steps to the other side of the bed, sitting on the edge. "You don't have to beg, Sonia. I'll help you and we'll get you through this. Besides," she looks over to me and Kira, "I think we're going to be in each other's lives regardless."

Sonia glances over to us as well and smiles up at Abby. "Thank you."

"Okay, with that settled, I think it's time you kids got back up to school," Mom says, looking around at us.

"But, I want to stay with Mom," Kira says.

Ryan also doesn't seem to like this idea, but I think he understands. For one, we have no place to stay.

"I'll call you the instant we know anything, so go home, get some sleep, and get to class."

I stand up and walk to Mom, wrapping my arms around her in a tight bear hug. "You're the greatest person I've ever met, and the best mom ever."

Her head nods against my chest. "Thanks, baby."

It takes us an hour to pack up and say goodbye before splitting up between my car and Dana's and heading back up to school.

Things have finally fallen into place. It was a long road, but for the first time I really feel like a weight has been lifted. Like my dreams can become a reality.

The price was high, but we'll be okay.

We'll all be okay.

THIRTY TWO
BRAYDEN

Sonia is at my mom's for now. Safe.

My father is on his way out of her life.

What happened to Sonia is a motherfucking tragedy. The only positive thing I can say is that my father will be gone soon. One way or the other, we'll all be free of him.

As soon as we are, I can finally move forward with what I've been planning.

What I've been planning for weeks.

Actually, I've been leading up to this my whole life. I just didn't know it.

My mom helped me out, and I threw all the money I've managed to save into it.

Worth it.

I can't wait to finally ask Kira that question. Make it clear to her and the whole world what this means to me.

First, that divorce has to be finalized. I know that.

So, for now, I'll wait.

I walk up to my front door, keys in hand—

What the fuck?

It's night out, and lately, my contacts haven't been helping as much. It's time for me to go get a new prescription. That's the main reason I stand here, on the porch, blinking at the open door and making sure I'm not seeing shit.

I'm not.

The lock to the door leading to my apartment is all scratched up.

Busted open.

Someone either broke into one of my neighbor's apartment downstairs—

Or they broke into mine on the second floor.

I drop my shit on the porch and take a cautious step inside.

Kira's supposed to meet me here in a few minutes. I should call her. Tell her not to come.

I should call the fucking cops.

I don't do any of those things. A weird, powerful autopilot takes over, luring me deeper inside. I hear no signs of movement, downstairs or upstairs.

See no signs of a theft in progress.

Instinct calls me toward my stairs, a cold premonition that I don't understand at first.

My neighbor's door is firmly closed. So is the one of the other side of the entry.

But there's a light coming from the second floor.

From my open doorway.

I creep up the stairs, palming my phone. As if it's a weapon or some shit. This is the stupidest thing I've ever done. There's nothing I can use to defend myself. What if whoever is there has a gun?

My mind yells at me to turn around, head back outside, and call the police.

My body and gut take me the rest of the way up the stairs.

The door to my apartment *is* open.

And that isn't regular light coming through the slightly ajar door.

Is that . . . is that fucking candlelight?

First thought: Kira is in there waiting to surprise me.

Second thought: she has a set of the fucking keys to my place. There's no way she would've busted the lock.

On the second floor landing, I pause and take a deep breath.

Scented candles.

Whoever is in there lit my entire house up with some sickly sweet smelling shit.

If it's not Kira inside . . .

God no. Please don't let her be that dumb.

I've flirted with no one here. Barely talk to the female population. I've given none of them any inclination that some shit like this would be welcome.

There's only one person—*woman*—I know that would think this shit is okay.

And Kira is on her way here any moment.

I push the door open, not sure if I'm praying I'm right, or if I'm praying that it's actually a very weird thief awaiting me in my apartment.

The door swings all the way and I hiss out a curse.

"I know. I look amazing, don't I?"

I'm too busy gawking at this woman's audacity to pay much mind to her outfit, but I do see enough of it to know her nipples are out, and her panties are crotchless.

"*What the fuck is wrong with you?*" I ask in a disgusted tone.

Jennifer doesn't even pretend to hear me. Her eyes . . . there's something odd about her eyes. They're too focused on my body. Too unhinged. She twirls in a circle, showing me her ass in that crotchless thong. "Remember when you used to use this body all you wanted?" She turns back around and smiles at me, this fucking *happy* smile that makes no sense. "Remember the night you fucked me for like six hours straight without stopping?"

No. I honestly don't. "Do yourself a favor. Get dressed and get the fuck out. *Now.*"

"Your little bitch isn't here, Brayden. You don't need to pretend."

I take a single step into the apartment. "Watch your fucking mouth."

Jennifer's eyes flash with malice, the first crack in her cheery facade. "I know it was her, you know? I know she sent that video to my parents to get rid of me once and for all."

I punch the door frame, fighting the urge to drag her out by her hair. "No, you fucking idiot. It was *me*." Shit, I don't know why I'm admitting that. Fine, I do. No one accuses or talks shit about Kira.

Jennifer shakes her head sweetly and approaches me with that tender, loving smile that honestly scares the hell out of me. "You would never do that to me, Brayden. You care about me."

"I did. Once. As a friend. And that's the only reason I'm warning you one last time, get the fuck out before I call the cops."

She doesn't listen.

Of course she doesn't listen.

For the first time I realize just how crazy she's gone.

Jennifer stops in front of me and reaches down to grab my crotch before I react.

It's an instant explosion of movement.

None of it from me.

Time slows down as I feel myself being pushed aside. I hit the door frame and out of the corner of my eye see an auburn blur.

It all happens too fast for me to track it.

I hear what sounds like a crack—the impact of a fist colliding with flesh, I realize.

Jennifer screams.

Then she's yanked out of the apartment.

I push off the door frame, the world returning to regular speed.

And see my girl.

Pulling Jennifer's hair.

Leading her toward the stairs.

"Kira, no!"

Too late.

Kira practically flings Jennifer down to the first floor.

Jennifer screams again.

Oh God. Oh God. Kira just threw her down the stairs.

And she isn't done. She flies down those stairs like a hell-bent demoness.

I don't know how bad that fall hurt Jennifer, but I do know Kira isn't going to stop until she kills her. I fly down the stairs, jumping down two at a time like Kira did.

Jennifer is on her feet, facing off against Kira. Both girls are locked in a struggle, but all I see is the blood pouring down the side of Jennifer's face.

She grabs the side of Kira's face and slams my girl's head into the open door.

Right where the busted hinge is.

When Kira jerks away, there's a trail of blood sliding down the door.

I hit the first floor and lunge for the both of them.

Kira growls a frightening, inhuman sound, and yanks Jennifer out onto the porch. Then, she kicks her out onto the walkway, jumps behind her, and starts dragging her out toward the parking lot by her hair.

I run after her. "Kira, baby, stop!"

Jennifer is kicking the air, clawing at Kira's hands, leaving bleeding welts on my girl's skin.

Kira feels none of it. The expression on her face, the look in her eyes . . .

"I've. Fucking. Had. Enough. Of. You!" she yells, throwing Jennifer out onto the asphalt of the parking lot.

People have come out of their homes. A few have stopped around the periphery of the parking lot.

More are joining every second.

I already see phone's in their hands.

Jennifer scrambles to her feet, seeming oblivious to the fact that there's a group of people staring at her almost naked ass. It's cold as hell outside, but she doesn't seem to notice that either. Her eyes are unhinged.

Kira faces off against her, uncaring, her chest heaving.

There's a small trail of blood on the fur fringes of her coat.

I run to her.

397

"You stupid bitch! I'll have you arrested!" Jennifer shrieks.

"For what, you dumb cunt? For defending myself when you broke into Brayden's apartment?" Kira asks calmly.

Jennifer's mouth falls open as she realizes Kira's intent.

My girl is going to claim self-defense.

As fucked up as it is, I plan on backing whatever version of the story she goes with.

"You lying, dirty bitch!" Jennifer starts running at Kira.

I grab Kira, trying to move her aside, but she digs her heels in and shrugs me off. "You have enough problems," is all she tells me before ducking and running head-first into Jennifer's midsection.

Linebacker style.

I can almost hear Jennifer's back scraping against the cement as they land.

Kira jumps off her and tries to back away. "Lay off, Jennifer. It's over. Just get your naked, disgusting ass home."

It isn't over. Jennifer's glare makes it clear. "You fuck your stepbrother behind everyone's back and are still a jealous, possessive bitch over him. He can't ever be yours! Don't you get it? He's your *stepbrother*, and you call *me* disgusting?"

"Shut the fuck up already!" I growl, torn between calling the cops on her or just getting her to leave.

Kira is an equal participant in this fight.

Actually, she's schooled Jennifer so far.

People no doubt saw her drag Jennifer out. The only part that is in question is what happened in the house before she did so. Jennifer definitely broke in. It'll be mine and Kira's word against hers.

I see some people with their phones in their hands and realize it's too late. Someone has probably already called the cops.

"You broke into my house, Jennifer. That's not normal," I say in the calmest tone I can muster. Shrugging off my coat, I throw it to her. "Now you're out here almost naked—"

"Because your bitch dragged me out here!"

I hold up a hand when Kira takes a step back in her direction. "Watch how you talk about her. This is the last time I'm warning you. And cover up for Christ's sake. Like I said, what you're doing right now isn't normal."

"But fucking your stepsister is?" she yells, wrapping my coat around herself before turning to face all the people gathered behind her. "Because he is! He's fucking *her*, and they're stepsiblings!"

Kira laughs.

It's a hollow laugh.

A deadened laugh.

A bitter sound that makes me turn in her direction just in time to see her storming back to Jenn.

"Is it your fucking business?" she growls.

Jennifer scrambles to her feet again, shrugging into my coat, and faces off against Kira.

I move to them.

"Stop Brayden! You can't do anything about this!" Kira snaps, still glaring at Jenn.

They're face to face now, a ticking time bomb of female aggression.

Both bleeding.

Both still blood thirsty for more.

399

And I can't jump in. I can't jump in for legal reasons, but also because Kira is right. There's nothing I can do about this. Short of slamming my fist into Jennifer's face—something I can only do if she threatens Kira's life—nothing I say gets through to that psycho.

I try one last time. "I don't want you, Jenn. I'm sorry I somehow built some fantasy up in your head. I don't know how the fuck I did it, but I'm sorry, okay? I thought I made it clear that it was only sex between us. We haven't fucked in years, man. Almost four years to be exact."

"I was the only one!" Jennifer cries, teary eyes locking with mine. "All the other girls came and went, none lasting more than a night. But me? Me you kept coming back to—"

"For two years only," I grit out, my patience dwindling. This level of self-delusion is more than I can bare.

"But I was still the only one you came back to! Until this little slut—"

Kira shoves her back. "I'm not the one fucking every guy *and girl* I can get between my legs. And it's none of your business what happens between us!"

It takes me a few seconds to assimilate what just happened.

What my girl just did.

"You don't own him, Jennifer," Kira says in a low menacing tone.

Jennifer shrieks with outrage and backhands my girl across the face. "Yes I do! You're just in the way!"

Kira takes the hit, her head turning slightly to the side. When Jennifer tries to aim for her again, Kira grabs her hand in hers and squeezes down tight. Then, with a well-placed knee to the gut, she brings Jennifer down to her knees.

Jennifer is on her knees, struggling to breathe, when Kira backhands her onto her back. "*Enough*. You don't own him. *I do*. And you can let that eat at you for the rest of your miserable life. I don't give a fuck. But back off my man, and back off *our* lives, you psychotic piece of shit!"

Holy. Shit.

Did Kira just . . .

She did. Kira just announced to the entire world that she owns me.

Our parents aren't officially divorced yet, but she did it anyway.

Now everyone's going to know that Jennifer's rumors were true.

They'll know we've been with each other on the down-low.

Cop cars come skidding into the parking lot, their sirens blasting.

Kira takes one look at them and runs to me, cupping my neck in her cold hands.

"You were defending yourself. She broke in. You came up behind me and she attacked. You had no choice but to throw her down the stairs in self-defense," I mumble hurriedly, desperate for her to get the story right so our accounts match up.

"I love you," is all she says in response, and it doesn't matter that the sirens are drowning out most of the noise around us, I have a feeling that the people closest to us hear her anyway. "It's going to be okay, okay? Just make sure *you* stay out of it."

I know what she means: in our account of the story, I was an innocent bystander. I had nothing to do with this.

Not that far from the truth, actually.

Kira pulls me down to her and kisses the breath out of me in front of everyone.

Everyone.

"Miss, step away from him. *Now*."

She doesn't listen.

I finally break out of my shock, and with a groan, crush her to me, kissing her like it's the last time I'm going to see her.

It's not. I'll move heaven and hell to make sure she serves no jail time.

The cops come up behind Kira. I let her go before they can think of manhandling her. It's the last thing I need to see. My life will be over because I'll kill a motherfucker, cop or not.

Kira holds her hands up and allows one of them to grab her wrists and twist her arms behind her back.

Fuck. Watching them handcuff her is one of the hardest things I've ever done.

"I'm calling Ryan, Dana, everyone. A lawyer."

Jennifer is screaming from beside one of the cop cars, hurling accusations.

"She broke into my house and attacked first," I tell the cop nearest me.

He holds up a hand impatiently. "Relax. We need to get an ambulance here first. They're both bleeding pretty bad from their heads. Then we'll get your statement."

I want to demand that they let Kira go but I can't, of course. Pulling out my cell, I dial Ryan.

Of course, he flips out in my ear. "What the fuck do you mean she's in cuffs?"

"I know. I know,   man." Running my hand through my hair, I stare at where Kira's sitting inside one of the police cars. Our eyes meet and I bet she can see how frantic I am.

402

"Why didn't you stop the fight?" Ryan asks. I can hear him slam into his car and peel away.

"At first? Because it happened too fast. Then I thought it was over—but Kira was furious, and Jennifer kept flipping out—and *fuck*, man. You're right, I should've done more to stop it."

"Calm down. I know my sister. You probably couldn't have stopped her if you tried, and you have enough shit on your plate without someone accusing you of manhandling one of the girls."

I look around at the growing crowd of people and all the pictures being taken. The videos being recorded.

This shit is already up on social media. I'll stake my life on it.

That and the kiss Kira and I shared, the words exchanged.

Fuck them.

Fuck them all.

I can't stand any of them.

"People are here. Recording and shit," I tell Ryan just as two ambulances come speeding into our parking lot. "Fuck. Thank God. The ambulance is here."

"Ambulance?" Ryan shouts. "What the fuck did Jennifer do to Kira?"

"It's more like what they did to each other. It's not bad. Fuck, I hope it's not bad." What if my girl has a concussion brewing? Or a blood clot builds from the hit?

I'm panicking, my mind flooded with the worst case scenarios, but I can't control it.

Kira is escorted out of the cop car so she can sit inside the ambulance while they check her head.

I rush to get as close as the cops will let me. "I have to call my mom. Get a lawyer ready. Just get over here."

"You can't get close to her," a cop says, stepping between me and the ambulance.

I'm so fucking feral that I almost bare my teeth at him. "That's the girl I love."

"Listen, I get that, but she's currently under arrest. Do her a favor and calm down."

His sympathy eases me a bit. He isn't trying to be a dick, he's just doing his job.

I call my mom and give her a quick run through of what happened, my eyes never straying from Kira.

"And who is this girl that broke into your apartment?"

I was dreading that question. Dreading it, and the honest answer I have to give. "Jennifer, mom. Jennifer Henrichs. Remember her?"

"That little blond that always followed you around when you were younger?"

"Yeah."

"Brayden, why on Earth would she break into your—" My mother stops abruptly and I can practically hear the conclusion she came to.

"It's not like that, Mom. It was a long time ago. I swear, I haven't been with her like that in years. She's just mentally unstable." And I probably made it much, much worse by sending that picture and video to her family. The stress of her father's judgement and subsequent punishment most likely pushed her over the edge further.

Fuck.

"Mom, can you just call Dan? Please?"

"Honey, it's ten o'clock. But I'll do my best to reach him. If not, we'll definitely get him tomorrow."

Kira spending a whole night in lock up? Every male, protective instinct in my body flares up. "Give me his number. I'll try reaching him, too."

She agrees to text it to me and we hang up.

I hear what sounds like Ryan speaking loudly and spot him at the edge of the parking lot. The cops are refusing to let him in.

I want to go up to him and calm him down, but I'm not leaving Kira's side. This is as close as they're letting me and I'm staying here until they tell me she's all right.

Thirty minutes later, Kira is escorted out of the ambulance and back into the cop car. Seeing her like that breaks my fucking heart.

My girl just gives me this small smile, though, as if trying to tell me it's all going to be all right.

I run to Ryan as the cops get into the car to take her to the station. "Go, go. We need to follow them."

He and Dana run with me to his car and we all jump in.

By the time we get to the station, I have confirmation from my mom that the lawyer actually agreed to come at this time. He's on his way to meet us here.

Some relief.

We all rush inside.

Kira and Jennifer are already in holding. Paperwork has just been started, so they refuse to let me in.

Now it's all a waiting game.

I'm going to lose my fucking mind.

All three of us trudge to the sitting area, the air between us heavy with hopelessness.

Two hours.

That's how long it takes for Jennifer's parents to arrive, their lawyer in tow.

My lawyer, Dan, walks in through the door right after.

The Henrich's lawyer pulls Dan aside almost immediately. We're too far for me to hear anything they're saying, but it's still obvious that they're speaking in hushed tones.

I'm out of my seat in an instant.

Ryan and Dana follow me and I realize that's what our little unit has become—a small family that follows each other no matter how fucked up things are.

My lawyer meets me halfway. "They don't wish to press charges."

"What?" Ryan and I ask.

"If Ms. Roth agrees not to pursue this, the Henrichs have no problem letting this drop."

"Why?" I'm finding it hard to believe Jennifer's parents would ignore this humiliation to their daughter.

For fuck's sake, the pictures and videos of them fighting must be all over social media by now.

"Ms. Henrich's parents are pulling their daughter out of the school. There's enough scandal surrounding this, as is. They wish to avoid more."

Plus, there's still the breaking and entering charge which isn't in the deal.

"Yes," Ryan says when it becomes obvious I'm still too shocked to respond. "My sister will take the deal."

My lawyer smirks with what seems like amusement. "That's up to Ms. Roth to decide. She's legally an adult."

I finally snap out of my apathy. "Of course she will. Just . . . Just get me in there and let me talk to her."

My lawyer nods. "Let me see what I can do. I'll have to talk to her first, of course."

Another half hour later, I'm escorted to the back near the holding cells.

Kira's already at the bars waiting for me.

Shit. We've changed places. This time it's me looking in from the outside.

It's sobering. This is what she must have felt seeing me all beat up and bloody, caged like an animal.

"Is it true that her parents don't want to press charges?"

I wrap my hands around hers, which are wrapped around the cell. "Come closer." She does. The bars make it impossible but I lean in as much as I can and kiss her forehead. "This is all my fucking fault."

"No, baby. It's mine. I had enough of her shit and couldn't control myself."

I'm shaking my head, silently denying her claim. "Her parents are taking her out of the school. I don't know for how long but if you agree to drop it, they will too."

"Why?"

"I think they've realized how out of control she is and they're worried about any more family embarrassment."

"Fine."

I blink in surprise. "What? Just like that?" I expected more of a fight from my enraged hellcat.

"I don't care about her anymore. If she's going to be out of our lives, good."

I reach through the bars and caress the side of her head. There's a bandage wrapped around, down to the bottom where her head meets her neck.

Where Jennifer slammed her into the broken hinge on the door.

"How bad is it?"

Kira turns her head and kisses my palm. "The EMTs said it's just a bad bump and cut. I'll be fine."

Heart heavy, I tilt her head to look into her eyes. This isn't the place to talk about this, but I want her prepared for what's awaiting us once she's out of here. "Kira, in the heat of the moment, you—"

"It wasn't the heat of the moment. I made a decision to stop hiding, Brayden. I'm sorry if that's not what you wanted."

My knees feel fucking weak. "What? You . . . You let the world know about us *on purpose*?"

Kira nods, expression somber. "Yeah. And I'm sorry if it's not what you wanted, but I don't care what they do to us anymore. I love you and that's all that matters to me."

Knees are definitely useless. Legs are, too. Shaking, I lean against the bars, eyes closed, my mind reeling.

She's choosing me.

Over the censure.

Over the chaos that's heading our way.

Her brother, mother, my mother, our friends . . . No one is going to be safe from this. People are malicious bullies. In some way or form, everyone in our lives will deal with some negative backlash from this.

But Kira doesn't care anymore. She just wants to be with me out in the open. "I fucking love you. I love you. *I love you.*"

I don't know how many times I chant it to her, but the entire time, my mind is on the little secret I've been hiding for weeks now.

The small box hiding in my apartment.

Fuck everything. She's choosing me, and I'm choosing her.

Soon, I'm making that clear to everyone.

Everyone.

Including her.

THIRTY THREE
BRAYDEN

"How's your head?" I ask as I step up behind Kira, wrapping my arms around her waist.

She smiles at me in the mirror and adjusts her hair in an attempt to cover the bruising and scab. There's a butterfly stitch near her hairline and bruises around her eye that she's tried to cover up. It won't change anything. We've been hiding all weekend at a hotel, partially thanks to my busted door, but we've seen the backlash on social media.

There's been righteous indignation from some of Jennifer's believers, and those who were silent, wanting to ride the "she was right" train. Then the Jenn haters and their "bitch had it coming."

Support, disgust, and the overwhelming silence from Jenn. Her parents had her delete all of her accounts and she was gone, back home, before dawn broke.

Kira shrugs. "It's okay. Need some aspirin though." She tilts her head back to look up at me, reaching up to caress my face. "Stop it."

I scrunch my brow at her, trying to figure out what she's talking about.

She heaves a sigh and turns in my arms, wrapping hers around my neck. "You keep blaming yourself for everything lately. You need to stop."

Leaning down, I rest my forehead on hers. "It's really hard not to, Kitty."

"It's going to be fine. We'll figure it all out."

I hope so. Today's our first day back at school after everything that went down.

Our first day out there, in front of everyone, as a couple.

Officially, that is.

I'm excited.

Wary.

Another thing I hope? That everyone understands I'll do anything to protect my girl.

They better leave her the fuck alone.

I kiss Kira on the forehead. "Come on. Let's go. We can't be late."

Kira

"Just look at her. Walking around here. Holding hands with him like she's proud of it."

"Let it go. It doesn't matter."

"Of course it does! They ruined that girl's life and the whole time she had been telling the truth. And God, who does that? Fuck their stepbrother? I wouldn't even think of mine like that!"

"Yours is twelve and nowhere near as hot as Brayden Hunt."

"Still, it's so disgusting and like I said, they ruined that Henrich's girl's life."

We ruined Jennifer's life.

Fucking laughable.

I leave it alone though and stay in the bathroom stall, not giving away my presence.

Yeah. It's that bad. A girl can't even take a piss without hearing this shit.

Oddly, it doesn't bother me as much as I thought it once would. Their ignorance and willingness to believe whatever is annoying as hell, but I also recognize this for what it is.

Jealousy.

I, Kira Roth, am officially the envy of the entire female population at OSU.

Brayden walked in with me this morning, his arm around me, and eyes blazing down at me with love and need.

And I've never loved him more.

Fuck the stares. I've been walking around all day with my head held high no matter what they throw at me.

The people that truly matter know the truth about what went down. That's enough for me.

The door leading into the bathroom opens. I hear a third girl greet the other two shit-talkers.

"You're still going on about the whole thing?" the newcomer asks.

"I told her to let it go."

"They both deserve all the shit they're getting. It's just so wrong."

The new girl laughs. "You're just jealous 'cause you had plans to hop on that dick."

See? Told you.

"Not now. He's gross as hell for fucking his sister."

"*Stepsister*. They aren't really related. And I heard their parents got married only three and a half years ago. *And* they knew each other their whole lives. You know that boy was already fine as hell by the time that all happened. I don't blame her for setting her sights on him."

"Whatever," the main hater in the group scoffs.

I hear them get their things together and head out. Sighing, I grab my own things and finally exit the stall to wash my hands.

It's been like this all day. It isn't heartbreaking, just exhausting.

My friends however?

Man, someone's going to go to jail.

Ironically, I think that someone's going to be Dana. Earlier, I got several texts. Most of them were a string of red-faced, enraged emojis.

Not the iPhone ones like her phone has, mind you. Dana took the time to screenshot the Samsung ones, their teeth bared in pure rage, and sent it to me so I'd understand how serious she was.

That girl is fucking nuts.

They were followed by, ***Your brother wants me to leave for the day. He doesn't understand I'm taking someone down with me when I go.***

I didn't know whether to laugh or cry.

This is what I mostly feared about the world finding out. The people I love are getting hit with this backlash even harder than me and Brayden are.

Because Brayden and I no longer care about anything but being together.

But fuck them. Seriously, fuck every single person attacking us at this school. I don't care.

I just can't wait to go home for Thanksgiving break and spend time surrounded by all the people that matter to me.

I hear Brayden on his cell in the other room and my heart melts at the tone of his voice.

He was always meant to be this. An older brother. He has such a big, loving heart, and he's slipped into the role so easily.

I chew on my thumbnail, nervous, waiting for him to come in.

Emily's been asking to meet me. From what I gather, she's been alone most of her life. Just her and her mom. She's eager to meet all of us, but mostly me.

Brayden says it's because he can't shut up about me.

I called him my adorable dork.

Which he is.

He opens the door to the bedroom and peeks inside. When he sees me destroying my thumbnail, he scowls and slaps my hand lightly away from my mouth.

I pout at him.

"Yeah, she's here. Worried about talking to you." He smiles down at me. "Emily says not to be worried. She loves you already because *I* adore you."

I don't know what's wrong with me lately, but everything he does brings tears to my eyes. I can't handle the force of the love I feel for this man.

Still smiling, he hands me the phone. "Here."

I *am* nervous to meet her. Well, talk to her. Swallowing, I bring the phone to my ear. "Hi Emily."

"*Hiiiiiiii!*"

I cringe and resist the urge to pull the phone away from my ear. A smile tugs at the corner of my lips. "How are you?"

"I'm awesome! Having Brayden in my life has made everything so much better."

That smile breaks free. "Yeah. Trust me, I know the feeling," I say, still staring up into his eyes.

He stares down at me questioningly.

"He talks about you all the time."

"He talks about you all the time, too," I tell her. We both giggle at that.

Brayden rolls his eyes and walks out of the room, leaving me alone to get to know his sister.

"Brayden said we'll all be together for Thanksgiving." The excitement in Emily's tone makes my heart clench.

"Yup. And you'll get to go shopping with me and Dana." I've just decided this now, and I'll have to get Dana to agree, but I want to do this for Emily.

"Oh my God! Really?"

I smile again.

"You guys are all so epic. I wish I had met you all sooner."

Blinking back tears, I stare at the closed door Brayden just went through. This situation is hard on me. This little girl is such a sweetheart and she's gone through a lot not having a father in her life.

I can only imagine how hard this has been on Brayden. "Trust me, we all feel the same way. But we're going to make up for lost time, right?"

Emily readily agrees and we spend the next thirty minutes on the phone, getting to know each other.

Hanging up the call, I go in search of Brayden. I find him in the living room, his laptop on his lap.

He takes one look at my face and jumps off the couch. "Baby, what's wrong? What happened?"

The tears I've been holding in start rushing out. "She's just so nice, and I feel so bad for the both of you—"

Brayden crushes me to his chest. "Oh, baby. There's nothing any of us could've done. Please don't cry."

I snuggle deeper into his arms, wrapping my arms tight around him. More than ever, I understand how he ended up screwing things up as much as he did. It's no excuse and doesn't erase all the years of pain, but how could he have done better?

He didn't know how.

Fucked up, emotionally scarred, he tried his best to deal with his screwed up life without having the skills needed to properly cope. To make the right decisions.

Just like me.

"Stop crying, baby. You know it breaks my heart," he whispers, kissing my cheek.

I turn my head and kiss his lips hard. "I love you, Brayden."

He exhales against my lips. It amazes me how I've said it to him so many times now, and his relief is still palpable every time I do.

"I love you, Kira. Forever, you hear me? *Forever*."

There's something in his tone when he says that. Something I can't quit place. "I'll love you even longer than that, Brayden."

"You better fucking mean that."

BRAYDEN

November 25, 2015

Pulling up to my mom's house is exciting. There's a smile covering my face, because I am the happiest I've ever been when coming here.

Kira's by my side, and seeing her place for only the second time—the first time when we moved Sonia in. Ryan is in the car behind us with Dana. They're headed to her family's house on Friday night after the girls go on a shopping trip with Emily.

Getting out of the car, we grab our bags and head to the door. I twirl through the keys, locating the house key, but Kira's to the door first and twists on the door handle.

"Shit."

Kira turns to me in the open door. "What?"

I stomp up the stairs. "Mom!"

417

"Hi, my baby," she says from the island. Her smile fades. "What's wrong?"

"The door was unlocked again. What have I told you about that?"

She folds her arms over her chest and I can hear a little giggle behind me that I'll deal with in a minute.

She rolls her eyes at me and steps forward, wrapping her arms around my shoulders. "Brayden, my sweet boy, you said you were coming at noon. Sonia and I ran an errand and just got back so I went ahead and unlocked it."

I glare at her but she just rolls her eyes at me and walks around me.

"Hi, honey."

"Hi Abigail," my girl says sweetly and they hug. "Where's my mom?"

"Here, my impatient daughter." Sonia comes walking down the hallway into the open kitchen/ living room area. She and Kira hug right as Ryan and Dana walk inside.

Sonia heads to greet them next.

I walk in front of my mother, blocking her path, and cross my arms. "We're not done here, mother."

"Yes we are, child of mine."

"Your safety. Important. When did you forget this?"

I'm ignored.

"You must be Dana," Mom says as she pushes past me.

Turning around, I glare after her again.

"You are sometimes too cute," Kira says, pulling me down for a kiss.

The touch of her lips silences any protest about being called cute.

Taking my hand, she tugs me over to where Sonia is. Her hand is still wrapped up in the splint from her surgery, but the rest of her looks a lot better than she did the last time I saw her.

In fact, she looks lighter, like a weight has been lifted. And it has, one the size of a forty-seven-year-old bastard.

Which is very telling for how her meeting went with the lawyers yesterday, a topic we've all very anxious to hear about.

Sonia's arms are wrapped tightly around Kira, kissing the top of her head.

"How are you doing?" Kira asks. It's more than just the usual, mundane question one asks someone they know. My girl's been concerned about her mother on a near obsessive level the last few weeks.

Sonia smiles, a genuine smile that lights up her eyes. I can almost feel Ryan vibrating with curiosity, even with his stone face. They both called yesterday, but she refused to tell them anything, waiting until we all arrived.

"Let's sit," she says.

We set our bags on the floor and move into the family room. Ryan sits on the couch, Dana next to him. There's no way I'm letting Kira away from me for this, so I pull her to one of the sofa chairs, and onto my lap. Mom takes the other chair and Sonia the far end of the couch.

"Spill," Ryan says, not wanting to be put off a minute longer.

Sonia takes a deep breath. "I've dropped the charges against Steven."

Silence blankets the room before an eruption of anger.

"What?"

"No!"

"Are you fucking kidding me?"

Each of us are practically screaming out our strong disapproval.

It doesn't even phase her. She simply holds up her hands to quiet us. "Are you going to let me finish?"

Ryan looks like he's about to commit murder, and I'm right there with him. I'm sure Dana and Kira will help us hide the body.

Once the room is silent, but vibrating, she continues. "We came to an arrangement and made a deal."

My fingers dig into Kira's thigh; her's into my shoulder.

"And?" Kira prompts.

"Due to what happened, Steven has agreed to a speedy divorce and it will be finalized in the next few weeks. He will be paying me alimony for the next two years while I get back on my feet."

"He should," Ryan says.

Sonia nods. "I have agreed to drop the charges against him in exchange for this."

Kira shakes her head. "Wait, that doesn't seem like it's enough."

"That was what was agreed to with the lawyers and it's binding. However, outside of that, I made certain he knew that should he try and fight Carrie's child support claim, *everyone* will find out what he did."

"A few weeks . . ." Ryan's jaw twitches. "How do you know he'll do it all, not fight it once you've dropped the charges?"

"I've made sure. My lawyer has arranged in the divorce that I get to sue him even if the state drops the charges against him, and that stands until the divorce is finalized."

"That way it ensures that no matter what, even if something should happen to you, he'll end up paying in some way," I say.

She nods. "I don't trust him without some sort of insurance. After meeting with the lawyer, I feel like I have that." A smile breaks out on her face. "For the first time in years, I feel so light."

Seeing her happy and excited, lightens the guilt I've been holding onto since I got that phone call in the middle of the night.

It was worth it. All the time, the lies, to see her like this.

Saving her from him saved us all.

"I just can't believe . . ." Sonia trails off sadly, her eyes flickering to my mother. "I was such a fool, Abigail. I can't ever apologize enough."

My mother waves her away. "You actually freed me from him, and for that I'm grateful. I'm just sorry you had to go down in the process."

Sonia covers her face with her hands.

Kira shifts on my lap. "Mom—"

Sonia raises her head. "Never again. I promise you, Ryan. Kira. I'll never be such an idiot ever again."

Kira's off my lap in a flash, rushing to hug her mother. Ryan joins them and I can only sit here and watch, my throat tight with emotion for all of them.

It's not a happy end. Not by far. But at least I know in my gut that we're all finally heading in that direction.

November 26th, 2015
Thanksgiving Day

I run my fingers up and down Kira's arm. She's asleep, her breath blowing across my chest. This right here, her in my arms, is what was always supposed to be.

Lying in my bed at my mom's is perfection. It isn't just her though. It's my mom down the hall, Sonia in the spare bedroom, and Ryan and Dana camped out downstairs. It's Carrie and Emily coming over, and spending the day with my family. My *whole* family.

These are the things I'm thankful for.

"That feels good."

I glance down. Her eyes are closed, but she snuggles in and lets out a contented sigh.

"Good, but we do need to get up. We promised to help."

She nods, her eyes fluttering open. "It's hard to get up when I'm so comphy."

"Oh, Kitty, don't say that."

"Why?"

"Because you make me want to stay."

She lets out a little giggle before placing her hand on my chest and pushing herself up to a sitting position. Her fingers crawl around my skin, around the *K* inked over my heart.

"I need to take a shower. Wanna join me?"

Fuck.

My dick twitches, morning wood in full affect. "Hell yes."

Three hours later we're in the kitchen, peeling a ten pound bag of potatoes when the doorbell goes off. Kira's eyes light up, the peeler slipping from her hand into the sink, and she runs down the stairs.

I join her, knowing who's at the door.

Emily throws herself at Kira immediately, as if they're long-lost best friends reuniting.

Kira catches my wraith of a little sister up against her and twirls her around.

So much love, and all for a girl she has never even met before.

It's not the first time I see Kira's potential to be a great mom one day.

The weight in my pocket feels heavier, taunting me, and my skin breaks out in a cold sweat.

I can't wait to do this. I won't wait a second longer.

But the girl better agree.

She'll say yes.

Won't she?

It's too soon for me to have forgotten everything we've gone through. Nothing stands between us now except years of brutal memories.

I'm willing to push past all of it, but can I really blame her if she's not?

"Brayden!" Emily comes running at me like a hurricane of sisterly love, ripping me out of my panicked thoughts.

I catch her up in a tight hug.

Carrie is smiling at the both of us with so much happiness that it breaks my heart.

It's a whirlwind of activity as Sonia, my mom, Ryan, and Dana all join us and welcome Carrie.

I'm not surprised when Dana hits it off with Emily right away.

Kira and Dana are sitting on the couch with Emily and I stand at the edge of the living room watching.

Ryan stops next to me, analyzing the scene as well. "Your little sis is really sweet."

I smile at him, surprised by the burst of warmth and pride in my chest. "Yeah. I still can't believe I have one sometimes, you know."

He nods in that wise way of his. "Yes. You do. And she looks like the blond version of you. It's scary how much you guys look alike."

"Like you and Kira?"

Another nod. "Exactly." Sighing, he claps my shoulder. "And now, my friend, one day, you're going to know."

My stomach drops suddenly at his hidden meaning. "Oh God, no . . ."

His smirk is pure evil. "Oh God, yes. It's going to happen bro."

I shake my head even though I know I'm being utterly ridiculous. My little sister is going to grow up one day. It's inevitable. Besides, I just met her. I shouldn't be suffocating on this much brotherly protectiveness.

I look at Emily, then look at Kira.

Then, making sure I bring out as much contrition as any human being can muster, I face Ryan again. "Dude, you're a better person than I can ever be. You were never going to stop me. Nothing was. But thank you for not breaking my face more than you did. I could never be like you."

He laughs good naturedly. "Tell that to my girl. Maybe one day she'll believe you. She thinks I'm full of shit sometimes and a little too 'holier than thou.'"

She might have a point but this isn't the time to even try and bring that up.

Mom and Sonia walk into the living room holding trays of snacks.

The panic returns.

Ryan catches one glimpse of my expression and his eyes widen. "Now? You're doing it now?"

Of course I spoke to him about this. Their father passed away a long time ago, so Ryan had to fill as a stand in.

I went traditional. Asked his permission and all that.

Sure, he threw in my face that I didn't ask for permission to be with her, but that was all in good fun. He agreed happily.

I nod at him and gesture for him to join everyone by the couches.

Holy crap.

Fuck me.

Help my heart.

I'm panicking big time and it's not just because I'm actually going to do this.

It's because that girl might just shatter me to ashes in the next few minutes.

Ryan sits next to Dana and his eyes cut in my direction. "Everyone?" he calls, making sure they all quiet down. "Can we chill for a sec? Brayden has something he wants to get off his chest."

Kira's eyes immediately find mine, worried, anxious.

I love how she cares for me.

And in that second, I decide, *fuck it*. She can say no if she wants. That's fine. I'll just keep asking again and again until she says yes.

425

Eyes on her, I walk straight to her, ignoring everyone around. She starts to stand but I shake my head, silently asking her to remain seated.

Then, before my fear can get the best of me, I pull the small black velvet box out of my pocket and drop down to one knee in front of her.

Everyone but Ryan gasps.

Shaking inside, I open it, letting Kira see the princess cut diamond ring I've been hiding for weeks now.

I can't tell if that's shock or horror on her face.

"Kira Paisley Roth, I refuse to be without you in my life for a single minute ever again. I know I'm fucked up, but I've been yours from the first moment I laid eyes on you. It doesn't have to be now, but someday. Will you marry me and be mine for the rest of our lives? Be with me always, because I can never be without you again."

Kira's mouth is hanging open. Tears are gathering in her eyes. She says nothing.

"We don't have to get married right away. We can have a really long engagement. I just want you to walk around wearing this ring. Knowing what it means. I want the whole world to see it on you, for *them* to know what it means."

Still, she says *nothing*.

Fuck. I'm really trembling now. "Woman, I'll hound you. I'll make your life annoying as hell every single day until you say yes."

Kira finally blinks and a tear leaks out of each eye. "*You* want to marry *me*?"

My heart breaks. "Baby, you're fucking everything to me. Please don't tell me you haven't realized that yet."

She starts sobbing.

Uncontrollably.

Body-shaking cries that completely overwhelm her.

Choking on her tears, she covers her mouth, little brow scrunched as if she's in pain.

What the fuck? "Kira?"

She moves so fast I can't keep up.

One moment, she's sobbing on the couch.

The next, her body is slamming onto mine and I'm falling backwards onto the floor.

Somehow, my fist tightens automatically around the box.

I blink up at the ceiling. On top of me, a sobbing Kira kisses me all over the face. Wrapping one arm around her, I twist my head and catch one of those wet kisses on my lips. "Tell me this is a yes."

"YES!"

God damn it. She almost killed me with worry. Melting with relief, I crush her to me, burying my face in her hair.

All around us, everyone breaks out into cheers.

"I love you," I whisper repeatedly in her ear, eyes closed as I breathe through the last of my nervous energy.

"I love you. You have no idea. I can't even believe—oh my God, Brayden."

I sit up, easing her back with me. It's hard to push her away when all I want is more of those kisses, but something more important has to be done.

I take her small hand into mine and slip the ring onto her ring finger.

The sight of it there floors me.

Kira starts crying harder. "It's beautiful. I love it. I love *you*. I don't know why I can't stop crying. I'm so happy, I swear."

Her emotional rambling brings a huge smile to my face.

I hear every one around us, congratulating us. My mom and Sonia very loudly agreeing that this better be a "very long" engagement, saying we're too young to get married and we have to get through school first.

I think I hear Dana ribbing Ryan about how I've outdone him. Ryan responds with, "You have no idea what's coming your way woman, so shut it."

Everyone is ignored because all I can do, as I sit on this floor with Kira sitting in front of me, her hand in mine and that ring glinting in the light, is stare into my girl's eyes as she stares into my own.

My woman.

The love of my life.

My best friend.

My reason for becoming the man I was supposed to be.

My future *wife*.

Every emotion I'm feeling right now is flashing through her eyes. We've been connected together, on a level that defies understanding, from the first moment we met.

That connection seems to take on an even greater meaning now.

Our road has been more fucked up than two people should ever have to deal with. It's been twisted, and downright dirty at times. For a while there, it also went wrong. So, so wrong.

But it was *our* road, and even when we were apart, somehow this connection got us through it together. And that connection is what kept everything right in the end.

I don't know if soulmates are real, but if they are, she's undoubtedly mine. A force in my very DNA I could never deny.

One I could never live without.

Things aren't perfect. They probably never will be, but that's okay. Coming out has put targets on our backs. The world has decided to brand us for now. Judge us.

But they'll never tear us down.

I have my issues.

Thanks to me, she now has her own.

But we're going to get through this next round, however bad or great it is, the way we should've gotten through the first one.

Together.

Always together.

And now, there's nothing anyone in the world can do to stop us.

STAY

Coming winter 2017-spring 2018

"Everything in my life was in the perfect place. Goals? Achieved. Life? Peaceful. Myself? In utter control. I had it all figured out . . . and then she came along and fucked all my shit up."

Lime—squeezed and slathered all over the flexed, tanned chest in front of me.

Salt—sprinkled right onto the juice of the lime.

His chest—racing with quick breaths, excitement making his skin break out into goosebumps.

I pound back the Patron. Make a show of licking my lips. His eyes flare and I don't have to look down to his see how hard his cock is. The subtle thrust of his hips toward me.

Taking my sweet time, I lean in close, letting him feel my breath over his wet flesh.

Tongue. Contact. A nice slow sweep.

Above the music and the roar of everyone cheering around us, I hear his low groan.

Mission: Accomplished.

Interest: lost.

Not that he ever had much of my interest to begin with.

I give him a friendly pat on the shoulder, what I know is a bland smile, and sashay away from him.

He calls my name. The disappointment in his tone brings out a real smile.

They're always calling me back. All of them. Sadly for them, none of them can keep my interest for more than a few seconds.

None of them.

Because none of them are him.

Just like that, my mood goes black.

Searching the crowd, I let my eyes bounce off faces, searching for my next prey.

That's all they are. Prey. Pieces of meat on display for my consumption. For my disposal.

I make my way onto the dance floor, through the gyrating, sexually charged mass of bodies.

The need to fuck tonight is so strong. It's been over a month. Too long considering the constant ache in my soul.

In my pussy.

And there is no dick on this Earth that can ever satisfy it for long. Why? I refuse to think on it.

Coming clean with the truth is torture. Only one dick ever comes close to doing it for me, and it just happens to be the one dick that's gone off to college to hoe itself around.

I really wish the rumors wouldn't get back to me. The information that kills me although I keep telling myself I don't care.

He's still as much of a whore as ever. Fucking his way through the female population of Earth like he's on a mission to leave his mark all over the place.

Whatever. I'll just fuck my way through the male population in return. Even the score.

Why the hell am I still even keeping score with him?

My heart twists in my chest, as if to answer my stupid question.

He shouldn't matter. At all.

A tall, muscular blond man pushes his way through the crowd toward me, his eyes eating me up.

Oooo. I like that. He thinks his predator is more powerful than mine.

I give him a saucy smirk and crook my finger, daring him to come try and get some.

He does.

Just as he comes up to me, his large hand pressing to the small of my back to fling me in close, a shiver goes down my spine.

A shiver that has nothing to do with this guy.

I try to subtlety look around the packed house. The lights are off and club lights were installed. Through the ever-changing, flashing colors, I see nothing but a confusing blur of people.

The guy holding me grinds his hips into me. I've barely looked at him and he's already hard as fuck.

I know why. It's my exotic coloring. Brown and blond hair. Aqua blue eyes. A deceptively innocent face. A body I bust my ass to maintain.

I've heard it all before. How dangerous my looks are. What they do to the men I come across.

All but one man, that is.

I push him out of my mind and focus on meeting the thrusts of the behemoth in front of me with my own.

He bites his lip, eyes glazed.

I know exactly where his mind is at and I try my hardest to get there with him.

But my heart is racing, and that sensation of being watched keeps slithering down my spine.

Struggling to breathe, I turn, pressing my ass back against the hard dick grinding on me.

I feel more than hear the guy's low groan against my back.

It distracts me for a bit, reminds me that this is now the only type of high I can truly get.

There's no alcohol, no drug powerful enough to bring exhilaration back into my life. Not after *he* ripped it from me all those years ago.

But this? The power I have over men? It's the only thing that comes close. It doesn't help me forget, not at all, but it makes the hollowness a bit easier to bear.

I lift my hair up, tilting my head to the side and down as I move my hips in slow circles. The large hands on my hips clench.

Biting my lip with a smile, I let my long hair fall down over my shoulders again and look up.

Hazel mixed with green.

Horror mixed with that addicting excitement I can never feel unless he's near.

And he is. He's *right fucking there.*

The ability to breathe almost deserts me.

I haven't seen him in months. He looks . . . He looks insanely beautiful.

The most gorgeous thing walking this motherfucking planet.

Bigger.

Meaner.

Damn, he's mean. He looks like he hasn't shaved in days, and in the dark, his auburn hair is almost black.

He glares at me with a hatred returned tenfold.

But it's that other thing I see that almost makes me stop dancing.

He wants me.

He always does.

This man treats me like I'm less than human, a husk with no emotions, but his dick hasn't gotten over me anymore than my pussy has gotten over him.

Don't let him see.

I can't.

I force my expression into nonchalance, staring at him like he means nothing.

He should mean nothing.

He still means everything and I fucking *hate* him for that.

On purpose, I wrap my arms around the guy behind me, around his neck, and lean all my weight on him.

Hazel-green flashes with malice.

He's always the epitome of calm with his yoda-type shit. Pretending to the world he's this uber-civilized being, on his mighty gold pedestal above us.

Only I bring out the truth in him.

Only I bring out the monster in his veins.

The main proof I would ever need of how much he hates me.

I'm not good enough to be anything more than a come receptacle when it suits him. Never a girlfriend. Never a date.

No longer his friend.

But he also wants me to suffer eternally. To belong to no one although he doesn't want me to belong to him.

Sadistic fucker.

I grind into the guy I'm dancing with, eyes locked with the man I despise, the man I can't forget, and ride the hard dick pressing into my ass as if I'm starving for it.

Murder leaks into his stare.

I gasp under my breath when he starts storming toward me, using those big, muscular shoulders to move people out of his way.

I'm wet. Soaking. My pussy is shivering with hunger for him.

It's been months since we last fucked.

I'll let him fuck me right on this dance floor if wants.

No, you dumb ass! Resist the voodoo dick. Stop being his own personal whore when he calls.

I can't.

The tragedy of my life: this man has left nothing but ashes of my existence and personality behind, and I can't resist him for shit.

He ignores the guy behind me, staring down into my eyes, and bends his knees to press against me.

Oh. My. God.

He starts dancing, and I'm suddenly sandwiched between two testosterone powerhouses.

And only one matters.

The only one that ever matters.

"Don't," leaves me in a pitiful whisper that's drowned out by the music.

He can't do this to me again.

I won't let him.

This time, it'll be the end of me. We'll fuck again. He'll take the last bit of my soul with him.

And he'll leave. Go back to all the bitches he loves to fuck.

He always leaves.

Jesus, are those tears I feel in my eyes?

The guy behind me keeps grinding into me, clearly thinking this is okay. That I want to be shared between them and he doesn't mind sharing.

He's nothing but an afterthought. A presence I barely acknowledge.

The tyrant in front me stares straight into my eyes with every move. His groin teases me, barely brushing along the part of me that's screaming for him.

I slap my hands against his chest, those bunched up pecs, and feel his heart pounding like a drum.

His name gets stuck in my throat.

He's still sharing me with this other dude I've all but forgotten, staring down at me with utter loathing.

And I'm about to come.

From having him near.

From every light brush of his pelvis along mine.

The feel of him.

His scent.

He bites down on his lip, expression harsher than ever.

A tiny gasp chokes out. Clit pulsating, I come on my panties and jeans, the horror of it doing nothing to ease how fucking *good* this feels.

Hazel-green eyes penetrate mine, and I can tell he knows. He knows I'm coming right now. He knows that it's all for him and has nothing to do with the guy behind me.

I push him away.

Break out of the other guy's hold.

Without looking back, I run through the crowd.

Exit.

Escape.

Distance.

My pussy continues to throb with mini aftershocks. I push past people, what's left of my world falling to pieces around me.

I can never come with any of the guys I fuck. Ever.

One dance with him and I creamed all over my panties.

A sob rises up my throat. I run blindly, into what I think is a stairwell, and push it down.

I've cried oceans for that man. I refuse to cry more.

Up the stairs, footsteps pounding. Closed doors, all around. I'm near incoherent in my emotional turmoil.

I spot a door open at the end of the hallway.

I'm on the second floor. It's not an exit. But at this moment, it's my only escape.

Mindlessly, I run into a dark room, wobbling in my heels. I'm so out of control, I don't stop running once I'm inside. I keep going, on a panicked autopilot, until a dresser stops my progress.

I slam to a halt, breaths heaving.

It isn't until I stop that I hear it—

A second, even rougher set of breaths.

Behind me.

I'm so tuned into this motherfucker that I recognize him by the sound of his breathing alone.

He followed me.

Hands land on my hips, pushing me forward into the dresser. Those same hands yank my jeans down so roughly that the button and zipper tear with the force.

"Wants to lick other guys. Dance with them like she's fucking them," he mumbles to himself behind me.

I'm going to collapse. My legs can't hold me up. My hands grab onto the top of the dresser, but they're useless.

I'm frozen all over again, fear and desire warring.

Lies. They're winning. Both. Equally.

I'm afraid of what this is going to do to me, but I'll hand over my very soul to have that cock inside me.

He shoves his hand inside my thong, forcing it aside. Just the sound of his zipper lowering makes me almost come again.

He bends me over the dresser, clearly not giving a fuck how I feel about the matter.

His huge, beautiful dick slides up and down my wet slit from behind. I bite down into my lip so hard I break my own skin.

"Tell me you want this," he demands in a deep voice.

No. I refuse. My pussy's drenched. He needs no other confirmation than that.

"Fine. This pussy's going to answer for you anyway."

"Fuck you," I gasp, hips circling back for his dick.

He impales me with it.

My world shatters.

Everything goes white.

He arches behind me with a loud, unholy groan, pushing his cock deeper and my body along the dresser.

I claw at the wood, destroying my nails, the pleasure robbing me of every ounce of my humanity.

"God. Fucking. Damn." He whips his hips back and gives me another hard thrust.

Another wave of pleasure.

I can't stop coming.

His dick . . . It's like finally coming home after years of brutal desolation in an empty desert.

Everything I am, everything I will ever be, centers on this one single moment.

My heart won't stop breaking.

"I hate you," I moan, lifting my ass higher so he can thrust deeper.

He wraps his hand around my neck and lifts my upper body off the dresser. Thrusting into me frantically, he tongues and bites my ear. "I hate you, too. God, I hate you."

But the way he says it almost makes me lie to myself. With that tone, it's easy to imagine he said *love* instead of hate.

"This pussy. Missed it. I fucking hate you. Missed it so much." His cock swells inside me as he fucks me faster.

Pulling my hair with one hand, he squeezes down around my neck with the other. "Say my name, damn you. Say it."

I'm too lost to fight him, my swollen pussy convulsing around his cock. "Fuck you, Ryan."

He growls out like a beast behind me.

"Fuck you, Ryan Roth. *Fuck you.*"

www.ingramcontent.com/pod-product-compliance
Lightning Source LLC
Chambersburg PA
CBHW051510250626
47156CB00001B/32